Giants in the Earth

"There were giants in the earth in those days; and also after that, when the sons of God came in unto the daughters of men, and they bare children to them, the same became mighty men which were of old, men of renown."

GENESIS vi:4

Giants in the Earth

A Saga of the Prairie

by

O. E. Rölvaag

Translated from the Norwegian
by Lincoln Colcord & the Author

PERENNIAL LIBRARY
Harper & Row, Publishers
New York • Hagerstown
San Francisco • London

GIANTS IN THE EARTH, the translation into English of the Norwegian *I de dage*, published by H. Aschehoug and Company of Oslo in two volumes in 1924 and 1925, was originally published in this country by Harper & Brothers in 1927.

PERENNIAL CLASSICS are published by Harper & Row, Publishers, Inc., 10 East 53rd Street, New York, N.Y., 10022.

LIBRARY OF CONGRESS CATALOG NUMBER: 65-6531
STANDARD BOOK NUMBER: 06-083047-6

16—76

TO THOSE OF MY PEOPLE
WHO TOOK PART IN THE GREAT SETTLING,
TO THEM AND THEIR GENERATIONS
I DEDICATE THIS NARRATIVE

Contents

Foreword

In offering this novel to the English-reading public, I feel the need of an explanation. Book I of *Giants in the Earth* was published in Norway (Aschehoug & Co.) as a separate volume in October, 1924; Book II, one year later.

I am aware of the slight similarity existing between Johan Bojer's *The Emigrants* and certain portions of the First Book of my novel; and lest the reader should consider me guilty of having plagiarized him, I find it necessary to offer the information that *The Land-Taking* was in the hands of the Norwegian book dealers a little better than one month before Bojer's book appeared. In a letter to me, dated January 11, 1925, Mr. Bojer writes: "It certainly was fortunate for me that I got my book finished when I did. Had it appeared much later, I should have been accused of having plagiarized you."

The work of translating this novel has been a difficult task. The idiom of the characters offered serious problems. These settlers came from Nordland, Norway; and though the novel is written in the literary language of Norway, the speech of the characters themselves naturally had to be strongly colored by their native dialect; otherwise their utterances would have sounded stilted and untrue. To get these people to reveal clearly and effectively their psychology in English speech seemed at times impossible; for the idioms of a dialect are well-nigh untranslatable. A liberal use of footnotes was unavoidable.

If the old saying, that many cooks spoil the broth, is true, then surely the English text cannot be of much account; for many have worked at it. The following friends have helped with the translation: Mr. Ansten Anstensen, Columbia University; Miss Ruth Lima, Concordia College, Moorhead, Minnesota; Dr. Nils Flaten, Miss Nora Sølum, Prof. Olav Lee, Miss Esther Gulbrandsen—all four of whom are fellow teachers in St. Olaf College; and Atty. John Heitmann, Duluth, Minnesota. I feel also greatly indebted to Dr. and Mrs. Clarence Berdahl, University of Illinois, for their many valuable suggestions and corrections. What I asked of these friends was a literal translation. They complied so willingly and so cheerfully. I take this opportunity to thank them all!

But most of all do I owe gratitude to my friend Lincoln Colcord, Minneapolis, Minnesota, who unified and literally rewrote the English text. As I got the translation from the others, I would wrestle with it for a while, and then send it on to him. When he had finished a division he and I would come together to work it over, he reading the manuscript aloud, I checking with the text of the original. How intensely we struggled with words and sentences! It would happen frequently that several pages had to be rewritten. But he never tired. His has been a real *labor amoris*. Were it not for his constant encouragement and for his inimitable willingness to help, this novel would most likely never have seen the light of day in an English translation.

St. Olaf College,
Northfield, Minnesota, O. E. RÖLVAAG
July 15, 1927

Introduction

I

It is a unique experience, all things considered, to have this novel by O. E. Rölvaag, so palpably European in its art and atmosphere, so distinctly American in everything it deals with. Translations from European authors have always been received with serious consideration in the United States; in Rölvaag we have a European author of our own—one who writes in America, about America, whose only aim is to tell of the contributions of his people to American life; and who yet must be translated for us out of a foreign tongue. I think I am right in stating that this is the first instance of the kind in the history of American letters.

There are certain points of technique and construction which show at a glance that the author of this book is not a native American. Rölvaag is primarily interested in psychology, in the unfolding of character; the native American writer is primarily interested in plot and incident. Rölvaag is preoccupied with the human cost of empire building, rather than with its glamour and romance. His chief character, Beret, is a failure in terms of pioneer life; he aims to reveal a deeper side of the problem, by showing the distress of one who could not take root in new soil. Beret's homesickness is the dominant *motif* of the tale. Even Per Hansa, the natural-born pioneer, must give his life before the spirit of the prairie is appeased. This treatment reflects something of the gloomy fatalism of the Norse mind; but it also runs close to the grim reality of pioneering, a place the bravest art would want to occupy. *Giants in the Earth* never turns aside from the march of its sustained and inevitable tragedy. The story is told almost baldly at times, but with an unerring choice of simple human detail. When we lay it down we have gained a new insight into the founding of America.

II

Ole Edvart Rölvaag was born April 22, 1876, in a small settlement on the island of Dönna, in the district of Helgeland, just south of where the Arctic Circle cuts the coast of Norway. The place is far up in the Nordland. Strictly speaking, the settlement has no name; the cove where it lies is called *Rölvaag* on the map, but it is merely an outskirt of one of the voting precincts on the island. Rölvaag, it will be seen, took his place name after coming to America; he has explained this practice in a footnote in the present work. His father's Christian name was Peder, and in Norway he would have been Pedersen; his own sons, in turn, would have been Olsen. The name is pronounced with umlauted *ö* rolled a little, as in *world;* the last syllable, *aag,* is like the first syllable in *auger.*

All the people in this settlement were fishermen. In summer they fished in small open boats, coming home every night; in winter they went in larger boats, carrying crews of from four to six men, to the historic fishing grounds off the Lofoten Islands, where the Maelstrom runs and the coast stretches away to North Cape and beyond. It was a life full of hardship and danger, with sorrow and poverty standing close at hand. The midnight sun shone on them for a season; during the winter they had the long darkness. The island of Dönna is a barren rock covered with gorse and heather—hardly a tree in sight. It looks like a bit of the coast of Labrador. An opening between low ledges of granite marks the cove named *Rölvaag;* at the head of the cove the houses of the settlement stand out stark and unprotected against the sky line. Behind them loom the iron mountains of the coast. A gloomy, desolate scene—a perilous stronghold on the fringe of the Arctic night. There Rölvaag's forebears had lived, going out to the fisheries, since time immemorial.

His father, who is still alive, is the image of a New England sea captain. The family must have been a remarkable one. An uncle, his father's brother, had broken away from the fishing life and made himself a teacher of prominence in a neighbouring locality. An older brother had the mind of a scholar; but something happened—he went on with the fishing, and died long ago. There was a brilliant sister, also, who died young. These two evidently overshadowed Rölvaag while he was growing up; his case as a child seemed hopeless—he could not learn. Nevertheless, he had a little schooling, mostly of a semireligious nature. The school lay seven miles away, across the rocks and moors; that gave him a fourteen-mile walk for his daily education. He went to school nine weeks a year, for seven years. This ended at the age of fourteen, when his father finally told him that he was not worth educating. That was all the schooling he had in Norway.

Once during the period of childhood he was walking in the dusk with his mother; they had been gathering kelp on the rocks which they boiled and fed to the cattle; and now they were on their way home. His mother took him by the hand and asked him what he wanted to be when he grew up. "I want to be a poet," he told her. This was the only time he ever revealed himself to a member of his family. He remembers the quiet chuckle with which his mother received the news; she did not take him to task, nor try to show him how absurd it was, but she couldn't restrain a kindly chuckle as they went along the rock path together. That winter they had only potatoes and salt herring to eat, three times a day; his mother divided the potatoes carefully, for there were barely enough to go around.

In place of education was the reading—for this was a reading family. The precinct had a good library, furnished by the state. Rölvaag had learned to read after a long struggle, and his head was always in a book. The first novel he ever read was Cooper's *The Last of the Mohicans* in the Norwegian. All of Cooper's novels followed, and the novels of Dickens and Captain Marryat and Bulwer-Lytton. Then came the works of Ingemann, the Danish historical novelist; the works of Zakarias Topelius, the great Swedish romanticist; the works of the German, Paul Heyse; and the complete works of their own great novelists, especially Björnson and Jonas Lie.

For miscellaneous reading there were such things as the tales of Jules Verne and H. Rider Haggard and Alexandre Dumas, Carlyle's *The French Revolution*, and Stanley's *Across the Dark Continent*. Neither did they lack the usual assortment of dime novels and shilling-shockers, in paper covers. The list could be extended indefinitely; the parallel with the reading of the better-class American boy of a generation ago is little short of astonishing.

This reading, promiscuous but intensive, lasted through the period of his youth. Once it was rumoured that at a certain village, fourteen miles away, a copy of *Ivanhoe* could be obtained; Rölvaag set out on foot to get it, and was gone two days on the journey. There is another incident, slight but deeply revealing, which shows the promise wrapped up in the husk of boyhood. In a moment of exaltation he decided to write a novel of his own. He may have been eleven or twelve when this creative impulse seized him. All one afternoon he spent in his bedroom writing; with infinite labour he had completed as many as five pages of the novel. Then his elder brother, who shared the room with him, came in—the brilliant brother of whom he stood in awe. "What are you doing there?" asked the brother. "Nothing," Rölvaag answered, hastily trying to conceal the fruits of his first literary effort. "Let me see it!"—the brother had quickly sensed what was going on. "I won't!" And so the battle had started—a terrific struggle that nearly wrecked the room, in the course of which the five pages were torn to shreds. But the brother had not seen a word of them. Rölvaag never attempted literary composition again until he was completing his education in America, fifteen years afterward.

Awhile later we find him reading Cooper and Marryat aloud to the fishermen at Lofoten, during the winter lay-up; there was a splendid library at this remote station, too, maintained by the state for the use of the fishing fleet. By this time Rölvaag had become a fisherman himself, like everyone else in the community. He went on his first trip to the Lofoten fishing grounds at the age of fifteen. In all, he fished five years, until he had just passed twenty. Every year he was growing more discontented. In the winter of 1893 a terrible storm devastated the fishing fleet, taking tragic toll among his friends and fellow fishermen. The boat he sailed in escaped only by a miracle. This experience killed his first romantic love of the fishing life; he sat down then and wrote to an uncle in South Dakota, asking him for a ticket to the United States. Not that he felt any particular call to go to America; he only thought of getting away. He longed for the unknown and untried—for something secret and inexpressible. Vaguely, stubbornly, he wanted the chance to fulfil himself before he died. But the uncle, doubtless influenced by Rölvaag's family reputation, refused to help him; and the fishing life went on.

Two more years passed, years of deepening revolt—when suddenly the uncle in South Dakota changed his mind. One day a ticket for America arrived. The way of escape was at hand.

Then a dramatic thing happened. All the fishermen went to the summer fair at the market town of Björn. At this fair, boats were exposed for sale, the finest fishing craft in all Norway. Rölvaag's master sought him out and took him down among the boats. His admiration for this master was extravagant; he speaks of him to-day as a sea king, the greatest human being he has ever known. The man led him directly to the best boat hauled out on the beach. They stood admiring her. He led him aft, under her stern, where they could see her beautiful lines. He patted her side as he spoke. He said: "If you will send back the ticket to your uncle, I will buy this boat for you. You shall command her; and when she has paid for herself she shall be yours."

The offer swept him off his feet. Never, he affirms, can he hope to attain in life again a sensation of such complete and triumphant success as came to him at that moment. A new boat, the backing of the man he admired and loved above all others, a place at the top of his profession at the age of twenty, a chance to reign supreme in his little world. And yet, nothing beyond—it meant that this was all. To live and die a fisherman. No other worlds—the vague, beautiful worlds beyond the horizon. "I will have to think it over," was his answer. He turned away, went up on a hillside above the town, and sat there alone all the afternoon.

This young man of twenty sitting on a hillside on the coast of Norway, wrestling with his immense problem, takes on the stature of a figure from the sagas. Which way will he make up his mind? "It was a fine, clear day in Nordland," he tells me, speaking of the incident thirty years afterward. A fine, clear day—he could see a long way across the water. But not the shape of his own destiny. The life he knew was calling him with a thousand voices. How could he have heard the hail of things not yet seen? Where did he get the strength to make his momentous decision? He came down from the hillside at last, and found his master. "I am sorry," he said, "but I cannot accept your offer. I am going to America."

III

Rölvaag himself has told about the journey in his first book, *Amerika-Breve* (*Letters from America*), published in 1912, a work which is largely autobiographical and which struck home in a personal way to his Norwegian-American readers. He landed in New York in August of 1896. He was not even aware that he would require money for food during the railway trip; in his pocket were an American dime and a copper piece from Norway. For three days and nights, from New York to South Dakota, he lived on a single loaf of bread; the dime went for tobacco somewhere along the vast stretches unfolding before him. Through an error in calculation his uncle failed to meet him at the country station where he finally disembarked. He had no word of English with which to ask his way. The prairie spread on every hand; the sun was going down. He walked half the night, without food or water, until at last he found Norwegians who could direct him, reached his uncle's farm, and received a warm welcome.

Then began three years of farming. At the end of that time he knew that he did not like it; this was not the life for him. He had saved a little money, but had picked up only a smattering of English. A friend kept urging him to go to school. But his father's verdict, which so far had ruled his life, still had power over him; he firmly believed that it would be of no use, that he was not worth educating. Instead he went to Sioux City, Iowa, and tried to find work there—factory work, a chance to tend bar in a saloon, a job of washing dishes in a restaurant. But nothing offered; he was forced to return to the farm. He had now reached another crossroads in his life; a flat alternative faced him—farming or schooling. As the lesser of two evils, he entered Augustana College, a grammar or preparatory school in Canton, South Dakota, in the fall of 1899. At that time he was twenty-three years old.

Once at school, the fierce desire for knowledge, so long restrained, took him by storm. In a short while he discovered the cruel wrong that had been done him. His mind was mature and receptive; he was able to learn with amazing ease; in general reading, in grasp of life and strength of purpose, he was far in advance of his fellow students. He graduated from Augustana in the spring of 1901; that fall he entered St. Olaf College, with forty dollars in his pocket. In four years he had worked his way through St. Olaf, graduating with honours in 1905, at the age of twenty-eight. On the promise of a faculty position at his *alma mater*, he borrowed five hundred dollars and sent himself for a year to the University of Oslo in Norway. Returning from this post-graduate work in 1906, he took up his teaching at St. Olaf College, where he has been ever since. Professor Rölvaag now occupies the chair of Norwegian literature at that institution.

IV

I have mentioned the *Amerika-Breve*, published in 1912. There is an earlier work, still in manuscript—a novel written during his senior year at St. Olaf College. In all, Rölvaag has published six novels, two readers for class use, a couple of handbooks on Norwegian grammar and declamation, and one volume of essays. In 1914 appeared his second book, *Paa Glemte Veie* (*The Forgot-*

ten Path), a relatively unimportant product. Then came the war, which threw consternation into all creative work. Rölvaag walked the hills of southern Minnesota, his mind a blank, facing the downfall of civilization, seeing the death of those fine things of life which he had striven so hard to attain. It was during the war period that he compiled his readers and handbooks, for the publishing board of the Norwegian-American Lutheran Church.

He had married in 1908. In 1920 a tragedy occurred in his family—one of his children was drowned under terrible circumstances. This seems to have shaken him out of the war inertia and stirred his creative life again. That year he wrote and published his first strong novel, *To Tullinger* (*Two Fools*), the story of a rough, uncultivated couple, incapable of refinement, who gain success in America and develop the hoarding instinct to a fantastic degree. This book, too, made a sensation among Norwegian-Americans.

Then, in 1922, came *Laengselens Baat* (*The Ship of Longing*), which seems to have been Rölvaag's most introspective and poetical effort up to the present time. It is the study of a sensitive, artistic youth who comes to America from Norway full of dreams and ideals, expecting to find all that his soul longs for; he does not find it, with the result that his life goes down in disaster. Needless to say, this book was not popular with his Norwegian-American audience. The truth-teller of *To Tullinger* was now going a little too far.

All of these works were written and published in Norwegian. They were brought out under the imprint of the Augsburg Publishing House, of Minneapolis, and circulated only among those Norwegian-Americans who had retained the language of the old country. The reason why none of them had reached publication in Norway is characteristic. In 1912 the manuscript of *Amerika-Breve* had been submitted to Norwegian publishers. They had returned a favourable and even enthusiastic opinion, but had insisted on certain changes in the text. These changes Rölvaag had refused to concede, feeling that they marred the artistic unity of his work. In anger and disappointment, he had at once published with the local house; and with each successive volume the feeling of artistic umbrage had persisted—it had not seemed worth while to try to reach the larger field.

But in the spring of 1923, an item appeared in the Norwegian press to the effect that the great novelist Johan Bojer was about to visit the United States, for the purpose of collecting material on the Norwegian-American immigration. He proposed to write an epic novel on the movement. This news excited Rölvaag tremendously; he felt that the inner truth of the Norwegian-American immigration could be written only by one who had experienced the transplanting of life, who shared the psychology of the settlers. His artistic ambition was up in arms; this was his own field.

He immediately obtained a year's leave of absence from St. Olaf College, and set to work. The first few sections of *Giants in the Earth* were written in a cabin in the north woods of Minnesota. Then he felt the need of visiting South Dakota again, to gather fresh material. In midwinter of that year he went abroad, locating temporarily in a cheap immigrant hotel in London, where he worked on the novel steadily. When spring opened in 1924, he went to Norway. There he met Bojer, visiting him at his country home. Bojer was delighted to learn that Rölvaag, of whom he had heard a great deal, was also working on a novel of the Norwegian-American settlement; the two men exchanged ideas generously. "How do you see the problem?" Rölvaag asked. The answer showed him that Bojer saw it from the viewpoint of Norway, not of America; to him it was mainly a problem of emigration. This greatly relieved Rölvaag's mind, for there was no real conflict; he set to work with renewed energy, and soon finished the first book of *Giants in the Earth*.

In the meanwhile it had been placed with Norwegian publishers—the same firm, by the way, which had lost *Amerika-Breve* twelve years before. It appeared in the latter part of 1924, under the title *I De Dage* (*In Those Days*), a month in advance of Bojer's *Vor Egen Stamme* (*Our Own Tribe*), better known to us by its English title of *The Emigrants*. A year later the second book of the present volume was brought out, under the title *Riket Grundlaegges* (*Founding the Kingdom*).

In Norway these two books have run through many editions; they have been hailed on every hand as something new in Norwegian literature. Swedish and Finnish editions will be published in 1927. Arrangements are being made for a German translation, and the book will probably be off the press in Germany soon after it has appeared in the United States. Rölvaag's vigorous, idiomatic style (which, incidentally, has been the despair of those who have worked over the English translation) is an outstanding topic of recent Scandinavian criticism. The eminent Danish critic, Jörgen Bukdahl, for instance, in his latest work, *Det Skjulte Norge* (*The Latent Norway*), devotes a whole chapter to Rölvaag and his novels of pioneering in South Dakota. A new name has been added to the literary firmament of Norway.

V

Does Rölvaag's work belong legitimately to Norwegian or to American literature? The problem has unusual and interesting features. The volume before us deals with American life, and with one of the most characteristically American episodes in our history. It opens on the western plains; its material is altogether American. Yet it was written in Norwegian, and gained its first recognition in Norway. Whatever we may decide, it has already become a part of Norwegian literature. Rölvaag's art seems mainly European; Rölvaag himself, as I have said, is typically American. His life and future are bound up in the New World; yet he will continue to write in a foreign language. Had he been born in America, would his art have been the same? It seems unlikely. On the other hand, had he remained in Norway—had he accepted the boat that fine, clear day in Nordland—how would his art have fared?

But such speculation, after all, is merely idle; these things do not matter. It has not yet been determined, even, what America is, or whether she herself is strictly American. And any sincere art is international. Given the artist, our chief interest lies in trying to fathom the sources of his art, and to recognize its sustaining impulses. What were the forces which have now projected into American letters a realist of the first quality writing in a foreign language a new tale of the founding of America? It is obvious that these forces must have been highly complex and that they will continue to be so throughout his working life; but beyond that we cannot safely go. The rest is a matter of opinion. When I have asked Rölvaag the simple question, Did Norway or America teach you to write? he has invariably thrown up his hands.

The same speculation, in different measure, applies to a considerable quantity of Norwegian-American literary production which as yet our criticism knows nothing about. The Norwegians are a book-loving people; no set of adverse conditions can for long restrain them from expressing themselves in literary form. Here in the Northwest, during the last thirty or forty years, they have built up a distinctive literature, written and published in the Norwegian language, but concerned wholly with American life. Until quite recently, in fact, the region supported a Norwegian fiction magazine.

There are the five substantial novels of Simon Johnson, for instance, with many short stories by the same author. There are the romantic novels of H. A. Foss; and the poetry, short stories, novels, and travelogues of Peer Strömme. There are the polemical and poetical works of O. A. Buslett, obscure and fantastic. There are the three novels and four collections of short stories by the able writer, Waldemar Ager. There is the lyric poetry of Julius B. Baumann and O. S. Sneve, the collected works of both of whom have now been brought out. There are the amazing Biblical dramas of the farmer-poet Jon Norstog—huge tomes with the titles of *Moses*, and *Israel*, and *Saul*, set up by his own hand and published from his own printing press, in a shanty on the prairies of North Dakota—works that reveal the flash of genius now and then, as I am told. Do all these serious efforts belong to Norwegian or to American literature? Their day is nearly done; the present generation of Norse stock has another native language. But it would be of value to have some of this early Norwegian-American product translated into English, to enrich our literature by a pure stream flowing out of the American environment—a stream which, for the general public, lies frozen in the ice of a foreign tongue.

LINCOLN COLCORD

Minneapolis, Minnesota,
January, 1927

Giants in the Earth

Book I

THE LAND-TAKING

I Toward the Sunset

I

Bright, clear sky over a plain so wide that the rim of the heavens cut down on it around the entire horizon. . . . Bright, clear sky, to-day, to-morrow, and for all time to come.

. . . And sun! And still more sun! It set the heavens afire every morning; it grew with the day to quivering golden light—then softened into all the shades of red and purple as evening fell. . . . Pure colour everywhere. A gust of wind, sweeping across the plain, threw into life waves of yellow and blue and green. Now and then a dead black wave would race over the scene . . . a cloud's gliding shadow . . . now and then. . . .

It was late afternoon. A small caravan was pushing its way through the tall grass. The track that it left behind was like the wake of a boat—except that instead of widening out astern it closed in again.

"Tish-ah!" said the grass. . . . "Tish-ah, tish-ah!" . . . Never had it said anything else—never would it say anything else. It bent resiliently under the trampling feet; it did not break, but it complained aloud every time—for nothing like this had ever happened to it before. . . . "Tish-ah, tish-ah!" it cried, and rose up in surprise to look at this rough, hard thing that had crushed it to the ground so rudely, and then moved on.

A stocky, broad-shouldered man walked at the head of the caravan. He seemed shorter than he really was, because of the tall grass around him and the broad-brimmed hat of coarse straw which he wore. A few steps behind him followed a boy of about nine years of age. The boy's blond hair was clearly marked against his brown, sunburnt neck; but the man's hair and neck were of exactly the same shade of brown. From the looks of these two, and still more from their gait, it was easy to guess that here walked father and son.

Behind them a team of oxen jogged along; the oxen were drawing a vehicle which once upon a time might have been a wagon, but which now, on account of its many and grave infirmities, ought long since to have been consigned to the scrap heap—exactly the place, in point of fact, where the man had picked it up. Over the wagon box long willow saplings had been bent, in the form of arches in a church chancel—six of them in all. On these arches, and tied down to the body on each side, were spread first of all two handwoven blankets, that might well have adorned the walls of some manor house in the olden times; on top of the blankets were thrown two sheepskin robes, with the wool side down, which were used for bed-coverings at night. The rear of the wagon was stowed full of numberless articles, all the way up to the top. A large immigrant chest at the bottom of the pile, very long and high, devoured a big share of the space; around and above it were piled household utensils, tools, implements, and all their clothing.

Hitched to this wagon and trailing behind was another vehicle, homemade and very curious-looking, so solidly and quaintly constructed that it might easily have won a place in any museum. Indeed, it appeared strong enough to stand all the jolting from the Atlantic to the Pacific. . . . It, too, was a wagon, after a fashion; at least, it had been intended for such. The wheels were made from pieces of plank fitting roughly together; the box, considerably wider than that of the first wagon, was also loaded full of provisions and household gear, covered over with canvas and lashed down securely. Both wagons creaked and groaned loudly every time they bounced over a tussock or hove out of a hollow. . . . "Squeak, squeak!" said the one. . . . "Squeak, squeak!" answered the other. . . . The strident sound broke the silence of centuries.

A short distance behind the wagons followed a brindle cow. The caravan moved so slowly that she occasionally had time to stop and snatch a few mouthfuls, though there was never a chance for many at a time. But what little she got in this way she sorely needed. She had been jogging along all day, swinging and switching her tail, the rudder of the caravan. Soon it would be night, and then her part of the work would come—to furnish milk for the evening porridge, for all the company up ahead.

Across the front end of the box of the first wagon lay a rough piece of plank. On the right side of this plank sat a woman with a white kerchief over her head, driving the oxen. Against her thigh rested the blond head of a little girl, who was stretched out on the plank and sleeping sweetly. Now and then the hand of the mother moved across the child's face to chase away the mosquitoes, which had begun to gather as the sun lowered. On the left side of the plank, beyond the girl, sat a boy about seven years old—a well-grown lad, his skin deeply tanned, a certain clever, watchful gleam in his eyes. With hands folded over one knee, he looked straight ahead.

This was the caravan of Per Hansa, who with his family and all his earthly possessions was moving west from Fillmore County, Minnesota, to Dakota Territory. There he intended to take up land and build himself a home; he was going to do something remarkable out there, which should become known far and wide. No lack of opportunity in that country, he had been told! . . . Per Hansa himself strode ahead and laid out the course; the boy Ole, or *Olamand*, followed closely after, and explored it. Beret, the wife, drove the oxen and took care of little Anna Marie, pet-named *And-Ongen* (which means "The Duckling"), who was usually bubbling over with happiness. Hans Kristian, whose everyday name was *Store-Hans* (meaning "Big Hans," to distinguish him from his godfather, who was also named Hans, but who, of course, was three times his size), sat there on the wagon, and saw to it that everyone attended to business. . . . The cow Rosie trailed behind, swinging and switching her tail, following the caravan farther and farther yet into the endless vista of the plain.

"Tish-ah, tish-ah!" cried the grass. . . . "Tish-ah, tish-ah!" . . .

II

The caravan seemed a miserably frail and Lilliputian thing as it crept over the boundless prairie toward the sky line. Of road or trail there lay not a trace ahead; as soon as the grass had straightened up again behind, no one could have told the direction from which it had come or whither it was bound. The whole train—Per Hansa with his wife and children, the oxen, the wagons, the cow, and all—might just as well have dropped down out of the sky. Nor was it at all impossible to imagine that they were trying to get back there again; their course was always the same—straight toward the west, straight toward the sky line. . . .

Poverty-stricken, unspeakably forlorn, the caravan creaked along, advancing at a snail's pace, deeper and deeper into a bluish-green infinity—on and on, and always farther on. . . . It steered for Sunset Land! . . .

For more than three weeks now, and well into the fourth, this caravan had been crawling across the plain. . . . Early in the journey it had passed through Blue Earth; it had left Chain Lakes behind; and one fine day it had crept into Jackson, on the Des Moines River. But that seemed ages ago. . . . From Jackson, after a short lay-up, it had pushed on westward—always westward—to Worthington, then to Rock River. . . . A little west of Rock River, Per Hansa had lost the trail completely. Since then he had not been able to find it again; at this moment he literally did not know where he was, nor how to get to the place he had to reach. But Split Rock Creek must lie out there somewhere in the sun; if he could only find that landmark, he could pick his way still farther without much trouble. . . . Strange that he hadn't reached Split Rock Creek before this time! According to his directions, he should have been there two or three days ago; but he hadn't seen anything that even looked like the place. . . . Oh, my God! If something didn't turn up soon! . . . My God! . . .

The wagons creaked and groaned. Per Hansa's eyes wandered over the plain. His bearded face swung constantly from side to side as he examined every inch of ground from the northeast to the southwest. At times he gave his whole attention to that part of the plain lying between him and the western sky line; with head bent forward and eyes fixed and searching, he would sniff the air, like an animal trying to find the scent. Every now and then he glanced at an old silver watch which he carried in his left hand; but his gaze would quickly wander off again, to take up its fruitless search of the empty horizon.

It was now nearing six o'clock. Since three in the afternoon he had been certain of his course; at that time he had taken his bearings by means of his watch and the sun. . . . Out here one had to get one's cross-bearings from the very day itself—then trust to luck. . . .

For a long while the little company had been silent. Per Hansa turned halfway around, and without slackening his pace spoke to the boy walking behind.

"Go back and drive for a while now, Ola.* . . . You must talk to mother, too, so that it won't be so lonesome for her. And be sure to keep as sharp a lookout as you can."

"I'm not tired yet!" said the boy, loath to leave the van.

"Go back, anyway! Maybe you're not, but I can feel it beginning to tell on me. We'll have to start cooking the porridge pretty soon. . . . You go back, and hold her on the sun for a while longer."

"Do you think we'll catch up with them to-night, Dad?" The boy was still undecided.

"Good Lord, no! They've got too long a start on us. . . . Look sharp, now! If you happen to see anything

* In most dialects of Norway the name Ole becomes Ola when spoken.

suspicious, sing out!" . . . Per Hansa glanced again at his watch, turned forward, and strode steadily onward.

Ole said no more; he stepped out of the track and stood there waiting till the train came up. Then Store-Hans jumped down nimbly, while the other climbed up and took his seat.

"Have you seen anything?" the mother asked in an anxious voice.

"Why, no . . . not yet," answered the boy, evasively.

"I wonder if we shall ever see them again," she said, as if speaking to herself, and looked down at the ground. "This seems to be taking us to the end of the world . . . beyond the end of the world!"

Store-Hans, who was still walking beside the wagon, heard what she said and looked up at her. The buoyancy of childhood shone in his brown face. . . . Too bad that mother should be so scared! . . .

"Yes, Mother, but when we're both steering for the sun, we'll both land in the same place, won't we? . . . The sun is a sure guide, you know!"

These were the very words which he had heard his father use the night before; now he repeated them. To Store-Hans the truth of them seemed as clear as the sun itself; in the first place, because dad had said it, and then because it sounded so reasonable.

He hurried up alongside his father and laid his hand in his—he always felt safer thus.

The two walked on side by side. Now and then the boy stole a glance at the face beside him, which was as stern and fixed as the prairie on which they were walking. He was anxious to talk, but couldn't find anything to say that sounded grown-up enough; and so he kept quiet. At last, however, the silence grew too heavy for him to bear. He tried to say indifferently, just like his father:

"When I'm a man and have horses, I'm going to make a road over these plains, and . . . and put up some posts for people to follow. Don't you think that'll be a good idea?"

A slight chuckle came from the bearded face set toward the sun.

"Sure thing, Store-Hans—you'll manage that all right.

. . . I might find time to help you an hour or two, now and then."

The boy knew by his father's voice that he was in a talkative mood. This made him so glad, that he forgot himself and did something that his mother always objected to; he began to whistle, and tried to take just as long strides as his father. But he could only make the grass say: "Swish-sh, swish-sh!"

On and on they went, farther out toward Sunset Land—farther into the deep glow of the evening.

The mother had taken little Anna up in her lap and was now leaning backward as much as she could; it gave such relief to her tired muscles. The caresses of the child and her lively chatter made her forget for a moment care and anxiety, and that vague sense of the unknown which bore in on them so strongly from all directions. . . . Ole sat there and drove like a full-grown man; by some means or other he managed to get more speed out of the oxen than the mother had done—she noticed this herself. His eyes were searching the prairie far and near.

Out on the sky line the huge plain now began to swell and rise, almost as if an abscess were forming under the skin of the earth. Although this elevation lay somewhat out of his course, Per Hansa swung over and held straight toward the highest part of it.

The afternoon breeze lulled, and finally dropped off altogether. The sun, whose golden lustre had faded imperceptibly into a reddish hue, shone now with a dull light, yet strong and clear; in a short while, deeper tones of violet began to creep across the red. The great ball grew enormous; it retreated farther and farther into the empty reaches of the western sky; then it sank suddenly. . . . The spell of evening quickly crowded in and laid hold of them all; the oxen wagged their ears; Rosie lifted her voice in a long moo, which died out slowly in the great stillness. At the moment when the sun closed his eye, the vastness of the plain seemed to rise up on every hand—and suddenly the landscape had grown desolate; something bleak and cold had come into the silence, filling it with terror. . . . Behind them, along the way they had come, the plain lay dark green and lifeless, under the gathering shadow of the dim, purple sky.

Ole sat motionless at his mother's side. The falling of evening had made such a deep impression on him that his throat felt dry; he wanted to express some of the emotions that overwhelmed him, but only choked when he tried.

"Did you ever see anything so beautiful!" he whispered at last, and gave a heavy sigh. . . . Low down in the northwest, above the little hill, a few fleecy clouds hovered, betokening fair weather; now they were fringed with shining gold, which glowed with a mellow light. As if they had no weight, they floated lightly there. . . .

The mother drew herself forward to an upright position. She still held the child in her lap. Per Hansa and Store-Hans were walking in the dusk far up ahead. For the last two days Per had kept well in advance of the caravan all the time; she thought she knew the reason why.

"Per," she called out, wearily, "aren't we going to stop soon?"

"Pretty soon." . . . He did not slacken his pace.

She shifted the child over into the other arm and began to weep silently. Ole saw it, but pretended not to notice, though he had to swallow big lumps that were forcing themselves up in his throat; he kept his eyes resolutely fixed on the scene ahead.

"Dad," he shouted after a while, "I see a wood over there to the westward!"

"You do, do you? A great fellow you are! Store-Hans and I have seen that for a long time now."

"Whereabouts is it?" whispered Store-Hans, eagerly.

"It begins down there on the slope to the left, and then goes around on the other side," said his father. "Anyway, it doesn't seem to be much of a wood."

"D'you think they are there?"

"Not on your life! But we're keeping the right course, anyhow."

"Have the others been this way?"

"Of course they have—somewhere near, at any rate. There's supposed to be a creek around here, by the name of Split Rock Creek, or whatever they call it in English."

"Are there any people here, do you think?"

"People? Good Lord, no! There isn't a soul around these parts."

The sombre blue haze was now closing rapidly in on the caravan. One sensed the night near at hand; it breathed a chill as it came.

At last Per Hansa halted. "Well, I suppose we can't drive any farther to-day. We and the animals would both drop pretty soon." With these words he faced the oxen, held his arms straight out like the horizontal beam of a cross, shouted a long-drawn "Whoa!"—and then the creaking stopped for that day.

III

The preparations for the night were soon made; each had his own task and was now well used to it. Store-Hans brought the wood; it lay strapped under the hind wagon and consisted of small logs and dry branches from the last thicket they had passed.

Ole got the fireplace ready. From the last wagon he brought out two iron rods, cleft in one end; these he drove into the ground and then went back to the wagon for a third rod, which he laid across the other two. It was also his duty to see that there was water enough in the keg, no matter where they happened to stop; for the rest of it, he was on hand to help his mother.

The father tended to the cattle. First he lifted the yoke off the oxen and turned them loose; then he milked Rosie and let her go also. After that he made up a bed for the whole family under the wagon.

While the mother waited for the pot to boil she set the table. She spread a home-woven blanket on the ground, laid a spoon for each one on it, placed a couple of bowls for the milk, and fetched the dishes for the porridge. Meanwhile she had to keep an eye on And-Ongen, who was toddling about in the grass near by. The child stumbled, laughed, lay there a moment chattering to herself, then got up, only to trip on her skirt and tumble headlong again. Her prattling laughter rang on the evening air. Now and then the voice of the mother would mingle with it, warning the child not to stray too far.

Store-Hans was the first to get through with his task; he stood around awhile, but, finding nothing more to do, he strolled off westward. He was itching to know how far it was to the hill out there; it would be great fun to see what things looked like on the other side! . . . Now he started off in that direction. Perhaps he might come across the others? They surely must be somewhere. Just think, if he could only find them! He would yell and rush in on them like an Indian—and then they would be scared out of their senses! . . . He had gone quite far before he paused to look back. When he did so the sight sent a shiver over him; the wagons had shrunk to two small specks, away off on the floor of a huge, dusky room. . . . I'd better hurry at once, he thought; mother will surely have the porridge ready by this time! His legs had already adopted the idea of their own accord. But thoughts of his mother and the porridge didn't quite bring him all the feeling of safety he needed; he hunted through his mind for a few strains of a hymn, and sang them over and over in a high-pitched, breaking voice, until he had no more breath left to sing with. . . . He didn't feel entirely safe until the wagons had begun to assume their natural size once more.

The mother called to them that supper was ready. On the blanket stood two dishes of porridge—a large dish for the father and the two boys, a smaller one for the mother and And-Ongen. The evening milk was divided between two bowls, and set before them; Rosie, poor thing, was not giving much these days! The father said that he didn't care for milk this evening, either; it had a tangy taste, he thought; and he drank water with his porridge. But when Ole also began to complain of the tangy taste and asked for water, the father grew stern and ordered him to go ahead and get that drop of milk down as quick as he could! There was nothing else on the table but milk and porridge.

Suddenly Ole and Store-Hans flared up in a quarrel; one blamed the other for eating too close to the edge, where the porridge was coolest. The father paused in his meal, listening to them a moment, then chuckled to himself. Taking his spoon and cutting three lines through the crust of the porridge, he quickly settled the matter between them.

"There you are! Here, Store-Hans, is your land; now take it and be satisfied. Ola, who is the biggest, gets another forty. . . . Shut up your mouths, now, and eat!" Per Hansa himself got the smallest share that evening.

Aside from this outbreak it was quiet at the table. A spell of silence lay upon them and they were not able to throw it off. . . . As soon as the father had eaten he licked his spoon carefully, wiped it off on his shirt sleeve, and threw it on the blanket. The boys did likewise as they finished; but And-Ongen wanted to tuck her spoon in her dress and keep it there till morning.

They sat around in the same silence after they were done. Then she who was the smallest of them repeated in a tiny voice:

"Thanks to Thee, Our Lord and Maker. . . .

"Now I want to go to sleep in your lap!" she said, after the Amen. She climbed up into her mother's lap and threw her arms around her neck.

"Oh, how quickly it grows dark out here!" the mother murmured.

Per Hansa gave a care-free shrug of his shoulders. "Well," he said, dryly, "the sooner the day's over, the sooner the next day comes!"

But now something seemed to be brewing back there over the prairie whence they had come. Up from the horizon swelled a supernatural light—a glow of pale yellow and transparent green, mingled with strange touches of red and gold. It spread upward as they watched; the colors deepened; the glow grew stronger, like the witching light of a fen fire.

All sat silently gazing. It was And-Ongen, hanging around her mother's neck, who first found her voice.

"Oh, look! . . . She is coming up again!"

In solemn grandeur the moon swung up above the plain. She had been with them many nights now; but each time she seemed as wonderful a sight as ever. Tonight a hush fell on their spirits as they watched her rise—just as the scene had hushed them the evening before, far away to the eastward somewhere on the plain. The silvery beams grew stronger; the first pale fen fire began to shimmer and spread; slowly the light mellowed into a mist of green and yellow and blue. And-Ongen exclaimed that the moon was much bigger to-night; but it had seemed bigger the night before also. Store-Hans again solemnly told her the reason for it—that the moon had to grow, just as she did! This seemed to her quite logical; she turned to her mother and asked whether the moon had milk and porridge every evening, too.

Per Hansa had been sitting on the tongue of the wagon, smoking his pipe. Now he got up, knocked out the ashes carefully, put his pipe in his pocket, and wound up his watch. These duties done, he gave the order to turn in for the night.

A little while later they all lay under the quilts, gazing off into the opalescent glow. When the mother thought that the children had gone to sleep she asked, soberly:

"Do you suppose we'll ever find the others again?"

"Oh yes—I'm sure of it . . . if they haven't sunk through the ground!"

This was all Per Hansa said. He yawned once or twice, long and heavily, as if he were very sleepy, and turned away from her.

. . . And after that she said no more, either.

IV

Truth to tell, Per Hansa was not a bit sleepy. For a long while he lay wide awake, staring into the night. Although the evening had grown cool, sweat started out on his body from time to time, as thoughts which he could not banish persisted in his mind.

He had good reason to sweat, at all the things he was forced to lie there and remember. Nor was it only to-night that these heavy thoughts came to trouble him; it had been just the same all through the day, and last night, too, and the night before. And now, the moment he had lain down, they had seized upon him with renewed strength; he recalled keenly all the scruples and misgivings that had obsessed his wife before they had started out on this long journey—both those which had been spoken and those which had been left unsaid. The latter had been the worst; they had seemed to grow deeper and more tragic as he had kept prying into them in his clumsy way. . . . But she wasn't a bit stupid, that wife of his! As a matter of fact, she had more sense than most people. Indeed she had!

. . . No, it wasn't a pleasant situation for Per Hansa, by any means. He had not seen a happy moment, day or night, since the mishap had struck them on the second afternoon this side of Jackson. There the first wagon had got stuck in a mud hole; in pulling it out they had wrecked it so hopelessly that he had been forced to put back to Jackson for repairs. Under the circumstances, it had seemed to him utterly senseless to hold up all the rest of the company four days. He simply wouldn't listen to their waiting for him; for they had houses to build and fields to break, if they were to get anything into the ground this season. They must go on without him; he'd come along all right, in his own good time. . . . So they had given him full instructions about the course he was to follow and the halting places where he was to stop for the night; it had all seemed so simple to him at the time. Then they had started on together—Tönseten, who knew the way, and Hans Olsa, and the two Solum boys. They all had horses and strong new wagons. They travelled fast, those fellows! . . .

If he only had paid some attention to Hans Olsa, who for a long while had insisted on waiting for him. But he had overruled all their objections; it was entirely his own doing that Hans Olsa and the others had gone on, leaving him behind.

But he soon had learned that it wasn't so easy. Hadn't he lost his way altogether the other day, in the midst of a fog and drizzling rain? Until late in the afternoon that day he hadn't had the faintest idea what direction he was taking. It had been after this experience that he had formed the habit of keeping so far ahead of the caravan. He simply couldn't endure listening to her constant questions—questions which he found himself unable to answer. . . .

The only thing he felt sure of was that he wasn't on the right track; otherwise he would have come across the traces of their camps. It was getting to be a matter of life and death to him to find the trail—and find it soon. . . . A devil of a jaunt it would be to the Pacific Ocean—the wagon would never hold out *that* long! . . . Oh yes, he realized it all too well—a matter of life and death. There weren't many supplies left in the wagon. He had depended on his old comrade and Lofot-man,* Hans Olsa, for everything.

Per Hansa heaved a deep sigh; it came out before he could stop it. . . . Huh!—it was an easy matter enough for Hans Olsa! He had ample means, and could start out on a big scale from the beginning; he had a wife in whose heart there wasn't a speck of fear! . . . The Lord only knew where they were now—whether they were east or west of him! And they had Tönseten, too, and his wife Kjersti,† both of them used to America. Why, they could talk the language and everything. . . .

And then there were the Solum boys, who had actually been born in this country. . . . Indeed, east or west, it made no difference to them where they lay that night.

But here was he, the newcomer, who owned nothing and knew nothing, groping about with his dear ones in the endless wilderness! . . . Beret had taken such a dislike to this journey, too—although in many ways she was the more sensible of the two. . . . Well, he certainly had fixed up a nice mess for himself, and no mistake!

He wondered why he had ever left Fillmore County; as he lay there thinking it over, he couldn't understand what had prompted him to do such a thing. He could easily have found a job there and stayed until his wife got up from childbed; then he could have moved west next spring. This had been what she had wanted, though she had never said it in so many words.

The quilt had grown oppressively heavy; he threw it

* A companion on the winter fishing grounds at the Lofoten Islands.

† The combination *kj* in this name is pronounced like *ch* in *church*; the final *i* has the sound of *y* in godly.

aside. . . . How long it took her to go to sleep to-night! Why wouldn't she try to get as much rest as possible? Surely she knew that it would be another tough day to-morrow? . . .

. . . Just so that confounded wagon didn't go to pieces again! . . .

V

The night wore on. The children slept quietly and peacefully. The mother also seemed to have found rest at last. Per Hansa thought that she was sound asleep; he began to move slowly away from her. He threw his hand over on the quilt between them as if making a motion in his sleep. . . . No, she didn't stir; he lay quiet for a while, then moved again. In so doing his hand happened to fall on that of Store-Hans; it was so chubby and round, that hand, so healthy and warm, and quite firm for the hand of only a child. Per Hansa lay still for a long time, holding the boy's hand with a desperate earnestness. . . . Slowly the troublesome thoughts seemed to lighten and lift; his courage ebbed back again; surely everything would come out all right in the end!

Little by little he slipped the quilt off, crept out of bed as quietly as a mouse, got into his trousers, and pulled on his shoes.

Outside, the misty sheen of the moonlight shimmered so brightly that it blinded him. Near at hand, the prairie was bathed in a flood of tarnished green; farther off the faint blue tones began to appear, merging gradually into the purple dimness that shrouded all the horizon.

Per Hansa looked for the North Star, found it, turned about until he had it over his right shoulder; then he glanced at his watch, took a few steps, hesitated, and looked back as if taking a bearing of the wagons and the star. The next moment he faced about resolutely, and hurried off westward.

It felt good to be moving again; he almost broke into a trot. There were the oxen, busily grazing; they needed to get their fill all right, poor devils! . . . Rosie lay closer to the wagons; his eyes had passed over her at first, a dark spot in the vague, deceptive light. The cow must have noticed the shadow gliding along so swiftly; she gave a long moo. . . . This enraged Per Hansa; he broke into a run and got out of her sight as quickly as he could, for fear she would moo again. . . . If she only hadn't waked Beret!

He set his course toward the point where he thought the crest of the ridge must lie. Now and then he stopped and looked around, to find out if he could still see the wagons. When he had lost them at last, and they were wholly swallowed up in the night, he gave an involuntary gasp—but clenched his teeth and went on.

The ridge lay farther off than he had thought. He had walked for a solid hour before he finally reached what he felt to be the highest point; he reckoned that he must be at least four miles from camp. . . . There he fell to examining the ground carefully; but first of all he looked at his watch again, and then at the North Star and the moon, trying to fix the bearings of the camp in his mind.

On the other side of the ridge the lay of the land seemed to be different; the slope was a little steeper; a thick underbrush covered it; through the tall bushes the moonlight shimmered strangely. . . . Per Hansa felt no fear, but every sense within him was alert. First he searched the northerly slope of the hill, beyond the edge of the thicket, stooping over as he went, his eyes scanning every foot of the ground. When he had found no trace of what he was looking for, he came back to the same starting point and searched an equal distance in the opposite direction; but he discovered nothing on this tack, either.

Now he began to walk along the edge of the thicket, in and out, crisscrossing the line in every direction; he pushed his way into each little grassless opening, and kicked over the earth there, before he went on. Sweat was running off him in streams. A quarter of an hour went by; he was still searching frantically. . . . All at once, right at the edge of the woods, he struck a piece of level ground with a larger clearing on it; in the middle of this clearing lay a wide, round patch in the grass. Per Hansa threw himself down on his knees, like a miser who has found a costly treasure; he bent over and sniffed the ground. His blood throbbed; his hands shook as he dug. . . . Yes, he was right—here there had been a fire! It couldn't have been many days ago, either; the smell of the ashes was still fresh. . . . His eyes had grown so moist and dim that he had to wipe them. . . . But he wasn't crying—no, not yet! . . .

He began to crawl around on all fours, farther and farther down the slope. Suddenly he stopped, sat up on his haunches, and held something in his hand that he was examining closely. . . .

"I'll be damned if it isn't fresh horse dung!" . . . His voice rang with a great joy. He tried the stuff between his fingers—crumbled it, sniffed at it . . . there was no doubting the fact any longer.

Now he got up, walking erectly with a confident step, like a man who has just made a lucky strike, and began to search along the whole slope. . . . He might as well go ahead and find the ford to-night; then he wouldn't be delayed by hunting for it in the morning. The underbrush thickened as he made his way down the slope. . . . Here, then, was Split Rock Creek; and here they had camped, as Tönseten had said they would! . . .

Once he had reached the edge of the creek, it did not take him long to find the ford that the others had used; the ruts still stood there plainly, as fresh and deep as if they had been made that very day. For a while he paused at the edge of the water, and looked about him. . . . Had they chosen the best crossing, after all? The bank of the creek on the other side formed a bend; the brink looked pretty steep. At last he waded out into the water, with his shoes still on. . . . Oh, well, the grade wasn't so steep that the oxen couldn't easily make it; there would be a bad jolt here at the edge, but after that they would have an even slope up the bank. . . . Stepping out on the opposite shore, he stood as if rooted to the ground.

. . . "What in the devil . . . !"

Per Hansa bent over and picked up the object that lay before him; he held it out in the moonlight, turned it over and over in his hands, smelled of it . . . then took a bite.

. . . "By God! if it isn't one of Hans Olsa's dried mutton legs!"

He straightened himself up and gazed with deep thankfulness into the quivering bluish-green haze that glowed all around him. . . . "Yes, that's the way it goes, when people have more than they can take care of!" . . . He stuck the mutton leg under his arm; whistling a love ballad of Nordland, which seemed to have come into his mind unconsciously, he crossed the creek again.

On the way back he took his own time. Nothing mattered now; the night was fair and mild; his aching weariness was gone; he felt refreshed and strengthened. His wife and children were sleeping safe and sound; of food they still had supplies for a couple of weeks; and now he had found the trail again and could be certain of it all the way to Sioux Falls. . . . That wretched wagon was the only difficulty; it would have to hang together for a few days more! . . .

When he drew near enough to the wagons to make them out clearly in the moonlight, he slackened his pace, and a shiver passed over him.

Wasn't some one sitting there on the wagon tongue? Surely that was a human form?

In growing apprehension he hurried on.

"Good Heavens, Beret! What are you doing out here in the middle of the night?" His voice was full of alarm, yet softened by his great concern for her.

"It felt so awful to lie there alone, after you had gone. . . . I could hardly breathe . . . so I got up."

The words came with difficulty; he realized that her voice was hoarse with weeping; he had to pull himself sharply together in order to keep his own tears back.

"Were you awake, Beret? . . . You shouldn't lie awake that way in the night!" he said, reproachfully.

"How can I sleep? . . . You lie there tossing back and forth, and say nothing! . . . You might have told me. I know very well what's the matter!"

Suddenly she could stand it no longer. She ran over to him, flung her arms around his neck, and leaned close against him. The dam of her pent-up tears broke in a flood of emotion; she wept long and bitterly.

"Now calm yourself, dear. . . . You *must* calm yourself, Beret-girl!" . . . He had put his arm lovingly around her, but found it hard to speak. . . . "Don't you see that I've got one of Hans Olsa's dried mutton legs under my arm?" . . .

. . . That night Per Hansa was good to his wife.

II Home-founding

I

On the side of a hill, which sloped gently away toward the southeast and followed with many windings a creek that wormed its way across the prairie, stood Hans Olsa, laying turf. He was building a sod house. The walls had now risen breast-high; in its half-finished condition, the structure resembled more a bulwark against some enemy than anything intended to be a human habitation And the great heaps of cut sod, piled up in each corner might well have been the stores of ammunition for defence of the stronghold

For a man of his strength and massive build, his motions were unusually quick and agile; but he worked by fits and starts to-day. At times he stopped altogether; in these pauses he would straighten himself up and draw his sleeve with a quick stroke across his troubled face; with each stroke the sleeve would come away damper; and standing so, he would fix his gaze intently on the prairie to the eastward. His eyes had wandered so often now over the stretch of land lying before them, that they were familiar with every tussock and hollow. . . . No—nothing in sight yet! . . . He would resume his task, as if to make up for lost time, and work hard for a spell; only to forget himself once more, pause involuntarily, and stand inert and abstracted, gazing off into the distance.

Beyond the house a tent had been pitched; a wagon was drawn up close beside it. On the ground outside of the tent stood a stove, a couple of chairs, and a few other rough articles of furniture. A stout, healthy-looking woman, whose face radiated an air of simple wisdom and kindliness, was busy preparing the midday meal. She sang to herself as she worked. A ten-year-old girl, addressed by the woman as Sofie, was helping her. Now and then the girl would take up the tune and join in the singing.

Less than a quarter of a mile away, in a southeasterly direction, a finished sod house rose on the slope of the hill. Smoke was winding up from it at this moment. This house, which had been built the previous fall, belonged to Syvert Tönseten.

Some distance north from the place where Hans Olsa had located, two other sod houses were under construction; but a hillock lay between, so that he could not see them from where he stood. There the two Solum boys had driven down their stakes and had begun building. Tönseten's completed house, and the other three half-finished ones, marked the beginning of the settlement on Spring Creek.

The woman who had been bustling about preparing the meal, now called to her husband that dinner was ready—he must come at once! He answered her, straightened up for the hundredth time, wiped his hands on his trousers, and stood for a moment gazing off eastward. . . . No use to look—not a soul in sight yet! . . . He sighed heavily, and walked with slow steps toward the tent, his eyes on the ground.

It was light and airy inside the tent, but stifling hot, because of the unobstructed sunlight beating down upon it. Two beds were ranged along the wall, both of them homemade; a big emigrant chest stood at the head of each. Nails had been driven into the centre pole of the tent, on which hung clothing; higher up a crosspiece, securely fastened, was likewise hung with clothes. Two of the walls were lined with furniture; on these pieces the dishes were displayed, all neatly arranged.

A large basin of water stood on a chair just inside the tent door. Hans Olsa washed his face and hands; then he came out and sat down on the ground, where his wife had spread the table. It was so much cooler outside. The meal was all ready; both mother and daughter had been waiting for him.

"I suppose you haven't seen any signs of them yet?" his wife asked at last.

"No—nothing at all!"

"Can you imagine what has become of them?"

"The Lord forgive us—if I only knew!"

Her husband looked so anxious that she asked no more questions. Out of her kind heart rose a hopeful, "Don't worry, they'll get here all right!" . . . But in spite of the cheerfulness of the words, she could not give them that ring of buoyant confidence which she would have liked to show.

. . . "Of course!" said the girl with a laugh. "Store-Hans and Ola have two good pairs of eyes. Leave it to them—they'll find us!"

The father gave her a stern glance; he didn't tell her in words to stop her foolish chatter—but she said no more. Without speaking once, he ate his dinner. As soon as he had finished, he tossed his spoon on the blanket, thanked them for the food, got up gloomily, and went back to the half-completed wall. There he sat down awhile, as if lost in thought . . . gazing eastward. His large, rugged features were drawn and furrowed with anxiety. . . . "God Almighty!" he sighed, and folded his big hands. "What can have become of Per Hansa?"

His wife was watching him closely as he sat there on the wall. By and by she told her daughter to finish washing the dishes, and started to go over where he was. When he saw her coming, he tried to begin working as if there were nothing on his mind.

"Hans," she said, quickly, when she had reached his side, "I think you ought to go out and look for them!"

He waited until he had got a strip of sod in place before he answered: "Easier said than done . . . when we haven't the faintest idea where to look . . . on such stretches of prairie!"

"Yes, I know; but it would make us all feel better, anyway . . . as if we were doing something."

Hans Olsa laid another strip of turf; then he stopped,

let his hands fall to his sides, and began thinking aloud as he gazed off into the distance. . . .

"I know this much—you don't often find a smarter fellow than Per Hansa. . . . That's what makes it so queer! I don't suppose he's able to get much speed out of his oxen; but one thing I'm certain of—he has been hurrying as fast as he could. And we surely didn't come along very fast . . . but now it's the fifth day since we arrived here! If he made use of these bright moonlight nights, as he probably did, I begin to be afraid that he's gone on west of us somewhere, instead of being still to the eastward. . . . It's certainly no child's play to start looking for him!"

Hans Olsa slumped down on the wall, the picture of dejection. His wife quickly found a place beside him. Together they sat there in silence. The same fear that she felt him struggling with, a fear thrown into sharp relief by the things he had just been saying, had long since gripped her heart also.

"I feel so sorry for Beret, poor thing . . . and the children. You must remember, though, that he couldn't go very fast on account of her condition. . . . I think she is with child again!" She paused. "I dreamed about them last night . . . a bad dream. . . ."

Her husband glanced sidewise at her. "We mustn't pay attention to such things. A bad dream is a good sign, anyway—that's what my mother always said. . . . But I suppose I'll never forgive myself for not waiting for him." He got up heavily and laid another strip of turf. "He's always been like that, Per Hansa; he never would take help from any man. But this time he's carried it a little too far!"

His wife made no answer. She was watching a short stout man with a reddish beard who had started up the slope from the direction of the house to the south of them. He had cheeks like two rosy apples, a quick step, and eyes that flitted all about; he was noted among them for his glib tongue and the flood of his conversation. With hands stuck into the waistband of his trousers, and elbows out akimbo, the man looked half as broad again as he really was.

"Here comes Tönseten," said the woman. "Why don't you talk it over with him? I really think you ought to go out and look for them."

"Seen anything of them yet, Hans Olsa?" asked the man, without further greeting, as soon as he arrived. . . . "Well, well! this looks fine! Ha, ha! It's a warm house, you know, that's built by the aid of a woman's hand."

Hans Olsa wheeled on him. "You haven't caught sight of them yourself, Syvert, have you?"

"Caught sight of them? Why, man alive, that's just what I've come up here to tell you! I've had them in sight for over an hour now. Seems to me you ought to be able to see them easy enough—you who carry your eyes so high up in the air! . . . Good Lord! it won't be long before they arrive here, at the rate they're coming!"

"What's that you say?" the others burst out with one voice. . . . "Where are they?" . . .

"I reckon Per Hansa must have got off his course a little. Maybe the oxen didn't steer well, or maybe he didn't figure the current right. . . . Look to the westward, neighbours! Look over there about west-northwest, and you'll see him plain enough. . . . No need to worry. That fellow never would drown in such shallow water as this! . . . I wonder, now, how far west he's really been?"

Hans Olsa and his wife faced around in the direction that Tönseten had indicated. Sure enough, out of the west a little caravan was crawling up toward them on the prairie.

"Can that be them? . . . I really believe it is!" said Hans Olsa in a half whisper, as if hardly daring yet to give vent to his joy.

"*Of course* it is!" cried his wife, excitedly. . . . "Thank God!"

"Not the least doubt of it," Tönseten assured them. "You might as well go and put your coffeepot on the stove, Mother Sörrina! * That Kjersti of mine is coming over pretty soon; she'll probably have something good tucked under her apron. . . . In half an hour we'll have

* The name properly is Sörine, with the accent on the second syllable; but in the dialect of Helgeland it is pronounced Sörrina, with the accent on the first. These people all came from the district of Helgeland, in Norway.

the lost sheep back in the fold!"

"Yes! Heavens and earth, Sörrina!" cried Hans Olsa, "fetch out the best you've got! . . . Per, Per, is it really you, old boy? . . . But why are you coming from the west, I'd like to know?"

Tönseten coughed, and gave the woman a sly wink.

"Look here, Mother Sörrina," he said with a twinkle in his eyes, "won't you be good enough, please, to take a peek at Hans Olsa's Sunday bottle? . . . Not that *I* want anything to drink, you understand—I should say not. Good Lord, no! But think of that poor woman out there, who has been suffering all this time without a drop! And I'd be willing to bet that Per Hansa wouldn't object to having his stomach warmed up a little, too!"

At that they burst out laughing, from mingled joy and relief; but Tönseten's laughter at his own joke was the loudest of all. . . . Work was resumed at once; Syvert began to carry the sods for Hans Olsa to lay up, while Mother Sörrina went off in a happy frame of mind, to make her preparations for the reception of the wanderers.

II

Before the half hour allotted by Tönseten had passed, the caravan came slowly crawling up the slope. Per Hansa still strode in the van, with Store-Hans at his side; Ole walked abreast of the oxen, driving them with the goad. Beret and And-Ongen sat in the wagon. Rosie came jogging along behind at her own gait; she gave a loud, prolonged "moo-o-o-o" as she discovered the other animals across the prairie.

Both families stood ready to receive them; Hans Olsa and Sörine, Tönseten and his Kjersti, all watching intently the movements of the approaching company; but the girl couldn't possess her patience any longer, and ran down to meet the new arrivals. She took Store-Hans by the hand and fell in beside him; the first question she asked was whether he hadn't been terribly scared at night? . . .

As the slope of the hill grew steeper, the oxen had to bend to the yoke.

"Hey, there, folks!" shouted Per Hansa, boisterously. "Don't be standing around loafing, now! It's only the middle of the afternoon. Haven't you got anything to do around here?"

"Coffee time, coffee time, Per Hansa . . . ha, ha, ha!" Tönseten was bubbling over with good spirits. "We thought we might as well wait a little while for you, you know."

. . . "You've found us at last!" said Hans Olsa, with a deep, happy chuckle. . . . He didn't seem able to let go of Per Hansa's hand.

"Found you? Why, devil take it, it's no trick to follow a course out here! You just have to keep on steering straight ahead. And you had marked the trail pretty well, all the way along. I found plenty of traces of you. . . . I guess we stood a little too far to the westward, between Sioux Falls and here; that's how it happened. . . . So *this* is the place, is it? . . . The pastures of Goshen in the land of Egypt—eh?"

"Just so, just so!" cried Tönseten, nodding and laughing. "Pastures of Goshen—right you are! That's exactly what we are going to call the place—*Goshen*—if only you haven't sailed in to mix things up for us!" . . .

Beret and the child had now got down from the wagon; the other two women hovered around her, drawing her toward the tent. But she hung back for a moment; she wanted to stop and look around.

. . . Was this the place? . . . *Here!* . . . Could it be possible? . . . She stole a glance at the others, at the half-completed hut, then turned to look more closely at the group standing around her; and suddenly it struck her that *here something was about to go wrong*. . . . For several days she had sensed this same feeling; she could not seem to tear herself loose from the grip of it. . . . A great lump kept coming up in her throat; she swallowed hard to keep it back, and forced herself to look calm. Surely, surely, she mustn't give way to her tears now, in the midst of all this joy. . . .

Then she followed the other two women into the tent; seeing a chair, she sank down in it, as if her strength had gone!

Sörine was patting her on the shoulder. . . . "Come, get your things off, Beret. You ought to loosen up your clothes, you know. Just throw this dress of mine around you. . . . Here's the water to wash yourself in. Let down your hair, and take your time about it. . . . Don't mind Kjersti and me being around."

After they had bustled about for a little while the others left her. The moment they had gone she jumped up and crossed the tent, to look out of the door. . . . How will human beings be able to endure this place? she thought. Why, there isn't even a thing that one can *hide behind!* . . . Her sensitive, rather beautiful face was full of blank dismay; she turned away from the door and began to loosen her dress; then her eyes fell on the centre pole with its crosspiece, hung with clothes, and she stood a moment irresolute, gazing at it in startled fright. . . . It looked like the giants she had read about as a child; for a long while she was unable to banish the picture from her mind.

Outside the tent, Ole stood with his hand resting on one of the oxen. He was disgusted; the older people seemed to have clean forgotten his existence. They never would get done talking—when he, too, might have had a word to put in! . . .

"Hadn't we better unhitch the oxen, Dad?"

"Yes, yes—that's right, Ola. We might as well camp down here for the night, since we've run across some folks we used to know. . . . How about it, you fellows?" He turned to the other two. "I suppose there's a little more land left around here, isn't there, after you've got through?"

"*Land?* Good God! Per Hansa, what are you talking about? Take whatever you please, from here to the Pacific Ocean!" Tönseten's enthusiasm got so far away with him that he had to pull one of his hands out of his waistband and make a sweeping circle with it in the air.

"You must take a look around as soon as you can," Hans Olsa said, "and see if you find anything better that meets your fancy. In the meanwhile I've put down a stake for you on the quarter section that lies north of mine. We'll go over and have a look at it pretty soon. Sam Solum wanted it, but I told him he'd better leave it till you came. . . . You see, you would be next to the creek there; and then you and I would be the nearest neighbours, just as we've always planned. It makes no particular difference to Sam; he can take the quarter alongside his brother's."

Per Hansa drew a deep breath, as if filling himself with life's great goodness. . . . Here Hans Olsa had been worrying about him, and with kindly forethought had arranged everything to his advantage! . . . "Well, well, we'll have to settle all that later, Hans Olsa. For the present, I can only say that I'm deeply thankful to you! . . . Unhitch the beasts, there, Ola! . . . And now, if you folks have got anything handy, to either eat or drink, I'll accept it with pleasure."

. . . "Or *both*, Per Hansa!" put in Tönseten, excitedly.

"Yes, both, Syvert. I won't refuse!"

Soon they were all gathered around a white cloth which Mother Sörine had spread on the ground. On one side of it lay a whole leg of dried mutton; on the other a large heap of *flatbröd*, with cheese, bread, and butter; in the centre of the cloth stood a large bowl of sweet milk, and from the direction of the stove the breeze wafted to them a pleasant odour of fried bacon and strong coffee. Mother Sörine herself took charge of the ceremony, bringing the food and urging them all to sit down. The stocky figure of Per Hansa rocked back and forth in blissful delight as he squatted there with his legs crossed under him.

"Come, Sörrina, sit down!" he cried. "I guess we've fallen in with gentlefolks, by the looks of things around here. . . . I suppose you think you're old Pharaoh himself—eh, Hans Olsa?"

"Who do you call me, then?" inquired Tönseten.

"You, Syvert? Well, now, I really don't know what to say. Of course you'd like to be His Majesty's butler, but you mustn't be encouraged—remember what happened to that poor fellow! . . . I think we'd better make you the baker—it might be safer, all around. What's your idea, Hans Olsa?"

By this time they were all laughing together.

In the midst of the jollification came Sörine, carrying a plate with a large bottle and a dram glass* on it. . . .

* This bottle and glass would have been old family pieces from Norway, the bottle shaped something like an hourglass, with a contraction in the middle to be grasped by the hand.

"Here, take this off my hands, Hans Olsa—you will know what to do with it!"

Tönseten fairly bubbled over in his admiration for her: "Oh, you sweet Sörrina-girl!—you're dearer to my heart than a hundred women! . . . What a blessing it must be, to have a wife like that!"

"Stop your foolishness!" said Kjersti, but her voice didn't sound too severe.

For a long while they continued to sit around the cloth, chatting, eating, and drinking, and thoroughly enjoying themselves. Hans Olsa seemed like a different man from the one who had eaten here at noon. His loud voice led the cheerful talk; his ponderous bulk was always the centre of the merriment; it seemed as if he would never tire of gazing into that bearded, roguish face of Per Hansa's.

Once, as Per Hansa was slicing off a piece of mutton, he regarded the cut thoughtfully, and asked:

"I suppose you brought all your supplies through safe enough?"

"Oh, sure," answered Hans Olsa, innocently. "We had no trouble at all—didn't lose anything; that is, except for the leg that we left behind somewhere, east on the prairie. But that's hardly worth mentioning."

Per Hansa paused with the piece of meat halfway to his mouth, and looked at Sörine with an expression of deep concern:

"The devil you say! Did you lose one of your legs . . . ?"

Mother Sörine laughed heartily at him. "Oh no—not quite so bad as that. . . . But a leg of mutton might come in handy later on, I'll tell you; there aren't too many of them to be had around here."

Per Hansa chewed away on the meat and looked very serious. At last he said:

"That's always the way with folks who have more of the world's goods than they can take care. . . . But I'll promise you one thing, Sörrina: if I can get my old blunderbuss to work, you're going to have your lost leg back again. . . . How about it, fellows? Have you seen any game that's fit to eat out here?"

III

They sat on until the first blue haze of evening began to spread eastward over the plain. The talk had now drifted to questions of a more serious nature, mostly concerned with how they should manage things out here; of their immediate prospects; of what the future might hold in store for them; of land and crops, and of the new kingdom which they were about to found. . . . No one put the thought into words, but they all felt it strongly; now they had gone back to the very beginning of things. . . .

As the evening shadows deepened the conversation gradually died away into silence. A peculiar mood came drifting in with the dusk. It seemed to float on the evening breeze, to issue forth out of the heart of the untamed nature round about them; it lurked in the very vastness and endlessness surrounding them on every hand; it even seemed to rise like an impalpable mist out of the ground on which they sat.

This mood brought vague premonitions to them, difficult to interpret. . . . No telling what might happen out here . . . for almost anything *could* happen! . . .

They were so far from the world . . . cut off from the haunts of their fellow beings . . . so terribly far! . . .

The faces that gazed into one another were sober now, as silence claimed the little company; but lines of strength and determination on nearly every countenance told of an inward resolve to keep the mood of depression from gaining full control.

Per Hansa was the first to rouse himself and throw off the spell. He jumped up with nervous energy; a shiver passed over him, as if he were having a chill.

"What is it—are you cold?" asked his wife. She had instinctively sensed his mood as she looked at him—and loved him better for it. Until that moment, she had supposed that she herself was the only one who felt this peculiar influence.

"Such crazy talk!" he burst out. "I believe we've all lost our senses, every last one of us! Here we sit around celebrating in broad daylight, in the middle of summer, as if it was the Christmas holidays! . . . Come on, woman, let's go over to our new home!"

Everyone got up.

"You must do exactly as you please about it, Per Hansa," spoke up Hans Olsa with an apologetic air. "Don't feel that you must take this quarter if you don't like it. But as far as I can see, it's as good a piece of land as you could find anywhere around—every square foot of it plowland, except the hill over there. Plenty of water for both man and beast. . . . As for my part, if I can only sit here between you and Syvert, I certainly won't be kicking about my neighbours. . . . But I don't want you to feel that you have to take this quarter on my account, you understand. . . . If you do take it, though, we must get one of the Solum boys to go down to Sioux Falls with you the first thing to-morrow, so that you can file your claim. You'll have to do that in any case, you know, whichever quarter you take. . . . There's likely to be a lot of people moving into this region before the snow flies; we five oughtn't to part company or let anyone get in between us. . . . You've heard my best advice, anyway."

"Now, that's the talk!" Tönseten chimed in, briskly. "And considering the size of the head it comes from, it isn't half bad, either. You're damned well right, Hans Olsa. Before the snow flies you're going to see such a multitude swarming around these parts, that the thundering place won't be fit to live in! Remember what I say, boys, in times to come—bear it in mind that those were Syvert's very words! . . . You've got to go straight to Sioux Falls tomorrow morning, Per Hansa, and no two ways about it! If one of the Solum boys can't go along to do the talking for you, why, I shall have to buckle down to the job myself."

Once more Per Hansa's heart filled with a deep sense of peace and contentment as he realized how matters were being smoothed out for him. They seemed to move of their own accord but he knew better. . . . Was he really to own it? Was it really to become his possession, this big stretch of fine land that spread here before him? Was he really to have his friends for neighbours, both to the north and to the south—folks who cared for him and wanted to help him out in every way? . . .

He was still chuckling with the rare pleasure of it as he asked, "You haven't discovered any signs of life since you came?"

"Devil, no!" Tönseten assured him. "Neither Israelites nor Canaanites! I was the first one to find this place, you know. . . . But there's no telling how soon the drift will loosen, the way folks were talking back East last winter. And now the land office for this whole section of country has been moved to Sioux Falls, too. That means business; the government, you may be certain, has good reason for doing such a thing." Tönseten spoke with all the importance of a man who has inside knowledge.

Per Hansa looked at him, and a bantering tone came into his voice:

"I see it clearly, Syvert—it would never do to keep you around here as a mere baker! We'll have to promote you to a higher office, right away. . . . Now, boys, I'm going over to see this empire that you two have set aside for me. Ola, you hitch up the oxen again and bring the wagons along."

With these commands he walked rapidly away; the others had almost to run in order to keep up with him. Strong emotions surged through him as he strode on. . . .

"It lies high," he observed after a while, when they had looked all the plowland over. . . . "There must be a fine view from the top of that hill."

They were bending their steps in this direction, and soon had reached the highest point. It seemed so spacious and beautiful to stand high above the prairie and look around, especially now, when the shades of evening were falling. . . . Suddenly Per Hansa began to step more cautiously; he sniffed the air like an animal; in a moment he stopped beside a small depression in the ground, and stood gazing at it intently for quite a while; then he said, quietly:

"There are people buried here. . . . That is a grave!"

"Oh no, Per Hansa! It can't be possible."

"No doubt about it," he said in the same subdued but positive tone.

Tönseten and Hans Olsa were so astonished that they could hardly credit the fact; they came over at once to where Per Hansa stood, and gazed down into the hollow.

Hans Olsa bent over and picked up a small stone that his eyes had lighted on; he turned it around in his hand several times. . . . "That's a queer-looking piece of stone! I almost believe people have shaped it for some use. . . . Here, see what you make of it, Syvert."

Tönseten's ruddy face grew sober and thoughtful as he examined the object.

"By thunder! It certainly looks as if the Indians had been here! . . . Now isn't that rotten luck?" . . .

"I'm afraid so," said Per Hansa, with a vigorous nod. Then he added, sharply, "But we needn't shout the fact from the house-tops, you know! . . . It takes so very little to scare some folks around here."

He waited no longer but walked hastily down the hill; at the foot he called to Ole, telling him not to drive any farther; but first he turned to Hans Olsa to find out whether they were well across the line between the two quarters.

"No use in building farther away from you than is absolutely necessary," he said. "It's going to be lonesome for the women-folks at times." . . .

. . . Awhile later, Tönseten was dragging his way homeward. For reasons that he wouldn't admit even to himself, he walked a good deal heavier now than when he had climbed the slope that afternoon.

Per Hansa returned with his other neighbour to the wagons, where Beret and the children were waiting. Again he inquired about the line between the two quarters; then asked Beret and Hans Olsa to help pick the best building place; his words, though few and soberly spoken, had in them an unmistakable ring of determination. . . . This vast stretch of beautiful land was to be his—yes, *his*—and no ghost of a dead Indian would drive him away! . . . His heart began to expand with a mighty exaltation. An emotion he had never felt before filled him and made him walk erect. . . . "Good God!" he panted. "This kingdom is going to be *mine!*"

IV

Early the next morning Per Hansa and one of the Solum boys set out on the fifty-two-mile journey to Sioux Falls, where Per Hansa filed an application for the quarter-section of land which lay to the north of Hans Olsa's. To confirm the application, he received a temporary deed to the land. The deed was made out in the name of *Peder Benjamin Hansen;* it contained a description of the land, the conditions which he agreed to fulfil in order to become the owner, and the date, *June 6, 1873.*

Sörine wanted Beret and the children to stay with her during the two days that her husband would be away; but she refused the offer with thanks. If they were to get ready a home for the summer, she said, she would have to take hold of matters right away.

. . . "For the summer?" exclaimed the other woman, showing her astonishment. "What about the winter, then?"

Beret saw that she had uttered a thought which she ought to have kept to herself; she evaded the question as best she could.

During the first day, both she and the boys found so much to do that they hardly took time to eat. They unloaded both the wagons, set up the stove, and carried out the table. Then Beret arranged their bedroom in the larger wagon. With all the things taken out it was quite roomy in there; it made a tidy bedroom when everything had been put in order. The boys thought this work great fun, and she herself found some relief in it for her troubled mind. But something vague and intangible hovering in the air would not allow her to be wholly at ease; she had to stop often and look about, or stand erect and listen. . . . Was that a sound she heard? . . . All the while, the thought that had struck her yesterday when she had first got down from the wagon, stood vividly before her mind: here there was nothing even to hide behind! . . . When the room was finished, and a blanket had been hung up to serve as a door, she seemed a little less conscious of this feeling. But back in the recesses of her mind it still was there. . . .

After they had milked the cow, eaten their evening

porridge, and talked awhile to the oxen, she took the boys and And-Ongen and strolled away from camp. With a common impulse, they went toward the hill; when they had reached the summit, Beret sat down and let her gaze wander aimlessly around. . . . In a certain sense, she had to admit to herself, it was lovely up here. The broad expanse stretching away endlessly in every direction, seemed almost like the ocean—especially now, when darkness was falling. It reminded her strongly of the sea, and yet it was very different. . . . This formless prairie had no heart that beat, no waves that sang, no soul that could be touched . . . or cared. . . .

The infinitude surrounding her on every hand might not have been so oppressive, might even have brought her a measure of peace, if it had not been for the deep silence, which lay heavier here than in a church. Indeed, what was there to break it? She had passed beyond the outposts of civilization; the nearest dwelling places of men were far away. Here no warbling of birds rose on the air, no buzzing of insects sounded;* even the wind had died away; the waving blades of grass that trembled to the faintest breath now stood erect and quiet, as if listening, in the great hush of the evening. . . . All along the way, coming out, she had noticed this strange thing: the stillness had grown deeper, the silence more depressing, the farther west they journeyed; it must have been over two weeks now since she had heard a bird sing! Had they travelled into some nameless, abandoned region? Could no living thing exist out here, in the empty, desolate, endless wastes of green and blue? . . . How *could* existence go on, she thought, desperately? If life is to thrive and endure, it must at least have something to hide behind! . . .

The children were playing boisterously a little way off. What a terrible noise they made! But she had better let them keep on with their play, as long as they were happy. . . . She sat perfectly quiet, thinking of the long, oh, so interminably long march that they would have to make, back to the place where human beings

* Original settlers are agreed that there was neither bird nor insect life on the prairie, with the exception of mosquitoes, the first year that they came.

dwelt. It would be small hardship for her, of course, sitting in the wagon; but she pitied Per Hansa and the boys—and then the poor oxen! . . . He certainly would soon find out for himself that a home for men and women and children could never be established in this wilderness. . . . And how could she bring new life into the world out here! . . .

Slowly her thoughts began to centre on her husband; they grew warm and tender as they dwelt on him. She trembled as they came. . . .

But only for a brief while. As her eyes darted nervously here and there, flitting from object to object and trying to pierce the purple dimness that was steadily closing in, a sense of desolation so profound settled upon her that she seemed unable to think at all. It would not do to gaze any longer at the terror out there, where everything was turning to grim and awful darkness. . . . She threw herself back in the grass and looked up into the heavens. But darkness and infinitude lay there, also—the sense of utter desolation still remained. . . . Suddenly, for the first time, she realized the full extent of her loneliness, the dreadful nature of the fate that had overtaken her. Lying there on her back, and staring up into the quiet sky across which the shadows of night were imperceptibly creeping, she went over in her mind every step of their wanderings, every mile of the distance they had travelled since they had left home. . . .

First they had boarded the boat at Sandnessjöen. . . . This boat had carried them southward along the coast. . . . In Namsos there had been a large ship with many white sails, that had taken her, with her dear ones, and sailed away—that had carried them off relentlessly, farther and farther from the land they knew. In this ship they had sailed for weeks; the weeks had even grown into months; they had seemed to be crossing an ocean which had no end. . . . There had been something almost laughable in this blind course, steadily fixed on the sunset! When head winds came, they beat up against them; before sweeping fair breezes they scudded along; but always they were westering! . . .

. . . At last they had landed in Quebec. There she had walked about the streets, confused and bewildered by a jargon of unintelligible sounds that did not seem like the speech of people. . . . Was this the Promised Land? Ah no—it was only the beginning of the real journey. . . . Then something within her had risen up in revolt: I will go no farther! . . .

. . . But they had kept on, just the same—had pushed steadily westward, over plains, through deserts, into towns, and out of them again. . . . One fine day they had stood in Detroit, Michigan. This wasn't the place, either, it seemed. . . . Move on! . . . Once more she had felt the spirit of revolt rising to shout aloud: I will go no farther! . . . But it had been as if a resistless flood had torn them loose from their foundations and was carrying them helplessly along on its current—flinging them here and there, hurling them madly onward, with no known destination ahead.

Farther and farther onward . . . always west. . . . For a brief while there had been a chance to relax once more; they had travelled on water again, and she could hear the familiar splash of waves against the ship's side. This language she knew of old, and did not fear; it had lessened the torture of that section of the journey for her, though they had been subjected to much ill-treatment and there had been a great deal of bullying and brawling on board.

At last the day had arrived when they had landed in Milwaukee. But here they were only to make a new start—to take another plunge into the unknown. . . . Farther, and always farther. . . . The relentless current kept whirling them along. . . . Was it bound nowhere, then? . . . Did it have no end? . . .

In the course of time they had come jogging into a place called Prairie du Chien. . . . Had that been in Wisconsin, or some other place named after savages? . . . It made no difference—they had gone on. They had floundered along to Lansing, in Iowa. . . . Onward again. Finally they had reached Fillmore County, in Minnesota. . . . But even that wasn't the place, it seemed! . . .

. . . Now she was lying here on a little green hillock, surrounded by the open, endless prairie, far off in a spot from which no road led back! . . . It seemed to her that she had lived many lives already, in each one of which she had done nothing but wander and wander, always straying farther way from the home that was dear to her.

She sat up at last, heaved a deep sigh, and glanced around as if waking from a dream. . . . The unusual blending of the gentle and forceful in her features seemed to be thrown into relief by the scene in which she sat and the twilight hovering about her, as a beautiful picture is enhanced by a well-chosen frame.

The two boys and their little sister were having great fun up here. So many queer things were concealed under the tufts of grass. Store-Hans came running, and brought a handful of little flat, reddish chips of stone that looked as though they had been carved out of the solid rock; they were pointed at one end and broadened out evenly on both sides, like the head of a spear. The edges were quite sharp; in the broad end a deep groove had been filed. Ole brought more of them, and gave a couple to his little sister to play with. . . . The mother sat for a while with the stones in her lap, where the children had placed them; at last she took them up, one by one, and examined them closely. . . . These must have been formed by human hands, she thought.

Suddenly Ole made another rare discovery. He brought her a larger stone, that looked like a sledge hammer; in this the groove was deep and broad.

The mother got up hastily.

"Where are you finding these things?"

The boys at once took her to the place; in a moment she, too, was standing beside the little hollow at the brow of the hill, which the men had discovered the night before; the queer stones that the children had been bringing her lay scattered all around.

"Ola says that the Indians made them!" cried Store-Hans, excitedly. "Is it true, mother? . . . Do you suppose they'll ever come back?"

"Yes, maybe—if we stay here long enough. . . ." She remained standing awhile beside the hollow; the same thought possessed her that had seized hold of her husband when he had first found the spot—here a human being lay buried. Strangely enough, it did not frighten her; it only showed her more plainly, in a stronger, harsher light, how unspeakably lonesome this place was.

The evening dusk had now almost deepened into night. It seemed to gather all its strength around her, to close in on every side, to have its centre in the spot where she stood. The wagons had become only a dim speck in the darkness, far, far away; the tent at Hans Olsa's looked like a tuft of grass that had whitened at the top; Tönseten's sod house she was unable to make out at all. . . . She could not bring herself to call aloud to the boys; instead, she walked around the hollow, spoke to them softly, and said that it was time to go home. . . . No, no, they mustn't take the stones with them to-night! But to-morrow they might come up here again to play.

. . . Beret could not go to sleep for a long time that night. At last she grew thoroughly angry with herself; her nerves were taut as bowstrings; her head kept rising up from the pillow to listen—but there was nothing to hear . . . nothing except the night wind, which now had begun to stir.

. . . It stirred with so many unknown things! . . .

V

Per Hansa came home late the following afternoon; he had so many words of praise for what she and the boys had accomplished while he had been gone, that he fairly bewildered her. Now it had taken possession of him again—that indomitable, conquering mood which seemed to give him the right of way wherever he went, whatever he did. Outwardly, at such times, he showed only a buoyant recklessness, as if wrapped in a cloak of gay, wanton levity; but down beneath all this lay a stern determination of purpose, a driving force, so strong that she shrank back from the least contact with it.

To-day he was talking in a steady stream.

"Here is the deed to our kingdom, Beret-girl! See to it that you take good care of the papers. . . . Isn't it stranger than a fairy tale, that a man can have such things here, just for the taking? . . . Yes—and years after he won the princess, too!" He cocked his head on one side. "I'll tell you what, it seems so impossible and unheard of, that I can't quite swallow it all yet. . . . What do you say, my Beret-girl?"

Beret stood smiling at him, with tears in her eyes, beside the improvised house that she had made; there was little for her to say. And what would be the use of speaking now? He was so completely wrapped up in his own plans that he would not listen nor understand. It would be wrong, too, to trouble him with her fears and misgivings. . . . When he felt like this he was so tender to her, so cheerful, so loving and kind. . . . How well she knew Per Hansa! . . .

"What are you thinking about it all, my Beret-girl?" He flung his arm around her, whirled her off her feet, and drew her toward him.

"Oh, Per, it's only this—I'm so afraid out here!" She snuggled up against him, as if trying to hide herself. "It's all so big and open . . . so empty. . . . Oh, Per! Not another human being from here to the end of the world!"

Per Hansa laughed loud and long, so that she winced under the force and meaning of it. "There'll soon be more people, girl . . . never you fear. . . . By God! there'll soon be more people here!"

But suddenly another idea took hold of him. He led her over to the large chest, made her sit down, and stood in front of her with a swaggering air:

"Now let me tell you what came into my mind yesterday, after I had got the papers. I went right out and bought ten sacks of potatoes! I felt so good, Beret—and you know how we men from Nordland like potatoes!" he added with a laugh. "This is the point of it: we're not going to start right in with building a house. The others are just foolish to do it." His voice grew low and eager. "They're beginning at the wrong end, you see. For my part, I'm going over to Hans Olsa's this very night and borrow his plow—and to-morrow morning I shall start breaking my ground! Yes, sir! I tell you those potatoes have got to go into the ground at once. Do you hear me, Beret-girl? If the soil out here is half as good as it's cracked up to be, we'll have a fine crop the very first fall! . . . Then I can build later in the summer, you know, when I am able to take my time about it. . . . Just wait, my girl, just wait. It's going to be wonderful; you'll see how wonderful I can make it for you, this kingdom of ours!" He laughed until his eyes were drawn out in two narrow slits. "And no old worn-out, thin-shanked, pot-bellied king is going to come around and tell me what I have to do about it, either!"

He explained to her at great length how he intended to arrange everything and how success would crown his efforts, she sitting there silently on the chest, he standing in front of her, waving his arms; while about them descended the grandeur of the evening. But with all his strength and enthusiasm, and with all her love, he didn't succeed in winning her heart over altogether—no, not altogether. She had heard with her own ears how no bird sang out here; she had seen with her own eyes how, day after day as their journeyed, they had left the abodes of men farther and farther behind. Wasn't she sitting here now, gazing off into an endless blue-green solitude that had neither heart nor soul? . . .

"Do you know," she said, quietly, as she got up once more and leaned close against him, "I believe there is a grave over there on the hill?"

"Why, Beret! Did you find it? Have you been going around brooding over that, too? . . . Don't worry, girl. He'll bring us nothing but good luck, the fellow who lies up there."

"Perhaps. . . . But it seems so strange that some one lies buried in unconsecrated ground right at our very door. How quiet it must be there! . . . The children found so many things to play with, while we were up on the hill last night, that I let them go again to-night. Come, we had better begin to look for them. . . . It is beautiful up there." She sighed, and moved away.

They climbed the hill together, holding each other's hands. There was something in that sad resignation of hers which he was powerless against. As he walked beside her and held her hand, he felt as if he could laugh and cry in the same breath. . . . She was so dear, so dear to him. Why could he never make her understand it fully? It was a strange, baffling thing! But perhaps the reason for it lay in this: she was not built to wrestle with fortune—she was too fine-grained. . . . Oh, well—he knew one person, at any rate, who stood ready to do the fighting for her!

Per Hansa had so much to think about that night that a long time passed before he could get to sleep. Now was a good chance to make his plans, while Beret lay at his side, sleeping safe and sound; he must utilize every moment now; he didn't feel very tired, either.

There seemed to be no end to the things he needed. But thirty dollars was all the money he had in the world; and when he thought of what would have to be bought in the near future, and of everything that waited to be done, the list grew as long as the distance they had travelled. . . . First of all, house and barn; that would need doors and windows. Then food and tobacco; shoes and clothing; and implements—yes, farming implements! If he only had horses and the necessary implements, the whole quarter-section would soon blossom like a garden. . . . The horses he would have to do without, to begin with. But he ought to get at least one more cow before fall came—no dodging that fact. . . . And pigs—he absolutely had to have some pigs for winter! . . . If the potatoes turned out well, there would be plenty to feed them on. . . . Then he would buy some chickens, as soon as he could run across any folks who had chickens to sell. Things like that would only be pleasant diversions for Beret. . . . There certainly seemed to be no end to all that he needed.

. . . But now came the main hitch in his calculations: Beret was going to have a baby again. . . . Only a blessing, of course—but what a lot of their time it would take up, just now! . . . Oh, well, she would have to bear the brunt of it herself, as the woman usually did. A remarkably brave and clever wife, that she was . . . a woman of tender kindness, of deep, fine fancies—one whom you could not treat like an ordinary clod.

. . . How hard he would strive to make life pleasant for her out here! Her image dominated all the visions which now seemed to come to him of their own accord. . . . The whole farm lay there before him, broken and under cultivation, yielding its fruitful harvests; there ran many horses and cows, both young and grown. And over on the location where to-day he was about to build the sod hut should stand a large dwelling . . . a *white* house, it would be! Then it would gleam so beautifully in the sun, white all over—but the cornices should be bright green! . . .

When, long ago, Per Hansa had had his first vision of the house, it had been painted white, with green cornices; and these colours had belonged to it in his mind ever since. But the stable, the barn, and all the rest of the outhouses should be painted red, with white cornices—for that gave such a fine effect! . . . Oh yes, that Beret-girl of his should certainly have a royal mansion for herself and her little princess! . . .

VI

As Per Hansa lay there dreaming of the future it seemed to him that hidden springs of energy, hitherto unsuspected even by himself, were welling up in his heart. He felt as if his strength were inexhaustible. And so he commenced his labours with a fourteen-hour day; but soon, as the plans grew clearer, he began to realize how little could be accomplished in that short span of time, with so much work always ahead of him; he accordingly lengthened the day to sixteen hours, and threw in another hour for good measure; at last he found himself wondering if a man couldn't get along with only five hours of rest, in this fine summer weather.

His waking dreams passed unconsciously into those of sleep; all that night a pleasant buoyancy seemed to be lifting him up and carrying him along; at dawn, when he opened his eyelids, morning was there to greet him—the morning of a glorious new day. . . . He saw that it was already broad daylight; with a guilty start, he came wide awake. Heavens! he might have overslept himself—on *this* morning! . . . He jumped into his clothes, and found some cold porridge to quiet his hunger for the time being; then he hurried out, put the yoke on the oxen, and went across to Hans Olsa's to fetch the plow. . . . Over there no life was stirring yet. Well, maybe they could afford to sleep late in the morning; but he had arrived five days behind the others, and had just been delayed for two days more; they had a big start over him already. His heart sang as he thought how he would have to hurry! . . . He led the oxen carefully, trying to make as little noise around the tent as possible.

Dragging the plow, he drove out for some distance toward the hillock, then stopped and looked around. This was as good a place as anywhere to start breaking. . . . He straightened up the plow, planted the share firmly in the ground, and spoke to the oxen: "Come now, move along, you lazy rascals!" He had meant to speak gruffly, but the thrill of joy that surged over him as he sank the plow in his own land for the first time, threw such an unexpected tone of gentleness into his voice that the oxen paid no attention to it; he found that he would have to resort to more powerful encouragement; but even with the goad it was hard to make them bend to the yoke so early in the morning. After a little, however, they began to stretch their muscles. Then they were off; the plow moved . . . sank deeper . . . the first furrow was breaking. . . .

It would have gone much easier now if Ole had only been there to drive the oxen, so that he could have given his whole attention to the plow. But never mind that! . . . The boy ought to sleep for at least another hour; the day would be plenty long enough for him, before it was through. . . . Young bulls have tender sinews—though for one of his age, Ole was an exceptionally able youngster.

That first furrow turned out very crooked for Per Hansa; he made a long one of it, too. When he thought he had gone far enough and halted the oxen, the furrow came winding up behind him like a snake. He turned around, drove the oxen back in the opposite direction, and laid another furrow up against the one he had already struck. . . . At the starting point again, he surveyed his work ruefully. Well, the second furrow wasn't any *crookeder* than the first, at all events! . . . When he had made another round he let the oxen stand awhile; taking the spade which he had brought out, he began to cut the sod on one side of the breaking into strips that could be handled. This was to be his building material. . . . Field for planting on the one hand, sods for a house on the other—that was the way to plow! . . . Leave it to Per Hansa—he was the fellow to have everything figured out beforehand!

By breakfast time he had made a fine start. No sooner had he swallowed the last morsel than he ordered both the boys to turn to, hitched the oxen to the old home-made wagon, and off they all went together toward the field, Per Hansa leading the way. . . . "You'd better cook the kettles full to-day!" he shouted back, as they were leaving. "We're going to punish a lot of food when we come in!"

Now Per Hansa began working in real earnest. He and Store-Hans, with plow and oxen, broke up the land; Ole used the hoe, but the poor fellow was having a hard time of it. The sod, which had been slumbering there undisturbed for countless ages, was tough of fibre and would not give up its hold on the earth without a struggle. It almost had to be turned by main strength, piece by piece; it was a dark brownish colour on the under side—a rich, black mould that gave promise of wonderful fertility; it actually gleamed and glistened under the rays of the morning sun, where the plow had carved and polished its upturned face. . . . Ole toiled on, settling and straightening the furrows as best he could, now and then cutting out the clods that fell unevenly. When Per Hansa had made a couple of rounds, he let the oxen stand awhile to catch their breath, and came over to Ole to instruct him. "This is the way to do it!" he said, seizing the hoe. "Watch me, now—*like this!*" He hewed away till the clods were flying around him. . . . When they quit work at noon a good many furrows lay stretched out on the slope, smiling up at the sun; they were also able to bring home with them a full wagonload of building material; at coffee time they brought another; at supper another. But when, arriving home at the end of the day, they found that supper was not quite ready, Per Hansa felt that he must go after still another load; they had better make use of every minute of time!

VII

He began building the house that same evening.

"You ought to rest, Per Hansa!" Beret pleaded. "Please use a little common sense!"

"Rest—of course! That's just what I propose to do! . . . Come along, now, all hands of you; you can't imagine what fun this is going to be. . . . Just think of it—a new house on our own estate! I don't mean that you've got to work, you know; but come along and watch the royal mansion rise!"

They all joined in, nevertheless . . . couldn't have kept their hands off. It gave them such keen enjoyment that they worked away until they could no longer see to place the strips of sod. Then Per Hansa called a halt—that was enough for one day. They had laboured hard and faithfully; well, they would get their wages in due time, every last one of them—but he couldn't bother with such trifles just now!

. . . That night sleep overpowered him at once; he was too tired even to dream.

From now on Per Hansa worked on the house every morning before breakfast, and every evening as soon as he had finished supper. The whole family joined in the task when they had nothing else to do; it seemed like a fascinating game.

To the eyes of Tönseten and Hans Olsa, it appeared as if nothing short of witchcraft must be at work on Per Hansa's quarter section; in spite of the fact that he and his entire family were breaking ground in the fields the whole day long, a great sod house shot up beside the wagon, like an enormous mushroom.

Per Hansa plowed and harrowed, delved and dug; he built away at the house, and he planted the potatoes; he had such a zest for everything and thought it all such fun that he could hardly bear to waste a moment in stupid sleep. It was Beret who finally put a check on him. One morning, as he threw off the blanket at dawn, on the point of jumping up in his reckless way, she lay there awake, waiting for him. The moment he stirred, she put her arms lovingly around him and told him that he must stay in bed awhile longer. This would never do, she said; he ought to remember that he was only a human being. . . . She begged him so gently and soothingly that he gave in at last and stayed in bed with her. But he was ill at ease over the loss of time. It wouldn't take long to lay a round of sod, and every round helped. . . . This Beret-girl of his meant well enough, but she didn't realize the multitude of things that weighed on his mind—things that couldn't wait, that had to be attended to immediately!

. . . Yes, she was an exceptional woman, this Beret of his; he didn't believe that her like existed anywhere else under the sun. During the last two days she had hurried through her housework, and then, taking And-Ongen by the hand, had come out in the field with them; she had let the child roam around and play in the grass while she herself had joined in their labour; she had pitched in beside them and taken her full term like any man. It had all been done to make things easier for him . . . and now she was lying awake here, just to look after him!

. . . He thought of other things that she had done. When they had harrowed and hoed sufficient seed ground, Beret had looked over her bundles and produced all kinds of seeds—he couldn't imagine how or where she had got them—turnips, and carrots, and onions, and tomatoes, and melons, even! . . . What a wife she was! . . . Well, he had better stay in bed and please her this time, when she had been so clever and thoughtful about everything.

However it was accomplished, on Per Hansa's estate they had a field all broken and harrowed and seeded down, and a large house ready for thatching, by the time that Hans Olsa and the Solum boys had barely finished thatching their houses and started the plowing. Tönseten, though, was ahead of him with the breaking—Per Hansa had to accept that—and was now busy planting his potatoes. But Syvert had every reason to be in the lead; his house had been all ready to move into when they had arrived. That little stable which he had built wasn't more than a decent day's work for an able man. And he had horses, too. . . . Of course, such things gave him a big advantage!

They finished planting the big field at Per Hansa's late one afternoon; all the potatoes that he had brought home from Sioux Falls had been cut in small pieces and tucked away in the ground. . . . "Only one eye to each piece!" he had warned Beret as she sat beside him, cutting them up. "That's enough for such rich soil." . . . The other seed, which she had provided with such splendid forethought, had also been planted. The field looked larger than it really was. It stood out clearly against the fresh verdure of the hillside; from a little distance it appeared as if some one had sewn a dark brown patch on a huge green cloth. . . . That patch looked mighty good to Per Hansa as he stood surveying the scene, his whole being filled with the sense of completed effort. Here he had barely arrived in a new country; yet already he had got more seed into the ground than on any previous year since Beret and he had started out for themselves. . . . Just wait! What couldn't he do another year!

"Well, Beret-girl," he said, "we've cleaned up a busy spring season, all right! To-night we ought to have an extra-fine dish of porridge, to bless what has been put into the ground." He stood there with sparkling eyes, admiring his wonderful field.

Beret was tired out with the labour she had undergone; her back ached as if it would break. She, too, was looking at the field, but the joy he felt found no response in her.

. . . I'm glad that he is happy, she thought, sadly. Perhaps in time I will learn to like it, too. . . . But she did not utter the thought; she merely took the child by the hand, turned away, and went back to their wagon-home. There she measured out half of the milk that Rosie had given that morning, dipped some grits from the bag and prepared the porridge, adding water until it was thin enough. Before she served it up she put a small dab of butter in each dish, like a tiny eye that would hardly keep open; then she sprinkled over the porridge a small portion of sugar; this was all the luxury she could afford. Indeed, her heart began to reproach her even for this extravagance. But when she saw the joyful faces of the boys, and heard Per Hansa's exclamations over her merits as a housekeeper, she brightened up a little, cast her fears to the wind, and sprinkled on more sugar from the bag. . . . Then she sat down among them, smiling and happy; she was glad that she hadn't told them how her back was aching. . . .

. . . They all worked at the house building that night as long as they could see.

VIII

Per Hansa's house certainly looked as if it were intended for a royal mansion. When Tönseten saw it close at hand for the first time he exclaimed:

"Will you please inform me, Per Hansa, what the devil you think you're building? Is it just a house, or is it a church and parsonage rolled in one? . . . Have you lost your senses altogether, man? You won't be able to get a roof over this crazy thing in a month of Sundays! . . . Why, damn it all, there aren't willows enough in this whole region to thatch a half of it! You might just as well tear it down again, for all the good it will do."

"The hell you say!" cried Per Hansa, genially. "But there it stands, as big as Billy-be-damned, so what are you going to do about it? . . . The notion I had was this: I might as well build for my sons, too, while I was about it. Then when they got married and needed more room they could thatch a new section any time. . . . What ails you, Syvert? Isn't there plenty of sod for roofing, all the way from here to the Pacific coast?"

But Tönseten took a serious view of the affair:

"I tell you, Per Hansa, there's no sense in such a performance. It isn't the sod, it's the poles—you know it damned well! . . . You'd better go right ahead and tear it down as fast as ever you can!"

"Oh, well, I suppose I'll have to, then," said Per Hansa, dryly.

As a matter of fact, it was hardly to be wondered at that Tönseten grew excited when he saw this structure; it differed radically from the one he had built and from all the others that he had ever seen. He wondered if such a silly house as this could be found anywhere else in the whole country. . . . His own hut measured fourteen by sixteen feet; the one that the Solum boys were building was only fourteen feet each way; Hans Olsa had been reckless and had laid his out eighteen feet long and sixteen feet wide. . . . But look at this house of Per Hansa's—*twenty-eight* feet long and *eighteen* feet wide! Moreover, it had *two* rooms, one of them eighteen by eighteen, the other eighteen by ten. The rooms were separated by a wall; one had a door opening toward the south, the other a door opening toward the east. Two doors in a sod hut! My God! what folly! In the smaller room the sod even had been taken up, so that the floor level there was a foot below that of the larger room. What was the sense of that? . . . If we don't look out, thought Tönseten, this crazy man will start building a tower on it, too!

Things surely looked serious to Tönseten. In the first place, Per Hansa plainly was getting big-headed; heavens and earth, it was nothing but an ordinary sod hut that he was building! In the second place, it wasn't a practical scheme. If he were to search till doomsday, he wouldn't be able to find enough willows for the thatching. Why, he might just as well thatch the whole firmament, and be done with it! . . . As soon as he had looked his fill, Tönseten trotted right over to Hans Olsa's, told him all about it, and asked him to go and reason with the man. . . . But, no, Hans Olsa didn't care to meddle in that affair. Per Hansa had a considerable family already; it might grow in the next few years; at any rate, he needed a fairly large house. Above all, he wasn't the man to bite off more than he could chew.

"But that's just it—he doesn't know what he's bitten off! He doesn't know anything at all about building a house!" With these drastic words, Tönseten went directly to the Solum boys; they had been born and brought up in America, and knew what was what. Now they must go, right away, and talk to Per Hansa about this crazy building that he was putting up! The only way out of it that he could think of was for them and himself and maybe Hans Olsa—to go in a body and show him what to do, and help him to build a house then and there. The thing that he had put up was frankly impossible; the poor man would ruin himself before he got a decent start! . . .

To his great disappointment, the Solum boys wouldn't go, either. It was Per Hansa's own business, they said, what sort of a house he wanted to build for himself. So Tönseten had to give it up as a bad job. He shook his head solemnly. . . . A damned shame, that a perfectly good man had to go to ruin through sheer folly!

Per Hansa had put a great deal of thought into this matter of building a house; ever since he had first seen a sod hut he had pondered the problem. On the day that he was coming home from Sioux Falls a brilliant idea had struck him—an idea which had seemed perhaps a little queer, but which had grown more attractive the longer he turned it over in his mind. How would it do to build house and barn under one roof? It was to be only a temporary shelter, anyway—just a sort of makeshift, until he could begin on his real mansion. This plan would save time and labour, and both the house and the barn would be warmer for being together. . . . He had a vague recollection of having heard how people in the olden days used to build their houses in that way—rich people, even! It might not be fashionable any longer; but it was far from foolish, just the same.

It will go hard with Beret, he thought; she won't like it. But after a while he picked up courage to mention his plan to her.

. . . House and barn under the same roof? . . . She said no more, but fell into deep and troubled thought. . . . Man and beast in one building? How could one live that way? . . . At first it seemed utterly impossible to her; but then she thought of how desolate and lonesome everything was here and of what a comfortable companion Rosie might be on dark evenings and during the long winter nights. She shuddered, and answered her husband that it made no difference to her whichever way he built, so long as it was snug and warm; but she said nothing about the real reason that had changed her mind.

This answer made Per Hansa very happy.

"Beret-girl, you are the most sensible woman that I

know! . . . Of course it's better all around, for us to build that way!"

He, too, had reasons that he kept to himself. . . . Now he would get ahead of both Hans Olsa and the Solum boys! None of them had even begun to think of building a barn yet; while according to his plan, his barn would be finished when his house was done.

IX

One evening Per Hansa came over with his oxen to Hans Olsa's to borrow his new wagon; the time had come to get his poles for the thatching. The others had been able to gather what they needed along the banks of a creek some ten miles to the southward, where a fringe of scattering willows grew; but it was small stock and a scanty supply at that; their roofs were certainly none too strong, and might not hold up through the next winter. . . . Per Hansa had a bigger and more original scheme in mind. If conditions were really as bad as Tönseten had made out, he'd have to find something besides willow poles for rafters on that house of his. The busy season of spring was over; now he proposed to rest on his oars awhile . . . take a little time to nose around the prairie at his leisure. He had been told that the Sioux River was only twenty-five or thirty miles away; big stands of timber were reported to lie in that direction, and several settlements of Tränders,* who had lived there for a number of years; many other interesting things would turn up, of course—things that he hadn't heard about; he wanted to see it all and get a running idea of the whole locality. He confided to Hans Olsa where he was going, but asked him not to mention it to anyone else. . . . "We might as well keep this matter to ourselves, you know. Besides, something has got to be done about getting fuel for the winter."

He brought the wagon home that evening, merely explaining that he and Store-Hans were going out to gather wood. Ole would have to look after the farm while they were away, and take the full responsibility on his shoul-

* People from the district of Trondhjem, Norway.

ders. Store-Hans, who had been chosen to go on the trip, was overjoyed at the news; but his brother was reduced to the verge of tears at such an outrageous injustice. The idea of taking that *boy* along, and letting a grown man loaf around the house with nothing to do! For the first time his faith in his father's judgment was shattered. . . . And the situation grew worse and worse as Ole watched the extensive preparations for the trip; it looked for all the world as if they intended to move out West! The father was taking along a kettle, and was measuring out supplies of flour, and salt, and coffee, and milk, besides a big heap of *flatbröd* and plenty of other food. But, heaviest blow of all, the rifle—Old Maria—was brought out from the big chest! Ole wept at that in sheer anger. Ax, rope, and sacks, too—everything was going! . . . And on top of it all, this youngster who wasn't dry behind the ears yet had grown so conceited that he wouldn't deign to talk to his brother; he kept fussing and smirking around his father all the time, speaking to him in low, confidential tones, and pushing himself to the front on every occasion! He seemed to be bubbling over with foolish questions. Shouldn't they take this along, and *this*, and *this?* . . . But when at last he came dragging a piece of chain, even Per Hansa had to laugh outright. "That's the boy, now! I might have forgotten the chain. And how could we go to the woods without a chain, I'd like to know?"

Beret got the food ready for the journey. Her face wore a sad, sober expression. . . . Yes, of course, the house must have a roof; she knew that perfectly well. How could they live in a house without a roof? . . . But now he was going to be away for another two-day stretch—two whole days and a night! . . . It wasn't so bad in the daytime . . . but at night . . . !

"You'd better take the children with you and go over to Mother Sörrina's to-morrow evening," Per Hansa advised her, cheerfully. "You can spend the whole evening there, you know, visiting and talking. It'll make the time pass quicker, and you won't be so lonesome. . . . You do that, Beret!"

To this suggestion she answered neither yes nor no. In her heart she knew very well that she wouldn't follow his advice. She never could forget that evening of his trip to Sioux Falls, when she and the children had come down the hill toward the wagons; the air of the place had suddenly filled with terror and mystery. The wagons had floated like grey specks in the dusk; and all at once it had seemed as if the whole desolation of a vast continent were centring there and drawing a magic circle about their home. She had even seen the intangible barrier with her own eyes . . . had seen it clearly . . . had had to force herself to step across it. . . . Now she went on getting the food ready for them as well as she could; but from her sad lips there came not a word.

This was destined to be a memorable journey, both for those who went and for those who stayed at home. . . . Before it was over the latter were in a panic of apprehension and fear. The second day passed as the first had done; the second night, too; the third day came . . . noon, but no one in sight.

Beret had not really begun to expect them until sometime during the second day; Per Hansa had told her not to begin looking before they came in sight. Nevertheless, she had found herself unconsciously doing it shortly after dinner on the very first day. She knew that it was foolish—they hadn't even got there yet; but she couldn't refrain from scanning the sky line in the quarter where they had disappeared. . . . She went to bed with the children early that evening.

The following evening she took them up on the hill; they sat there silently, gazing eastward over the plain. From this elevation her sight seemed to take flight and carry a long, long distance. . . . In the eastern sky the evening haze was gathering; it merged slowly into the purple dusk, out of which an intangible, mysterious presence seemed to be creeping closer and closer upon them. They sat trying to pierce it with their gaze; but neither wagon nor oxen crossed the line of their vision. . . . Ole took no interest in keeping watch; it was more fun for him to look for queer stones around the grave. . . . When the day was well-nigh dead and nothing had appeared, Beret suddenly felt that she must talk to some one to-night . . . hear some human voice other than those of the two children. Almost in spite of herself, she directed her steps toward Hans Olsa's.

—Hadn't Per Hansa returned yet?

—No. She couldn't imagine what had become of him. He surely ought to have been home by this time.

—Oh, well, she mustn't worry; he had probably travelled a long way on this trip; no doubt he had made use of the opportunity to look around for winter fuel.

—Winter fuel? . . . She had never given a thought to that before; but of course they would need wood if they were going to stay through the winter. It suddenly occurred to her how much there was for Per Hansa to plan about and worry over; but she also felt a twinge of jealousy because he had not confided in her. . . . Winter fuel? Of course; it was the thing they needed most of all!

Mother Sörine was well aware that her neighbour did not have any courage to spare. She realized, too, how lonesome it must be for Beret, to sleep over there in the wagon with only the children. As the visitors were leaving she got up, called her daughter, and insisted on accompanying them back to the wagon. They chatted gaily and freely all the way . . . and that night there was no magic circle to step across!

Some time after noon on the third day Per Hansa and Store-Hans came home with a load so big that the oxen were just barely able to sag up the slope with it. It was like an incident out of a fairy tale, that famous load. There was a stout timber for the ridgepole, there were crossbeams and scantlings, and rafters for the roof; but Ole only sneered at such prosaic things. Was *that* all they had gone for, he'd like to know? Farther down in the load, however, lay six bundles of young trees; their tops had been trimmed off, and the soil had been carefully wrapped around their roots with strips of bark. . . . "Those are to be planted around the house!" Store-Hans explained. "Would you believe it, Mother—in this bundle there are twelve plum trees! They grow great big plums! We met a man who told us all about them." Store-Hans caught his breath from sheer excitement. . . . There were still stranger things in that load. In the back of the wagon, as the father unloaded, an opening almost like a small room was gradually revealed. Here lay two great bags—two bags brimful of curious articles. One of them evidently contained fish; the other seemed to hold the flayed carcass of a calf; at least, Ole thought so, and wanted to know where it had come from.

"*Calf!*" exclaimed Store-Hans. "What makes you think it's a calf?" . . .

Per Hansa winked slyly at his travelling companion; the wink warned him that he'd better say no more—for a little while! . . . Store-Hans assumed a knowing silence; but it could be seen with half an eye that he was bursting with important secrets. At last he was no longer able to contain himself.

. . . "*Antelope!*" he burst out, ecstatically.

Beret watched with speechless admiration the unloading of all the wonderful things that they had brought; she was so overjoyed to have her dear ones with her again that she could have burst into hysterical tears; as she stood beside the oxen she stroked their necks fondly, murmuring in a low voice that they were nice fellows to have hauled home such a heavy load.

. . . "Well, there!" said Per Hansa at last, when he had cleared the wagon. "Now, this is the idea: Store-Hans and I have figured on having fresh fish to-day, cooked in regular Nordland fashion, with soup and everything. We nearly killed ourselves, and the beasts, too, to get here in time. . . . Beret, what the devil have we got to put all this meat and fish into?"

Store-Hans ate that day as if he could never get enough; there seemed to be no bottom to the boy. . . . When he had finished the father chased him off to bed at once; and strange to say, he wasn't at all unwilling though it was only the latter part of the afternoon. When evening came the mother tried to shake life into him again, but without success; once he roused enough to sit up in bed, but couldn't get so far as to take off his clothes; the next moment he had thrown himself flat once more and was sleeping like a log.

As time went on this first expedition of Per Hansa's came to be of great consequence to the new settlement on Spring Creek. . . . In the first place, there were all the trees that he had brought home and planted. This alone excited Tönseten's enthusiasm to such a pitch that he was for leaving at once to get a supply of his own; but Hans Olsa and the Solum boys advised him to wait until the coming fall, so Tönseten reluctantly had to give up still another plan.

. . . But there were other things to do when fall came, and several years went by before the others had followed Per Hansa's lead. This is the reason why, in the course of time, a stout grove of trees began to grow up around Per Hansa's house before anything larger than a bush was to be seen elsewhere in the whole neighbourhood.

But the most important result of all, perhaps, was the acquaintance with the Trönders eastward on the Sioux River, which sprang out of this journey. Amid these strange surroundings, confronted by new problems, the two tribes, Trönder and Helgelander, met in a quite different relationship than on the Lofoten fishing grounds. Here they were glad enough to join forces in their common fight against the unknown wilderness. . . .

. . . The Great Plain watched them breathlessly. . .

III "Rosie!—Rosie!"

I

The food supply was steadily vanishing. Bags and sacks yawned empty and had nothing to yield. The settlers shared freely with one another as long as they had anything left; but even at Hans Olsa's, where plenty usually reigned, the food at last began to give out. Among the menfolk a crumb of tobacco was as rare as gold. . . . High time that they took the situation in hand and did something about it! Besides, the season was getting so far advanced that they would soon have to start in haying. No two ways about it—they must make a trip to town.

All the men, accordingly—Per Hansa, and Tönseten, and Hans Olsa, and the two Solum boys—met together one Sunday to discuss the matter. A trip to town in those days was a serious affair, which had to be planned carefully from beginning to end. The seventy or eighty miles through desolate country was in itself no trifle; one couldn't expect to be back in less than four days, even with horses. And under pressure of time, it was hard to accomplish everything that one wanted to do. Provisions of all sorts must be replenished for the next season; first of all came food, and after that clothing; then tools and farming implements, as far as their money would go. If it wouldn't go far enough they would have to find some other way out of the fix, but they must hold down to essentials in order to keep alive. . . . As yet, no one in the Spring Creek settlement was in a position to carry any produce along, to be sold for cash or given in exchange for wares. But they all looked forward to the time when this would be possible; it would be harder work to haul a load both ways, of course; but what a help it would be—and what a satisfaction—to have their own products to barter!

They at once agreed that some of the menfolk would have to stay at home, in case anything untoward happened. . . . It was a singular thing, not a soul in this little colony ever felt wholly at ease, though no one referred to the fact or cared to frame the thought in words. All of a sudden, apparently without any cause, a vague, nameless dread would seize hold of them; it would shake them for a while like an attack of nerves; or again, it might fill them with restless apprehension, making them quiet and cautious in everything they did. They seemed to sense an unseen force around them. . . . The men grew taciturn under the strain; they would cast about for some task or other on which they could work off the spell. With the women it found an outlet in talk; they often became extravagantly loud and boisterous over nothing at all. Few realized what this strange feeling was; none of them would have admitted that he was afraid.

. . . Yes, God defend them! Man's strength availed but little out here. They had already experienced it more than once. Terrible storms would come up—so suddenly, with such appalling violence! . . . Mother Sörine had reason to be frightened of these storms. Less than a week ago their tent had been carried away in one of them; Sörine, trapped inside and half choked, had been swept along with the canvas. Hans Olsa had laid the tent rope across his shoulder, planted his feet solidly in the ground, and summoned all his giant strength; but he had been whirled away like a tuft of wool. It had turned out all right, however; no one was seriously hurt . . . this time.

And then, the Indians! . . . "*Injuns,*" as the red children of the great plain were called in common speech. Kjersti, Tönseten's wife, didn't mind the storms so much;

they never committed inhuman outrages . . . weren't out for your scalp, at any rate! But fear of the Indians was ever vividly present in her mind. Not a day passed that she didn't search the sky line many times. . . . Why, one of the savages actually lay buried over on Per Hansa's land! And where the dead had their abode, the living were sure to come. . . . Since she had learned of the grave she was always on the lookout. . . .

Truth to tell, her fear of the Indians was very natural. She and Syvert had heard the tale of the terrors of '62 so often that they could have repeated it word for word, as if from an open book. When they were living in Fillmore County, Minnesota, two refugees from the Norway Lake massacre had drifted into the place; the story of the horrors they had undergone had taken on new and gruesome details as it passed from mouth to mouth; out here now on the open prairie, where no hiding place could be found, the form in which Kjersti remembered it had assumed the fantastic proportions of a myth.

Tönseten, however, wasn't a bit afraid of the Indians—not he! Who ever heard of such nonsense? Why should he or anyone else fear them, now that they had become peaceful and civilized? He tried his best to instill this idea into the others. . . . Per Hansa would sit listening to Tönseten with a quizzical smile on his face. "That's right, Syvert—go on," he would agree. "All the Indians have turned into honest-to-God gentlemen these last ten years, with red skull-caps, and wooden shoes, and long pipes, and everything else they need. It's no trick at all, you know, for a savage to learn fine manners, as crowded with folks to teach him as it is out here!" . . . From the Trönders on the Sioux River, Per Hansa had learned a great deal of valuable information about the Indians; he had heard of a place, not very far away, called Flandreau or some such outlandish name, where they had a permanent colony; west from this place an Indian trail ran all the way through to Nebraska, and along this route the red man was said to make his yearly journeys. More than likely, Per Hansa thought, his own quarter-section lay directly in their path; he inferred this from the grave on the hill and from what he had heard. . . . If it were true, the fact would be certain to come to light before the summer was over. In the meanwhile—well, no use to cross a bridge until you came to it.

The men never spoke of the Indians while the womenfolk were around. But at other times, whenever the subject came up for discussion, Ole and Store-Hans stood listening with open mouths. . . . The grave where they found the stones had now begun to strike a chill into their hearts; but it also exerted a strange and irresistible fascination.

. . . So here they all were, afraid of something or other. But the women were the worst off; Kjersti feared the Indians, Sörine the storms; and Beret, poor thing, feared both—and feared the very air.

The outcome of their deliberations that Sunday was only what might have been expected; it seemed the logical thing for Hans Olsa and Tönseten and Henry Solum, each of whom owned horses and wagon, to make up the party for the journey. That would give three men and three separate teams; such a caravan ought to be able to haul home on one trip whatever the settlement could afford to buy.

Per Hansa was badly out of sorts that day; every word that he let fall had a bitter sting to it; he said little and sat morose and silent most of the time. In his eyes, the whole affair had the appearance of having been settled beforehand. He and the other Solum boy were to stay at home and look after the settlement; that was the plan, though it hadn't been stated in outright terms. It looked to Per Hansa like a pretty mean piece of business. . . . For his part, he took it as a matter of course that he was a better man for the trip to town than Syvert Tönseten or Henry Solum—neither of whom, God knows, had any more wits than he could get along with! . . . In all their talk, no one had even hinted at that side of the question. And certainly Per Hansa wasn't the sort of man to force himself down anybody's throat. . . . But, by God! it was disgusting to have to lie around the house with the womenfolk while the others were off on such a fine expedition! . . . The thirst for adventure was burning in his blood.

When the party left on Monday morning Per Hansa was in a towering ill humour; he rose with the others at dawn, woke Ole, and hitched the oxen to the plow. On that day he broke up an acre and a half of prairie, with only the crude implements at hand—a record that stood for many years in that part of the country.

But at quitting time that night, when he paced around the field and discovered what an enormous day's work he had done, he felt so elated that he began to whistle the tune of an old ballad. . . . Just look at that! If they didn't hurry back, he'd have the whole farm broken up before they arrived. . . . By God! he'd show them! He'd give them a chance to see for themselves who was the better man!

II

The next day he did not drive himself so hard; but he turned off a good day's work, just the same.

Per Hansa was again in a good humour that afternoon as he and Ole sauntered home from the field; he felt that during this interval he would easily get ahead of Tönseten. Ole's tired feet dragged at every step; his voice was hoarse from steadily shouting at the oxen.

They had not got far on their way home when Store-Hans came running out to meet them; he began shouting as soon as he caught sight of them, and arrived all out of breath.

"Dad . . . quick . . . people are coming!" . . .

The news sounded so incredible that Ole stopped short in his tracks and stared at his brother with his mouth wide open, but the father only laughed as he looked indulgently at the boy.

"Of course people are coming!" he said with a chuckle. . . . "And you'll grow up to be a man, too, some day—at about the same rate, I guess! You've both got a long distance yet to travel."

But Store-Hans was too excited to be thrown off the track by his father's kindly sarcasm.

"Look! . . . *look there!*" he cried, pointing toward the southwest. . . . "Mother thinks they may be Indians!" . . .

Per Hansa took in the whole western horizon in one swift glance . . . "Huh!" he grunted . . . and immediately began to walk faster. The longer he looked, the more haste he made. At last he was taking such mighty strides that the boys had to run in order to keep up with him.

Beret was standing just beyond the wagon, holding And-Ongen in her arms.

"They have come," she said in a calm voice; but her sad, resigned face was pale and drawn.

"Well, don't stand there! . . . Go and look after the cooking as if nothing had happened!" . . . He spoke rapidly, with a metallic ring in his voice.

In an instant he was over at the new house, which as yet was only half thatched. The boys followed close at his heels; he spoke to them in quick, low tones; all his words had the same hard, metallic ring.

"Hans, run over to Sam's and tell him what's up. . . . Hurry, now!"

"Yes." . . . The boy hesitated.

"*Hurry*, I said!"

"Yes, sir!" . . . Store-Hans found his legs and was off like lightning.

Per Hansa turned to Ole. "You go and get Old Maria. You'll find her in the big chest—and something to load her with in the till. Stand the gun and everything just inside the door here. . . . And listen"—his face was hard set—"when I *whistle*, I want her—but not before! . . . Are you afraid?"

"N-n-no." . . . Ole ran to execute the order.

Per Hansa began to work away at the thatching as if nothing unusual were going on; but his eyes were steadily fixed on the approaching train. Little by little, as he watched, he grew calmer; the look of anxiety slowly faded away from his features, to be replaced by the half-sly, half-roguish expression of his lighter moods. . . . No war party, this—nothing but harmless families roaming over the plain!

Just then Ole arrived with the rifle.

"Never mind," said Per Hansa. He was laughing now. "Go back and hide those things where you found them. . . . That fellow Store-Hans is a regular little rascal—the way he nearly scared us out of our wits!"

"But don't you want the gun, Father?"

"No, I guess not. . . . Go and put her back—then come and run an errand for me."

The boy ran inside, and returned in a moment empty-handed. Per Hansa was sitting on the edge of the roof; he kept looking off to the westward as he gave his orders:

"Run over and tell Sörrina that the Indians are coming, but don't frighten the life out of her. Tell her it's only a wandering tribe—just peaceful people like ourselves. . . . And tell her they are likely to camp for the night over here on the hill; if she is afraid, she can stay with us. . . . Don't get off a lot of wild talk, now. Be sensible!"

Almost before he had heard the words, Ole was gone. . . . Per Hansa came down to the ground, heaved an armful of sod up on the roof, and then climbed back unconcernedly to his work.

The band of Indians crawled slowly toward them out of the west. Per Hansa counted the teams—fourteen in all, he made it—but he couldn't be certain of the exact number; they drove close together and were headed straight in the direction of the settlement. . . . No doubt about it any longer—here lay an old Indian trail!

He was kneeling on the roof awhile later, trying to fit a strip of sod in place, when suddenly a figure stood below him; it had appeared so swiftly and silently that Per Hansa was startled in spite of himself. . . . The next moment he saw that it was Sam Solum, frightened and excited, gun in hand. He had run so fast that Store-Hans had been left far behind.

"You must be going hunting to-night," Per Hansa observed, dryly.

"Haven't you seen 'em? . . . Don't you know . . . ?" Sam had to stop to catch his breath.

"Seen who?"

"The Indians! . . . They're right on top of us!"

"I see you look like the scared fool you are, all right! . . . What are you ramming around with that rattletrap of a gun of yours for? Put it out of sight as quick as you can! Then come here and help me with the thatching. . . . Store-Hans, you'd better go and stay with mother."

Sam did as he was bid, without half understanding; he took his gun inside the house, stood it against the wall, and came out again; in front of the door he paused, staring open-mouthed at the approaching train. . . . Seated above him on the roof, Per Hansa glanced alternately westward and down at the puzzled youth.

"I supposed we ought to warn Kjersti—she's always so skittish," he said with a grin. "Why don't you go down and tell her that our red neighbours are coming? . . . But don't scare the wits out of the poor woman!"

Sam hesitated; the task obviously wasn't to his liking. . . . "Or should we wait, and let the Indians take her scalp?"

At these words Sam jumped, then suddenly broke into a run.

Per Hansa laughed heartily as he watched him go.

"Hey, there! Don't tear off as if your pants had caught fire!" he shouted. "You needn't be in such an awful sweat about Kjersti, either!"

But Kjersti herself had seen the enemy; she must have been on the lookout, as usual. . . . At that moment she hove in sight on the slope of the hill, leading her cow.

At the same time Ole arrived, with Sörine and the girl close behind him; but Sörine, unfortunately, hadn't thought of her cow, which was grazing off on the prairie to the westward, some distance from Hans Olsa's house.

Soon they were all gathered in a little knot—the three women, Ole, and the Solum boy; but Store-Hans felt that it would be safer with his father, and had gone over to where Per Hansa was still working. . . . Kjersti was moaning and wailing because her Syvert was away at a time when the Lord sent such tribulations upon her; Mother Sörine was comforting her as best she could, saying that, after all, Indians were only people—human beings . . . just human beings! . . . Beret listened in stony silence to it all.

At last Per Hansa took a quick slide down from the roof and went over to the agitated group.

"What have we here—a sewing circle? . . . By George! It seems to me that three nice modest girls like you oughtn't to be standing around and making eyes at strange menfolk! They've got their own women with 'em, too. . . . Maybe the squaws would have a word or two to say about that!"

Per Hansa's sally broke the tension; Beret immediately resumed her preparations for supper, and Mother Sörine began to help her; Kjersti found a pail and milked her cow; and Per Hansa himself went back to his roof and laid a few more strips of sod before supper was ready.

III

. . . While they sat waiting for the porridge to cool, they watched with anxious attention the Indian band as it crept up the slope of the hill toward the crest. The foremost team reached the summit, passed some distance beyond it on the other side, and came to a halt; at that they all drew up, the whole train forming a crescent around the brow of the hill, facing the house of Per Hansa. One by one the horses were unhitched from the rickety wagons and turned loose on the prairie. . . . Per Hansa's face brightened still more as he noticed this move. People who did a thing like that could have no evil intentions!

Just then, however, Sörine's cow, which was still grazing some distance off on the prairie, suddenly seemed to go crazy. She bellowed loud and long, lifted her head and tail high in the air, and galloped away toward the wagons of the newcomers. All watched her in amazement. Sörine burst out crying, blaming herself for being so shortsighted as to forget all about her precious cow. . . . As he saw the beast gallop away, Per Hansa cursed it from the bottom of his heart.

In an instant, before the little company sitting there had found time to gather their scattered wits, all the rest of their cattle were smitten by the same craze. At the first bellow of Sörine's cow they had looked up inquiringly, had caught sight of the new arrivals, and at once had started off behind their leader—Rosie first, then Kjersti's Brindlesides—both rearing their tails on high and galloping straight toward the camp of the Indians.

. . . "Damn the luck!" muttered Per Hansa between

his teeth. "There goes the milk for our porridge! . . . The devil salt and burn their blasted tails!"

A far-away "moo-o-o" drifted in from the north, and there the Solum boys' Daisy came running at full speed, to join the deserters! *

At that Per Hansa burst into a loud laugh. . . . "You'd better go after your cow," he said to Sam, "unless you want to munch dry porridge all winter!"

The women took the matter each in her own way, according to her feeling for her particular cow. Kjersti wept and took on, vowing that this was the worst thing that had ever happened to her—it was just awful; Sörine's eyes were moist, but she believed that her cow would come back, just the same; she had never seen a better cow than Dolly and had tended her like a mother. . . . But Beret remained quite calm; she seemed more annoyed than frightened. Why didn't one of the men go after the cows? . . . When they remained sitting and made no move, she rose and laid her spoon aside.

"We must get them at once," she announced, firmly. "If the Indians were to leave to-night, the cows would follow—that is perfectly plain!" . . . She took And-Ongen in her arms and started for the hill.

"Good Heavens, Beret," cried Kjersti in despair. "You must be crazy!"

Per Hansa gazed fondly at his wife; across his face came a light that almost made him handsome. . . . *There* was a woman for you! . . . He got up before she had gone many steps, and ran to her side.

"Go back and eat, Beret-girl! There isn't anything to worry about, really and truly. . . . Leave the cows to me. It can just as well wait till after we have eaten. . . . We must behave like well-mannered folk, you know."

As they sat over the last of their porridge Per Hansa drew such ghastly pictures to Sam of the cruelty with which the Indians would probably treat the cows, that the women shuddered at his words. . . . "I've often heard—have read it in books, too—that Indians would

* The cattle of the first settlers, from the wandering habits they had formed during the outward journey, had to be watched, for they wanted to join every caravan that came along.

rather take the scalp of a cow any day, than of a man. . . . Haven't you ever read about it? Huh! that's strange! . . . Well, they're just crazy, you see, for the scalp of a cow. They dry them out and use them for winter caps!" . . .

Beret looked at him reproachfully. It seemed to her that it ill behooved him to talk in this fashion; if they were all afraid, they couldn't help it; the words sounded coarse in his mouth, and seemed to coarsen him also. . . . "Can't you shut up with that talk!" she said in her quiet, cutting way, without looking up. "It isn't such a brave and manly thing, to terrorize poor womenfolk who are frightened already."

Per Hansa fell suddenly silent; his face grew burning red. In all the years that they had lived together it had never happened till now that she had shamed him before others. And she had spoken so quietly—hadn't even looked up! . . . He ate his porridge slowly and thoughtfully. What she had said kept repeating itself in his mind, and cut deeper each time.

At last he laid his spoon aside and got to his feet; he stuck his pipe in his mouth—the pipe that had been empty and cold so long now, for lack of fuel—and began sucking the stem.

"I suppose in all fairness, Sam, you ought to go chasing your own damned beast—you who are such a sharper in both the American and Indian languages!" he snapped out. . . . "But—oh, well, there might be some women over there who were worth having a look at!" he muttered with plain insinuation. "I guess I'd better go myself and make it a good *job!*"

Store-Hans jumped up like a flash and put his hand in his father's. . . . Per Hansa glanced down into the beaming, ruddy face that smiled up at him and begged so earnestly. . . . But the boy uttered never a word.

"Come along, then," said the father. Still holding the outstretched hand, he began to walk away.

"Hans, come here!" his mother cried out, sharply. A wild anxiety had come into her voice—a note of desperate pleading.

"No," said Per Hansa, shortly. "Hans is going with

me." . . . He waited for no answer, but grasped the boy's hand firmly and started off.

IV

Store-Hans had been too absorbed in what was going on to notice the clash between his parents. As they went along, his whole being was athrill with excitement; he took long, manly strides, and chattered on in a low, rapid voice, but always returned to the same question:

—What was his father going to do to the Indians?

—Do? . . . Per Hansa's mind refused to act any further. The biting words of his wife, spoken in the plain hearing of all, kept ringing in his ears.

"Yes, Dad, what are you going to do?"

"We'll see about that later." . . . He tried to wrench himself out of his abstraction, repeating in a loud tone: "We'll see later—when the time comes!"

"Are you . . . are you going to fight them, Dad?"

Per Hansa gave the boy's hand a good squeeze. "I guess we'll have to be satisfied with a scalp or two!"

The only thing Store-Hans knew about scalping was that it was the most dreadful thing in the world; as to the actual process, he had only a hazy idea. Now he asked, fearfully, what did it mean, anyway—to scalp some one?

—Oh, nothing much. . . . Didn't he know how it was done?

"No. . . . Please tell me, Dad?"

Per Hansa shifted the empty pipe to the other corner of his mouth; he laughed as he said:

"You see, Store-Hans, when the hide begins to get good and dry on the heads of some people, then the Indians peel it off."

"Does it grow out new again?" Store-Hans gave a sidewise glance at the top of his father's head; before he realized it, his hand had gone up under his own cap.

"Oh, I suppose so."

"But . . . but doesn't it hurt awfully?"

"No, not at all . . . that is, when the skin is good and dry."

That seemed quite logical; Store-Hans grasped it immediately.

"But what do they do with the scalp?"

"What do they do with the scalp?" Per Hansa spoke slowly, as if his mind were elsewhere. . . . "They use it, I guess . . . for mittens, and things like that. . . . They turn the hair side in, you see." . . .

"Oh, you're only fooling!" cried Store-Hans, lengthening his stride in order not to fall behind.

"Maybe I am fooling. . . . I thought you knew all about it, though."

The boy was dying to ask about other things; but he was getting afraid to raise his voice now—his throat, too, seemed very dry. . . . And, besides, they were drawing so near to the Indian camp now, that his eyes kept him fully occupied.

There was a good deal to see, up there on the hill. . . . A big tent, or wigwam, had been pitched in the centre of the crescent, with four smaller ones on each side. A troop of brown, half-naked children were running around among the tents. . . . They seemed to be playing games, thought Store-Hans; and immediately he picked up courage. He saw women moving about, too. . . . There couldn't be any real danger here!

The rough tents, constructed of poles and hides, stood some distance back of the semicircle of oddly-assorted vehicles. Halfway between, a group of dusky squaws were busy at a fire, carrying wood from the wagons and throwing it on; around the fire several bronzed men were sitting motionless, with their legs crossed under them. . . . These men were smoking—that was the first thing that caught Per Hansa's eye. The flames of the camp fire threw a lurid glare over the figures sitting around it, turning their copper-coloured faces to a still deeper hue, their raven hair to a more intense and glistening black. They smoked on in silence.

When the two visitors had arrived within the illuminated circle, one of the Indians pointed to them with his pipe; a few words were spoken among them in a guttural tongue; beyond this the coming of Per Hansa and his son created not a ripple of excitement.

Per Hansa stepped forward and greeted them in

English—he had picked up enough words for that. The greeting was returned in the same language. . . . One of the braves put something that sounded like a question; two of the others, sitting beside him, added to it. . . . Per Hansa stood helpless for a moment; he could not understand a word.

But in this crisis Store-Hans, who had been half hiding behind his father, came to his aid; he whispered, rapidly:

"They want to know if we live here."

"How the devil could you tell that? . . . By God! I guess we do!" Per Hansa nodded emphatically toward the Indians. "Tell them there isn't any doubt of it—not the least doubt in the world—but say it *nicely*, now!"

Store-Hans stepped out in front, facing the seated redskins; he tried his best to make them understand, using what little English he had learned during the past winter.

The visit was soon over; after that strange, impassive meeting there seemed to be nothing else for Per Hansa to say or do. The stray cows, all four of them, had finally lain down beside the Indian wagons; he would only need to round them up and drive them home. . . . Yet there was something that made it almost impossible for him to tear himself away. The odour from the pipes wafted to him so enchantingly on the evening breeze, enthralled and held him captive. He hadn't had a decent smoke for over two weeks, and he could smell that this was good strong tobacco.

At last the temptation grew altogether too powerful; he simply couldn't resist it any longer. He glanced around the circle, picked out the face that looked to him the most approachable, then took the empty pipe from his mouth and indicated by signs that he needed something to fill it with.

The man he had chosen understood him perfectly. He gave a laugh, remarked something to the others, pulled a large leather pouch from his shirt, and held it out with a dignified gesture. Per Hansa grasped the pouch with an eager hand, took a deep dive into it, and gave his pipe a good fill. . . . "Many thanks, good friend! If Hans Olsa happens to get back before you're gone, I'll see that you are well repaid! . . . Hans, translate that to him the best way you know how. . . . What a thundering shame that we can't talk with such good folks!" . . . Per Hansa went over to the fire, raked out a glowing ember, lit his pipe, and pulled at it long and deeply, while an expression of rare contentment passed over his face.

V

Turning away from the fire, as he stood there enjoying his smoke, he noticed a face on the ground at his side—a face that peered out of the folds of a gaudily coloured blanket, so close to the fire that it startled him. . . . Good Lord! was the man trying to singe himself?

Per Hansa stared down into the face incredulously; the form in the blanket gazed up as fixedly at him in return. It struck him at once that the Indian must be suffering terrible pain; his features were distorted in agony.

"Store-Hans!" he called, hastily. "Come here and ask this fellow what's the matter with him. It looks to me as if he were fighting death itself!"

Again Store-Hans had to try out his meagre stock of newcomer English on the Indians. The face moaned; in a moment it gave answer. The boy repeated his question; a second answer came, and then another long moan.

"He says his hand is hurt," Store-Hans reported.

"Is that it? Too bad! . . . Tell him I'd like to take a look at that hand of his."

But Store-Hans didn't have to repeat the request. The man had been lying there watching them as they spoke together, looking closely and intently at Per Hansa. Now he got up beside him without a word; first he removed the blanket from his arm, and then unwound a bundle of dirty coloured rags that were wrapped around his hand.

When this was done, he held out an ugly-looking claw, swollen to the size of a log; not only the hand, but the wrist and a large part of the arm as well were badly swollen and infected. The evil seemed to have its source in a festering wound in the palm of the hand. . . . Per

Hansa examined the hand, felt of it, squeezed it, and turned it over, as if he had done nothing else all the days of his life but tend to such cases. The flesh was as hard to the touch as a block of wood; but the wound itself didn't look serious.

"Sure enough!" he observed, wisely. "If this doesn't end up with blood poisoning my name isn't Per! Maybe it's come to that already. . . . Tell him"—he turned to Store-Hans—"tell him we've got to have some warm water at once—and more rags. But they must be clean—*clean white* rags, tell him! . . . See what a good job of talking you can do, now!" With these words, he went back to his examination.

The job of talking, however, was more than Store-Hans could handle—he stuck in it halfway. That his father wanted warm water he could make them understand; but the other request for clean white rags was either beyond his English or a little too much for their comprehension.

The sick Indian had kept his eyes intently fixed on the man who was examining his hand with all the assurance of an expert. Others had now risen and come up to them, one by one. A close circle had formed about the little group. The women were also joining it; the children stopped playing and slipped in among their elders; at last the whole camp had gathered in a silent ring around the three. . . . Per Hansa's face wore a sober expression, but all the while he kept drawing long, deep puffs from his pipe.

"Seventeen devils of a claw you've got, man!" he exclaimed at last, when he had finished his diagnosis. . . . "I can't see any way out of it, Store-Hans. You'll have to run home and get mother. Tell her an old chief is lying over here almost ready to die—tell her it's blood poisoning. She must bring the small kettle, and all the clean rags she can spare. Can you remember to say *white* rags? . . . And she must bring a pinch of salt, too. . . . The man has got to have help this very night, tell her. . . . Now run along. You aren't afraid, are you?"

Certainly Store-Hans wasn't frightened any longer; this was the greatest experience he had ever had or ever expected to have. . . . He had already pressed his way through the throng when his father thought of something which he had forgotten, and called him back.

. . . "Tell Sörrina to go home and see if there isn't a drop left in Hans Olsa's bottle. Even if it isn't more than a thimbleful, we ought to have it; it's a matter of life or death here. . . . And mother must bring some pepper. . . . Let's see, now, how well you can remember everything!"

The boy was off like a flash. As soon as he had gone, Per Hansa began treating the hand. First of all, he made them understand that he needed water to wash his own hands. . . . "Yes, water, *water!*" he said, going through the motion of dipping his hands and rubbing them. They caught his meaning at once; the word was passed among them, and a woman immediately brought some water in a tin bucket.

Per Hansa washed his hands very carefully; then he poured out the water and motioned for more. . . . "Yes, yes—more, more!" . . . He got it at once and began to wash the wound—first the hand, and then the wrist and the arm, but particularly the hand, and the wound itself most of all. . . . Brown it had been in the beginning, that skin—and brown it remained; Per Hansa couldn't be certain whether he had got it clean. But now he led the man as close to the fire as the heat would allow; there he sat down with him, and began to draw on the great store of experience he had gathered as a fisherman on the Lofoten seas. First he massaged the flesh around the wound for a long time; then he moved upward to the wrist, and afterward to the arm. He rubbed with the palm of his hand, making circular motions, gently for a while, then stronger and firmer; from time to time he bent over the hand, breathed heavily on the wound, and continued the rubbing.

At last Store-Hans returned, bringing his mother, who carried all the articles his father had sent for. Per Hansa noticed that she had put on her Sunday clothes; for some reason, this pleased him. When she stepped within the circle of the camp fire, she paused, greeted the strangers quietly, and dropped a curtsy.

"What do you think you are doing here?" she asked

in a low voice; the words seemed to carry more of reproach than fear. . . . He suddenly remembered the incident at supper awhile ago; the wave of bitterness rose again in his heart. . . . What a silly question for a grown woman to ask!

When she received no answer, she continued:

"Kjersti is crying her eyes out—and the rest aren't much better off. . . . These people have got to look after themselves! You must come home at once!"

Per Hansa still remained silent. . . . This speech was so unlike the Beret that he knew, that he glanced up at her quickly.

"Give me that kettle! . . . Yes—water, *water!*" he shouted at them, pointing to the kettle. But then he remembered Store-Hans. . . . "Tell them that I want *clean* water—yes, clean, that's it! And it must be hot, too!"

Now he found time to turn to his wife. . . . "Oh, well, Kjersti isn't going to miscarry to-night! . . . But if you don't want to stay here, to help save a human life in dire distress, you'd better go home. . . . Here, give me the rest of the things!" Her words of an hour before were again ringing loud in his ears; his own voice had taken on an added harshness; he knew it and felt glad.

Beret said no more; she stood looking silently at him, flushed and confused.

The kettle had now been placed on the fire.

"Where is the salt? . . . We need salt in the water."

He took the antique whisky bottle that Sörine had sent; it was still a good half full. The pepper, done up in a little package, had been brought over in a cup. Per Hansa looked at it for a moment in grave doubt. . . . "No, it's too much—never in the world can he stand all that! . . . Hold out your apron, Beret, to catch this. . . . There's too much pepper."

"Now, don't be so hasty!" she said. She took the pepper from him, made a funnel of the bag, and held it out for him to pour in as much as he wanted.

Then Per Hansa concocted for the sick Indian that "horse cure" which is famous among all the inhabitants of Nordland. A goodly tablespoonful of pepper lay in the cup; he filled it up with whisky, stirred it around, put the bottle down on the ground, and motioned to the Indian to drink.

The man took the cup, sniffed at it, and smiled; then he put it to his mouth and took a draught, smacking his lips and making a fearful grimace.

"Tell him to drain it off at once, Store-Hans! . . . He'll live through it—though it does kick powerfully to begin with!"

The Indian downed the rest of the mixture without wincing.

As Per Hansa was pouring the whisky from the bottle a couple of the others had suddenly grown restless; as soon as he set it down, one of these rose to his feet with a jerk and sauntered in their direction; the other followed close at his heels.

"They're taking the bottle!" whispered Beret, frightened at their manner.

Per Hansa whirled like a flash and caught hold of a brown arm; he grasped it firmly and gave it a violent twist. A howl of pain echoed through the camp. . . . "What the hell are you doing!" cried Per Hansa, wrenching loose the bottle with his other hand. "That bottle belongs to Hans Olsa. Don't you dare to touch it!" He looked so fiercely at the pair that they slunk off, afraid.

"Now come here and help me, woman! . . . Hold this bottle, and let the liquor drip down on his hand while I rub it in. . . . Right on the wound—only a drop at a time . . . God! did you ever see a nastier-looking hand?"

Beret did as he told her, but her own hand was shaking violently. He looked at her closely. Her face was flushed; tears hung in her eyes. . . . And all at once the loud ringing of bitter words died away in his ears.

He massaged the hand of the Indian for a long while, pouring the whisky on freely. Then he asked for the rags which she had brought. These he dipped in the kettle, where the water was now boiling; he wrung them out slightly and began swathing them around the hand—one rag over the other. The man gasped and moaned in his great agony.

"Now, Beret, we ought to have a clean, dry cloth to

wrap around the whole business. . . . But probably you didn't bring anything like that?"

She hesitated for an instant, then untied her apron and handed it over to him. He knew that it was her very best apron. He could not bear to take it, but he did not say so.

"That's just it, Beret-girl—the very thing! If that doesn't help him, I don't know anything in the wide world that would cure his hand! . . . Now, take mother with you and go home, Store-Hans. You can see for yourselves, there's nothing to be afraid of here. I'll bring the cows back with me when I come."

"But when will you come?" she asked with a tremor in her voice.

"Oh, I shall have to stay here part of the night, at least. If we can't make the swelling go down, and that right quick, there's nothing under God's heaven that can save him! I'll have to change the rags every half hour. . . . But you go right along, now, and don't worry!"

Beret paused a moment; she gazed at him, saying not a word, but her mouth quivered. Then she took Store-Hans by the hand and walked away.

VI

During the first part of the night Per Hansa kept constant vigil over the sick man, frequently looking at his watch and changing the bandages; every time the hand was exposed he rubbed in a few more drops from Hans Olsa's bottle. It was evident from the man's face that the pain was growing no worse; he even slept at intervals.

Midnight passed. The whole camp was now asleep; the men lay around like mummies, wrapped in their gaudy blankets, their feet towards the fire. Occasionally one of them would rise and throw on more wood; Per Hansa noticed that it was always the same man. . . . The night was vast and still; the glow of the fire spread a strange light a little way around . . . beyond hovered impenetrable darkness.

Per Hansa felt tired and drowsy; he realized that he would have to pull himself together in order to keep going through the middle watch. . . . Suddenly he pricked up his ears; in an instant he was wide awake. He had heard a sound like steps in the grass, off on one side—steps that seemed to be hesitating as if in fear. They trod cautiously, drawing closer and closer; then they stopped, as if the person were listening. . . . He glanced around; the sick man slept at his side; all the others seemed to be sleeping. Who could it be, reconnoitring so quietly out there? . . . He got up abruptly, stepped closer to the fire, and stood fully revealed against the glare. Now the steps were heard again, firmly approaching. . . . The next moment Beret stood within the circle of the camp fire, silently looking at him.

Per Hansa's eyes leaped out and embraced his wife's form: a great glow of love and tenderness surged through him. . . . "Beret-girl, come here!" he called in a low voice. "Don't be frightened; the whole crew is asleep!"

She advanced slowly to the side of the fire where he stood; but she did not look at him. Her face was flushed and swollen with weeping. . . . "How she must have been crying!" he thought; and the memory of his harsh words filled him with deep remorse. He went up to her timidly, took her by the hand, and led her nearer the fire . . . "Beret, you ought to be sleeping at this hour of the night! . . . Have you been frightened again?"

Her body shook with sobs; they tore her so convulsively that she could not speak a word. Like a crushed thing she sank inertly to the ground. He threw himself down beside her, put one arm around her waist, and sought her hand. . . . Then she began to weep softly; he heard it, and stroked the hand he had found. After a while he had tried to say, lightly: "I guess the old fellow is going to pull through, all right." . . . But the moment the words were out of his mouth he felt that he hadn't said the right thing; in his confusion, he asked her how all the others were at home.

She made no response to either of his attempts; then he heard the sick Indian stir, and looked around at him. The man lay wide awake, staring at them fixedly with his black, beady eyes.

For a while Per Hansa busied himself once more with the injured hand; the man sat up as the treatment went on; Beret rose and stood close by, watching the operation.

"If you had a string to tie around the rags, so that they wouldn't loosen when they got dry, they would keep the heat longer," she said in a low voice, but calm and clear.

"Oh yes! . . . If I only had it!"

She turned away for a moment and began fumbling at her clothes; then, with a bashful but determined air, she handed him one of her home-braided garters. . . . "Will this do?" she asked.

"*Do?* . . . My God! Beret, that's exactly what we need!" . . . He bound up the sick hand tightly, and tied the garter around the bandage. . . . "The fellow's better already!" he cried. "I can see it in his eyes—and his hand feels softer. . . . But it's still bad enough; he isn't over it yet, by any means!"

When the bandage had been firmly fastened the Indian got up, went to one of the wagons, and fetched three heavy blankets; these he gave to Per Hansa, motioning that they should cover themselves and lie down.

"Now, doesn't that show, Beret, what decent people they are? . . . I think the fellow will be able to take care of himself for a while. We might as well turn in!" . . . He wrapped one blanket around her, another around himself; then they both lay down with their feet to the fire, and pulled the third blanket over the two of them. Per Hansa put his arm around his wife and held her close in a fond, protecting embrace. "Now try to sleep, my dear Beret-girl!" he whispered, reassuringly . . . She dropped off almost at once, and slept until the crimson dawn fell on the eastern prairie.

The Indians remained for another day and night. During their stay Per Hansa spent more time with them than he did at home. Store-Hans practically lived on the hill, keeping an eye on things. And Ole, too, strolled over to the Indian camp at odd times. . . . But Sam Solum let the savages severely alone; and the women, though they were curious to see the camp, felt too timid to venture near.

The Indians, for their part, kept strictly to themselves. They did not once approach the houses of the settlement;

neither, strange to say, did they allow their women to come over.

It was noon of the third day before they broke camp, to continue the journey northward. The hand of the sick man still looked very bad, but the immediate danger seemed to be over. Per Hansa had made a sling for him, in which he carried his arm. When the long train of queer-looking teams had got well under way, they saw the sick Indian coming down the hill toward the house, leading a fully saddled pony by the bridle; one of the wagons stood waiting for him farther along the hill.

The fellow is probably coming to say good-bye, thought Per Hansa; he got up and went to meet him. Beret and the children followed slowly a little way behind. The man walked straight up to Per Hansa and uttered a few unintelligible words; he laid in Per Hansa's hand the bridle by which he was leading the pony; then he said a few more words, made a short, stiff bow, turned on his heel and stalked away. . . . He was a tall, broad-shouldered savage, well built and handsome.

"Has the old boy gone stark crazy?" exclaimed Per Hansa. "Can you imagine what he means?"

"He wants to give you the pony!" shouted Store-Hans, his eyes round with wonder.

Per Hansa roared out an emphatic protest, and started after the stranger. . . . "No, no!" he cried. "That will never do!" . . .

But the Indian only strode to the waiting wagon, climbed in, and rode away.

"I've never seen the beat of it in all my born days!" said Per Hansa, solemnly. He stood as if dumfounded, holding the bridle over his arm. . . . "Saddle and everything!" . . .

Store-Hans gave a leap into the air, turned a somersault, which immediately had to be repeated. Never in his life had he felt so supremely happy. . . . Then he and his brother ran over to claim the prize.

VII

In the evening of the following day the loaded wagons arrived from town; they brought great stores of curiosities, and the men who drove them had many remarkable tales to tell.

Hans Olsa, who had carried fifteen dollars in cash from Per Hansa to buy merchandise with besides going surety for him for a plow and a horse rake, came first to their house to unload, before going home. There was a great mountain of bags and packages, sacks and boxes; but best of all were the plow and the rake. The latter, especially, —it was painted in such beautiful, rich colours, red, blue, and green; it looked so impressive standing there in the yard, with its seat reared high in the air . . . like a veritable throne! Nothing would do but Store-Hans must climb up and try it at once; he was wondering if they couldn't hitch their new pony to this wonderful rig! . . . Still more marvellous things than this had come from town; but Store-Hans was fully occupied for a while and did not see them till later. Over at Tönseten's stood a mowing machine, which could cut both hay and wheat; this also had a seat high up in the air; and at the Solum boys' the sights were equally remarkable.

There was a grand celebration at Hans Olsa's house that night. Tönseten and Per Hansa arrived long before the others to have a talk together. They found much to do, and many important matters to discuss and settle. Everything that had been borrowed during the past season must now be paid back, and that was a complicated affair; for at one time one kind of measure had been used, at another time another; they were all in the same boat. Everyone owed everyone else—and now it was time to square the accounts. Hans Olsa, who during the shortage had had the most to lend, was now left with enough supplies to stock a good-sized store.

But the goods were what interested Per Hansa least of all just now; he was eaten up with curiosity, and only wanted to ask questions; he had to hear every detail of their difficulties and adventures on the way. . . . Had they run across many people? What news had they picked up? Did there seem to be many settlers moving west? How did the prospects look where they had been? . . . Was he a fair-minded man, this fellow they had bargained with—the one who had trusted them for the plow and the rake? Did he look like a chap who would extend still further credit to a poor devil who had an honest face and came to him in a straightforward way? . . . God knows, Per Hansa needed such a blessed lot of things!

—Yes, Hans Olsa would say that the man seemed to be a pretty decent sort of fellow; he spoke only English, however, so one couldn't get far with him in the way of talk; this was a bad piece of news for Per Hansa. His goods were fairly expensive, too; but one couldn't expect anything better out here. . . . On second thought, Hans Olsa seriously doubted whether it would be possible to get further credit from him. At the start of their dickering, the man wouldn't listen to a word of extending credit; but Syvert had argued with him so long and sensibly that he had finally yielded, on condition that they both sign their names as security for the plow and the rake. . . . By this time, anyway, he knew they were going to buy so much from him that it wouldn't have paid him to be unreasonable.

The returned voyagers, however, thought that the folks at home had stranger tales than their own to tell. It seemed nothing short of a miracle that Per Hansa had been able to bring back to life an Indian chief with one foot in the grave—those were the very words Kjersti had used to her husband. Tönseten swore that he had never heard anything so strange; by George! it was more exciting than any storybook ever written!

. . . "I declare, Per Hansa," said Hans Olsa, looking at him in open admiration, "it's a queer thing about you! No matter how hard you're put to it, you always give a good account of yourself! . . . I was dead set on having you go along with us this trip; we could have arranged it somehow, you know. Syvert and I were speaking about it only the night before we left; but then we both decided that we could feel so much more comfortable about going away, knowing that you were here. . . . It was an act of Providence, I say, to leave you home this time!" . . . Tönseten nodded yes-and-amen to all that Hans Olsa had said.

Per Hansa accepted their homage very modestly; he drew a deep breath and started to reply; but words failed him, and he had to begin all over again.

. . . "Oh, well—so much for that, boys. Forget it, now! I didn't do anything out of the ordinary. But I might as well own up that when I told Ole to get Old Maria I didn't have any courage to spare! . . . There came the band of Indians, thirty strong or more—and here I stood, alone with three crazy women! . . . It looked like far from plain sailing, I can tell you!" . . .

"I don't doubt it a bit!" agreed Hans Olsa. "It's a wonder to me that you didn't take the women and try to run away!"

"Yes, but where could I run to? Besides, they had horses. . . . The women were crying and carrying on, you know. . . . And just then it crossed my mind, Hans Olsa, that if you were only near enough to sing out to —and you, too, Syvert—I'd gladly have given my right hand, or both of them!"

"Sam wasn't much use to you, eh?" asked Tönseten.

"No, Syvert, Sam isn't quite equal to such a job." But then Per Hansa felt that he had been too harsh; he quickly added: "Let's hope that he, too, will have guts some day. . . . The boy has plenty of good qualities. . . ."

Meanwhile Beret and Kjersti had arrived; the Solum boys turned up at last, and then they were all gathered. The women had gone with Sörine into her new house; they were curious to see what her husband had brought; she had to give both of them a taste from this bag and that. The menfolk remained sitting behind the barn; they had many weighty matters to discuss, and didn't want to be interrupted; just now the hay cutting seemed to be the all-absorbing topic. . . . Per Hansa's boys and Hans Olsa's girl were chasing one another around the sod hut, playing "Indian."

It was a strange thing, however, the number of trips the men had to make into the barn to look at the window and door which Hans Olsa had brought. There must indeed be something very odd about that window and that door. The men never seemed to be done looking at them; they went in and came out—came out only to go in again; each time they reappeared they were laughing and talking more glibly. The children sneaked close to the walls whenever the men were inside. . . . It must be some very secret business they were about! Their voices sank so low—most of the time nothing but whispering could be heard. . . . And such a volley of hawking and coughing and clearing of throats came from the interior of the barn, such a smacking of lips, such a steady gurgling—like water running out of a bottle—that the children pressed against the wall outside couldn't help laughing. . . . There, one of them had given a tremendous sneeze! . . . "Hush!" whispered Sofie. "That was Syvert—he must have swallowed wrong!"

. . . Something very strange, indeed, whatever it was. . . . Now they heard Tönseten swear that it was his turn. He had forgotten himself and spoken out loud: "Can't I treat Per Hansa to an honest drink, when he has saved both my wife and my cow from dire death and scalping! . . . Toss it off, Per, old boy, and let the rest of us get a chance!"

Then more jolly laughter and smacking of lips.

"What do you suppose they're doing?" whispered Sofie, making a wry face.

"Drinking, of course!" said Ole, curtly, furious because he was not allowed to be in on this. . . . Surely he was grown-up enough to take a drink or two! He could drive the oxen fully as well as his father.

Then Sörine appeared in the doorway, shouting to them that now they must all come in. In one of the boxes which her husband had brought she had found two bottles. As far as she could make out, it was neither kerosene nor liniment; she felt pretty sure that it wasn't syrup! . . . It would do no harm to find out exactly what the stuff was—to-night they had good reason for rejoicing. She brought a glass, treated both of the neighbour women, took a wee drop herself, and then called in the men.

All five of the menfolk entered in a body and drew up in a close group at the door; at sight of the whisky they had suddenly become bashful and cautious.

"You shouldn't be handing around costly Christmas treats in the middle of the haying season!" said Tönseten, craftily. . . . "What sort of a housekeeper is this that you've got, Hans Olsa?"

"Oh, come on, Syvert!" laughed Sörine.

—What, *he?* Good gracious! *no*—he wouldn't have anything! He couldn't stand liquor right after supper, anyway. . . . She ought not to lead a weak brother into temptation!

But he was chuckling, and his four companions were chuckling with him.

Per Hansa pushed Hans Olsa forward.

"Here, Hans Olsa, you are the boss of this house. Show us how the thing ought to be done. . . . Syvert, you see, isn't feeling well, poor devil!"

—Now, it would never do for him to be first—this was Hans Olsa's ruling. Where he had been brought up, that wasn't considered proper.

"If you don't come at once and take this glass," said Sörine with mock severity, "I'll pour it back into the bottle. . . . Then you can stand there wishing for it as much as you please!"

. . . "Hold on, there, Sörrina—not so hasty, not so hasty! Be careful with the blessings of the Lord! . . . Of course I'll sample it for you, if you've got to have it done!" . . . It was Tönseten, after all, who had first spoken and come forward. But it seemed to take him an awful while to swallow that dram; he hawked and grinned over every little sip, and said the liquor burnt his throat so unmercifully that he could hardly get it down. . . . "Tell me, Hans Olsa, where did you find this stuff?"

"Now, heave it in, Syvert, so that the rest of us can have a whack before it gets too cold!" laughed Hans Olsa. "You've got to help me with that window, you know, before you leave to-night."

"Right you are! . . . Yes, right you are!" agreed Tönseten, solemnly, and emptied the glass without more ado.

Sörine treated them all. . . . And now the menfolk were sorry, but they really had no time to stay indoors; Hans Olsa needed all their help to get that window in before it came dark; and out they trooped in a body again, as soon as they had emptied their glasses.

When the celebration was over and they finally set

out for home that night, it seemed to Kjersti that Syvert walked very queerly. No matter how she adjusted her own steps, he would either range ahead of her or lag behind; when the latter took place, he would suddenly discover it and lurch forward, struggling hard to keep his balance; once he had caught up with her again, he would come to a stop and stand there babbling.

"What in the name of common sense are you mumbling about? What ails you, Syvert dear? . . . You act as if you were walking and talking in your sleep on the open prairie!"

"Hic! . . . Don't know!" he sighed. . . . "Feel awright . . . Maybe li'l' queer. . . . Sort o' diz' . . . sort o' dizzy, y' know. . . . Feet don't work prop'ly!" He lurched ahead like a boat scudding down the slope of a wave. . . . "You know, I think . . . abs'lutely I do . . . must be that stuff . . . that damned stuff of Sörrina's!"

"Oh, well," said Kjersti, consolingly, laughing to herself, "if it isn't anything worse than that, you'll soon be all right again."

VIII

It was two days later that the great misfortune befell them. And according to the manner of such events, it came while everything seemed safe and serene and even the thought of ill luck was far away.

They had finished their afternoon lunch. Hans Olsa was cutting hay; his new machine hummed lustily over the prairie, shearing the grass so evenly and so close to the ground that his heart leaped with joy to behold the sight. . . . What a difference, this, from pounding away with an old scythe, on steep, stony hillsides! . . . All the men had gathered around to see him start; Per Hansa had returned home from that send-off firmly determined to get another cow for the winter, even if he had to steal one; for with such a machine it would be nothing to cut the hay.

Per Hansa was finishing his thatching that afternoon. Ole and Store-Hans were helping; even Beret came out from time to time to lend a hand. The father was chatting with the boys, who answered him gayly; now and then they became so boisterous and laughed so heartily together that little And-Ongen wanted to get up on the roof with them. Some distance away the pony was tethered; the boys petted him constantly, and already he seemed so tame that in a short while it would be safe to turn him loose.

Tönseten was breaking some new land, with Sam as helper; from his high lookout, Per Hansa had just noticed how well Syvert was getting along with his field. But wait a bit, my good Syvert, wait a bit! . . . Per Hansa simply didn't feel like hurrying to-day. He shouted down once more to Beret, asking her to see whether the roof would hold water; that was one of his little jokes. The point was this: it had sounded so pleasant to hear her voice in the room below while he had been working on the roof; but now that the thatch was on, the low tone in which she naturally spoke didn't carry through the thickness of the sod; he missed hearing her, and liked to make her shout now and then. . . . He seemed to notice that she was growing better satisfied with things as they were out here.

Henry Solum was digging a well down by the creek. Everyone was busy with his own particular task; the little frontier settlement hummed with the keen joy of labour.

. . . Then the blow fell upon them—suddenly!

Kjersti noticed it first. At lunch time she had brought out a bite to eat and a drop of coffee for the men. Plenty reigned just now, after the trip to town. As she was about to enter her own house again it occurred to her that she hadn't seen Brindlesides, either on the way over or on the way back. . . . The cow must have been in sight, somewhere around. She turned and walked a little way beyond the corner of the house, then stopped and surveyed the scene. . . . Kjersti kept on looking until her eyes watered—until she could hear the heavy pounding of her heart; but her cow was not to be seen on the whole wide prairie . . . and not a single one of the other critters, either!

In her wild excitement she ran straight to Sörine's and rushed into the house, crying:

"Have you any idea where your cow is?"

"My cow . . . ?" Sörine noticed her agitated face, and could not say another word.

"That's just what I said, Sörrina! . . . Where is she —where is she? . . . Oh, merciful Heaven!" . . .

"You are scaring the life out of me, Kjersti! The cow must be right around here." . . . But she didn't wait for an answer; the women rushed out of the house together.

. . . Sure enough, no cows in sight anywhere!

"I can't understand it!" exclaimed Sörine. . . . "Can you?"

"They've run away!" cried Kjersti is despair.

"Of course they couldn't have sunk through the earth!" Sörine was always a sensible woman in a crisis.

"Oh, where are they?" wailed Kjersti. "Where have they gone?"

"We must tell the men this minute!" declared Sörine, firmly. She saw that it was no use to waste time in waiting for her neighbour; leaving Kjersti to look after herself, she hastened over to where her husband was working.

Hans Olsa pulled up the horses abruptly when he saw the two women straggling across the field.

. . . The cows? Oh, nothing worse than that! . . . Well, he hadn't seen hide nor hair of the cows; but they must be around somewhere. . . . He was in such spirits because of the smooth way the new machine was running, and of the ease with which they would now be able to get all the hay they needed, that he felt as if nothing could worry him to-day. . . . It was a sin how nervous these women were. Good Lord! the cows would show up all right at milking time!

"We must begin to search for them at once!" . . . Sörine was so earnest and determined about it, that almost unconsciously he found himself looking around. . . . Strange, not a beast to be seen! . . . Then he, too, became serious; he unhitched the horses, tied one of them to the mowing machine, mounted the other, and rode up the hill.

"We must go and tell Per Hansa!" said Sörine, briskly.

"Oh, what's the use!" wailed Kjersti, wringing her hands. "You can see for yourself that they are gone! . . . Yes, gone—and if anyone is to find them, we'll have to do it!"

Sörine was now both angry and frightened—angry with Kjersti, frightened over the cows. She hurried on ahead, the other trailing after.

But there was no information to be had at Per Hansa's either. None of them there had thought of keeping an eye on the cows; the animals had gone around loose every day, and had invariably come home at milking time in the evening; they never had been in the habit of straying so far away that they couldn't be seen. . . . Ole could distinctly remember having noticed them over by the creek, that very forenoon.

Per Hansa took the matter calmly and made a comforting suggestion; the cows were probably lying down in the tall grass, somewhere along the creek; they'd turn up safe and sound when it came milking time. . . . But just then Hans Olsa rode up with a very sober face and related that he hadn't seen a sign of life stirring on the whole prairie!

When Hans Olsa took it that way, and spoke so seriously, Per Hansa, too, began to get worried; he and the boys at once came down from the roof.

"Take the pony, Ola, and ride down to the creek. Search upstream first, then turn and go south. If you don't see anything, you'd better notify the Solum boys and Tönseten." . . . Per Hansa still believed that the cows would come back all right of their own accord; but he proposed that they all should quit work fairly early; then if the cows hadn't shown up they could get together and decide what was best to be done. For surely the gnomes hadn't taken them underground! . . .

IX

The evening wore on; outside of every hut the settlers stood watching, but no cows appeared. The uneasiness deepened, and that sneaking dread which comes to all when life about them has suddenly and mysteriously disappeared. . . . The wind blew from the southwest, driving heavy rain clouds; they hung so low that the grass seemed to bend as they swept over it where the plain swelled up to meet the sky.

A depressing gloom hovered over each of the four families sitting around the supper table. At Per Hansa's, little And-Ongen wept bitterly and inconsolably because she hadn't been taken along to pet Rosie while her mother milked. As they were sitting down to supper, the child had asked if they weren't going to milk the cow to-night; Beret didn't have the heart to tell her what had happened, and said hastily that she had milked already. The child felt that a great injustice had been done her—that she had been defrauded of something which was hers by right. She had burst out crying and had wanted to go to Rosie at once; but the mother had said: No, Rosie had gone away as soon as she had given her milk, and would not come back till to-morrow. And-Ongen had hung tearfully around her mother's neck, trying to make her promise never to go milking again unless she took her along. The mother had comforted her as best she could; although she had not said much, it had been more affecting to look at her than at the child.

Store-Hans listened to them until, all at once, he had to lay his spoon aside. He couldn't have swallowed another mouthful of his porridge. He got up quietly, his eyes on the floor, slipped outside, and ran behind the house. . . . The very thought of eating was horrible; every spoonful had threatened to choke him. It had seemed as if he were dipping the spoon in Rosie's very blood. . . . And dear Rosie, around whose neck he had put his arms so many times, resting his cheek against her soft skin. . . . He felt now that he loved her almost more than any living being in the world!

The elder brother, who considered himself a full-grown man, had remained at the table, gulping down large mouthfuls of milk and porridge with an indifferent air. He noticed his brother go out; then he said in a loud voice, just let the cows wait till he got hold of them! He'd lash their hides so thoroughly that they wouldn't ever dare to play that trick again! . . . His father shot a glance at the boy, which silenced him immediately. The next moment he, too, had lost his appetite and laid his spoon aside. After a while he went out; though he could hear where his brother was, by certain unmistakable sounds, he did not try to find him; instead he climbed up on the roof and sat there alone.

A little later the whole colony gathered on top of the Indian hill near Per Hansa's. Per Hansa himself, with Beret and the child, came last of all, although they had the shortest distance to walk. Away behind them Ole sauntered along; but Store-Hans was nowhere to be seen. The evening lay heavily on the plain. Toward the south, where the clouds were massing together, it was already deepening into night. No life, no sound—only the wind moaning under a lowering sky. . . . The evening brought memories to them—memories of half-forgotten tales which people had heard and repeated long, long ago, about happenings away off in a far country. There it had been known to have actually taken place, that both man and beast would be spirited away by trolls. . . . So many strange things were hovering between heaven and earth, if one stopped to think . . . and remember! . . . But that anything of the sort could happen out here on the open prairie, where not so much as a single jutting cliff or wooded ridge appeared, that was the strangest of all!

The folk stood around in gloomy silence; each was thinking the same thoughts.

. . . "They *must* be down by the creek!" repeated Tönseten for the hundredth time.

The hopelessness in his voice struck the same chord of desolation that possessed them all; no one had courage to ask Tönseten what he supposed could have happened to the cows down there. When he got no answer, he added with an even deeper note of melancholy:

. . . "Talk about mystery!"

The wind swept over them with a chilly breath, now and then flicking a drop of rain from the dense clouds.

Sam Solum rose from where he had been sitting on the ground, and began to walk up and down as if he had made up his mind.

"In my opinion," he announced, firmly, "it's the doings of the red man! . . . He's at his work again!"

All turned to look at him.

"You saw how crazy mad the cows acted that night when the Indians came? Well, most likely they noticed it, too, and have come back here after them. That's where we'll have to look for our cows, my friends!" . . . Sam spoke in a bold, convincing voice; now he had solved the riddle for them and felt very superior.

His idea at once gained general acceptance; it was at least a natural explanation. To the women it sounded very reasonable; they wondered why they hadn't thought of it themselves; for they had all seen how crazy the cattle acted that night. . . . Hans Olsa and Tönseten pondered deeply over the problem for a while; they said nothing at first; this explanation had at least dispersed the feeling of weirdness that had gripped the colony; but the longer they thought, the more they realized that scant consolation lay in the theory that the Indians had enticed the cattle away; for where could they find the Indians, or how could they recover the cattle after they had been found? If they had stolen them, they meant to keep them—and keep them they could.

Tönseten marched straight up to Per Hansa; he spoke rapidly, in a voice of great determination:

"If that's the case, by God! you've got to go and get the cows the first thing in the morning—you who are so friendly with the Indians. . . . We must have our cows right away!"

"Yes, good Heavens!" Kjersti put it. "How can we get along if that drop of milk is taken away from us? . . . You ought to go this very minute!"

Per Hansa sat gazing steadily off into the distance; but he said never a word. At Kjersti's remark, however, it seemed as if something had suddenly stung him; he bounded up from the ground like a rubber ball.

"That's just the job for you and Sam! . . . Come on, wife, let's go home and get to bed."

With these words he stalked away; everyone could see that now Per Hansa was thoroughly angry.

x

Rest was a long time in coming to them at Per Hansa's that night; a strange uneasiness had entered there and would not leave the house.

Store-Hans had not accompanied them to the hill; his brother found him sitting outside when he came home, and told him what Sam had said; he added it as his own opinion that undoubtedly the Indians had been there and stolen all the cows! . . . Ole had then left his brother and gone in to bed; the father and mother were inside already, getting ready for the night; but time went on and the other boy did not come. . . . After a while the mother had gone out to look for him; she had called several times and had walked around the house; finally she had received a gruff answer from the gable of the roof. There sat the boy, staring out into the darkness. He refused to come down until she spoke to him harshly, saying that she would call his father if he did not mind her at once. . . . Then he slid down quickly and silently, ran into the house, slipped off his clothes, and flung himself into bed.

Quiet gradually settled on the room; the father and mother had at last retired. As they were on the point of falling asleep, a violent sob came from the boys' bed; silence immediately followed—breathless silence; then came another sob, more violent than the first—a strangled gasp of anguish. . . . The mother called across the room, asking what was the matter—was Store-Hans sick? At that he broke down in earnest, with long heaves and gasps, with sobs so violent that they threatened to choke him. Beret spoke to him gently and soothingly; little by little the storm over there in the dark abated, lulled away, and finally seemed to die out altogether . . . except for a flutter or two. . . . Suddenly there arose a hoarse sound like that of bellows inhaling the air, which ended in a tear-choked gasp: "Rosie! . . . *Ro-o-sie!*"

"Stay where you are, Beret," said Per Hansa. "I'll get up and tend to the little fellow!" He pulled on his trousers, and went over in the dark to the boys' bed; his voice was so low that it could hardly be heard.

. . . "Come, Hansy-boy, I'll tell you a secret!"

He put his arm around the youngster, lifted him out of bed, took a coat from the wall and wrapped it around him, then carried him outside. Over by the woodpile, which they had hauled home together from the Sioux River, he sat down with the boy in his lap. . . . They began to talk. At first only the father did the speaking; but after a while, between sobs, Store-Hans began to join in. The wind, driving warm raindrops full in their faces, seemed to ask if they had gone crazy, sitting out here at this hour of the night; but they paid not the slightest attention. . . .

Store-Hans was finding consolation in his father's wise and kindly chat.

. . . "It's a burning shame," Per Hansa was saying, "that we haven't got two ponies! Then you could go with me to-morrow when I ride out to fetch those pesky cows!"

—Oh! . . . Did he know where they were, then?—slipped out between two sobs.

"Of course I do!"

Store-Hans snuggled deeper into his father's lap at this assurance, feeling an infinite, blissful safety there.

—Was it the Indians who had taken them?

"Certainly not! Those were honest Indians. . . . You could see that for yourself."

—But where were the cows, then?

"Oh, they've just strayed off so far that they can't find their way home again. . . . But don't worry, boy. Tomorrow morning I'm going to ride out and get them, never fear!"

A long silence followed this promise; Store-Hans felt a blissful happiness settling upon him; the sobs gradually ceased.

"The Indians don't scalp cows, do they?"

"No, indeed! . . . They aren't such barbarians!"

"They are good people, aren't they, Dad?"

"Yes, just ordinary folks."

"Cows wouldn't be anything for Indian braves to fight for, would they?"

"I should say not! . . . And much less for *chiefs!*"

It was growing very late; the raindrops were still falling steadily; the father said that they ought to be getting back to bed. But Store-Hans seemed well contented where he was.

"Are you going to start early to-morrow?"

"I suppose so."

"How long will you be gone?"

"That depends on how far I have to go."

"There won't be any danger if the Indians come back while you are away. . . . I can talk to them, you know!"

"Right you are, son! . . . Nothing to worry about as long as I have you here at home!"

Then Per Hansa got up and carried the boy back to bed.

Store-Hans fell asleep almost as soon as his head touched the pillow. But some time later in the night he suddenly rose to his knees.

"Here I come, Rosie!" he cried out, clearly—then sank back in a heap on the pillow, and slept on.

XI

At the first faint streaks of day Per Hansa slipped out of bed, made a fire, and put on the coffeepot. His wife, he noticed, was already awake. He told her to stay in bed; to this she made no reply in words, but she got up immediately, dressed herself, and began to prepare him a meal. A small lamp burned in the room; the day was yet too young to give much light.

Per Hansa sat down at the table and began to eat; the coffee wasn't quite ready; his wife stood over by the stove, waiting for it to boil. An air of fixed determination hung about her; although she had not spoken, he felt it just the same.

All night long Beret had been lying there with her eyes wide open, staring up at a picture that would not go away; a picture of a nameless, blue-green solitude, flat, endless, still, with nothing to hide behind. . . Some cows were grazing on it. . . . Yes, animals of flesh and blood were there . . . and in the next moment they were not there! . . .

The picture had been full of unearthly, awful suggestions. She had lain awake in terror, lost in her own imaginings, wrestling with fearsome thoughts that only increased the dread in her soul. . . . And now he was leaving her—now he would probably stay away for a long time and she would have no knowledge of where he was faring. . . . It must have been the Indians who had taken the cows. Could it have been anything else—could it have been? . . . She knew too well how hasty and fearless her husband was, plunging headlong into whatever lay before him! . . . The thought made her tremble.

. . . It seemed plain to her now that human life could not endure in this country. She had lived here for six weeks and more without seeing another civilized face than those of their own company. Not a settled habitation of man lay nearer than several days' journey; if any visitor came, it was a savage, a wild man, whom one must fear! . . . To get what supplies they needed they must journey four whole days, and make preparations as if for a voyage to Lofoten! . . . What would happen if something sudden should befall them . . . attack, or sickness, or fire . . . yes, *what would they do?*

. . . Ah no, this wasn't a place for human beings to dwell in. . . . And then, what of the children? Suppose they were to grow up here, would they not come to be exactly like the red children of the wilderness—or perhaps something worse? . . . It was uncivilized; they would not learn the ways of man; no civilization would ever come. . . . Never, never, would it be otherwise!

. . . Perhaps, then, it was an act of Providence that the cattle had been lost. . . . It ought to show them how things stood out here—that man could not exist in this savage, desolate wilderness; they ought to be able to see that much, at any rate. . . . Even he might see it, too! . . .

She could not tell whether she had slept at all that night; it did not seem so; she had heard her husband's first move when he began to stir. She remembered, too, the last thought she had been struggling with in bed;

she shuddered at it, now that there was a light in the house. There in the darkness she had felt that it would be a blessing if the cows never turned up. . . . How could she ever have thought it? That, too, was only a part of the hideous evil out here! . . .

"You aren't going alone?" she asked, from over by the stove.

He had not mentioned going yet; he gave her a quick look.

"We'll see."

"Will you be gone long?"

"You'd better not look for me till you see me. . . . I may be gone overnight."

She asked no more for a time; in a few moments she came and poured out his coffee.

"Which way are you going?"

"I don't exactly know yet. . . . Eastward, I suppose."

"You are doing a wrong thing, and I must tell you so!" she said, decisively, putting the coffeepot back on the stove. . . . "A wrong thing!" she repeated with even more emphasis.

The vehemence of her tone took hold of him.

"Perhaps it is," he answered, rather meekly. . . . "But we must try to get the cows back somehow, just the same."

"No more than the others!" she exclaimed, her agitation suddenly flaring up. . . . "If they can do without them, we can too!"

"But look here, Beret," he reasoned, trying to calm her, "you know that it's necessary for some one to go and look for the cattle. Hans Olsa hasn't time to do it, because of the haying; and as for the others, I haven't much faith in them. . . . There aren't many to choose from here, you know."

"Does it seem right to you, then," she burst out, wildly, "that I should be left alone here with the children while you are chasing around in the wilderness? . . . You may be gone for a day or a week—how can I know? . . . Why can't Sam or Henry go? They have no one sitting at home waiting for them!" She did not look up from the floor while she was speaking; deep passion burned in her words.

. . . Now she has fallen into one of her unreasonable moods, thought Per Hansa; but perhaps she couldn't help it, poor thing! . . . "It's this way, Beret, you see: I don't believe it would be any use for those fellows to go."

"Then Tönseten will have to do it!" . . . Now she was going to cry—he heard it in her voice.

"Oh, God Almighty! . . . then the cows would surely come home!" he groaned, not far from tears himself.

She did not answer; her rigid form remained standing over by the window, staring out into the drab, dismal dawn.

Per Hansa said no more, either; he gulped down his coffee hurriedly, found his hat and put it on; then he went to the door, paused an instant, opened it quietly, and stepped outside. There he stood still for a moment. . . . No, no—he couldn't leave Beret this way! . . . But what had struck her? It was beyond his comprehension! She had more common sense than any other person he knew; yet here she was, talking more unreasonably than a cross child. What strange influence had come over her since they had arrived out here? . . . He oughtn't to leave her this way—but what could he do? . . . In a deep quandary, he walked over to the woodpile, saddled and bridled the pony, which was tethered close by . . . then paused again.

XII

Before he could make up his mind to jump into the saddle he heard footfalls behind him, and turned toward the house. It had flashed through his mind: here she is coming now; everything will be all right and I can be off at once. . . . I need to hurry!

But in the same flash he had realized that it wasn't from the direction of the door that the sound had come. . . . He turned to find Hans Olsa rounding the corner of the house. Did Hans Olsa think of going? Well, that was another matter; that man was equal to any task. But who would drive the mowing machine while he was gone? And it looked like fine weather for making hay—it seemed to be clearing. . . . All these thoughts passed through Per Hansa's head as he watched his neighbour draw near; he wished that Hans Olsa hadn't come just now . . . no, not just now! His usual frankness was lacking in his greeting:

"You seem to be out early, Hans Olsa."

"And so are you, I see. I sort of expected it; I wanted to talk to you before you went. . . . You're going, aren't you?"

Per Hansa glanced aside and did not answer immediately; at last he said, after a long pause: "Some one will have to go, I suppose. . . . It seems best for you to keep on with the haying, so that we can get the job done. . . . I am no hand at machinery, you know."

"I know that you can ride faster than I can—that is the better reason. . . . Guess what Sörrina told me last night?"

Per Hansa made no attempt at it; he wasn't in a mood to solve riddles just now. His eyes were on his neighbour, but his thoughts were in the house. . . . She must have heard their voices by this time. . . . Would she come out?

. . . "Well," said Hans Olsa, raising his eyebrows significantly, "yesterday morning Sörrina suspected that cow of ours of wanting male company!"

Per Hansa came back to reality with a violent jolt. "What's that you say, Hans Olsa?"

"Those were her very words—'male company'! . . . Do you suppose that old cow of mine could have taken it into her head to ramble all the way back to Fillmore County, just for *that*—and the others followed her? . . . The idea occurred to me, anyway; and I thought it best to tell you at once, before you got away."

"Ha-ha! . . . Ha-ha! . . . She had to have a man, that old dame of yours—and led the others with her into temptation!"

. . . "Well, who knows?"

"Good enough!" . . . Per Hansa leaned forward and untied the horse; he sprang quickly into the saddle. . . . "I was thinking of the Trönders all last night; now I'm going over and make them a visit. There's no telling when you'll see me back. Perhaps you'll keep an eye on things for me here, while I am gone?" . . . He paused, glanced toward the house, and added in a low voice: "Be sure and send Sörrina over here to-night. . . . And you keep on with the haying as hard as you can; it looks to me as if it were going to clear up soon!"

He headed the pony past the house and around it to the side where the door lay; there he drew up, coughed loudly, listened a moment—then rode away.

. . . In the window looking toward the east a woman's face, tear-stained and swollen with weeping, watched his figure grow less and less in the dim grey light of the breaking day, until at last it had disappeared altogether. . . . To her it seemed as though he were sinking deeper and deeper into an unknown, lifeless sea; the sombre greyness rose and covered him.

Soon the word was passed around that Per Hansa had set out eastward to the Sioux River, to look for the cattle; everyone was willing to let the matter rest at that. His pony was fleet-footed; there was no need for any of the others to take up the search; they had better wait to see what luck he had. . . . Not that Tönseten had any faith or hope in the trip. He had kept turning the matter over in his mind all night; he had got from Kjersti a detailed account of how the cattle had behaved when the Indians came, and when he had risen that morning he had been fully convinced that Sam's solution of the riddle was the right and only one. To Tönseten's mind, all that remained of the problem was how to get hold of the beasts again without causing bloodshed and war—how to wrest them from the possession of the redskins before they had gobbled them all up. . . . When he heard of Per Hansa's intended visit to the Trönders, he spluttered with anger; he was disgusted, too, with Hans Olsa because he had not dissuaded him from such a brainless move. . . . But his anger at Per Hansa simply knew no bounds. So—he was not the courageous fellow, then, that he posed as being! Didn't he know that the responsibility for getting the cattle back rested solely on him? For he had been the one who was so friendly with that robber brood. He hadn't chased them back where they had come from, as he should have done. Oh no, he had taken gifts from them instead—and been gloriously fooled into the bargain! And why did he waste his time now, in revelling with the Trönders on the Sioux River? The man had better be made to understand that they needed their cows at once! . . . Tönseten went about breathing fire and brimstone, and didn't care who heard him.

The gloom of this loss lay heavy upon the others as well; they went about their work as usual, but their eyes strayed elsewhere.

Evening came, but neither Per Hansa nor the cattle. Folks did not care to go to bed; they sat about staring and waiting. All of Hans Olsa's family went over to Beret's; Tönseten and Kjersti, having first stopped at Hans Olsa's and found them out, went there, too. The Solum boys could see no reason for moping around their hut alone; they soon joined the others. . . . But none of them found cheer in this place, either. Beret seemed distant and strangely calm, as if the whole affair didn't in the least concern her. They wondered at her manner, it was so unnatural.

When they were leaving, however, she said, quietly, as if musing to herself:

"Somehow, I can't figure this out. . . . Night has come now; Per Hansa is wandering off there alone in this endless wilderness. And four grown men are sitting here talking the time away. . . . But aren't the cattle just as much theirs as his? . . . No, I can't seem to figure it out at all. . . ."

Over in the bed little And-Ongen began to cry for her father; the mother went and sat down beside her; she kept her eyes on the floor. Her words still lingered in the air; not a voice cared to answer. There seemed to be nothing to say, and the silence only made the gloom deeper. . . .

When the others had gone and the children were asleep, Beret rose and hung some heavy clothes up over the windows—the thickest clothes she could find—

to shut out the night. She felt that she could never go to bed, with all the eyes out there staring in upon her. . . .

. . . Last of all, she pulled the big chest in front of the door.

XIII

The following day there was no getting the boys down from the roof; they climbed up immediately after breakfast and sat there hour after hour. The forenoon passed; noon came. Ole jumped down to eat, but Store-Hans remained at his post; the mother let him stay. Coffee time finally went by, yet no one in sight. . . .

Then, all of a sudden, eager shouts rang out from the roof; Store-Hans was screaming in an excited voice that now . . . right over there . . . dad was coming! . . . Yes, now he was coming! Ole's voice joined in. . . . And he has the cattle with him, too!

"Come on—let's run and tell the others!" cried Ole. . . . "Mother first!" shrieked Store-Hans, forgetting that they had both been shouting the news. They jumped down from the roof together, jerked open the door, and announced in one breath that their father was coming; the next instant they were gone. The word was first carried to Hans Olsa, then to Tönseten, last of all to the Solum boys. In each place the same message: "Dad is coming!"—that from Ole. . . . "And he's got the cows!"—this from Store-Hans.

Sure enough, here came Per Hansa riding the pony, and driving before him a small herd of cows. As the caravan came in sight from the several huts, each family proceeded to count the animals. . . . What was the meaning of this? Were they seeing double? . . . They counted over again with the same result; every person who tried his hand got one cow too many! There should be only four—now there were five. No getting away from it: *five there were!* They were easy enough to count; they straggled over the prairie one by one, like beads on a string. . . . Per Hansa on the pony brought up the rear.

As the people stood outside, looking at the approaching train, they instinctively set out for Per Hansa's. Each had to get his own cow; all were eager to learn where Per Hansa had been these last two days, and to find out about that fifth cow!

The last question had already been answered in part; before the train had arrived they had made out that the fifth animal wasn't a cow at all! No cow, indeed—but a yearling bull! . . . Per Hansa himself was barely recognizable; his face was grimy and streaked with sweat, which had been running down it in streams, and still ran as freely as ever. But what they first noticed about the man was that he carried something strapped to his chest—some sort of a box, it looked like. . . . No—wonder of wonders!—it was a bird cage, made of thin slats; and inside lay a rooster and two hens!

Beret had stepped outside the house at last; she came forward without paying any attention to the others; they felt embarrassed now, and did not dare to approach her; some of them even shrank back as she came near.

. . . "Per, what have you brought?" she asked in a low, tender voice, as if she were shy of him.

Per Hansa was unfastening the cage; he seemed wearied to the point of stupor.

"Oh, well," he said with an effort, "since I had to go so far, I thought I might as well do something worth while." . . . He handed her the cage. . . . "Here are your chickens, Beret. . . . I don't know whether there's any life left in them yet, or not."

Beret took the cage, turned slowly away, and walked toward the house. The others all thronged about him, eager to hear what adventures he had met with.

Tönseten pushed in ahead:

"I say, Per Hansa, who is that fellow you brought with the rest of the cattle?"

The shadow of a grin brightened the grimy face:

"That fellow? . . . Oh, just a Tönder."

"Oh-ho! . . . then he must be a good one! Tönders, they say. . . . But where did you pick him up?"

Per Hansa pretended not to hear; he dismounted and threw the bridle to Store-Hans. . . . "Water him now, and feed him well! . . . Where did I pick that fellow up? Oh, I beguiled a kind Trönder woman into letting me take him for a year. I promised her ten dollars into the bargain; that makes exactly two dollars and a half for your share, Syvert. But that'll be cheaper for you in the long run, you see, than to chase up and down the whole of Dakota Territory looking for your cow!"

Sörine and Kjersti were both very outspoken in their gratitude to Per Hansa; they plainly meant every word that they said. But it seemed to Per Hansa that the deepest word of wisdom on this occasion was offered by Kjersti. She stood listening patiently until the story of his long ride had come to an end; then she remarked, as if quietly musing:

"When lust can be so strong in a dumb brute, what mustn't it be in a human being! . . . I shall never forget this trick you have turned, Per Hansa!"

. . . At that they all laughed heartily.

IV What the Waving Grass Revealed

I

That summer Per Hansa was transported, was carried farther and ever farther away on the wings of a wondrous fairy tale—a romance in which he was both prince and king, the sole possessor of countless treasures. In this, as in all other fairy tales, the story grew ever more fascinating and dear to the heart, the farther it advanced. Per Hansa drank it in; he was like the child who constantly cries: "More—more!"

These days he was never at rest, except when fatigue had overcome him and sleep had taken him away from toil and care. But this was seldom, however; he found his tasks too interesting to be a burden; nothing tired him, out here. Ever more beautiful grew the tale; ever more dazzlingly shone the sunlight over the fairy castle.

How could he steal the time to rest, these days? Was he not owner of a hundred and sixty acres of the best land in the world? Wasn't his title to it becoming more firmly established with every day that passed and every new-broken furrow that turned? . . . He gazed at his estate and laughed happily, as if at some pleasant and amusing spectacle. . . . Such soil! Only to sink the plow into it, to turn over the sod—and there was a field ready for seeding. . . . And this was not just ordinary soil, fit for barley, and oats, and potatoes, and hay, and that sort of thing; indeed, it had been meant for much finer and daintier uses; it was the soil for *wheat*, the king of all grains! Such soil had been especially created by the good Lord to bear this noble seed; and here was Per Hansa, walking around on a hundred and sixty acres of it, all his very own!

A beautiful, alluring thought had begun to beckon him. His first quarter-section was rightly only tillage land; the quarter next to it to the east would be about what he needed for hay and pasture for the cattle; yes, he could even use the one to the west of it, too, if his plans worked out; but he wanted the one to the east first, for it had open water on the creek. These two quarter-sections would make an estate more magnificent than that of many a king of old. . . . He never mentioned this dream to anyone; he could see no way at present of getting hold of another quarter; but his boys were growing bigger day by day; in time they would be able to earn the wherewithal. . . . No hurry yet . . . this was just the beginning!

And there were many other tantalizing, delectable thoughts, of things that would have to come first, before the fine estate was won. The live stock, for instance; in the course of time he would have great numbers—horses and pigs and cattle, chickens and ducks and geese—animals both big and small, of every kind. There would be quacking and grunting, mooing and neighing, from every nook and corner of the farm. . . . The place would need plenty of life, for his Beret to mother!

But dearest to him of all, and most delectable, was the thought of the royal mansion which he had already erected in his mind. There would be houses for both chickens and pigs, roomy stables, a magnificent storehouse and barn . . . and then the splendid palace itself! The royal mansion would shine in the sun—it would stand out far and wide! The palace itself would be white, with green cornices; but the big barn would be as red as blood, with cornices of driven snow. Wouldn't it be beautiful—wasn't it going to be great fun! . . . And he and his boys would build it all!

And stranger things than this transpired in fancy—just

as in the fairy tale: they seemed to lie enchanted under the most prosaic and deceptive semblances, invisible to the eye of man; but then he came and touched them, pouring on a few drops from the magic horn; the charm was instantly broken, and behold, treasures sprang forth, shining in all their newborn freshness and beauty! . . . Just now, for instance, he beheld a vision so fair that his face shone with a glowing light that transfigured his coarse features; he had suddenly discovered a new object outside the palace of his dreams. . . . Yes, sir—there it was! Nothing less than a snow-white picket fence around a big, big garden! And many trees grew there, both within and without; some bore apples, others various kinds of fruit: and some . . . *some had cones* . . . yes, trees with *pine cones* on them! . . . Per Hansa's eyes swam and shone; a sudden moisture dimmed his sight; dear God, there really were pine cones hanging from some of the trees! . . . He didn't know where they waited for him, those trees . . . but they would come! . . .

And so Per Hansa could not be still for a moment. A divine restlessness ran in his blood; he strode forward with outstretched arms toward the wonders of the future, already partly realized. He seemed to have the elfin, playful spirit of a boy; at times he was irresistible; he had to caress everything that he came near. . . . But he never could be still. To remain inactive over the Sabbath would drive him into a fit of ill humour; by noon he had to go outdoors and stir around. If nothing else turned up, he took a long jaunt over the prairies; on these trips he selected many a pretty spot that would be a fine site for a home. . . . Some day a settler will locate here, he thought; I'll remember this, and show him where to build! . . . Wherever he went, no matter how far, he found the same kind of soil.

. . . Endless it was, and wonderful! . . .

II

One Sunday evening the boys had come home wild with excitement. They had made a long trip westward on the prairie to some big swamps which lay out there, with tall grass growing from them, and long stretches of open water in between. They told of thousands upon thousands of ducks, so tame that you could almost take them in your hand. Store-Hans vowed that never in his life had he seen anything like it. He described the ducks, how many and how tame they were, until the words stuck in his throat, and his whole body trembled; his brother raged on even worse.

From then on the boys were always talking about the ducks. Was there no way to get them? . . . But they had no shotgun, the father said, and Old Maria had not been built for that purpose; as it was, they had only a small supply of "feed" for her, which must be kept in case . . . well, no one could tell. Just what it was that "no one could tell," he didn't say; but they understood this much that no ducks would ever be shot with that gun. So the ducks continued to live there, swimming leisurely about in countless numbers, and flying from one pond to the next whenever the boys came too close. And not even a good-sized pebble to be found . . . plague take it all!

Ever since the boys had first discovered the ducks they had made a practice of going out to look at them every Sunday. Each time the birds seemed to have multiplied in numbers. Soon the boys never pretended to speak of anything else between themselves; they thought only of the ducks, and of how to get hold of them. . . . Their father had not yet found time to go with them and behold this wonder.

Then one Sunday afternoon, in the early part of August, Per Hansa went for a stroll westward with Store-Hans. Ole was told to stay at home; it would never do to let mother sit there alone, the father said, when she had three grown men in the family; Ole, the older of the two boys, would have to take his turn first. The boy raised such a commotion over this disappointment that his mother said they had better take him along. The father was firm, however; next Sunday he himself would stay at home, and then Ole could go; but to-day the boy must do as he had been told.

So it fell to Per Hansa and Store-Hans to make the trip alone. Plenty of ducks there were, no doubt about that. When he first saw the place Per Hansa was reminded of the great bird cliffs in Finmarken. Store-Hans pointed at the birds, whispering hoarsely to his father, until he choked, and tears came in his eyes.

—Wasn't there any possible way to get a few of 'em?

—Well—the father seemed quite serious—one might try salt on their tails.

—Salt on their tails? Was that any good?

—Oh yes—they often did it in the olden days.

But then the father had to laugh, and that spoiled it all. As he stood there gazing longingly at the birds no boy could have been more thrilled by the wonderful spectacle. By George! there would *have* to be some way out of this fix; he'd have to *make* a way when he got time to cast about! . . . Maybe the fairy tale had nothing to say about the king's having a shotgun; but he ate plenty of ducks, just the same! . . . What had been done once could be done again!

Store-Hans didn't exactly approve of his father's jocular air; this was no fooling matter. If he only wanted to, he could easily rig up some sort of a contrivance for catching them; he could work miracles when he tried . . . Well then, why didn't he begin to get busy. He certainly saw how thick they were! . . .

But Store-Hans had to possess his soul in patience awhile longer; no birds were captured on their first trip to the swamps.

It was on the way home from this trip that Per Hansa made his startling discovery. Store-Hans had taken a short cut home; he had to hurry back and tell his brother what they had seen. But the father never liked to follow an old path while there was still unexplored land left around him; accordingly, he made a long détour to the westward. He had often wondered how far west his land extended, but had never taken the time to pace it off. Since he was headed in that direction now, he might as well pace down the western border line of his and his neighbours' new kingdom.

He had a pretty good idea of the location of Tönseten's south line, as well as of the corners on it where his east and west lines began; the southeast corner, in fact, was near Tönseten's house. He cut across country until he judged himself to be about on this south line, and walked east for some distance; then he decided that it would be too far to go all the way in, just to pick up the corner; so he turned west again. He would have to be satisfied with an approximate position of Tönseten's southwest corner to-day. . . . About *here*, it ought to be, he thought; he stopped, gazed around, and took his bearings for the walk north. He had been following this course for perhaps a hundred paces when the toe of his boot suddenly struck against a small stake—a little fellow who stood hiding there, nodding in drowsy lonesomeness, just at the edge of a thick tuft of grass. Per Hansa looked down, saw the stake, and brought up with a violent start. . . . Here was Tönseten's southwest corner! What, had Syvert been so cautious as to put down stakes here, too? A very careful man was Syvert, indeed!

Per Hansa bent down closer to examine the stake. Yes, he was right—it was a corner stake; there stood the description, indicating both section and quarter. But the name below . . . *the name* . . . good God! what was this? He dropped to his knees and peered at it until the letters danced before his eyes; he wondered if he were dreaming. The name on the stake wasn't *S. H. Tönseten* at all, as it should have been; it was just *O'Hara* . . . nothing else but *O'Hara!* The letters had been carved on the stake with a knife, and the arrow pointed east, to Tönseten's quarter! . . . When Per Hansa finally rose, he smoothed the grass carefully over with his hand, where his knees had bent it to the ground; the action was quite involuntary.

. . . "Well!" he exclaimed, and walked hastily away. But presently he stopped, turned around, and went back to the stake, to read the name once more. In order to be sure that his eyes hadn't deceived him, he spelled it out letter by letter, tracing the carving with his forefinger. . . . No doubt about it—the thing was true!

And now he laid his course to the northward, walking slowly. The radiant, happy look had vanished from his face; it looked old and worn. All at once, as if struck by a new thought, he quickened his pace. He hurried on until he had reached the vicinity of Hans Olsa's south line, dividing his land from Tönseten's; here he began to search the ground, first to the eastward, then to the westward, working slowly forward into the next quarter-section.

At last he found it—another stake, Hans Olsa's south-west corner! . . . He looked carefully around; no one was in sight. Then he fell on his knees and examined the stake; he didn't bother to glance at the description this time; but the name—the name! Tears suddenly came to his eyes as he stooped over; for an instant he found it hard to see. . . . But there it was, exactly as he had feared; this stake had *Joe Gill* carved on it . . . *Joe Gill*, when it should have been *H. P. Olsen!* . . . He got up at last; his round, jóvial face now looked drawn and sinister.

Moving mechanically, he strode toward the north until he had reached the line between Hans Olsa's quarter and his own; there he repeated his tactics of a while before, zigzagging back and forth over a broad space; but though he kept tacking around for a long time, he was unable to locate any stake. That a stake was there, however, he felt very certain; it was unthinkable that this misfortune should have befallen both Tönseten and Hans Olsa, and not have run him down at the same time. . . . He searched until he had to give it up in despair; then he went north to the line between himself and Henry Solum, and fell to searching in this locality; but no, he couldn't find any stake here, either. It was now growing so late that he had to quit and go home. . . . A short while before, he had been as happy and light-hearted as a child; he came home full of a weariness greater than he had ever known. . . .

III

. . . By God! the trolls must be after him! It was only natural that he should meet them somewhere out here; but to think of their coming in just this dirty fashion! . . . Ah, well, trolls were trolls, no matter how they came! . . .

Per Hansa didn't know what to do with himself that evening; he felt that the only thing that would relieve him just now would be to hitch the oxen to the plow and break a stretch of new land. He looked longingly at the oxen, and at the plow over yonder. . . . No, it was the Sabbath—and evening already.

His discovery had been so utterly disheartening that he could not have mentioned it to anyone for the price of his soul. He would have liked to tell his wife about it, and hear her opinion; but that was out of the question; she was disturbed enough already. . . . But Per Hansa had to do something, or he would go mad; he walked across the yard and sat down on the woodpile; there he remained a long while, staring listlessly at the ground.

. . . These trolls would not be easy to cope with—not if he knew them! . . . But why hadn't he been able to discover their tracks on his own quarter? That was the strangest thing of all!

The boys were only waiting for a chance to talk with their father, now he had been west to the swamps and had seen how thick the birds were there. They came up and spoke to him, but got no response; first one of them tried, and then the other; soon they both were talking at him together; a little later their mother came out and asked him something, but he paid no attention. He sat there in a silence like a stone wall. . . .

He's probably thinking of the ducks, Store-Hans decided; the knowledge made him very happy. Of course he was thinking of the ducks, and would soon hit upon some fine way to capture them! . . . At last Store-Hans could no longer restrain himself; he edged over to his father's side, laid his hand on the stout thigh, and said in a deep joy:

. . . "Weren't there a lot of 'em, Dad?" . . .

"*What?*"

"Did you ever see so many ducks in all your life?"

"Ducks? . . . No."

"You think we can get some of them, don't you?" asked the boy, in a hushed, confidential tone.

But the father made no answer; he was already far away and did not hear. Just then the mother came out with the milk pail on her arm and called loudly to Rosie. This reached Per Hansa's ears; he got up and took the pail from her. . . . "I might as well do the milking, since I'm only sitting here idling away my time." . . . He seemed so absent-minded that she looked hard at him; as he walked away his head drooped forward, his shoulders were slouched down, his whole body seemed strangely shrunken. . . .

The next morning he was up earlier than usual; he left the house without saying a word. As soon as he was gone, Beret got up and went to the window to see what became of him. The early dawn was still in the sky; she saw him stride off westward; soon the slope of the hill hid him from view. . . . It's only the ducks, she thought; I'm glad that he and the boys have found some diversion; but just the same, he ought not to wear himself out over such trifling things. . . . Beret turned away from the window, her face heavy with sadness.

The boys were up and the food was on the table when Per Hansa returned. . . . He was heated as if from a brisk walk, his wife noticed. She had to look at him a second time; there was something queer about his face this morning; it seemed so hard set and forbidding; although it glowed with the heat of his body, it lacked any warmth of expression. Instinctively she asked:

"Is anything wrong with you, Per?"

"No." . . . But he did not look up.

As soon as he had eaten he left the table, telling the boys to come along and help him; now was a good time to pace out the west line of their land; it had to be done soon, anyway; perhaps they would break a stretch of ground out there. . . . His words sounded cold and distant; he went out, and said no more.

Beret watched him narrowly. . . . There's certainly something the matter with him, she thought.

Striking west from the house, Per Hansa paralleled his own south line, between his land and Hans Olsa's; he knew exactly how far in from this line the house had been built; so he merely kept along with it, counting the paces. When he had reached the western limit of his quarter, he stood still; the grass had been trampled down all over the place. . . . "This is where it ought to be; the line should run straight north from here." . . . He walked a few paces north to show them the direction. . . . "There ought to be a small black stake driven down in the grass here somewhere, but I can't seem to find it. Let's go south first; look sharp and see if you can't pick it up. If we don't find it there, we'll go the other way. Keep your eyes open, now, every step!"

"When did you put a stake down here?" asked Ole.

His father apparently didn't hear him. . . . "It ought to be right here; funny, that we can't find it! . . . The cattle must have tramped it into the ground."

All three of them kept searching steadily the whole forenoon; the father seemed so excited, and walked so fast, that the boys could hardly keep up with him. They made tack after tack, north until they stood on Henry's land, south to Hans Olsa's; they did not go in single file, but walked abreast, four or five paces apart.

. . . "Look in the grass, boys—look carefully in the grass!" the father repeated a thousand times.

Whenever they reached the end of the line they zigzagged east and west; they looked everywhere, and combed the ground; but with all their labour and painstaking care, no stake could be found. The boys noticed something very odd about their father's manner: the longer their search went on unsuccessfully, the less impenetrable became that wall of isolation around him. When they finally stopped on the last tack, looked around, and saw that they had covered every possible place, his voice sounded almost joyful. . . . "It must be that the cows have tramped it down! . . . Well, no harm done . . . it was nothing but an old stick, anyway."

IV

Beret soon came to realize that he was absorbed in things of which she was not to know. Whenever she happened to speak to him unexpectedly he seemed to be present and yet absent; even when he made an effort to converse naturally, he kept her at a distance; all his ardour seemed to have disappeared, and with it the childlike joyousness that she had loved so much in him, though she had been unable to respond to it. . . . No more did she hear his cheerful, fairy-tale banter about the royal mansion, and the king and queen; she was aware how often he lay awake at night, or tossed restlessly about in his sleep. . . . In a short while she became fully convinced that something had happened at last which he had to conceal from her; but she could not imagine what it might be. The whole affair was so unlike him, that it worried her night and day. . . . What, in Heaven's name, could there be to conceal out here?

This mood lasted with him throughout the week. On the morning of the next Monday he was up early. . . . Beret had been lying awake the latter part of the night, feeling keenly that he was wrestling beside her with a monster which would not leave him in peace; but after a while she had fallen asleep again. When she finally opened her eyes the dim grey of dawn was creeping through the window; her husband was up and gone. The room somehow gave her the sensation that he must have left a long time ago; not a sound could be heard anywhere. . . . Beret got up, dressed herself hurriedly, and went outdoors. The plow was still there, she noticed, and the oxen lay a short distance from the house; but Per Hansa was nowhere in sight. . . . She felt so forlorn, so helpless, filled as she was with gnawing loneliness. Here she stood, abandoned in the great solitude, not knowing where he had gone nor what the trouble was. . . . What had happened to him? What was he struggling with, that had to be kept from her? . . . She called his name aloud a couple of times; but her voice trembled so strangely that she did not dare to call again. The sound died away unheeded. . . . It seemed to Beret that she had never felt the awful desolation of the place weigh so heavily upon her as on this morning.

In the meantime Per Hansa was engaged in a very curious task west on the prairie. He had risen before daylight; had gone out and hunted up the spade, which he had stuck under his arm; then he had started off in a general westerly direction. He made a longer détour than necessary around Hans Olsa's house, watching closely as he went by to see if anyone there was up and stirring; once safely past, he quickened his gait. . . . So he came to a place at the southwest corner of Hans Olsa's land, where a black imp stood nodding sleepily in the grass; there he came to a halt and looked about in all directions. . . . Not a soul to be seen. His eyes were snapping now; his mouth was tight and drawn; all his features seemed hardened into solid rock. . . . "God!" he muttered, "Hans Olsa has got himself into a nice mess!" . . . He grasped the thing firmly, pulled it slowly out of the ground, and laid it aside with great care. Then he examined the hole, planning what he had better do; when he was finished, it was going to be hard to see that *here* a stake had ever been standing! He worked now with deep forethought and cunning; first he brought some loose soil from a distance in the spade, and filled the hole almost to the top; next he stopped it up with a sod plug; the grass of the plug grew as stout and green as that around it; he also took good care not to tramp down the grass near the hole, placing his feet lightly, as if he were afraid to rest his full weight on them.

At last he had finished and stood regarding his handiwork. . . . "If they only give the grass time to grow a little. I'll be damned if they can chase Hans Olsa away on account of that stick of wood!" . . . Then Per Hansa went on to the place when he had found the stake of Tönseten's land; here he repeated the performance, but was even more careful not to trample down the grass.

When he returned home that morning he did not arrive from the west, but from the north. The boys were eating breakfast; the mother was busy, but she kept a watch through the window; she saw him come into the yard, stop by the woodpile and throw down the spade—then pause and glance hastily toward the house; but she went on with her work as if she had noticed nothing. Soon after she heard his footfall outside, passing along the wall. . . . He had gone into the stable! . . . He stayed there for some time before he came into the house.

As he entered the room Beret glanced at him from the corner of her eye. . . . Yes, there he stood, the man she knew . . . but in his face shone something hard and menacing. . . . To-day they were going to plow, he told the boys—yes, *plow!* Both they and the oxen would get their bellyful. . . . His voice had the same unnatural, metallic hardness as his face; it seemed as if sparks flew when he spoke.

The stable was unoccupied as yet; at present it served as tool room, carpenter shop, and storehouse combined; Beret also used it for hanging spare clothes. . . . After they were gone, she happened to go into the stable looking for some garments that needed mending. There, quite by chance, she found the stakes; Per Hansa had hidden them behind the clothes. Burnt black to withstand the moisture, they hardly differed in colour from the walls; she would not have seen them at all, except for the carved letters; these stood out in the natural colour of the wood and looked like large worms in the black sod; they startled her—she had to see what they were. She picked the two stakes up and stood turning them over in her hands. . . . Here were some figures and letters . . . more letters, that joined together and made something like names. . . . "Joe Gill," said one; the other, "O'Hara." . . .

. . . What strange names, she thought. . . . Did people really have such names? If so, they must be Indians! . . . She kept turning the stakes over and over. The ends tapered down to a sharp point; they must have been made to stand in the ground; in fact, little particles of soil were clinging to them now. Where could Per Hansa have found them? . . . She put them back, found the garments she was looking for, returned to the house, and sat down to mend. . . .

But she could not dismiss those mysterious stakes from her mind. . . . What did the numbers mean . . . the numbers and letters . . . and then, the names? . . . They must be landmarks. And they had been standing in the ground, too. . . . It suddenly occurred to her that he must have put them in there recently; it was only last week that she had hung up those clothes. . . . Perhaps . . . could he have done it this very morning? . . . She laid her work aside and went out to the stable to examine them once more. . . . Yes, certainly they had been in the ground—just so far down they had been!

Back at her sewing again, her hands moved more and more slowly as she thought. . . . He had been struggling with something which must be kept from her. . . . His voice was sharper to-day, his face more determined. . . . It *must* be that he had brought them back with him this morning. . . .

. . . Her thoughts slowly began to spin; the longer they spun, the less she liked the web; after a while she became so frightened that her hand shook and she had to drop her sewing. . . .

When he came home for dinner, she told herself, she would ask him for an explanation of this matter; her fear was somewhat appeased by this resolution. . . . But then he came, still in a rigid, forbidding mood; and her thoughts grew so unspeakably dark and ugly that she could not utter them. At the same time, he seemed relieved in a measure, and more like himself.

After supper that night she heard him go into the stable and rummage around; then he came out and went across the yard. She stole to her post at the window; there he stood by the block, chopping up a stick of wood; it was burnt black, and tapered at one end; it had stood in the ground. He picked up every piece that he had split and cut them into short kindling wood! . . . He took another black stick and did the same with it. . . . Then he went down on his knees and began to gather the kindling, piece by piece, on his arm. . . . Now, what in the world. . . . Here he came, bringing it all into the house! . . .

Beret had timidly withdrawn to the corner by the stove; he saw her standing there but did not look at her directly; then he took off the lid of the stove and dumped in the armful of kindling.

. . . "Are you making a fire now?"

"Just some rubbish I picked up around the chopping block."

She wanted to run around the stove and stop him, but could not; she felt that her knees would not carry her even those few steps. A question trembled on her lips; she *must* ask him now . . . but the words would not come . . . her tongue refused to obey.

. . . No, she could not ask such a question! . . . It was so hideous, so utterly appalling, the thought which she harboured; God forgive him, he was meddling with other folks' landmarks! . . . How often she had heard it said, both here and in the old country: a blacker sin than this a man could hardly commit against his fellows! *

* In the light of Norwegian peasant psychology, Beret's fear is easily understandable; for a more heinous crime than med-

She stood motionless in the corner beyond the stove, watching her husband burn the proofs of his guilt; the terror that possessed her now was immeasurably greater than that which she had felt in the morning, when she had called his name and got no answer. . . .

. . . That night Per Hansa slept the sleep of the righteous in spite of what he had done; now it was Beret who had a monster to wrestle with. . . .

V

During the weeks that followed, Per Hansa's temper made him hard of approach; the man seemed driven by a restless energy, an indomitable will that knew but one course—to break as much new land as possible each day. . . . "Do you intend to break the whole quarter-section this fall?" Hans Olsa asked him more than once. He had broken a large part of it already; a new piece was added every day; but still he found no rest, nor would the joyous peace of the early summer return to him. . . . His face now always wore that forbidding, menacing look, which often would flare up into a flame, and his voice would suddenly be hard as flint.

Before his thoughts stood ever the same problem: How would it turn out when the trolls came? Would he be able to hack off their heads and wrest the kingdom from their power? . . . It might happen that he would be going about with some object in his hand, and would suddenly grip it hard; all his strength would be needed to wield the enchanted sword. . . . For these would be archtrolls, no less. Here they had come and, disregarding all law and justice, had taken land in an unlawful manner.

There was another chain of thought which frequently led him on: Perhaps these men would never come back? They might just have happened along here the previous fall, before Tönseten arrived; have taken a liking to the place, and put down their stakes; and then have failed to

---

dling with other people's landmarks could hardly be imagined. In fact, the crime was so dark that a special punishment after death was meted out to it. The visionary literature of the Middle Ages gives many examples.

go to the land office until *after* Tönseten's visit there, at which time they would have found their claims taken up and recorded by another; or still more likely, for some reason or other they had never gone to the land office at all, but had allowed their claims to go by default. . . . that *might* have happened.

. . . But no, the explanation didn't sound reasonable; those stakes hadn't stood in the ground all winter—they didn't look that way. . . . By God! the trolls had arrived *after* Tönseten's sod house had been built; they had "beheld the land, and seen that it was good"! . . . So, there was nothing to do but wait for them to come back. . . . Not by a breath or a syllable did Per Hansa betray the secret of what he had done. At one time he had strongly considered telling Hans Olsa, but had finally given up the idea; better to keep him out of this for the time being! . . . In all this trouble, it never once occurred to him that had there been a prior claim on these quarters, Tönseten and Hans Olsa couldn't have filed on them, and that the act of putting down claim stakes made no difference at all.

Beret's thoughts continued to spin; the web had grown so dreadful to look at that she longed to cast it aside; but lacked the power. . . . He has done it, he has done it!—the thoughts spun on. . . . Here we are sitting on another man's land, and Per Hansa intends to stay! . . . He has destroyed another man's landmarks. . . . Oh, my God! . . .

In a certain sense, however, his guilt began to appear less fatal in her eyes as she continued to look at it; surely there was enough land out here for everyone; whether they got this quarter or another made no difference. She could not understand why one should make a fuss over a thing like that. . . . But the dishonourableness of the act made her shrink back in disgust. . . . And now a new terror—the terror of consequences! Per Hansa, poor fellow, could not even speak the language. How would he ever defend himself, when the case came up? . . . The stories that she had heard, both in Norway and east in Fillmore, of how people in this wild country would ruthlessly take the matters of law and justice into their own hands, also crept into the web of her thoughts. Here he was, unable to give a satisfactory explanation, guilty before the law of one of the blackest crimes that it was possible for man to commit. . . . He was so hasty and quick-tempered, too, whenever things went wrong; and now he was in a mood which made people afraid to approach him. . . .

. . . Beret would look at her web until her whole body trembled and she had to reach out and grasp something to steady herself.

VI

Beret had now formed the habit of constantly watching the prairie; out in the open, she would fix her eyes on one point of the sky line—and then, before she knew it, her gaze would have swung around the whole compass; but it was ever, ever the same. . . . Life it held not; a magic ring lay on the horizon, extending upward into the sky; within this circle no living form could enter; it was like the chain inclosing the king's garden, that prevented it from bearing fruit. . . . How could human beings continue to live here while that magic ring encompassed them? And those who were strong enough to break through were only being enticed still farther to their destruction! . . .

They had been here four months now; to her it seemed like so many generations; in all this time they had seen no strangers except the Indians—nor would they be likely to see any others. . . . Almost imperceptibly, her terror because of the stakes which her husband had burned had faded away and disappeared. . . . They had probably belonged to the Indians, so it did not matter; he had become fast friends with them. . . .

People had never dwelt here, people would never come; never could they find home in this vast, wind-swept void. . . . Yes, *they* were the only ones who had been bewitched into straying out here! . . . Thus it was with the erring sons of men; they were lost before they knew it; they went astray without being aware; only others could see them as they were. Some were saved, and returned from their wanderings, changed into different people; others never came back. . . . God pity them: others never came back! . . .

At these times, a hopeless depression would take hold of her; she would look around at the circle of the sky line; although it lay so far distant, it seemed threatening to draw in and choke her. . . .

. . . So she grew more taciturn, given to brooding thoughts.

But then the unthinkable took place: some one from outside broke through the magic circle. . . .

It happened one evening. Ole had ridden the pony west to the swamps; on the way home he noticed a large white speck moving along through the haze on the eastern horizon. It did not seem so very far away; as he watched it came creeping closer; the boy was so startled that he could hear the beating of his own heart; he had to investigate this thing. The pony was fleet-footed; he had plenty of time to make a turn to the eastward; he rode directly toward the speck. When he had satisfied himself that west-movers were coming—the wagons indicated that—he turned toward home and urged the pony till his body lay flat to the ground. On the way in he stopped at Tönseten's with the news, then at Hans Olsa's; hastening on to his own house, he shouted loudly for them to come out and look . . . come out in a hurry!

. . . What a strange feeling it gave them! . . . Two horses in front of a wagon; the wagon covered, just like their own! . . . And like their own, it came slowly creeping out of the eastern haze; like them, these folks were steering for Sunset Land. . . . Alas! thought Beret, some one else has been led astray!

The wagon held on toward Tönseten's; it reached his place and halted. The incident was so unusual and startling that all in the little settlement forgot their good manners and rushed pell-mell over to Tönseten's. Even Beret could not keep away; she put on a clean apron, took And-Ongen by the hand, and joined the others. . . . The whole colony, young and old, were gathered there when she arrived—everyone except Per Hansa. . . . He came up silently at last, carrying a heavy stick.

The company consisted of four men; they were from

Iowa. . . . No, they didn't intend to stop here; they were bound for a place about seventy miles to the southwest; the land was nearly all taken up around here, they had been told. . . . Tönseten and the Solum boys were conversing with them in English; Hans Olsa, together with the women and children, stood respectfully listening; as for Per Hansa, he was all eyes and ears, scrutinizing the four visitors from head to foot, trying to make out what they were saying. . . . His grip on the stick relaxed; hadn't he understood that they were going seventy miles farther? . . .

At last he grew impatient, because he was unable to follow the conversation as well as he wished; he grasped Tönseten by the arm and pinched it so hard that he turned around angrily; but the next second he was talking again.

"What sort of people are they?"

"Germans. . . . Don't bother me now!"

"You must tell them not to stop. . . . We want only *Norwegians* here, you know!"

But Tönseten had no time now to waste words on Per Hansa; that could be attended to in due season; he was deep in a long discussion with the strangers, all about the prospects for the future out here.

These four unexpected evening arrivals stayed with them overnight, and went on their way the next morning; the Spring Creek settlers had never seen them before; they would perhaps never see them again; but they all felt that this was the greatest event which had yet happened in the settlement. . . . Seventy miles farther into the evening glow these fellows were going—seventy long miles! Then this place would no longer be life's last outpost! . . . Folks were coming, were passing on . . . folks who intended to build homes! . . .

. . . A living bulwark was springing up between them and the endless desolation! . . .

Before the Germans left in the morning they came to examine Per Hansa's house; Tönseten had told them of one of his neighbours who had built a dwelling and stable under one roof; they thought it would be well worth the trouble to go and look at a structure of that kind; they themselves were just beginning, and needed ideas. While they were there Per Hansa got a chance to sell them some potatoes and vegetables, to the amount of two dollars and seventy-five cents; this was the first produce to be sold out of the settlement on Spring Creek. . . . Tönseten didn't take it kindly at all; he could have done as much himself; but who would ever have thought of such a thing? . . . He certainly watches his chances, that fellow Per Hansa!

VII

The strangers finally managed to make a start late that forenoon; the Spring Creek folks stood watching the wagon as it grew smaller and smaller, until it was only a dot on the horizon, receding farther and farther under the brow of the heavens; at last it disappeared—but whether into the earth or into the sky, no one could tell. . . .

This visit affected each one differently, according to his own traits and peculiarities; but with all it was a new incentive to let their eyes scan the prairie. They had always done this, of course; but more often it had been with the object of straightening their tired backs for a moment, than to seek for actual traces of wandering fellow beings. . . . This visit had encouraged them all, but Tönseten and his wife were especially firm and optimistic in their faith; from now on Syvert always spoke of the future with fervent conviction, and Kjersti went about listening to him in a glow of silent but none the less ardent devotion. The Solum boys also had little doubt of the omen—this wagon was only the forerunner of more to come! The next in order of enthusiasm was Sörine, to whom faith imparted a glad calmness. Hans Olsa let every day be sufficient unto itself, enjoyed the confident spirits of the others, and set himself every day to accomplish something needful; he was not a fast worker, but got things done with a peculiar sureness of purpose and steadiness of gait; it did not seem of great importance to him how many new people came; the important thing was how they got along—the folks who were here already.

Per Hansa was even louder in his optimism than Tönseten. Now there were settlers to both the east and the southwest of them; far away to the northeast, too, folks were known to have taken up land; the time wasn't far distant when they would have near neighbours all around. There were moments, even, when he felt confident that he would live to see the day when most of the land of the prairie would be taken up; in such moods, there was something fascinating about him; bright emanations of creative force seemed to issue out of his square, stocky figure; his whole form became beautiful, the lines of his face soft and delicate; whenever he spoke a tone of deep joy rang in his words. . . . But these moods did not last; when there came a pause in the fairy tale, Per Hansa fell silent about the future, worked intensely and grew cross and irritable; at such times he was a hard man to deal with.

To Beret the visit had seemed nothing but a brief interruption to the endless solitude. The facts were unchangeable—it was useless to juggle with them, or delude oneself; nothing but an eternal, unbroken wilderness encompassed them round about, extending boundlessly in every direction; that these vast plains, so like infinity, should ever be peopled and settled, would be a greater miracle than for dead men to rise up and walk! . . .

It happened about a week later, that another caravan came creeping slowly out of the evening. This was a great procession—six teams of horses, with the same number of wagons. . . . Darkness was already falling when they were sighted. Per Hansa's boys wanted to start out at once, and were quarrelling over who should ride to meet the strangers; but the father suddenly came and told them both to stay at home; he spoke in such a determined voice that they understood it would be useless to mention the matter again. . . . They shouldn't be running out to meet every stranger, he went on, as though they had never seen people before! Time enough to speak with these newcomers to-morrow. He was going over now to find out if they needed any potatoes. . . . He suited the action to the word.

At Hans Olsa's house the caravan had not yet been sighted; Per Hansa saw a light in the window as he passed. Tönseten was standing outside when he arrived there; the caravan lay some distance off to the southward, steering too far west to fetch the settlement.

"You're going to have visitors," Per Hansa greeted his neighbour.

"It looks that way!" chuckled Tönseten. . . . "Though I'm afraid they're heading a little too far west."

They stood gazing at the train of wagons, now less than a hundred yards away; through the dusk they could just make out the forms of the men driving. Kjersti stood behind them in the door, laughing to herself and wondering how she could put them all up for the night. . . . Oh, well, if it couldn't be arranged here, Per Hansa would have to take some of them home to his place.

. . . "I wonder what kind of people they are?" Tönseten mused. . . . "Are they going to pass right by an open door?"

"That's just what they're doing!" said Per Hansa, curtly, fearing that now the trolls were upon them.

"But surely they can see us?"

"They ought to, if they have eyes!"

The caravan had now drawn abreast of them to the southwest; it was so near that they could hear the panting of the horses; then the foremost wagon swung off a trifle and took a more westerly course; they evidently had no intention of camping here for the night.

"You'd better go over and talk to them, Syvert," said Kjersti. . . . "We'll make room for them somehow."

Tönseten gazed at them open-mouthed; tears of disappointment stood in his eyes. . . . "That's a fine way to act!" he spluttered. . . . "Hadn't we better go over and invite them?"

Per Hansa's eyes flashed daggers; his face lighted up with irresistible forcefulness. . . . "We won't bother about that just yet. . . . They might be high-toned, you know—heading for Hans Olsa's place, or mine!"

The train moved slowly on toward the northwest, until it was on the line between Hans Olsa's and Tönseten's; there the wagons stopped and the horses were unhitched; the newcomers had evidently decided to pitch their camp for the night.

. . . "It's the strangest thing I ever saw!" said Tönseten, as if speaking to himself. "Can you imagine anyone coming into a neighbourhood where the houses are standing around as thick as fleas on a dog's back, and not even wanting to talk to the folks who live in 'em? . . . I call it a damned outrage! What's the matter—are they afraid of us?"

"It doesn't seem as if they can really be civilized people!" put in Kjersti.

"Most likely they've got some nice-looking girls aboard, and are afraid the place is full of knock-about single men!" Per Hansa explained, calmly.

The three puzzled folks stood there watching and wondering; through the deepening dusk they couldn't make out clearly what the strangers were doing. . . . Apparently they were building a fire down on the slope; a glare of flames intermittently rose and spread, waned and reappeared; it seemed to flit back and forth on the ground.

"Do you know what, Syvert?" Per Hansa suggested, mischievously. . . . "Since those fellows won't come and talk to us, we'd better take a trip over and visit them. We might even talk them into buying some potatoes—eh? We must watch our chances, you know." . . . He was anxious to get a look at them.

Tönseten could see no particular objection, especially since Per Hansa had an errand with them; but it did seem rather humiliating to go and shake hands with folks who had refused to say "hullo" to them. . . . But after a moment they started on their way.

They had walked only a few steps, however, when he drew up with a jerk. "Let's go over to Hans Olsa's and take him along; he'd like to shake hands with them too, you know."

—Not at all—certainly not!—was Per Hansa's decisive reply. Hans Olsa knew no more English than he did; and it was devilish awkward to stand around and stare strangers in the face, without knowing a word they said; he himself would never have thought of going if it hadn't been that they ought to make use of the opportunity to sell some potatoes! . . .

They went on a few steps farther, and then Tönseten stopped again; his courage was dripping away. . . . Suppose they were Scandinavians?

—What nonsense! . . . Per Hansa kept right on walking. Neither Swedes nor Danes behaved in that boorish fashion; anyway, they probably had all gone to bed at Hans Olsa's; they always turned in early there.

The fire burned lustily over on the prairie; four women went to and fro placing dishes of food on a big green cloth spread on the ground; some of the men had already gathered around it; others were occupied with the wagons. . . . As they drew near, Per Hansa counted ten men in all; he scrutinized their faces closely, one by one; but he found none that he liked. . . . Tönseten went briskly up to the fire and greeted those who were sitting around; Per Hansa did likewise. The strangers plainly sneered at their greeting; they said something among themselves which Per Hansa did not understand. . . .

—Where did these men come from? Tönseten asked, boldly.

—From down in Iowa.

—Were they going far west?

—No!

This much Per Hansa was able to follow; but here he began to lose the meaning; the men spoke English too fast, and Tönseten wasn't much better; not that it made any difference, however; Per Hansa knew all that he needed to know. . . . *They had come at last!* . . . Of the conversation that followed he only understood that it was about land and that the men were making sport with Tönseten, who had grown angry and now spoke still faster. . . . It was unbelievable how fast Syvert could rattle off the English! . . . The strangers' mockery was getting rather ugly now; he could tell it by the sound of their laughter. . . . Damn it all, to think that he couldn't talk to them!

"Huh!" exclaimed Tönseten, turning suddenly to his neighbour . . . "Can you imagine what they are saying? . . . They . . . they insist that both my quarter and Hans Olsa's belong to them!"

"You don't say! . . . What about *mine?*"

But Tönseten paid no further attention to him; he was off again in his squabble with the Irishmen, and growing more and more excited with every word. . . . It struck Per Hansa that if Syvert didn't stop a moment to catch his breath, he was either going to explode, or else he would burst into tears; he grasped his arm firmly.

"What do they say, Syvert?"

"They say they've taken up all the land between the creek and the swamps over to the westward, a strip two quarter-sections wide. . . . And they talk rougher and wilder than anything I ever heard; they're threatening murder, and fire, and state's prison!"

"Do they say when they were here?"

"Last summer, and late in the fall, and early this spring, too!"

"What cultivation have they done to meet the law?" . . . Per Hansa spoke calmly and thoughtfully.

"They claim that they've been granted exemption from the government because they were soldiers in the Civil War! . . . Isn't that the devil's own luck?"

"Ask to see their papers."

"They say they've got the papers. They'll produce them in the morning, all right!"

"Then we might as well go home and get to bed!" said Per Hansa, calmly. . . . "But be sure to ask whether they need any *potatoes!*" he added with a flash of roguishness.

But Tönseten had not heard; he was once more absorbed in wrangling. The men about the fire had now all risen; those who were working at the wagons had joined them; a close circle had formed around the pair. Per Hansa watched in silence, his pipe hanging unlighted from one corner of his mouth; when his eyes caught those of one of the strangers he held on some time before letting go.

"Well," he put in, dryly, as Tönseten stopped to catch his breath, "don't they want to buy any potatoes?" . . .

"*Potatoes!*" cried Tönseten. . . . "You ought to hear how savagely they talk! They say they don't need to show any papers to thieves and claim jumpers like us!"

"All right. . . . Have they got their stakes down here, too?"

"On both quarters, they say!"

Per Hansa saw that if Tönseten kept on much longer, he would go to pieces entirely; that would be rather embarrassing for both of them.

"Come on, Syvert, let's go home to bed. . . . It looks as though we couldn't make a deal in potatoes, anyway!"

At that he calmly began to elbow his way out of the circle; Tönseten saw him going, grew alarmed, and hurried after. Some one of the Irish must have tripped him; he stumbled and nearly lost his balance; this made them all laugh—but one man in particular roared with glee; his jeering voice had an offensive, deliberately insulting tone.

. . . Per Hansa wheeled suddenly and stood glaring at them; Tönseten glanced at him and grew frightened in earnest.

. . . "Come on!" he cried with chattering teeth, and took to his heels.

. . . "Hell, Syvert—wait a minute!"

Per Hansa kept searching the crowd until he found the face from which that insolent jeering came; a grim, cold sneer had spread over his own. At last he located the fellow, close at hand; he held his clenched fist under the man's nose, drew his head well down between his shoulders in order to get more power, and said in a dry, rasping voice, in the broadest Nordland dialect:

"Now, by God! you'd better shut up your mouth or I'll wipe that grin off your face for you!"

His eyes actually seemed to scorch the man; then he let up, straightened his shoulders, and glanced around at the crowd.

. . . Apparently no one was anxious to have anything to do with him; the jeering laughter died away. Then he let his gaze travel slowly back to the first man; the fellow had sense enough not to laugh any more. . . . And so, since he couldn't talk to them, there was nothing left for Per Hansa to do but go away. . . .

Off in the dark he could hear a faint calling; by the sound of Tönseten's voice he was not far from tears now.

"I'll take all our papers along to-morrow and show them—they'll see what's what!" he blubbered, as Per Hansa came up. . . . "You shouldn't be so hasty! Suppose they had all fallen upon us! . . . Good heavens! . . ."

"Well, you can try your papers on them, if you want to. . . . But let me tell you this, my good Syvert: with these people you can't use either the 'Catechism' or the 'Epitome'; they don't live according to the Scriptures!" . . .

Tönseten drew a long and heavy sigh. . . . "My God! what troubles a man may fall into! . . . It makes me shudder to think how wild they talked!"

When they parted it was agreed that all the menfolk should meet early next morning, to counsel together as to what must be done. Per Hansa was to notify Hans Olsa and the Solum boys, and bring all three over to Tönseten's.

"Don't breathe a word to Kjersti about how things are!" Per Hansa warned him. . . . "If the women ever get hold of this, they'll die of fright! . . . We'll find a way out somehow—I tell you we will!"

VIII

As he walked homeward Per Hansa was a totally different man from the one who had gone over to Tönseten's a couple of hours before. Then he had carried a heavy burden of worry and care; but now he walked with a lightsome, buoyant step, very well pleased with the turn events had taken. His mood lightened and brightened as he figured things out and added up the total. The problem came out just right. . . . These fellows were nothing but a pack of scoundrels; the thought was so comforting to him that he felt like thanking the Lord. They had not filed their claims at all; he doubted very much if they were soldiers; if they had had a clear case, they would have produced their papers at once. . . . Why, one only needed to look at their faces! Next moment he began to whistle, striking up the merry tune of an old polka. It wasn't so much because they would not be able to chase him away that he was glad; but because now he was once more a guiltless man! He felt so lighthearted and free again that he could have leaped up and soared through the air. . . . How fine life was, after all! He didn't know, just at present, exactly how he was to snatch his neighbours out of the grip of the trolls; but matters would straighten themselves out somehow; the magic sword would be there when he needed it! . . .

When he got home the boys were sitting up in bed, undressed and waiting for him; Beret stood by the stove, roasting a substitute for coffee which she made from potatoes; the room was filled with smoke and the door stood open. She looked at him in the faint glimmer from the lamp; his face bore nothing but signs of good, she saw; then no danger hung over them! Perhaps a few more settlers would arrive as the years passed. . . . The boys were asking questions both together in a steady stream; now and then she quietly slipped in a question of her own; but the flood of talk from the bed was so torrential that she could scarcely be heard. The father had to go over and give them a box or two on the ears, to quiet them down; but it turned into skylarking instead of chastising, with screams of laughter and a new flood of questions; they had forgotten their anger at not being allowed to go with him! . . . The wife asked, and the boys asked over and over again: what nationality the newcomers belonged to, how many they were, and whether they were going to settle here; how many horses they had, how many cattle; whether they had any women; what they had brought in their wagons; if they had bargained for many potatoes; and the like. It seemed as if their curiosity could never be satisfied. . . . But the father was in such a good humour that he had a bantering answer for everything, no matter what silly questions they asked; he entered wholeheartedly into the hilarity of the boys, till he too was talking only nonsense. . . . These folks were all Irish, he explained; their women were terrible trolls, with noses as long as rake handles. . . . Settle here? Not they! No, they were going on to the end of the world, and a long way farther. They were much, much uglier than the Indians, and spoke so terribly fast that it sounded like *this*. . . . He hardly thought there would be a chance to sell any potatoes; troll women ate the flesh of Christian men, instead of potatoes—didn't they know that? Just the same, he was going to take a couple of sacks along to-morrow, to see whether he couldn't tempt them away from their regular fare. . . . His banter grew so boisterous at last that Beret was half-frightened; but his voice sounded so bright and cheerful, and had such a warm, infectious gladness running through it, that she could not find it in her heart to reprove him. When they went to bed later in the evening he put his arm lovingly around her and fell asleep almost immediately. . . . She felt sure there could be no danger this time.

But before she was awake, and long before the faintest light of day shone into the room, Per Hansa was up again; he ate some cold porridge left from the night before, put the deed into his pocket, and went over to the Solum boys' place; there he roused them, and waited till they had eaten a mouthful or two; then all three continued on to Hans Olsa's.

As they walked along Per Hansa reviewed the situation for them; with the help of their questions, he gradually explained his plan:

"It's this way, boys: there's no danger for any of us three; our neighbours are the ones who are in trouble and stand in need of help; but as for that, you realize as well as I do that we wouldn't have a very pleasant future ahead of us, either, if they were chased away from here. . . . Now, you're a pretty good talker, Henry, and had better be spokesman for the rest of us; Tönseten gets excited so easily you know; then you, Sam, must translate for Hans Olsa and me, in order that we may follow what's going on. Those fellows must be made to show their papers; be sure to look closely at dates and signatures and that sort of thing, to satisfy yourself that they haven't been tampered with. . . . After that, we want to know if they have planted *stakes* here, and where they are! Just tell them straight from the shoulder, in good plain English, that here we are, and here we intend to stay until some one kicks us out. . . . Put all the guts into it that you can!"

The Solum boys took a sensible view of the whole matter; to Henry it seemed just an amusing interruption to their loneliness; the idea of chasing people away from a place that was nearly destitute of human beings already, seemed comical. . . . Even Sam was brave to-day; these were *white* folks, with whom one could talk and reason; that wasn't so dangerous! . . .

Per Hansa told them to keep on to Tönseten's; he and Hans Olsa would come as soon as they could.

IX

Everything about Hans Olsa was of unusual dimensions; his great body made strangers stop and look; it loomed up like a mountain when he rose to his full height; his strength was in proportion to his bulk; things that he took hold of often got crushed in his grip. New ideas found their way behind that big forehead with great difficulty; he had to look at a thought for some time before he could comprehend it; on the other hand, it invariably held true that when an idea had once become well lodged in there, it would remain clear and unchanged forever. His mind worked in the same way as his body; he was slow to grasp, but rarely dropped anything after he had picked it up; on this account he always found it difficult to turn back, once he had chosen his path. Right and wrong were eternal verities with him, which could not be changed and must not be tampered with; right was right, and wrong was wrong; thus it had always been, and thus it must remain as long as the world should stand.

When Per Hansa entered his neighbour's house that morning, he found himself immediately embarrassed; both husband and wife were up, and he did not care to speak of their predicament while Sörine was listening; the women ought to be kept out of this! Time was pressing, however, and he couldn't waste it in lengthy explanations; besides, Hans Olsa and his wife had already discovered the camp to the westward and were planning to go over and visit the strangers, with Tönseten as an interpreter. . . . Per Hansa hardly knew which way to turn; he looked at Sörine's face, and again, as so often before, was impressed by the goodness and intelligence in it; then he made up his mind and related frankly the whole experience which had befallen him and Tönseten the night before.

. . . "Now, Sörrina, I know you are a sensible woman

and will keep your mouth shut," he added, *quickly, when he was through.* "Beret doesn't know anything about this, neither does Kjersti; there's no need of alarming folks who are in a bad way already. . . . Not that we need to worry over this business; I'm sure they'll take it peaceably when we show them our papers. . . . Now we must hurry. Get your deed, Hans Olsa!"

But it was a sheer impossibility for Hans Olsa to hurry in a matter of this kind; he had to ask about it over and over again. Facts were facts, which in this case were clear beyond questioning: He himself had gone to the land office in person; Tönseten had put his finger on precisely this quarter-section on the map, and had asked in Hans Olsa's name if it could be taken up; there had been nothing in the way, not the slightest claim; it was so stated in the document; and he had moved directly on to his land and had done everything that the law prescribed. If anything was wrong, the government would have to clear it up; but how could anything possibly be wrong? . . .

"Why, certainly," said Per Hansa, with shrewd common sense. . . . "The government is all right in its place—no one questions that! But out here this morning, the government is a little too far away . . . that's where the trouble comes in."

"You don't mean that they actually intend to *kick us out?*" demanded Hans Olsa in an astonished voice, unconsciously stretching his huge frame.

"That's just what they intend to do, as I understand them. . . . We'll have to show them where we stand, in black and white!" . . . Per Hansa looked at the woman.

"You don't say, Per Hansa! Are there . . . are there many of them?"

"I counted ten men and four women; I believe that's all there are." . . . The ghost of a smile passed over Per Hansa's face.

Hans Olsa sat in silence for a while, with the deed folded up in his hand: then he smoothed it out again and looked at it closely. The greater part of it was unintelligible to him, but he understood all the essentials: the date, the description of the land, the signature of the government, and his own. All this was correct in every way; and up to this very minute he had kept his part of the contract to the letter of the law. He handed the paper to Per Hansa, and said in a ponderous voice:

"Do you see anything wrong there?"

Per Hansa was growing impatient; here they sat, wasting precious time; his laugh had a hard, short ring:

"No! It isn't you who are wrong in this case, you see; it's those devils who have squatted here on your land!"

"Do they look like peaceable folks?" asked Sörine, calmly.

"One would suppose so . . . they have their women along!"

Hans Olsa spoke slowly: "We'd better go over and talk to them."

"That's the idea! . . . Just put the deed in your pocket, and let's get started!"

X

Tönseten and the Solum boys were waiting impatiently when the others arrived. Later on, Tönseten let it out that he had told his wife the whole story as soon as he had come home the night before; neither of them had slept a wink all night. He was nervous and jumpy this morning, and wanted to start out immediately.

"No, this won't do," said Per Hansa, firmly. "We mustn't go without a plan. How are we going to tackle the business when we get there?"

"We've got to drive them away from here!" cried Tönseten, excitedly.

"Fine! . . . But the question is: How are we going about it?"

"We've got to convince them that we are here with the full sanction of law and justice," said Hans Olsa, solemnly.

"You're damned right we must!" flashed Per Hansa. . . . "Have you got your paper, Syvert?"

—No, Tönseten had thought of bringing the deed with him, but he feared it would be too risky. . . . "They might take it away from me, and then I'd be in a devil of a hole!" Tönseten's face was so agitated that it was a pity to look at.

But Per Hansa now took charge in a determined manner. . . . "Go in and get that deed immediately, Syvert, so that we can get going! . . . Don't worry—we'll see to it that no one molests you!"

And so they started. On the way over, Per Hansa explained the tactics they were to follow; Henry Solum and Tönseten should be the spokesmen, Sam the interpreter; Per Hansa took pains to impress upon Sam how important it was that he translate correctly and rapidly, so that he and Hans Olsa could keep abreast of proceedings. . . . "I think it will be best for you, Henry, to cut loose; then you, Syvert, can put in your oar when you think it's needed. But don't say much; and for Heaven's sake, be careful not to talk too fast; you know how quickly you get short-winded. Remember we have the whole day ahead of us!"

Tönseten was highly displeased with this plan of Per Hansa's, but he lacked the strength to protest; matters had reached such a bad pass already that they could hardly get worse. . . .

It was plainly evident that the strangers had not overslept themselves that morning; although the hour was still very early—full daylight had barely come—all hands were busily at work when the five settlers reached the camp. Two of the wagons had already been unloaded; a few of the men were beginning to open up the others, while the rest of the crew were putting up a large tent.

Per Hansa and Henry Solum walked ahead; then came Hans Olsa and Sam; Tönseten, who at first had trotted along with the van, had now quietly dropped back to the rear.

"Ah-ha!" observed Per Hansa to his companions. "They're planning to settle here, it seems! . . . Now, first you must ask to see their papers; and then the stakes—insist on the *stakes!* Talk pleasantly to begin with . . . but it won't do any harm to have a little sport with them, you know. If they get ugly, just tease them on awhile."

Their friendly greetings were returned in a churlish fashion; the strangers didn't seem anxious for company;

each man went about his task without paying the slightest attention to the visitors.

—What were they doing here? Henry demanded.—This quarter had been taken up long ago.

—Indeed? Two of the men stopped their work and entered the conversation.

—Yes, the man who owned the land was standing right there—Henry pointed to Hans Olsa.—That fellow; he had his papers along, too; and now they must show their papers! If the land office had granted the same quarter-section to two different men, a bad mistake had been made, but it could easily be cleared up.

—Well, so they wanted to see the papers—was that the idea? Had they brought their *spectacles?* A roar of laughter from the others greeted this sally; but the man who had spoken wasn't exactly laughing—he held his head tilted on one side, his whole face screwed into an ugly leer. . . . Sam translated as accurately as he could.

—Yes, Henry continued in a firmer and more imperative tone, they had come to see both their papers and their stakes! Furthermore, there was a court in Sioux Falls to settle such matters. They had been living here all summer, breaking and planting, and hadn't the least thought of moving away. . . . Per Hansa sensed by the tone of Henry's voice that he was speaking well.

"That's right, Henry. . . . Give 'em hell!"

The man who had spoken with such an evil look a moment before, now threw down his sledge hammer and came up to them.

—All right, boys! Since they wouldn't take his word for it, he'd soon show them in black and white! The papers had been packed away somewhere and couldn't be found just now. They would have to wait awhile to look at them; but he would show them the stakes! They'd better come right along with him now; he was in a devil of a hurry; he had both plowing and building to do before the snow flew.

The stranger began to walk rapidly westward; Per Hansa was right at his heels; as they hurried on, he breathed a prayer that the grass might have sprung up freshly where he had done that little piece of work! . . .

The man seemed very certain about his direction. As

they approached Hans Olsa's southwest corner, he slackened his pace and began pushing the grass aside with his foot; Per Hansa had in the meanwhile discovered with his eyes the exact spot where the stake had stood. He all but laughed aloud; indeed, the rain and the sun of the good Lord had done their work well; not a blade of grass seemed displaced, not a broken stalk could be seen! . . . Besides, the man was mistaken about the location of the spot; he had gone too far to the north and west before he got down on his knees to scan the ground. He did a thorough job, however; walked a few steps, knelt and examined the ground round about; rose, went forward a little distance, got down on his knees again; but all the while he was moving farther and farther away from the right spot. . . . Per Hansa could hardly restrain himself; quiet chuckles were beginning to rise in his throat; but he realized the danger in time, and coughed them away.

The man searched and searched, back and forth, around and around; at first he went at it hastily, as if finding that stake were the easiest thing in the world; after a while he looked more slowly and cautiously. . . . He was swearing like a trooper now; Per Hansa knew enough English to understand most of it; he didn't wonder that the fellow felt moved to say a little something, under the circumstances. . . .

At last the searcher got up and called loudly to the others. . . . A man came over from the camp—a small man with reddish hair and a face as freckled as a moor dotted with heather. They began to talk together in low tones, from time to time casting angry glances at Hans Olsa; they searched the whole region again, but found no trace of what they were looking for.

Hans Olsa made strenuous efforts to take in what was happening; his big, rough-hewn face, with the rugged features that ordinarily were the picture of trust and honesty, had become strange to behold. He gazed at these two men, hurrying here and there, trying to prove that he was a scoundrel; he heard what Sam managed to translate of their complimentary remarks about him; and it all seemed to awaken a new and ominous force behind that impassive countenance; his big childlike eyes blazed with astonishment, occasionally emitting sharp flashes; he trembled slightly all over, though he was not aware of it.

Suddenly the two men abandoned the search, exchanged a few heated remarks, turned away, and went back to the camp without saying another word. . . . The five settlers followed.

"If they have no better luck with the papers," said Per Hansa, "things don't look very bright for them!"

When the five reached the camp all ten of the strangers stood in a group, talking angrily together. The women were nowhere in sight; as the Nordlanders came up a burly, red-faced man stepped out from the group, evidently their leader. . . . "God be with you, Henry. . . . Stand right up to him and talk him down!" Per Hansa whispered to the Solum boy. . . . It was clearly evident from the man's face that a storm was brewing; the fact that the big Irishman carried a sledge hammer in his hand also attracted Per Hansa's attention.

"Where are the men who claim to have taken up this land?" he snapped at them.

—Right there, those two!—Henry pointed to Tönseten and Hans Olsa.—That one—Tönseten—owned the quarter to the south; this one—Hans Olsa—the one they now stood on.

The Irishman singled out Hans Olsa and looked him up and down.

—What was the matter with that fellow—was he deaf and dumb? He couldn't seem to get his mouth open! The man fingered his sledge hammer, and glared around at Henry as if he would swallow him up.

—Oh no, Hans Olsa had his faculties, all right! He just couldn't talk English.

Sam was translating all this as best he could.

—Well, he could tell this dirty son-of-a- —— that he was a thief and a blackguard who had destroyed another man's landmarks!

Sam translated rapidly, trembling with fear.

The Irishman came closer.

—If the whole damned gang of sneaking swine didn't get off their land right away, he'd give them something to start with!—Perhaps they'd understand that language better!—The man swung his sledge hammer.

"Look out, now!" shouted Per Hansa. "Here the trouble starts!" . . .

And so it did, only much faster than he or any of the others had anticipated. When Hans Olsa saw the Irishman loom up before him in that threatening attitude, he stared at him blankly, and stood for a moment as if rooted to the ground. Then, all of a sudden, the upper part of his body seemed to stretch; he stepped aside to evade the onslaught . . . his left fist shot out and struck the man below the ear. There was a crashing sound; with a loud groan the man sank in a heap and lay perfectly still.

"Look out there, Henry!" cried Per Hansa. . . . "See that you get your man, and I'll get mine! . . . Wait a minute!"

The crowd had drawn back in front of one of the empty wagons; they stood as if dazed. Hans Olsa stared at them wildly, took a step forward, and stumbled over the heap on the ground. Regaining his balance, he stopped, bent over, and plunged both hands into the inert heap of flesh; the next instant he lifted it high in the air and flung it bodily over the heads of the crowd, where it crashed into the wagon standing behind. The wagon shook violently at the impact. . . . At the same moment the group scattered and took to their heels southward across the prairie. From one of the wagons, still covered by its canvas, sounded a scream of terror; four women came tumbling out and followed after the men.

Hans Olsa stood motionless, quivering in every muscle; he seemed like a man half stunned.

Per Hansa jumped to his side and slapped him on the shoulder:

"Goodness! Hans Olsa, that was beautiful! I don't believe there's another man in the whole country who could do such a thing! . . . Now I think we can safely go home; those folks aren't likely to start any more arguments about land!"

Hans Olsa was slowly regaining his natural poise; he stroked his face and sighed deeply, like one recovering from an attack of delirium.

"I'm afraid I handled him pretty roughly; you'd better go and look at him, Per Hansa."

Per Hansa laughed confidently. . . . "No, leave him alone; just do as I say, now! We're going straight home, the whole lot of us. . . . Later in the day I'll take a little trip of my own out westward!"

They did as he bade them—though Tönseten could not be found anywhere; he had vanished from the scene long before. In the latter part of the afternoon Per Hansa returned to the camp of the Irish, to find out what they were doing and how they were getting along; he took Store-Hans with him as interpreter. . . . He found the whole camp moved to one of the two quarter-sections lying west of Tönseten's and Hans Olsa's land.

Per Hansa made frequent visits to them during the next few days; before the third day was over, he had sold them more than ten dollars' worth of potatoes; he felt that he had struck up a profitable business.

The Irish finally settled on these two quarters west of them. They returned east to Iowa just before the snow fell in the fall; but early the following spring they came back with a large company, and started their permanent settlement.

XI

On the morning when the men had gone out to parley with the Irish, Kjersti was left all alone in the house. She felt gloomy and depressed; there had been little or no sleep for either of them during the night; Syvert had tossed to and fro in bed, telling and retelling the same unhappy story—of the terrible folks who had come, of what they proposed to do, and of the dreary future that awaited him and Hans Olsa, who would now be forced to start everything anew. . . . Perhaps they had better just move east again, and be done with it! He had lain twisting and turning as he bemoaned their fate, his mood steadily growing gloomier and gloomier. . . . This had kept up so long that it had driven her nearly distracted; at last she had grown tired of his everlasting whimpering and had told him so in plain words. As yet, she pointed out, no one in the settlement had lost either life or limb; their papers were all correct, law and justice ruled the land, and five strong men were here on hand to look after things . . . *four*, at any rate! And at the worst, these were white people, thank the Lord! . . .

All this and more she had said to Syvert; every word of it had been well meant and fully considered. But he had grown angry and had accused her of not having a particle of common sense; then one word had led to another. When the quarrel had finally worn itself out they had found themselves at opposite ends of the earth, though lying side by side in the same bed.

It was lonesome after the men had left that morning; Kjersti kept the coffeepot on the stove, and laid on a couple of fresh sticks of wood; he would be sure to look in for a drop when he came back! . . . Then she put on Syvert's old hat and went over to see Beret; she wanted to find out what Per Hansa had told her when he came home the night before.

She got little information or comfort there, however. . . . First she recounted most of what Tönseten had let out to her—that people had arrived who claimed to own Hans Olsa's land, as well as his own; that these people wouldn't listen to reason, so in all probability they would have to seek the aid of the law. . . . Hadn't Per Hansa told her what had happened?

The boys were eating their breakfast; Beret sat over by the stove, dressing the child; she made no answer to Kjersti; her face flushed but she did not look up.

Ole, however, laughingly began to repeat some of the crazy stories his father had told them the night before; Store-Hans remembered more of them, and helped his brother out when his memory failed; the boys were still highly excited, and kept on making such a noise and chatter that Kjersti threw up her hands, begging them for the Lord's sake to be quiet! . . .

Beret listened in a rigid, frozen silence; she let the boys say anything they wanted to, as if she lacked the strength to make them stop. . . . One thought seemed to possess her whole being: he had destroyed the stakes on other people's land—and now he was going to drive them away! . . . Good God! could this be possible? . . .

But at last the boys went so far that she had to interfere; they had begun to laugh together in a coarse, bold way, and use evil words. . . . How truly it is said, she thought, that the seed which is sown in secret bears fruit openly! . . . With the child in her arms, she got up decisively, crossed the room, and flashed out at the boys; she was very stern now, and scolded them harshly.

All the while Kjersti had been growing more disturbed; she had to find consolation somewhere, and said, as if trying to bolster herself up:

"This can't be anything to worry about! Why, we have been given this quarter, and were the first to arrive here!"

"What about Per Hansa's land?" asked Beret.

"It seems they don't intend to claim that, according to what Syvert says. . . . I don't know why!"

"Probably nothing can be done about it," said Beret, quietly. "There is no telling who may have been wandering around out here before we came. . . . Many may have been here."

This aimless talk only irritated Kjersti.

"I should think they would keep all that straightened out—the people whose business it is to look after such things! If Syvert weren't such a milksop of a man, he would have gone after the sheriff at once. . . . Folks are put in prison for such deeds in America!"

Beret was silent for a moment; she bent over the child, while a deep flush slowly covered her face; then she said in a low voice:

"The guilty will receive their punishment in the end!" . . . As soon as she had spoken, she got up and left the house abruptly; outside, she put down the child, and stood like a stone image looking westward; there she remained standing until Kjersti came out.

"I see them coming now," she said, as the other appeared.

At that, Kjersti had to hurry off home, to get the breakfast for Syvert.

But Tönseten had returned long before the others; he was in bed when she came in; though the fall day was mild, he had covered himself up with the heavy blanket. At first she couldn't get a word out of him; she thought he must be ill, especially as he refused the coffee which she poured out for him. . . . They can't possibly have done him an injury? she thought. She began plying him with questions, and kept on until he finally admitted that they had come to blows out there on the prairie. His words were thickly interspersed with moans and groans; she began to fear in earnest that they had maltreated him; she felt him all over, and demanded to know where he had been hit.

. . . "Where did they hit me? . . . Why talk!" He would say no more on the subject. Then he gave a heavy sigh, adding: "It's terrible!" . . .

It was impossible for him to lie there long, however, without seeking an outlet; he had to confide in some one, or he would burst; so he finally told her his version of everything that had taken place that morning. Some of the things he had seen; the rest were phantoms of his own terror; he enlarged on certain points in his narrative very fully—especially the awful language which the Irish had used, and the effective replies which he had made to them. The general impression given by his story was that in all probability he would have brought the Irish around all right, if Per Hansa and Henry Solum hadn't stirred them up to fight; they had done just exactly the wrong things. And so a big ruffian had rushed forward with a sledge hammer; and Hans Olsa had gone into a mad rage and killed the man! From now on there would be nothing but war and bloodshed; so they might as well pack up and move right away! What a tragedy it was! . . .

Tönseten stayed safely in bed until late in the afternoon; then Kjersti came and told him that the strangers had gone. He got up immediately to see if it was true. . . . After that he seemed quite like himself again.

For a long time the Irish were the standing topic of discussion in the little settlement.

But whenever they were mentioned, Beret kept silent; she took no part in the joy and relief of the others, for there were certain circumstances connected with the affair which she couldn't get out of her mind; the longer she looked at them the uglier they appeared.

. . . He had destroyed the stakes; and worse than that, he had kept it secret from everyone . . . even from her!

. . . Shame had probably made him do that. . . . To be sure, she knew now that the stakes had been put down unlawfully. But suppose it had been otherwise—would he have done any different? . . . Was this the person in whom she had believed no evil could dwell? . . . Had it always been thus with him?

. . . Lives might have been lost; that, too, would have been his fault. . . . Nevertheless, he seemed to feel nothing but joy over the thing that he had done! . . .

. . . The explanation was plain; this desolation out here called forth all that was evil in human nature. Land fully as good as theirs extended round about them for thousands of miles; but then these people had come, and had immediately wanted to seize what had already been taken, thinking that it would be an easy matter, since they were the stronger; then her own husband had used deceit and force to drive them away; and now all was well! . . .

What would become of children who had to grow up in such an atmosphere? . . . Their own children! . . . She listened to her boys gloating over the incidents of the recent encounter—and her soul shuddered.

. . . No, she knew *one* who could not endure it forever out here!

One afternoon a few days later the Irish came over to Per Hansa's to buy more potatoes; they stayed for some time and asked for information on various matters; the boys translated the questions to their father as well as they could; Per Hansa thought the Irish were excellent folk!

At both Tönseten's and Hans Olsa's they had noticed the strangers come and go; in the evening they all went to Per Hansa's to learn how the Irish had behaved.

. . . "Finest people in the world!" Per Hansa assured them, pacing the floor, uplifted by a surge of high spirits that somehow had to find an outlet. No sooner did he sit down than he was up again; his sallies of humour had a dashing quality that made them positively contagious. Tönseten was in a continual gale of hilarity; Kjersti and Sörine, who sat on the big bed with their knitting, had to let their work drop at intervals to laugh at Syvert's and Per Hansa's extravagances. Beret had just laid the child in the other bed, and was sitting beside her on the edge; both boys were listening eagerly to the talk of their elders.

That evening Per Hansa told them all about the stakes; of how he had found them, of what he had thought, and of the way he had finally disposed of them. He related the story in a loud voice, with boisterous, care-free zest; he made it sound exactly like a fairy tale. . . . Many words of praise were bestowed on his wise action; Tönseten was especially effusive—there was a neighbour for you! As for Kjersti, she was moved almost to tears over such a man. What a difference from that spineless jellyfish of a husband of hers!

"I'll have to admit," said Hans Olsa, soberly, "that you played a risky game; and it was the hand of the Lord that kept you from telling. For if they had been able to show that their stakes had ever been on my land, we'd probably be building a new house now, somewhere out to the westward. All our work this summer would have been for others. . . . My thanks to you, Per Hansa!"

As Beret listened to the tale, she had to examine the narrator closely; surely this couldn't be Per Hansa! She remembered the morning when he had brought the stakes home; how he had chopped them up and put them furtively into the stove; and how his temper had taken hold of him at that time. . . . This was an entirely different person!

. . . So it had come to this, that he no longer felt ashamed of his sinful deed . . . and that respectable folks sat around, rejoicing with him over it! . . . She got up quickly, overcome by a sudden feeling of suffocation; involuntarily, without stopping to think, she said in a level, biting tone:

"Where I come from, it was always considered a shameful sin to destroy another man's landmarks. . . . But here, I see, people are proud of such doings!"

Her outburst shocked the others into silence—all but Per Hansa. With a loud laugh he reached out clownishly, trying to catch her in his arms.

"Oh, Beret, come on, now! . . . Just kick the dog that bites you—that's always the easiest way out, and the simplest, too!"

"I understand that perfectly well—though it makes poor Christianity. . . . But you were anything but confident, I noticed, that night when you stood over by the block, chopping up the stakes." She turned away from him and seemed to speak to them all. . . . "Remember what the Book says: 'Cursed be he that removeth his neighbour's landmarks! And all the people shall say, Amen.' . . . words like these we used to heed. . . . In my opinion, we'd better take care lest we all turn into beasts and savages out here!" . . .

Per Hansa laughed again with unnecessary loudness; but in the midst of the laugh he stopped, a wave of anger suddenly surging over him:

"We need a preacher, I hear. . . . Well, now we've got one!"

To this Beret made no reply; instead, she left the room abruptly. Outside, it was pitch dark; she knew not where to turn nor what she did; then she stumbled over the plow standing in the yard, and sank inertly on the plow beam. . . . As she sat there the storm within her slowly died away; deep melancholy came instead. . . . Long after the others had gone she remained in the same position. Per Hansa had not come out to look for her. . . . When she went in at last he had gone to bed; she could not make out if he was sleeping, but she did not speak to him. The boys also had gone to bed. . . .

During the days that followed, words were few and distant between Per Hansa and his wife.

V Facing the Great Desolation

I

In the beginning of October a memorable event stirred the little Spring Creek settlement. This, the greatest happening of the year, chose an opportune moment for its arrival.

It was shortly after dinner. In the early morning Per Hansa, Hans Olsa, and Henry Solum had gone east to the Sioux River after wood; Tönseten was so sorely troubled by rheumatism that he hadn't been able to go along; anyway, he had wood enough on hand to last until after Christmas, and hauling would be easier on the snow. He did want some trees for planting; but as it was getting so late in the fall, with little likelihood of their taking root, he had given up the project.

Beret sat by the window at home; she was knitting some sort of a round affair—something so tiny that Store-Hans had asked her whether it was a new thumb for one of dad's mittens? . . . His mother had given him a queer smile, and answered, maybe it was. . . .

Beret had grown more sober as the autumn came, more locked up within herself; a heavy heart lay all the time in her bosom, but she tried her best to hide it from her husband. . . . Her knitting needles worked rapidly, with an involuntary rhythm; but her mind was not on her task; she barely glanced at the knitting as she emptied a needle; her gaze constantly wandered out-of-doors, flitting back and forth over the section of the plain that lay in her view. Her face wore that weary, abandoned expression which had now become habitual to it whenever she was left alone; a sense of such deep melancholy lay upon her, that her whole appearance seemed to reflect a never-ending struggle with unreality. . . . Round after round was added to the knitting; her gaze continued to wander. . . .

. . . Without volition, it fastened on an object somewhere out there—and stayed. The knitting sank to her lap; she sat and gazed for a long time, motionless, self-absorbed. Deep compassion was mingled with her melancholy, as in the heart of one who would gladly give up life to save another from destruction.

. . . There must be many in that caravan! . . . She leaned forward, trying to count the wagons. . . . No, she could not make them out; the wagon train had already crossed the sky line and had come some distance toward her, settling into the blue-green stillness that lay over the intervening prairies.

. . . Some one else has gone astray! . . . Poor folks—poor folks!

Suddenly a strong impulse took hold of her to do something to save these people; she felt as if she ought to go and tell them to turn back; yes, turn back—turn back—before they had strayed any farther into destruction! . . .

She laid her knitting on the table, went outside, and stood at the door to look at them more clearly. . . . Were there five wagons in the caravan? . . . That meant a good many people.

. . . "Almighty God!" she sighed, "show mercy now to the children of men! Let not these folks be altogether lost in the trackless wilderness. . . . For it is only I who have sinned so sorely against Thee!"

Ole had gone to the woods with his father; Store-Hans at that moment came riding up from the creek, where he had been to water the pony; he saw his mother standing outside the door in an attitude of constrained attention, and rode rapidly toward her.

"What do you want, Mother? . . . What are you looking at?"

His words brought her out of her deep abstraction; she took a few steps forward, then halted again. . . . What was the use of trying? She couldn't even speak the language of these people! . . . A feeling of unfathomable loneliness settled upon her; the cruelty of her fate suddenly took on fanciful proportions. . . . Here she was, an exile in an unknown desert; even when human beings passed, her own kind, she could not talk with them! How could the Lord have found it in His heart to smite a soul so heavily? . . . Beret put her hand up under her breast, where her own heart was beating, and pressed convulsively. . . .

"What is it, Mother—what is it?"

"Ride . . . ride over to them and see if you can't do something . . . help them out!"

The boy was suddenly all aglow with life; he wheeled the pony around, followed the direction of his mother's gaze, and immediately discovered the caravan.

"We must tell Syvert at once!" . . . Store-Hans turned his head, waiting for his mother's opinion.

. . . "Syvert?" . . . A shadow spread over her face. . . . What possible help could Syvert be to these poor people in their grievous need? She sighed in hopeless impotence. . . . "No, just ride over and ask them if you can do anything. . . . Tell them your father isn't at home."

Store-Hans couldn't remember when he had ever heard his mother talk so sensibly; he straightened himself in the saddle, sitting like a grown man; then he spoke to the pony, gave it a slap with the flat of his hand, and shouted to his mother: "Now I'm off! . . . You had better go and tell Syvert!"

But other eyes than hers had wandered across the prairie to the eastern sky line that day. All at once Sam came running to tell the news; he stopped only an instant, then continued on toward Tönseten's. Beret went into the house, roused And-Ongen, who was asleep on the bed, and took her along to tell Sörine; she, too, would be glad over a bit of news. . . . On the way over she prayed fervently to the Lord for these people, that they should not be lost in the blue-green endlessness. . . . She felt secretly glad because her husband was away from home.

II

Soon they were all gathered in front of Tönseten's house, gazing with absorbed curiosity at the approaching train; it had drawn so close now that each wagon could be clearly distinguished; Store-Hans was riding abreast of the foremost team.

Tönseten fussed about excitedly, constantly thrusting his hands in and out of the waistband of his trousers; he was here, there, and everywhere, muttering incoherently all the while. . . . Good Lord! he thought, were these more Irish—as tough a gang as their last visitors? And Hans Olsa far away at the Sioux River! . . . Here was a fine mess, indeed!

Then Store-Hans came galloping in, and told a story so strange that all were lost in amazement.

"They are *Norskies!*" he shouted as he pulled up.

"What's that you say?" exclaimed Tönseten.

"Yes, Norskies, every single one, I tell you! A whole shoal of them—and they are coming right here! They talk Norwegian, too."

"Are you crazy!" shouted Tönseten. . . . At once he began to assume a great dignity and authority; he ordered Kjersti indoors to put on the coffeepot, and sent the other women to help her. . . . "Don't you hear Hans say that they are Norskies! Decent folks must get a decent reception!"

And now he took Sam with him, and did like the patriarch of old: he went out to meet the strangers, entreating them to enter in under his humble roof.

A great event, indeed! The company consisted of five wagons and the same number of horse teams; they were good horses, too—Tönseten could see that they were in fine condition. There were twenty men in the company, all Sognings and Vossings*—but mostly Sognings; the majority of them were married men; some had large

* People from the districts of Sogn and Voss, in Norway.

families back east in Minnesota; all were out seeking new homesteads; they intended to go back east in the fall, but would move west permanently as soon as spring came next year. They had passed through Sioux Falls and had been told at the land office of a settlement out here somewhere; so they had thought they'd better look the place over; but they were heading farther southwest, making for the James River or thereabouts. . . . Still, it was no small joy to these west-movers, to come across a cluster of sod huts inhabited by Norwegians out here on the endless prairie, and to find this hospitable, talkative man who was everywhere bustling about, trying to be of service to them.

They camped in the yard in front of Tönseten's house. When he discovered how many they were he said no more about coffee; but he brought them potatoes and other vegetables, and generously shared the evening milk with them. He would not hear of their sleeping in the open that night . . . Stay outside, he shouted, when they had come to Norwegians who owned a new-built house? That would never, never do! . . . At turning-in time, he and Kjersti crawled into bed first; then the floor space was packed with as many of the strangers as it would accommodate, the rest seeking shelter in the barn.

Tönseten didn't get much rest that night; the worst of it was that he couldn't talk to Kjersti, at a time when he so sorely needed her counsel. . . . Good God! how could he sleep, with this tremendous responsibility suddenly thrust upon him? A whole settlement of Norwegians snoring right in front of his bed! . . . Fine people, excellent people, every one! And there would be still more in the company when they moved west next spring. . . . Hang the luck!—that Per Hansa should be far away on the Sioux River at this important moment! . . . If he could only persuade them to settle here, the future would be secure for both himself and his neighbours. . . . Yes, let him bring that about, and things would look so bright that he could turn over in bed and drop asleep every night with a thankful heart! . . . He ought to start out right now, and get Per Hansa, who had such a wonderfully persuasive gift of tongue. But he couldn't discuss it with Kjersti; neither could he see any way to get out of the house; men lay snoring side by side, from the edge of the bed clear over to the door! . . .

When all the strangers finally left the room in the morning, so that he and Kjersti could get out of bed, Tönseten felt as if he hadn't slept a wink all night; he realized full well that now he rose to confront his day of days.

He had no time to eat breakfast—he hardly noticed Kjersti when she called him; already he was deep in conversation with the west-movers, telling them all about the land around Spring Creek. . . . Surely they wouldn't leave without first looking at it? . . . What? . . . No, that would be a great mistake, he'd better go along with them and show them around; he was just the man for the job, he dared to say, for here he was thoroughly at home. Hadn't he been the original discoverer of the place, the first to select it, and the first to build here and move in? He ought to have known what he was about when he chose *this* particular spot—he who had been to Fox River, had visited Muskego and Koshkonong, had travelled all over Minnesota, and even through large parts of the Dakota Territory! * . . . Tönseten gave them a full account of his expedition last fall to the western region where they were bound; the land around Vermilion was quite familiar to him; Yankton he had seen with his own eyes. At this point he spun into the narrative a little yarn which he had fabricated last night in bed; it wasn't exactly gospel truth, but—well, it might have happened! It was all about a man whom he had met in Yankton, an impoverished Scotchman, who had tried homesteading for two whole years up in the James River country; but the Indians and the fleas had been so annoying that they had finally driven him out of the place; his wife had died, and his cow had been stolen by the Indians! . . . Tönseten related the incident with a great show of sympathy.

The Sognings and Vossings were an inquiring people;

* These are the first three Norwegian settlements in the Northwest.

they had many questions to ask; of course they would consider the Spring Creek locality before leaving it—that was their business on this trip.

Immediately after breakfast they started out to survey the place. Sam Solum went with them, talking and explaining volubly; Store-Hans also tagged along, and with him was Sofie; but by noontime she was so tired from scurrying around with Store-Hans, looking for badger holes, and still more from listening to the ceaseless talk of Tönseten, that she could endure it no longer and ran home. After she left Store-Hans joined the rest of the group; now and then he would put in a word that sounded grown-up when he thought the occasion called for it.

The prospective settlers kept asking and looking, and were still undecided about the matter; they liked the place, and yet they didn't; the land seemed good; it lay nicely enough, and was easily tillable; but how bare and endless the scene was for the eye to rest upon! . . . Nothing but naked sky line all the way around! . . . It must be a desolate place in winter, without even a bramble bush for shelter. . . . And what were people to use for fuel? What for building material? Surely they couldn't live in sod huts all their lives! . . . These were a few of the objections; and many more were added as the survey went on.

Tönseten fully realized what was at stake; he trembled with excitement; that day he argued and chattered until the small of his back ached and he had to sit down in sheer exhaustion. . . . But they were not able to advance a single objection that he couldn't meet and do away with.

. . . "Wood for fuel and shelter?" . . . His voice lowered with fervent zeal; his hands fought the air. . . . Wood? Man alive, this was exactly one of their most valuable assets! Here folks could have just as much woodland as they wanted—no more, and no less! One of his neighbours had planted half an acre of trees this summer, and had now gone for more seedlings; he would probably bring enough to plant another half acre when he returned—more than he and his descendants could ever use. . . . "I'll just tell you, fellows, if it's only wood, you can go east to the Sioux River as soon as you've unloaded your wagons, and get enough trees planted this very fall to last you for a thousand generations! I'll go along and help you, and it won't cost you a cent! . . . You see, folks, it's really a matter to be thankful for, that there aren't any woods already standing here; in these few months since we arrived, we've broken more land than one could break in ten years in a cut-over country; in two years I'll have my whole quarter-section under the plow! . . . For Heaven's sake, fellows, don't talk to me about *wood!*"

In this fashion Tönseten talked against time; he pictured the future to them with a fervour that was prophetic; his reddish beard glowed as if with a living fire; his eyes beamed; his voice shook with emotion; his body trembled; his arms made magnificent sweeping gestures in the air. . . . He told about the schools which they would found, and the church which they would build together; about the thriving town which would spring up on the spot where they stood, and the railroads that would crisscross the prairie in every direction; for the railroad had already reached Worthington—soon it would be at Sioux Falls! Then they would have only a twenty-five-mile journey to town—did they realize that? *Only twen-ty-five mi-les!* . . . Tönseten chopped the words up into syllables, and showed them each piece. . . . And just look at Sioux Falls! Why, only a year ago he had been obliged to go all the way down to Vermilion —not a sign of a land office in Sioux Falls at that time! But you could just bet that the government knew what it was about in coming so far north—just wait and see! . . . Tönseten apparently had the future all charted and laid out in detail before him; he never stumbled, never made a mistake; the man burned with an unquenchable fire.

. . . If they would settle here now, more would be sure to follow next spring; then they would all be Norskies here—a settlement made to order for all of them! . . . But suppose they went to a place where no one had come yet? Couldn't they understand that all of Dakota Territory would never be peopled? Why, there weren't enough folks in the whole world for that, and never would be, either! . . . Or if they should be so unfortunate as to choose a location where no one fol lowed after? . . . What then? . . .

The strangers listened seriously to him; they were forced to admit that there was a good deal of common sense in what he said.

The party did not get back to camp until late in the afternoon. Then they cooked a substantial meal from the potatoes which Tönseten had given them; after that they held council; the majority were for settling down right here.

When Tönseten heard the decision, he gave an excited laugh; he ran hurriedly into the house and told Kjersti, who wept over the news; the next instant he had bounced out again. He felt now that Destiny had used him as her tool. He had only reached out his hand, and, lo! he had brought in twenty neighbours with a single stroke—Norwegians, every last mother's son of them! . . . This good fortune seemed so overwhelming, it had befallen him so suddenly, that he wasn't willing to trust it too far. . . . When the strangers hitched up their horses and crossed the creek—they had decided to settle on the east side, with a chance to expand southward—he felt obliged to go along with them; but after night had fallen and they had pitched their tents, and he was forced to leave them—then he was full of alarms.

. . . Many things might happen during the night!

III

They would soon have to make another trip to town. Beret looked forward to it with dread; it meant that Per Hansa would be gone for a whole week's time. The evenings were long and the nights hung heavy over the hut; she had to struggle with so many fearful fancies—fancies that multiplied as time went on; though she felt unable to speak to him about it—though he would be unable to help her if she did—yet it was a great relief to have him near, for then it seemed as if the horror dared not touch her. She dreaded each occasion which took him away from home, even if it was only for half a day's work with one of the neighbours. . . . And now he would be gone for a whole week's time!

. . . She realized, too, that they would have to have provisions for the winter; the children were sadly in need of clothes, and Per Hansa himself needed many things. But in her condition, these material affairs became more and more unreal to her; it seemed as if she stood apart from them—they did not concern her. . . . All this she kept to herself, however; ah, what was the use of speaking where no one could hear! . . . She helped him get ready for the journey as if nothing were wrong; whenever he begged to know what he could buy for her and for the house, she would stop to ponder the question with a distant look in her eyes, as if trying to think of many things which she couldn't for the moment remember. At that he would joke her, saying she mustn't be backward about it, for now they had plenty of money; what was she standing there thinking of? . . . To this question he either would receive no answer at all, or else he would hear her repeat what she had just been saying; or perhaps she would make some absent-minded, irrelevant remark, as if she had not heard him. . . . At such times Per Hansa would look at his wife and sigh; then he would take hold of her and swing her around, trying to cheer her. . . .

But beyond that he was too busy to pay much attention to her. On this trip to town he was going himself; Tönseten had offered to lend him his horses and wagon, and had promised to stay home and look after things. The Sognings and Vossings were still here; they needed advice and help in so many ways; and he, Tönseten, was just the man for that; he held himself like a father to them—yes, like Providence itself! . . . Per Hansa had a lot of plans to make before starting out; he wasn't so short of money now; the Irish were fond of potatoes and had been good customers; as for the Sognings, they seemed even fonder of potatoes than the Irish; he had managed to sell them more than ten dollars' worth; however it had happened, his cash supply was a good deal larger to-day than when he had first arrived in the early summer.

On the other hand, there was no end to all the things

he needed; he had jotted down a long list of articles that simply had to be bought, and a still longer list that he ought to get if the money only held out.

When the mother wasn't listening he talked earnestly to the boys of how they must look after the place during his absence. Ole, who was the bigger, would have to assume responsibility for everything out-of-doors; Injun, and Rosie, and the two oxen must be well taken care of; and then the wood—he must promise to chop up stacks of wood! . . . Store-Hans should serve as handy man to mother indoors; that was no easy job, even for a clever fellow like him—he understood that, of course? . . . The boys were far from enthusiastic over this arrangement; Ole had been hoping that his father would let him go along this time; he had taken pains to make himself useful on every occasion, ever since the trip had first been mentioned. Store-Hans, for his part, had harboured a secret hope that his father would bear in mind how exceedingly practical it was to have him along—he was so quick and handy about everything; he, too, had watched for every opportunity to please his father; he and his brother had often fought for the chance to run an errand. The disappointment hit Store-Hans the harder; here he would have to go pottering around like a hired girl—just like another woman! He fell to nagging, sulking, and fighting with his brother, all of which did not help in the least.

The father pitied him more than his older brother; he called him into the stable and talked to him long and confidentially, as though he were an old man with a long beard on his chin. . . . "You see, mother isn't in such condition that we can both leave her," he explained in a tone of open comradeship. "So if you go, I'll have to stay at home!" . . .

This was more than Store-Hans could understand; there wasn't anything the matter with mother, was there? She looked well enough, except for her face; but wasn't that probably because cold weather was coming on?

. . . "Oh, she's healthy enough, Store-Hans—it isn't that, you know. But"—the father's voice grew low and queer—"You'd better not tell this to your brother—but there may be another little Store-Hans coming around here, say about Christmas time; and mother will have to bear the brunt of that business! . . . You understand, now, we mustn't both leave her."

My, but this was strange! Deep wonderment rose in the eyes of Store-Hans. How could another come here—another boy? . . . He didn't dare to ask; he turned his head away from his father; a glowing blush covered his face. . . . Now he saw what the dream had meant that he had had the other night; he had seen both Joseph and Benjamin playing just beyond the house; and with them had been a tiny little fellow, who wasn't mentioned in the Bible story!

. . . Oh yes . . . of course he would take care of mother!

But, here was another thing: couldn't father get hold of a shotgun when he went to town? The last time Store-Hans had been to the swamps the ducks had been thicker than ever. . . . And the Irish had settled awfully close to them!

. . . Well, the father didn't know; he would see what he could do; he had thought of another way to catch those ducks, but what it was he wouldn't let out now.

Indeed, Per Hansa's mind was full of busy thoughts. . . . In the cellar were many more potatoes than they could consume during the winter or use as seed next spring; and now he was going to town with horses and wagon; it would be strange enough if he couldn't find people who needed food. Alas! however, it was now already the twelfth of October; some nights it froze—and potatoes were sensitive to cold! But ever since the world was made the people of Nordland had known how to bring potatoes safely all the way up to Lofoten, even in the middle of January. . . . It could certainly be done again, with a little care!

Per Hansa pondered, looked at the weather, sniffed and tried the air. On the afternoon before their departure he came to a decision: there were more potatoes than they could use; if they froze, they froze. Yes, sir! he would give it a try! And so he went over to Tönseten's and brought the wagon; he padded it thickly, bottom and sides, with soft hay; then he loaded it with potatoes in bulk. On top of the load he placed two sacks of rutabagas, and one of carrots; finally he picked out some of the nicest melons that were left in the cellar; these he tucked in between the sacks, covering everything with hay, and spreading some old clothes over the load.

Early the next morning they started off; Henry Solum and Hans Olsa went with him.

IV

The wagons drifted slowly through the outspread day, creeping on through indolent, drowsy fall sunshine and blue-green haze, toward a distant sky line from which hung a quivering yellow veil. For all they drove, the sky line came no closer; but when the purple shadows of evening fell, there seemed to be a chance, at least, that they might reach it.

This was a great day for Per Hansa. Now he was travelling the very trail he should have followed on his way out last summer; but in one day's march he traversed a stretch that then took him four times as long. . . . All day the landscape was the same, yet its details seemed ever changing and ever new; prairies that extended to the end of the world; prairies that billowed into slopes, rose in low hills, then flattened out again and sank away into an endless plain.

The caravan headed for the sky; it steered straight onward. Now, at last, Per Hansa had time to look about him and rejoice in what he saw. . . . And all he saw was beautiful! Even the others, who had gone this way before, found many strange new things to look at, the farther they advanced into the bluish-yellow haze. . . . Here and there a sod hut peeped up from the ground, where last summer there was nothing but gopher hills.

Their goal that first day's journey was Split Rock Creek, where they intended to camp for the night. They took turns with three teams at hauling Per Hansa's load, in order to ease up on his horses and so make faster progress; thirty-eight miles they had come that day when they finally reached Split Rock Creek, on the other side of the Sioux River; there they found a ford over the creek, and pitched their camp on the eastern shore. . . .

When they had been crossing the Sioux River earlier in the day—it seemed an almost unbelievably long while ago—they had stopped long enough to catch three big pickerel. Now Per Hansa slung a kettle over the fire and cooked the fresh fish for supper; he buried some potatoes in the ashes next to the kettle. Soon they were all seated on the bank, partaking of a lordly feast for them, even though it was only of fish and potatoes. . . . The water purled by below, murmuring gently, reminding them of much that was dear and half forgotten. . . . Conversation flowed freely while they ate, but after they had finished it began to lull away. They laid more wood on the fire and got out their pipes; then they could better hear what the crooning waters told. Deep silence fell. . . . A big star stood in the western sky, looking into their faces.

When the pipes had been emptied a second time they rose, tended to the horses for the night and crawled under the wagons; there they slept dreamlessly until the day began once more to gild the blue wall of the east. The coffee was boiled; enough cold fish and potatoes were left from supper to make a meal; very soon each one was seated in his wagon again, jogging still farther away from a place they knew . . . a place they seemed to remember . . . a place far off under the western skies, where a group of sod huts ought to be lying! . . . Wasn't there such a place out there somewhere? But it seemed strangely vague and distant now! . . . Per Hansa braced up in his seat, put his mind intently on Beret and Store-Hans—and then the sod huts stood out more vividly. . . .

. . . Poor Beret-girl! If only she wouldn't be too lonesome while he was away!

This day's journey also turned out to be full of interesting things. As they went along, sod huts stood here and there moping dejectedly, where, according to Hans Olsa and the Solum boy, no house should have been. . . . Good Heavens! where had they all come from? Settlers must be swarming out of the ground like ants in summertime! . . . Well, no—not so terribly many; it was only this, that there shouldn't have been any at all! . . . Too bad! Why hadn't these folks crossed a few more sky lines to the westward before they settled down for good!

Late in the forenoon they came upon two sod houses which must have sprung up since they were last here; neither Hans Olsa nor the Solum boy could remember a trace of them. Low and forlorn they lay there on the face of the prairie—only two sod huts, but situated so directly in their course that they couldn't resist stopping to learn what kind of folks lived here. . . . Beyond the huts a man and his wife were hard at work, breaking prairie; here, too, the sod must be tough of fibre, for the job didn't seem to be going very fast. What first arrested the eyes of the travellers was the team that pulled the plow; an ox with shining brass sockets on the ends of his huge horns had been yoked together with a skinny poll-cow. The woman walked alongside the team, driving; the man, whose patriarchal beard swept his chest, steered the plow, pushing from behind with all his might.

These folks were Hallings;* Per Hansa and Hans Olsa were very glad to hear it. A Halling is usually easy of approach; they at once struck up a conversation with these people. . . . Only another incredible fairy tale! With nothing but this team, the man related, he had brought his family and all his earthly possessions the whole distance from Iowa, a matter of over four-hundred miles—"a long, laborious journey," as he quaintly expressed it.

—They surely hadn't made the whole trip with those horses? asked Per Hansa.

—Why, certainly they had! . . . The Halling laughed.

—How long had it taken?

—Oh, not so very long—seven weeks and two days, to be exact. They hadn't been able to hurry, because of the cow; she was the one who supplied most of their food, and so they had to be reasonable with her.

"Do tell me!" said Per Hansa, flabbergasted. "You don't mean to say that she's milking, that cow of yours?"

"Certainly she's milking! . . . That is, when we don't drive her too hard."

"By God! that must be a wonderful cow! . . . But say, now: don't you need some potatoes with the milk? I've got a whole load of 'em here that I'm trying to sell."

* People from Hallingdal, in Norway.

The Halling looked at him, his jaw dropping, and evidently wanted to say something; but no sound came. A force was working there under the long beard which gave his whole face a comical expression; it seemed for a moment as if the man might be chuckling; but when Per Hansa looked at him more closely, he discovered a film of moisture in the man's blinking eyes.

. . . "*Potatoes*, you say? . . . Well, now!" . . .

The man wiped his eyes and regarded Per Hansa dumbly. His wife stood beside him; her face was long and drawn. . . . Suddenly she wept. . . .

"Have you got any food in the house?" demanded Per Hansa.

"Er—yes . . . as long as the cow gives milk!" . . . It was the woman who supplied this information.

Then Per Hansa burst out laughing. . . . "Listen here, woman—you run in after a pail, and we'll treat you to a decent meal . . . since we're the visitors!"

And this is sure: it didn't take the woman long to produce the pail! Per Hansa grabbed it from her, filled it with potatoes, and gave her a quick look—then looked again; at that, he poured the potatoes out on the ground, filled the measure once more, and gave her a second pailful.

. . . "There you are—one for each of you; don't kill yourselves eating, now!"

The man gazed at Per Hansa, blinked his eyes, coughed emphatically, and said: "So far, so good. . . . But give me four more pailfuls, and I'll pay you a whole dollar when I get the money; you'll probably be passing here again. . . . If you should happen to die before that time, the potatoes wouldn't do you any good."

"No, but I might need the dollar!" laughed Per Hansa. "But never mind—thanks for your offer, just the same! . . . What do you say to eight pailfuls and two dollars—when you get the money?"

Then the Halling laughed so that his big beard shook. . . . "Listen here, man; why not sixteen pailfuls and four dollars? You'll get your money sometime. . . . To tell the truth, there's very little to eat in our house." . . .

The woman had already taken one pailful inside; now

she was down on her knees, gathering the loose potatoes in her skirt; she worked with feverish haste, using both her hands, and eying Per Hansa askance from time to time.

Per Hansa laughed good-naturedly at the Halling. . . . "Now I'll just tell you how we'll do this: you have enough here for the time being; you can wait till I get back home—and then I'll bring you a whole load. . . . You need food, man! . . . I'll take the money when I get it."

So the agreement was made; before they went on, however, Per Hansa gave them one of the left-over fishes, half a pailful of carrots from the sack; and the nicest melon he could find on the load. . . . "Don't kill yourselves eating, now!" were his parting words to the Hallings.

. . . Again he sat on the wagon, creaking along toward a yellowish-blue horizon; he couldn't remember when life had been so much fun!

V

Around noon of the day after their visit with the Hallings, the three wagons entered Worthington. There was nothing much of an urban air about the place; as yet, the town consisted merely of a couple of dozen houses scattered all about, some just rough shanties, others only sod huts; all bore the earmarks of having been hurriedly constructed, and intended only for temporary shelter. The place had much the appearance of a camp, that to-day would be here, but to-morrow might have moved miles away. However, it contained a couple of stores; and most important item of all—the railroad, the main artery of life in this far region, had made its way thither.

Per Hansa drove from house to house, greeting the people with a cheerful grin and asking in his broadest Nordland dialect if they didn't want any potatoes; he said nothing of the other wares which he had brought. Luck wasn't sitting in every doorway waiting for him, however; the peddling proved to be a slow business. Not until he reached a sod hut at the other end of the town did he make a bargain worth mentioning; here he happened on a widow with two half-grown boys; the widow was Danish and ran a small poultry farm.

. . . Yes, indeed, she needed potatoes, for both herself and the boys, and for the birds as well; she hadn't any money in the house, but she had the chickens. . . . Wouldn't he trade some potatoes for a fowl or two?

—Of course he would! Per Hansa was more than willing; after dickering awhile, he bartered nine pails of potatoes for three young chickens.

—This is a mighty profitable deal!—he thought—The Hallings are good people, but the Danes are even better. . . . "Listen, Mother, perhaps you'd just as soon take three pailfuls more and give me the fourth hen?" . . . The widow agreed to that at once and Per Hansa felt that now he had made a fine bargain indeed.

The widow, too, seemed very well satisfied; they beamed in mutual gratitude, filled with generous thoughts. Their eyes looked into each other's. . . .

. . . Per Hansa started to leave. But the widow wouldn't hear of such a thing; of course he mustn't leave yet awhile! She had an old rooster cooking on the stove; it had been boiling since early in the forenoon and ought to be tender pretty soon; he must unhitch his horses and tie them to the wagon, and then come inside; where there was enough for three, there would always be something left over for a fourth. . . . Now he must go and do as she said, and then come right in! . . . Per Hansa wasn't refusing!

But when he saw the inside of the hut he grew more enthusiastic over it than he had been over the widow; if her face had been bright and cheerful, the face of the room in which he now found himself was even more attractive; it seemed that he had never seen anything so cozy as this room! It was only a sod hut, smaller than his own, with three tiny chambers; but a homely feeling pervaded every nook and corner of it. But best of all, the walls were not a dirty black like those in his house; they were a dazzling white—a white so pure and gleaming that it caught up and reflected the gold of the sun! . . . A real fairy house, that's what it was!

Per Hansa looked and looked—and forgot to sit down.

. . . "No, never mind the food, Mother," he said. "I'd rather you would tell me how you've gone about it to make things so extra fine in here! Is this *paint*, I'd like to know? . . . It must be terribly expensive!" . . . His face showed nothing but sheer good nature and open admiration as he stood there looking into her eyes; she gave him a merry laugh, as though she had known him for many a year.

—Oh no, it wasn't paint at all—far from it! Just ordinary lime and water!

—*Lime?* . . . What did they call that in English? . . . Lime, lime. . . . He said the word over to himself a number of times. . . . My, how strange everything was! . . . How did they mix it? Could it be bought in town? Was it very expensive?

The widow gave him all the desired information while she prepared the meal; she rattled on in a steady stream as she went about her work. He needn't worry about remembering the name; there was a Norwegian lumberman in town who sold the stuff; perhaps he might be able to barter potatoes for it! . . . *Thus* and *thus* he must mix it.

"You're crazy, Mother!" interrupted Per Hansa; he stood in the middle of the floor, overcome by a wild impulse to hug the cheery widow. . . . "Do you actually think he might take potatoes? I've got some carrots and melons, too! . . . I swear, Mother, that if I had met you in time, I would have courted you!"

The man's happiness was so rollicking and genuine that the widow suddenly burst out laughing. . . . He might have done a worse thing than that for himself! she answered. No telling how that courting might have turned out! . . .

But now dinner was ready. In came two little boys, with ruddy, beaming faces, just like their mother's; it seemed to Per Hansa as if he would never tire of looking at them; then he remembered the melons, and went out for the best one he could find; he brought it in and placed it on the floor. . . . He sat there eating the rooster with the widow and her boys—and it all seemed exactly like a fairy tale. As clear as daylight, luck was with him now! . . . Before he took his leave, he gave the boys another melon, and half a pailful of carrots to the mother.

. . . "It's a sin to ruin good-hearted people!" he said.

Indeed, luck followed Per Hansa that day. From the widow's he drove straight to the lumberman's, and asked if he would barter some building materials for a load of potatoes and other such delicacies; the man came over to look at his load. . . . Yes, that wasn't at all impossible. What did he want, and how much of it, for his load?

Per Hansa gave a loud laugh at this question: "I really should have everything you've got in the place! . . . But I'll be reasonable and take a few sacks of lime and a few pieces of boards. You carry lime, don't you?"

The dicker finally resulted in Per Hansa's getting all the lime he needed, more lumber than he expected, and even some nails thrown into the bargain. The boards were planed smooth; Per Hansa handled them as if they had been the fine leaves of some costly book.

. . . "A dandy boat this is going to make for the little fellow to rock in! . . . Now he can come along any time!" . . . He turned to the lumberman: "Next fall I'll show up here and buy out your whole shebang; I need all you've got, and lots more too, let me tell you!"

After that he had to chat a little while with this man; it seemed so pleasant to meet a Norwegian here; Per Hansa felt as if a part of the town belonged to him. He found so many questions to ask, so many matters that he wanted to be posted on; the lumberman, who wasn't very busy just then, seemed more than willing to talk and to hear how things were getting on, out to the westward where they lived. Per Hansa sat chatting with him a long time.

In the meanwhile his companions had finished their trading and had eaten their dinner; when he finally drove up to the general store they were loading their wagons with the merchandise they had bought. As soon as this was done all three entered the store again.

The moment he got in there among the many different kinds of merchandise, Per Hansa began to grow uneasy. Pleasant odours from all the wares mingled in the air; a strong scent of whisky permeated the whole place;

he went sniffing about and stamping on the floor, moving restlessly from one thing to another.

. . . "Oh, the devil! If I wasn't so short of money! . . . But it won't do any harm to know where they keep things, when once we get the cash—eh, boys?"

Before he started trading, Per Hansa had to make an agreement about the plow and the rake, which stood on the books against him; the Solum boy acted as interpreter.

—He could pay the whole amount, of course?—the trader asked, as if taking it for granted.

—Is the fellow plumb crazy! Per Hansa shouted.

—Huh! how much could he pay, then?

"Tell him fifteen dollars, Henry—and that's the last cent, too!"

The trader's voice grew hard as he asked: Was *that* all?

—Yes, that was all!—said Per Hansa; a hard note had come into his voice, too.—He hadn't anything more, unless the fellow wanted to take his hide. But as for that —here he laughed and looked the man in the eye—the hide was so old and wrinkled that it wasn't good for much.

—We-ell—drawled the merchant—this was pretty poor business; but he would let it pass this time. He'd be ashamed to take such a weather-beaten hide. . . . Did Per Hansa have anything at home?

—You bet he had!—laughed Per Hansa.—A wife and three youngsters, and one cow! . . . And something more coming! . . .

—Huh!—said the other, his face hardening again.—He could keep his wife and youngsters; but the cow he would have to forfeit eventually, if he couldn't raise other means. . . . Business was business!

The matter was finally arranged, however, in the way that Per Hansa wanted it; the balance of the amount should stand until next fall, at fifteen per cent interest.

Then Per Hansa started to trade. The first thing he called for was *net twine!* . . . The Solum boy and Hans Olsa burst out laughing; was he planning to knit a net out here on the open prairie? . . . Never mind; he needed *twine*—twine first and foremost! When he finally had found a kind that he thought might do, he bought several balls; and then he called for rope—he had to have rope for the sheeting—how could he get along without *that?* . . . It seemed to his companions that he was wasting good money; it was a long way to the Sioux River and few trips could be made during the year! This they pointed out to him emphatically. But it did not affect him at all. . . . "Just order that rope for me, Henry!" commanded Per Hansa.

Now the real provisioning, for which he had come all this distance, was ready to begin; he ordered a few trifles, in such a low, bashful voice, that Henry had to ask him a second time before he understood; just some calico of a gaudy pattern, a few bits of ribbon and thread, and some soft, dainty white cotton goods. And, listen here —this was very important—some Hoffman's drops, and a small bottle of sweet oil! . . . It was awfully awkward to have to use the Solum boy as interpreter in such matters—he was only a bachelor and had tried so few things in this world! Per Hansa managed to get what he wanted, however. . . . Next, the real needs of the household had to be met; flour was the most important item, and came first on the list; then cloth, and tobacco, and matches, and kerosene; after that coffee, and molasses, and *salt*. This item of salt again threw his companions into consternation; Per Hansa ordered such an unreasonable quantity of it, and still he wondered if it wouldn't be too little! . . . Lord! there was no limit to all the things Per Hansa thought he must have; but his money soon ran out and that put an end to the trading.

At last they were ready to leave.

"Aren't we going to have a single drop on this trip?" Hans Olsa mused aloud.

"There you said something!" exclaimed Per Hansa. "That reminds me—I was to get three bottles for Syvert! But not a word about it to Kjersti—bear that in mind when we get home. . . . He's going to use it as liniment for his rheumatism, you know!"

The trader treated them all around before he filled the bottles. Henry got two bottles for himself, and one for his brother; Hans Olsa had brought along his Sunday bottle to be filled; as that would hardly be enough he bought a smaller one, which he put in his pocket; Per

Hansa got two for himself, and three for Tönseten. . . . When the trader had filled all their orders he felt that he had had such good business with these fellows that he could well afford to stand another round of treats—they seemed to be such decent folk, too! And before they left they felt obliged to follow the good old custom of sampling one another's bottles. Good Lord! it wasn't every day that they came to town. . . . Hans Olsa was stepping very cautiously when he climbed into his wagon; he planked himself down upon the seat with slow and ponderous movements; but once down, there his big bulk sat secure.

It was late in the afternoon when they finally set out for home. Ninety long miles lay ahead of them, but no one thought of that; they had plenty of food, the vaulted heavens for a roof wherever they chose to camp, and fair weather to send them on. . . .

Per Hansa drove in the van; he was continually clucking to his horses. His eyes were fixed on the western sky, already tinted by the strong glow of evening. . . . God! how beautiful these prairies were! . . . Why couldn't they keep on driving all night long? . . .

When they at last pitched camp at the end of the day, and Hans Olsa had made the fire and hung the porridge pot over it, Per Hansa sat down by the firelight and began to whittle some shuttles for net knitting; he made two shuttles, and then a reel.

His companions laughed at him and told him he must be crazy; first he had thrown away good money on a lot of twine, and now he was wasting his time over such nonsense!

. . . "Never mind," said Per Hansa with his merry laugh. "One only talks according to his sense!" . . . He kept on working till he had finished the reel.

VI

The days were long for the boys during their father's absence. Ole soon tired of standing at the chopping block without the company of his brother; he idled aimlessly about, and made frequent errands into the house to see whether he couldn't hatch up something to break the monotony. Store-Hans wasn't much better off; the secret which his father had entrusted to him was certainly interesting; but it wasn't quite fascinating enough to hold its own with the vision of the ducks out there in the swamps. The father would surely bring something home from town to solve this problem; he and his brother ought to be over west reconnoitering every spare minute of the time. And now the Irish had all gone away, too; their sod huts were standing empty; there would be many curious things to look at and pry into! . . . Besides, their mother said so little these days; it was no fun to be with her any longer. Often when he spoke to her she was not there; she neither saw nor heard him, said only yes and no, which seemed to come from far away. . . . Probably she was brooding over the strange thing about to happen, Store-Hans told himself; he often looked wonderingly at her, thinking many thoughts beyond his years. . . . He remembered his father's words, and never left her for long, although it was very lonesome for him in the house.

A couple of days after the men's departure, she sent the boy over to Kjersti to borrow a darning needle; she had hidden her own away so carefully that she could not find it. Such things occurred commonly now; she would put something away, she could not remember where, and would potter around looking for it without really searching; at last, she would forget altogether what she was about, and would sit down with a peculiarly vacant look on her face; at such times she seemed like a stranger. . . . Ole was sitting in the house that morning, finishing a sling-shot which he had just made.

Suddenly Store-Hans came darting back with the needle; he had run until he was all out of breath. He burst out with the strangest news, of Tönseten's having killed a big animal; it was awfully big—almost like a bear! . . . Tönseten said it *was* a bear, so it must be true! Tönseten and Kjersti were skinning him right now; Kjersti had told him that if he would bring a pail, they could have fresh meat for supper. Both boys immediately began pleading for permission to go and see the animal; their mother scarcely answered; she gave them a pail and asked them not to stay long.

The boys came running down the hill just as Kjersti was cutting up the carcass; Tönseten was struggling with the hide, trying to stretch it on the barn door; his mouth bristled with nails, his hands were bloody—he was a frightful spectacle!

"What's that you've got?" asked Ole.

"Bear, my boy—bear!" . . . Tönseten wagged his head, took the nails out of his mouth, and spat a gob of tobacco juice.

"Bear!" snorted Ole, scornfully.

"That's no bear!" put in Store-Hans, though less doubtingly.

"By George! boys, to-day he had to bite the dust!" . . .

"But there aren't any bears out here, I tell you!" Ole protested.

"Is that so—huh? . . . There isn't an animal living that you can't find out here!" Tönseten spoke with such certainty that it was difficult for the boys to gainsay him.

"Where did you get him?" Store-Hans asked.

"Out west of the Irish a little way. . . . There were two of 'em; they had gone into the ground for the winter; this is the young one, you see—the old mammy got away from me!"

"But you didn't have any gun!" was Ole's next objection.

"Better than that, my boy! . . . I went for him with the crowbar!" Tönseten spat fiercely and looked at the boys. . . . "I smashed in his skull! . . . With that old bar I'd tackle either a tiger or a rhinoceros!"

"What became of the old she-bear?" Ole asked, falling under the spell of Tönseten's enthusiasm.

"She went north across the prairie, lickety-split! . . . Come here, now—take some of these chunks of meat home with you. . . . This will make delicious stew, let me tell you!"

"Is it fit to eat?" asked Store-Hans, still doubting.

"Fit to eat? No finer meat to be found than bear meat—don't you know that?"

The boys followed him over to where Kjersti was still cutting up the animal; it must have been a large carcass, for the cut meat made a sizable heap.

"Is it . . . is it really bear?" asked Ole, in a more humble tone.

"He's meaty enough for it! . . . Here, give me the pail; Beret needs some good, strengthening food. . . . Maybe you'll take a little to Sörrina, too; you can stop in with it on the way. . . . Careful—don't spill it, now!"

The boys loitered along on the way home; from time to time they had to put down the pail, in order to discuss this extraordinary event. . . . So there actually were bears slinking about this country! . . . If bears, there must be lions and tigers and other such wild beasts; this was worth while! . . . Suppose they were to go home and get Old Maria, hunt up the she-bear herself, and put a big bullet clear through her head? They thrilled with excitement. . . . "Do you dare to shoot her off?" Store-Hans demanded of his brother; Ole scowled ominously and clenched his fists. . . . "*I!* . . . I'd aim straight for her temple, and she'd drop deader than a herring!" . . . "Yes, aim at her *temple!*" Store-Hans advised, soberly. "And if it's close range, you must draw the bead very fine!" . . . "Fine as a hair!" said Ole, excitedly.

They picked up the pail at last, and finally succeeded in reaching Sörine's, where there was another long delay; a detailed account had to be given of the marvellous feat which Tönseten had performed.

When they were about to leave Sofie came out and wanted to know if they weren't frightened; maybe the old mother bear was slinking about the prairie right now, looking for her cub! The boys lingered to talk with her; they drew a glowing picture for the girl of how they were going home this minute to get Old Maria, and then go hunting for the she-bear herself . . . just watch them bring home a real roast pretty soon! . . . But weren't they scared? she asked. . . . "Scared?" exclaimed Store-Hans. . . . "Oh, fiddlesticks!" cried Ole. "Only girls and old women get scared!"

Sofie only laughed; at which they affected a swaggering gruffness and tried to spit like Tönseten—but theirs wouldn't come brown. . . .

They were gone such a long time that their mother

grew anxious; when they came over from Sörine's at last she stood outside the door watching for them. She had dressed And-Ongen, and was almost on the point of starting out to search; the boys were too preoccupied to notice this; Store-Hans spoke first:

"Just think, there's a big she-bear over there to the westward!" . . .

"We're going to take the gun and shoot her!" exclaimed Ole, gleefully.

"We'll aim straight for her temple!" Store-Hans assured his mother.

"Now we'll have plenty of bear meat!" continued Ole in the next breath, with absolute confidence.

The boys were all raging excitement; their mood frightened Beret still more; she grasped them frantically, one hand on the shoulder of each, and gave them a hard shake. . . . They were to go inside this very minute, and take their books! They weren't going out of this house to-day! . . . "Go in, don't you hear me! . . . Go in!" . . .

. . . But this wasn't fair! Ole began reasoning with his mother; he used strong words, his eyes flaming. . . . Didn't she realize that there was a real *bear* over to the westward—a real full-grown *grizzly* bear! . . . Mother . . . please . . . *please!* . . . Dad wasn't home, but the gun was all loaded and ready; they could easily manage the rest of it! In an hour's time they would have that bear's hide! Store-Hans even thought that he could go straight to the lair. . . . *Right through the temple* they would put the bullet! . . . The boys carried on like a raging hurricane.

The mother had to use force to get them indoors. . . . "Go in, I say, and take your books! Can't you hear what I'm saying?" . . .

This was hard on them; they burst into the house like two mad bull calves; she had to repeat the order several times more before they finally submitted and began to hunt for their books. At last Ole snatched up the "Epitome," his brother the "Bible History." They sat down to read by the table in front of the window, in a state of mutinous rebellion.

Trouble soon arose. Each wanted the seat immediately

in front of the window, where the most light fell; and neither would give up the position. A terrible battle broke out; Ole was the stronger, but his brother the quicker. On account of his age and size Ole considered himself the legitimate master of the house in the absence of his father, and therefore had the right to do anything; he now burst out with words which he had heard in the mouths of the men when something went wrong with their work. As soon as Store-Hans heard this he too began to use vile language; if Ole dared, he certainly did; he knew those words, and plenty more! . . . The boys kept up their scrimmage until they almost upset the table; their books suffered bad treatment and lay scattered about on the floor. And-Ongen watched them open-mouthed until she suddenly grew frightened and set up a howl.

Over by the stove the mother was washing the meat, putting it into a kettle which she had placed on the fire. . . . Although she heard every word, she kept on working in silence; but her face turned ashen grey.

When she had finished the task she went out hurriedly; in a moment she came back with a willow switch in her hand. Going straight over to the table, she began to lay about her with the switch; she seemed beside herself, struck out blindly, hit whatever she happened to aim at, and kept it up without saying a word. The switch whizzed and struck; shrieks of pain arose. The boys at once stopped fighting and gazed horror-stricken at their mother; they could not remember that she had ever laid a hand on them before. . . . And now there was such a strange, unnatural look in her eyes! . . .

They flew out on the floor to gather up their books, while the blows continued to rain down upon them; And-Ongen stood in the middle of the floor, screaming with terror. . . .

Not until the mother struck amiss, breaking the switch against the edge of the table, did she stop. . . . Suddenly she seemed to come to her senses; she left the child screaming in the middle of the floor, went out of the house, and was gone a long time. When she came back, she carried an armful of wood; she went over to the stove and fed the fire; then she picked up And-Ongen, and lay down on the bed with her. . . . The boys sat quietly at the table reading; neither of them had the courage to look up. . . .

The house seemed strangely still after the passage of the storm. Ole put his fingers into his ears to shut out the terrible silence; his brother began to read aloud. It was bad enough for Ole, but worse for Store-Hans; he now recalled clearly what his father had confided in him; he thought of his own solemn promise; here he had been away from the house nearly the whole day! He felt burning hot all over his body. . . . He had opened the book where it told about the choosing of the twelve disciples, and now he tried to read; but *that* wasn't the stuff for him just now! . . . He turned the pages forward to the story of Samson, and read it diligently; then to David and Goliath; then to the story about Joseph and his brethren. The last eased his heart somewhat. . . . Joseph was just the sort of boy that he longed to be!

Ole had felt ashamed at the sight of his mother bringing in the wood, though that was not his task; his brother was to be the hired girl! . . . Suddenly anger seized him; this time it certainly was the fault of Store-Hans—he should have given him the place! . . . He dragged himself through the *Third Article*, which he knew perfectly well already; when the tumult within him had somewhat subsided he sat there thinking of how shamefully Tönseten must have deceived them. . . . *He* kill a bear! It was nothing but a measly old badger! And now this nasty stuff was cooking on the stove—they were going to have it for supper! And mother was so angry that one would never dare to explain it to her! . . . There sat his younger brother, snuffling and reading his brains out; plain to be seen that he would never amount to anything! . . . Ole closed his book with a bang, got up, and went outdoors to chop more wood; but he did not dare to look at the bed as he passed. . . .

Store-Hans sat over his book until it grew so dark that he could no longer distinguish the letters. . . . From time to time he looked up; his mother lay on the bed perfectly still; he could not see her face; And-Ongen was fast asleep with her head high on the pillow. The boy rose quietly, looked around—then took an empty pail and went out for water. He left the pailful of water outside the door; then he brought Rosie and Injun and the two oxen into the stable, and tied them up for the night. He spoke loudly and gruffly to the animals; mother should hear that he was tending to business! . . . When he finally brought in the water his mother was up again; he could see nothing unusual about her.

. . . No, she hadn't been crying this time! The thought made Store-Hans so happy that he went straight to his brother, who was toiling over the chopping block as if possessed, and made friends with him again. The boys stayed outside until it was pitch dark; they talked fast and nervously, about a multitude of things; but that which weighed most heavily on their hearts—the way their mother's face had looked when she whipped them —they could not mention.

Inside the house the lamp had been lit. And-Ongen toddled about the floor, busy over her own little affairs; the boys came in quietly and sat down to their books again; but very little reading was done now. . . . At last the kettle of meat that had been boiling on the stove was ready; the mother put the food on the table; the boys drew up, Ole somewhat reluctantly. . . . "You get that troll stuff down!" he whispered to his brother, making a wry face. To this command Store-Hans made no answer; he had stuck his spoon into a crack between the boards of the table; they were large, those cracks—he could see a broad section of floor when he laid his eye down close. The earthen floor had such a rich brown colour in the dim sheen of the lamp; the cracks in the table made stripes across the shadow down there; it looked pretty, too—and just then it had occurred to Store-Hans how nice it would be if they could only have the floor looking like that by daylight.

The mother filled the big bowl from the kettle and put it on the table; she had made a thick stew, with potatoes, carrots, and pieces of the meat; it looked appetizing enough but somehow the boys felt in no hurry to start. The mother came and sat down, bringing And-Ongen with her; the child was so delighted over the holiday fare they had tonight that she hurried to say grace.

She and the mother immediately began to eat; the

boys no longer had an excuse to sit watching. Store-Hans dipped up a spoonful of the stew, blew on it, closed his eyes, and gulped it down. Ole did the same, but coughed as if he had swallowed the wrong way; then he leaned under the table and spat it out. . . .

The mother asked quietly how they liked the supper. . . . At that, Ole could no longer restrain himself; he looked at his mother imploringly, and said in a tear-choked voice as he laid his spoon aside:

"It tastes like dog to me!"

To Store-Hans it seemed a shameful thing for Ole to speak that way of food which their mother had prepared for them; he swallowed spoonful after spoonful, while sweat poured from him.

"I have heard it said many times," the mother went on, quietly, "that bear meat is all right. . . . The stew has a tangy taste, I notice, but not so bad that it can't be eaten. . . . You'd better leave the meat if you don't like it."

"It isn't bear at all!" Ole blurted out.

"What?" cried the mother in alarm, lowering her spoon.

"It's only a lousy old badger! . . . I've heard dad say often that they aren't fit to eat!" . . .

"It's true, every word of it!" cried Store-Hans, suddenly feeling frightened and jamming his spoon farther down into the crack. . . . "I could tell it by his tail—Syvert had forgotten to cut it off! . . . Oh, I'm going to be sick—I can feel it coming!"

Beret got up, trembling in every limb; she took the bowl and carried it out into the darkness; a long way from the house she emptied it on the ground; And-Ongen cried and toddled after her. . . . The boys sat on at the table, glaring reproachfully at each other; in the eyes of both blazed the same accusation:

"A nice mess you've made of things! Why didn't you keep your mouth shut?"

The mother came in again; she set the empty kettle on the stove and scoured it out carefully. . . . Then she cooked porridge for them, but when it was ready she could eat nothing herself. . . .

. . . That night she hung still more clothes over the

window than she had the evening before. She sat up very late; it seemed as if she was unable to go to bed.

VII

She had been lying awake a long time; sleep would not come. Her thoughts drifted. . . .

. . . So it had come to this; they were no longer ashamed to eat troll food; they even sent it from house to house, as lordly fare!

All night long as she tossed in bed, bitter revolt raged within her. *They should not stay here through the winter!* . . . As soon as Per Hansa came home they must start on the journey back east; he, too, ought to be able to see by this time that they would all become wild beasts if they remained here much longer. Everything human in them would gradually be blotted out. . . . They saw nothing, learned nothing. . . . It would be even worse for their children—and what of their children's children? . . . Couldn't he understand that if the Lord God had intended these infinities to be peopled, He would not have left them desolate down through all the ages . . . until now, when the end was nearing? . . .

After a while the bitterness of her revolt began to subside; her thoughts became clear and shrewd, she tried to reason out the best way of getting back to civilization. That night she did not sleep at all.

The next morning she got up earlier than usual, kindled the fire, got the breakfast and waked the children. The food was soon prepared; first she poured some water into the pot, put in a spoonful or two of molasses, and added a few pieces of cinnamon; then she cut into bits the cold porridge from last night, and put them into the big bowl; when the sweetened water was hot she poured it over the porridge. . . . This was all they had—and no one asked for more.

While she ate she looked repeatedly at the big chest, trying to recall how everything had been packed when they came out last summer. Where did she keep all the things now? She had better get the packing done at once

—then that job would be out of the way when he came home. . . .

The greatest difficulty would be to obtain wagons. . . . Alas! those old wagons! The smaller one he had taken apart and used in making the very table around which they were now seated; as for the larger wagon, she knew only too well that it would never hang together through the long journey back; only the other day she had heard Per Hansa mention that he intended to break it up, and see if he couldn't make something or other out of it. . . . Well—how to get the wagons would be his business! They certainly couldn't perish out here for want of a wagon or two! Was there not One who once upon a time had had mercy on a great city full of wicked people, only because one just human being interceded? . . . One just human being. . . . Alas! . . . Beret sighed heavily and put her hand up under her breast.

When there was no more porridge left in the bowl she rose, washed the dish, and put it away on the shelf. Ole had nothing to do in the house that morning; he walked toward the door, motioning to his brother to follow; but Store-Hans shook his head. Then Ole went out; the other boy sat there looking at his mother, not knowing what to do, unhappy and heavy-hearted; he felt a sudden impulse to throw himself down on the floor and weep aloud.

The mother was pottering about at some trifles, her thoughts constantly occupied with the idea of returning to civilization. Into her serious, grey-pale face, still soft and beautiful, had crept an expression of firmness and defiance; soon this aspect grew so marked that her face appeared to simulate anger, like that of one playing at being ferocious with a child.

As soon as she had finished her housework she went over to the big chest, opened the lid, sank down on her knees beside it, and began to rearrange the contents. The task was quickly done; then she took the clothes from the last washing, folded them up, and laid them carefully in the chest; there weren't many clothes left now! He ought to realize that they would soon be naked if they stayed here much longer! And where were they to get money for everything they needed out here? . . . Beret stood up and looked around the room, trying to decide what to pack first. On the shelf above the window lay an old Bible, a gift to her from her grandfather; it was so old that it was hard to read now, because of the many changes the language had undergone since then; but it was the only one they had. This book had been in her family many generations; her great-grandfather had owned it before her grandfather; from her it should pass on to Store-Hans; thus she had always determined when she thought of the matter. On top of the Bible lay the hymn book, in which she had read a little every Sunday since their arrival here. . . .

She put both books in the chest.

Again Beret rose and glanced around the room. Perhaps she had better take the school books, too; the boys were none too eager to use them; they might as well be excused for the rest of the day; either that day or the next the father would surely come. . . . She asked Store-Hans to bring the books to her so that she could pack them.

Not until then did the boy fully take in what his mother was doing; it startled him so that for a moment he could not get up.

"Mother, what are you doing?" . . .

"We must begin to get ready!" . . . She sighed, and pressed her hands tightly under her burden; it was painful to her, stooping over so long at a time.

"Get ready? Are . . . are we going *away?*" . . . Store-Hans's throat contracted; his eyes stared big and terror-stricken at his mother.

"Why, yes, Hansy-boy—we had better be going back where people live before the winter is upon us," she told him, sadly.

The boy had risen, and now stood at the end of the table; he wanted to go to his mother but fear chained him to the spot; he stared at her with his mouth wide open. At last he got out:

"What will dad say?" . . . The words came accusingly but there were tears in them.

She looked at him like one in a dream; again she looked, but could not utter a word. . . . The sheer impossibility of what she was about to do was written as if in fire on the face and whole body of the boy—as if in rays that struck her, lighted everything up with an awful radiance, and revealed the utter futility of it all. . . . She turned slowly toward the chest, let down the lid, and sank on it in untold weariness. . . . Again the child stirred within her, kicking and twisting, so that she had to press her hand hard against it.

. . . O God! . . . now *he* was protesting, too! Was it only by ruthless sacrifice of life that this endless desolation could ever be peopled?

. . . "Thou canst not be so cruel!" she moaned. . . . "Demand not this awful sacrifice of a frail human being!" . . .

She rose slowly from the chest; as she walked across the floor and opened the door she felt as if she were dragging leaden weights. . . . Her gaze flitted fearfully toward the sky line—reached it, but dared not travel upward. . . .

Store-Hans remained at the end of the table, staring after her; he wanted to scream, but could not utter a sound. Then he ran to her, put his arms around her, and whispered hoarsely between sobs:

"Mother, are you . . . are you . . . getting sick now?"

Beret stroked the head that was pressed so hard against her side; it had such a vigorous, healthy warmth; the hair was soft and pleasant to the touch; she had to run her fingers through it repeatedly. . . . Then she stooped over and put her arm around the boy; his response to her embrace was so violent that it almost choked her . . . O God! how sorely she needed some one to be kind to her now! . . . She was weeping; Store-Hans, too, was struggling with wild, tearing sobs. Little And-Ongen, who could not imagine what the two were doing over there by the door, came toddling to them and gazed up into their faces; then she opened her mouth wide, brought her hand up to it, and shrieked aloud. . . . At that moment Ole came running down the hill, his feet flying against the sky, and shouted out to them:

"They are coming! . . . Get the coffee on!"

. . . Gone was the boy like a gust of wind; he threw

himself on the pony and galloped away to meet the returning caravan.

Beret and Store-Hans had both sprung to their feet and stood looking across the prairie. . . . Yes, there they were, away off to the southeast! . . . And now Store-Hans, also, forgot himself; he glanced imploringly into his mother's face, his eyes eagerly questioning:

"Would it be safe to leave you while I run to meet dad?"

She smiled down into the eager face—a benign, spreading smile.

"Don't worry about me. . . . Just run along." . . .

VIII

The father sat at the table eating, with And-Ongen on his knee; the boys stood opposite him, listening enthusiastically to the story of his adventures along the way; the mother went to and fro between the stove and the table. There was an enchanting joyousness about Per Hansa to-day which coloured all he said; no matter how much he told, it always sounded as if he were keeping back the best till later on. This had a positively intoxicating effect on the boys; it made them impatient and eager for more, and caused a steady flood of fresh questions.

Even Beret was smiling, though her hand trembled.

At last the boys had to give an account of how they had managed affairs at home. When, after much teasing and banter, Per Hansa had finally heard the whole absurd story—it came little by little, in disjointed outbursts—of Tönseten and the bear, and their ill-starred badger stew of the night before, he laughed until the tears came and he had to stop eating. His mirth was so free and hearty that the boys, too, began to see the real fun of the incident, and joined in boisterously. Beret stood over by the stove, listening to it all; their infectious merriment carried her away, but at the same time she had to wipe her eyes. . . . She was glad that she had remembered to take out of the chest the things that she had begun to pack awhile before!

"Come here, Store-Hans," said the father, still laughing. "What's that across the back of your neck?"

The question caught the boy unawares; he ran over and stood beside his father.

"Why, it's a big red welt! . . . Have you been trying to hang yourself, boy?"

Store-Hans turned crimson; he suddenly remembered the fearful blows of last night.

Ole glanced quickly at his mother. . . . "Oh, pshaw!" he said with a manly air. . . . "That was only Hans and me fighting!"

"Ah-ha!" exclaimed the father, with another laugh. "So that's the way you two have been acting while I was away? Mother couldn't manage you, eh? . . . Well, now you'll soon be dancing to a different tune; we've got so much work on our hands that there won't be any peace here day or night. . . . Thanks for good food, Beret-girl!"

He got up, took the boys with him, and began to carry things in from the wagon. Most of the load they stored away in the house; some extra things, however, had to find a temporary place in the stable.

At length Per Hansa brought in a small armful of bottles and set them on the table.

"Come here, Beret-girl of mine! You have earned a good drink, and a good drink you shall have!" . . . He went over to the water pail with the coffee cup from which he had just been drinking, rinsed it out with a little water, and emptied it on the floor; then he poured out a good half cupful of whisky and offered it to her. She put out her hands as if to push him away. . . . Yes, indeed, she would have to take it, he told her, putting his arm around her waist and lifting the cup to her lips. She took the cup and emptied it in one draught. . . . "There, that's a good little wife! . . . You're going to have just another little drop!" He went to the table again and poured out a second drink, but not so much this time. "Two legs, and one for each! Just drink it down! . . . And now you take care of the bottles!"

That was a busy day in the humble dwelling of Per Hansa. First of all, he had promised a load of potatoes to the Hallings, who waited back east somewhere under a bleak sky, without even a potato peeling to put in their pot; he must carry food to them. When Beret heard how poorly things were in that hut—about the woman with the drawn cheeks and the starved look in her eyes—she straightway began to hurry him up; he must go while he had the horses and wagon here. Couldn't he get started to-day?

"Not so hasty there, my girl, not so hasty!" laughed Per Hansa, his face beaming. . . ."I'm not going to sleep with any *Halling woman* to-night—that I can tell you!"

Now he was his old irresistible self again. How strong, how precious to her, he seemed! . . . She felt a loving impulse to grasp his hair and shake him. . . .

Ole was immediately put to work knitting the net. The father had already knitted four fathoms of it, by the light of the camp fire the night before; he had sat up working over the net long after the others had turned in. . . . The boys grew wild with enthusiasm at the sight of the net; were they going fishing in the Sioux River? Both of them immediately began begging to be taken along. . . . "Just keep your fingers moving, Olamand—hurry them up, I tell you!" . . . The father made a great mystery of it, and refused to give any further explanation.

As for himself and Store-Hans, they busied themselves over the lime; it was all carried inside and placed in a corner where no moisture could reach it. The preparations for the mixing required a good deal of work; the first thing was to make a wooden box sufficiently tight to hold water. Well, there was plenty of lumber now, at any rate! Per Hansa built the box and carried it down to the creek; there he placed it under water, hoping that it would swell enough to be tight by the time he needed it.

Evening fell all too soon on a wonderfully busy and joyful day. The boys were at last in bed, fast asleep.

But Per Hansa had no time for rest; to-night that net simply had to be finished. He finally made Beret go to bed, but she wasn't a bit sleepy; she lay there talking to him and filling the shuttles whenever they were empty.

He explained fully to her how he intended to use the net; first he would set it in the Sioux River as he passed by there tomorrow; he knew of just the place; he would leave it there until he came back from the Hallings'. Unless the cards were stacked against him he would bring back a nice mess of fish. . . . That, however, wasn't his great plan with the net, he told her; but she mustn't say a word about this to the boys. It was to be a big surprise for them; they were such brave fellows! The fact of the matter was, he planned to catch *ducks* with that net; that had been the real reason for his buying the twine; there would be other fare than badger stew in this hut, he would just let her know, if the weather only held a few days more!

All at once it occurred to Beret that she had forgotten to cover up the windows to-night; she smiled to herself at the discovery. . . . What was the need of it, anyway? Cover the windows . . . what nonsense! . . . She smiled again, feeling a languorous drowsiness creep over her.

Per Hansa knit away on the net, chatting happily with her as he worked; a confident ring of joy sounded in all he said. He had fastened the net to the bedpost, just as her father always had done. She listened peacefully to his warm, cheerful voice, which after a while began to sound more distant, like the indolent swish and gurgle of lapping ocean waves on a fair summer's night. Gradually she was borne away on this sound, and slept the whole night through without stirring.

When she awoke next morning Per Hansa, still fully dressed, lay beside her, over against the wall; he evidently had thrown himself down to rest only a little while before. Light was creeping into the room; directly in front of the bed lay a big white heap of something. . . . Those careless boys—had they thrown their clothes on the floor again? . . . She stooped over to pick the clothes up and put them on the bench; she grasped hold of the heap—and it was a new net, sheeted and fully rigged, as a new net ought to be!

. . . Poor man!—he must have sat up all night! . . . She spread the quilt carefully over him.

That morning Beret took some of the precious white flour and made a batch of pancakes. He deserved to have one good meal before he went away again!

He left right after breakfast. Beret worked industriously throughout the day, while many thoughts came and went. . . . It must be her destiny, this! There was One who governed all things. . . . He knew what was best, and against His will it was useless to struggle! . . .

. . . Often that day she went to the window to look eastward. Every time she looked, it seemed to be growing darker over there. . . .

. . . That evening she again covered the window. . . .

VI *The Heart That Dared Not Let In the Sun*

I

During the first days of October a few white, downy snowflakes hung quivering in the air . . . floated about . . . fell in great oscillating circles. They seemed headed for nowhere; they followed no common course; but finally they reached the ground and disappeared.

The air cleared again. There came a drowsy, sun-filled interval . . . nothing but golden haze . . . quiet bereft of all life. . . .

The sun had no strength these days. It peeped out in the morning, glided across the sky as before, yet life it had not until toward evening, as it was nearing the western rim of the prairie. Then it awoke, grew big and blushing, took on a splendour which forced everyone to stop and look; the western sky foamed and flooded with a wanton richness of colour, which ran up in streams to meet the coming night. Folks would walk about in the evenings speaking in low tones. . . . Never in their lives had they seen such sunsets! . . .

. . . Day after day the same . . . evening after evening. Strangely still the days . . . the evenings more mysteriously quiet. How could one lift one's voice against such silence! . . .

Then one morning—October was nearly passed—the sun could not get his eye open at all; the heavens rested close above the plain, grey, dense, and still. The chill of this greyness drove through the air though no wind stirred. People went indoors to put on more clothes, came out again, but froze worse than ever. . . . Bleak, grey, God-forsaken, the empty desolation stretched on every hand. . . .

Sometime in the afternoon snowflakes began to fall. They came sailing down from the north until the air was a close-packed swarm of greyish-white specks, all bound in the same direction. The evening was short-lived that day, and died in a pitch-black night that weighed down the heart. . . .

. . . Again day came, and brought no other light than that which the greyish-white specks gave. . . . All that day the snow fell—all the next night. . . .

At last it grew light once more—but the day had no sun. A cold wind howled about the huts—left them, and tore down into the white snow blanket, shaking out of it blinding swirls. . . . The swirls vanished and reappeared—died down, flared up again and tore on. . . . New ones constantly rose . . . many. . . .

II

Per Hansa and his boys worked like firebrands during the last days before winter set in. Every task that came to their hands delighted them; they went from one fairy tale into the next—came out again, and there was a new one at hand; they gave themselves no peace, either by night or by day. . . . But Beret could not share their mood; she would watch them absently as they left the house; or when they were due to return, she would wander about with And-Ongen on her arm, looking for them through the window, and keeping a hot dish in readiness on the stove. They were sure to be cold, poor fellows! . . . Then when they were seated around the table, wrapped up in all their remarkable experiences, the talk would jump from one incident to another, and she would find herself unable to follow it. Their liveliness and loud laughter only drove her heavy thoughts into a still deeper darkness.

She had to admit, however, that Per Hansa could accomplish the most marvellous things; she could not imagine where he had learned it all. . . . There were the walls, for example, of which he himself was especially proud, and which Store-Hans never tired of admiring. He had begun work on these walls immediately after he had returned from the trip east to the Hallings' with the potatoes. The lime had been mixed according to directions, and spread over the walls—three coats of it, no less; now the sod hut shone so brightly inside that it dazzled the eyes. . . . Before the snow came, Beret thought it delightful to have such walls; but after there was nothing but whiteness outside—pure whiteness as far as the eye could see and the thought could reach—she regretted that he had touched them. Her eyes were blinded wherever she looked, either outdoors or indoors; the black-brown earthen floor was the only object on which she could rest them comfortably; and so she always looked down now, as she sat in the house. But hint at it, and thus ruin his pleasure, she could not. . . . And it really didn't matter much to her; she would endure it for the brief time that remained! . . .

She was thankful enough, though, for all the fine fish that he had brought home. Per Hansa had taken both boys with him on the great expedition east to the Sioux River; there they had made a tremendous catch with the help of the net, and Per Hansa had talked with the Tronders about many extraordinary things, and had gained much valuable information. . . . Heaps of frozen fish now lay outside all along the wall; Per Hansa explained to her what a God-send it was that the snow finally had come. Hm! Good Heavens! If it hadn't come soon he would have been obliged to go out and get it! Now he was spared that trouble; with the aid of the snowdrifts they could have fresh fish through the whole winter. . . . "Hey, woman!" he said with a laugh, whenever she complained of how desolate it was since the snow had come. "Can't you understand that we could never manage things without the snow? . . . Hey, wife—white and fine, both outdoors and indoors! . . . Wonder if something couldn't be done to the floor, too?" . . .

Now it came to light what had been working in Per Hansa's mind when he had bought all that salt; he salted down quantities of the fish, and packed them away in all the vessels they could spare.

But in the opinion of the boys, the duck hunt with the net was the crowning adventure. Never had there been such an enthusiastic party; the father was almost the worst of the three! Now the great secret of his planning and scheming over the ducks was revealed. While Store-Hans and his brother had only talked about capturing them and wondered what could be done, Per Hansa had figured out every detail in his mind; if the ducks got the best of him on one tack, he would fool them on another; into the net somehow they must go! . . . For three nights they had all stayed out in the swamps to the westward, toiling and fighting among the myriads of birds; in the morning they would come home after daylight, wet as crows, numb all over, and blue in the face with cold. But they always brought a catch! . . . As soon as the evening came they would be off again.

Each time Beret pleaded sadly, both by word and glance, for them to stay at home. . . . They would wear themselves out this way. What could they possibly do with all these fowl? Just wait and see; they might not need so much food—something might happen. . . . The boys only laughed at these objections; their mother sounded just like Sofie; probably all women were alike—they had no sense. Just imagine such a ridiculous idea—catch no more birds! . . . The father joined in with them and poked mild fun at the mother. How silly it would be not to grab good food when it lay right at their door! Suppose the swamps were to freeze up to-night? And after they had picked the ducks, there would be fine feather beds for both herself and Little Per! . . . Per Hansa's voice softened. . . . And besides, there was no more delicate fare than those ducks on any king's table! . . .

But she would not be carried along. . . . "We won't need them!" she said, dispiritedly . . . and fell into silence.

Dusk settled, the menfolk left—and she was alone with the child again.

But at last winter shut down in earnest; the swamps froze up and duck hunting came to an end for that year.

"I think we ought to carry some soup meat to our neighbours," said Per Hansa. . . . "This time it'll be something better than badger stew!" . . .

Every person in the little settlement had been rushed with work during the last days before Father Winter came. They all had a feeling that he wasn't very far away, that old fellow, and thought it best to be well prepared to receive him. Hans Olsa, Tönseten, and the Solum boys had been east to the Sioux River again for wood; they had made two trips, and home had seen very little of them lately. Few visits had been made; everyone had been busy with his own affairs. . . . For other reasons than this, visitors came but seldom to Per Hansa's now; there was something queer about the woman in that place; she said so little; at times people felt that they were unwelcome there. She was apt to break out suddenly with some remark that they could only wonder at; they hardly knew whether to be surprised or offended.

But on the day when the boys carried a gift of ducks to all the houses in the neighbourhood, proud of the dainty food they brought, and relating what sounded like a fairy tale, everyone went over to Per Hansa's to learn how he had gone about catching these birds. For Ole and Store-Hans wouldn't tell, though they plied them with questions. . . . The Solum boys came first, with Tönseten and Kjersti hard upon their heels; last of all came Hans Olsa and Sörine.

Once inside, they completely forgot their curiosity about the duck hunting; they stood with their mouths open, looking up one wall and down the next.

. . . Why . . . why . . . what in the wide world was this? Had they plastered *snow* on the walls? Sam thought it really was snow, and touched it gingerly with his finger. . . . What *was* it, anyway? Could it possibly be paint? . . . My stars, how fine it looked! . . . Per Hansa sat there, sucking his pipe and enjoying his little triumph; it seemed to him that he had never liked his neighbours so well as at this moment. . . . Beret went about listening quietly; in her face was a troubled expression. Not for all the world would she have had the work on the walls undone! . . .

Amazement was universal. . . . Sörine smiled in her

pleasant, kindly way; she went over to Beret and said with warm sympathy:

"Now you certainly have got a fine house! . . . You'll thrive all the better for it." . . . At that, she began to help her with the work. But Kjersti, with an emphatic slap on her thigh, voiced it as her opinion that it was a dirty shame that she and Sörrina had picked up such poor sticks for husbands! Why couldn't *they* ever hatch up some nice scheme? Why was Per Hansa the only man among them with his head on the right end? Yes, they certainly ought to feel ashamed of themselves, sitting there! . . . Tönseten took offence at this; he felt constrained to remind her that he was the fellow who had risen to the occasion and captured the Sognings! She'd better remember that; for what would have become of them all in the long run if the Sognings hadn't joined them? . . . "And I don't exactly see what this new notion of Per Hansa's is really good for," he spluttered on. "It's getting to be so damned swell in here that pretty soon a fellow can't even *spit!*" . . . Tönseten looked accusingly at Beret; it was from her that Per Hansa got these stuck-up airs. She was never willing to be like plain folks, that woman! . . . The Solum boys took great delight in the white walls; this was really beautiful. When they got married they would do the very same thing!

Hans Olsa sucked his pipe and said but little. This seemed very queer to him; he turned it over and over in his mind, but couldn't solve the problem. Was this like Per Hansa, who had always confided everything to him? . . . But here he was going about doing everything alone! When he had learned how a black earthen wall could be made shining white at so small a cost, why hadn't he told the others? There was so little cheer out here; they all sorely needed to share whatever they found. . . . The big, rugged features were very sober; he had to look hard at Per Hansa. No, it was the same good-natured face that one liked so well to have near by! This affair was just one of his many pranks; the longer Hans Olsa gazed at his neighbour, the more plausible grew this solution inside that big head of his.

Awhile later, as the two men stood together outside the door, watching the falling snow, he said, quietly:

"You have made it pretty fine inside, Per Hansa; but He Who is now whitening the outside of your walls does fully as well. . . . You shouldn't be vain in your own strength, you know!"

"Oh, nonsense, Hans Olsa!" laughed Per Hansa. "What are you prating about? . . . Here, take along a couple more ducks for Sörrina!" . . .

III

It was well enough that winter had come at last, thought Per Hansa; he really needed to lay off and rest awhile. After a good square meal of ducks or fresh fish, he would light his pipe and stretch himself, saying:

"Ha!—now we're really as well off here, my Beret-girl, as anybody could ever wish to be!" . . . He did not always expect an answer, and seldom got one. Then he would throw himself on the bed and take a good after-dinner nap, often sleeping continuously on into the night. . . . Life seemed very pleasant now!

In this fashion he spent quite a number of days; the bad weather still held out. Per Hansa continued to do full justice to the fare. When he had eaten his fill he would point out again to Beret how well off they were, and go to his couch to sleep the sleep of the righteous. It was almost uncanny—he could never seem to get sleep enough! He slept both day and night; and still he felt the need of more rest. . . . Now and then he would go to the door to look out at the weather, and glance across toward the neighbours. No . . . nothing to do outside—the weather was too beastly! He would come in again, and stretch himself, and yawn. . . .

The days wore on.

Yes, they wore on. . . . One exactly like the other. . . . Per Hansa couldn't grasp the strange contradiction that had begun to impress him; he knew that the days were actually growing shorter—were being shorn more closely by every passing night; but—weren't they growing longer?

Indeed they were—no question about it! They finally grew so long that he was at a dead loss to find something to do with which to end them. He assured himself that all this leisure was very fine; that he needed to ease up a bit; during the fall he hadn't spared himself; now it felt like a blessing to sit around and play the gentleman. Times would be strenuous enough for him once more, when spring came with fair weather and his great estate needed to be planted; he would just lay off and rest for a while yet! . . .

The days only grew longer and longer.

In the end, this enforced idleness began to gall him. The landscape showed a monotonous sameness . . . never the slightest change. . . . Grey sky—damp, icy cold. . . . Snow fell . . . snow flew. . . . He could only guess now where the huts of Hans Olsa lay. There wasn't a thing to do outdoors; plenty of wood lay chopped and ready for use; it took but a little while to do the chores. . . . Beyond this, everything took care of itself outside.

Per Hansa sat by the table, or lay down on the bed when he got tired of sitting up; tried to sleep as long as possible; woke up with a start; turned over and tried to sleep again; rose and sat by the table once more, when he grew weary of lying down.

The days wore on, and yet got nowhere. . . . Time had simply come to a standstill! He had never seen the like; this was worse than the deadest lay-up in Lofoten!

The boys were almost as badly off; they too sat restless and idle; and because they had nothing at all to occupy their minds they often came to blows, so that the father had to interfere. . . . But he was never very rough with them, poor boys, what else could they find for amusement? . . . The mother always reminded him of their books. . . . Yes, of course—certainly they must learn to read, the father said; no heathen were going to grow up in his house! He tried to be stern with them over this matter; but then . . . after all, boys were boys, he remembered!

At length he realized that this sort of life could not go on. He didn't give a hang for the weather—put on his coat and bade the boys do the same; then they went out and attacked the woodpile. They sawed and they chopped; they lugged in wood and piled it up; first they stacked up as much chopped wood as they could stow in the odd corners of the house; then they built a curious little fort of chopped wood out in the yard—very neatly and craftily constructed—and piled it full, too; this work cheered them up and kept their minds occupied, though the weather was bitterly cold and inclement. They toiled at it from early morning until late at night, and hardly took time off to eat their dinner; the boys began to get sick of the job and complained of being tired. The woodpile lasted exactly four days; when they had chopped up the last stick there was nothing left for them to do outside.

Then they sat idle again.

The bad spell of weather held out interminably. A cold, piercing wind from the northeast blew the livelong day, and moaned about the corners at night. . . . Snow flew . . . more snow fell.

No sun. . . . No sky. . . . The air was a grey, ashen mist which breathed a deathly chill; it hung around and above them thick and frozen. . . . In the course of time there was a full moon at night, somewhere behind the veil. Then the mist grew luminous and alive—strange to behold. . . . Night after night the ghostly spectacle would return.

Per Hansa would gaze at it and think: Now the trolls are surely abroad! . . .

One evening Tönseten and Kjersti came over. They sat and talked until it grew very late. One could readily see that Syvert was out of sorts about something; he puffed at his pipe in glum, ill humor, glared at Per Hansa's walls, and didn't have much to say. When he did speak his voice was unnecessarily loud.

Kjersti and Beret sat together on the bed; they seemed to be finding a good deal to chat about.

Kjersti was in an unusually neighbourly mood; she had come over to ask if . . . well, if she couldn't do something for Beret? She had some woollen yarn at home in her chest, very soft and very fine. Would Beret be offended if she knitted a pair of socks for the little newcomer they were all awaiting? . . . It was fine yarn, the very finest! Beret must just try to imagine how lonesome she was, sitting at home all alone with that useless husband of hers—and no little newcomer to wait for! . . . She had plenty of yarn; she could easily make the socks long enough to serve as leggings, too. The work would really bring joy to her—and to Syvert, too, poor fellow, to whom no little newcomer would ever arrive!

. . . Ah, well! . . . God pity us, Syvert wasn't so bad, after all—far be it from her to complain! . . . At that, Kjersti happened to think of a story she had heard, about a couple who couldn't seem to get a child though they wanted one very badly. Here the story was, since they happened to be talking about such matters. . . . This wife had so little sense that she sought the aid of a witch woman, who gave her both *devil's drink* and *beaver-geld;* she rubbed herself with the stuff and drank some of it, too, but no change came; that is, not until one summer when a shoal of herring came into the fjord and with it a fleet of strange fishermen. . . . Alas! desire makes a hot fire, once it has been kindled! But what do you suppose?—her husband became just as fond of that child as if he had been the father of it! . . . Wasn't that a queer thing? . . . But when the boy was a year old and was on the point of being christened—well, on that very Sunday it happened, as they were sailing across the fjord, that the boat capsized and the Lord took both mother and child, right there and then! He had taken away what he had refused to give in honour, and more besides. . . . There was something mysterious about such things, didn't Beret think so? And wasn't it strange that the father should have been so fond of *that* child? . . . Kjersti had known them both very well.

Beret listened attentively to this tale, putting in a word here and there.

Over at the table, the men had pricked up their ears as the story began; they heard it all. Per Hansa looked at Syvert and laughed; Syvert, in turn, glared at the wall and said, angrily:

"I should think you'd be able to find something American to talk about! . . . We're through now with all that troll business over in Norway!" . . . He got up and started to go. . . .

But Per Hansa wouldn't listen to their leaving just yet; since they had braved the weather to make a call they might as well sit awhile longer. . . . "You'll have the wind astern, Syvert, going home! . . . Come on, sit down and behave yourself!"

On another afternoon all of Hans Olsa's household came over. They stayed till dark; then they began to say that perhaps they'd better be going now—but they made no move to leave. . . . Sörine had brought a gift for Beret. There had been a few bits of cloth lying around the house, for which she could find no use; it had been rather lonesome these days and she had needed something to do, so she had made a little article for this newcomer whom everyone was waiting for! . . . At that, Sörine drew out from her ample bosom a child's cap, of red, white, and blue stripes, with long silk ribbons, all sewed with the greatest care. It was a beautiful cap; all had to see it; there were many warm words of praise. Beret received it in silence; her eyes were wet as she took the cap and laid it carefully in the big chest. . . .

To-night it was Beret who refused to let the visitors leave. She absolutely insisted. Such quantities of food lay outside around the house—far more than they would ever need—that they might as well stay for supper and help to eat it! . . . This proposal overjoyed Per Hansa. It was the plain truth, as Beret said, they had more than they needed—and there was plenty left in the Sioux River, for that matter; to-night they were going to celebrate with fresh fish for supper! . . . He went outside and brought in a generous supply of the frozen fish, which he scaled and cut up; he was in the finest of spirits—it seemed just like the good old days in Lofoten. . . . That evening was a happy interlude for them all.

IV

. . . No, the days would not pass! . . . Why, here it was, only the middle of November! It seemed to Per Hansa, as he sat by the table puffing his pipe and following Beret around with his eyes, that many winters must have gone by already.

He found himself watching Beret very often; during the last two weeks he had discovered many things about her which he had never noticed before. Just trifles, they were, but so many of them—one thing after another. Sitting here now with nothing else to occupy his mind, he began slowly and carefully to piece together what he had observed; the result pleased him less and less as he went on adding. He tried to wave the truth aside—to deny the plain facts; he even succeeded for a while—in the beginning. . . . Goodness! nothing but trifles—things that were always likely to happen under such circumstances! . . . Oh no! There was no danger that Beret couldn't stand her watch; things would right themselves when the time came; for it was only the law of nature, which man must obey. . . . Of course she couldn't help dreading it, poor thing!

. . . Did her face seem a good deal more wasted this time—or was he mistaken? She didn't look well at all. . . . No. . . . Then why didn't she eat more? Good Heavens! she wasn't trying to save on the food? Here was everything—quantities of it: meat aplenty, and any amount of flour! . . . She should help herself, this Beret-girl of his, or he would make her dance to another tune!

One day at table he burst out with it, telling her that she mustn't act the stranger in her own house! He made his voice sound gruff and commanding: Now she must sit up and eat like a grown woman. . . . "Here, help yourself!" . . . He took a big piece of fish from the platter and put it on her plate; but she merely picked at it, and left most of it lying there.

"It is hard when you have to force every mouthful down," she complained.

"But look here, you've got to eat, both for yourself and —Of course you must eat!"

"Oh, well," she said, wearily, as she got up and left the table. . . . "It doesn't matter much about the food." . . .

Lately he had also begun to notice that she lay awake the greater part of the night; he always dropped off to sleep before she did; yet she would be wide awake in the morning when he first stirred, although he was by habit an early riser. And if by chance he woke up in the night, he would be almost certain to find her lying awake beside him. . . . One night she had called him; she had been sitting up in bed, and must have been crying—her voice sounded like it. And she had only wanted him to get up and see what ailed Store-Hans; he had been moaning in his sleep all night, she said. Per Hansa had risen to look after the boy, and had found nothing the matter, as he had expected. . . . That night he had been seriously frightened. When he had come back to lie down she had started crying so despairingly; he hadn't been able to make any sense of the few words he got out of her. . . . From that time on, he had been scared to show her any tenderness; he had noticed that when he did so, the tears were sure to come. And that, certainly, was not good for her!

As he sat through the long, long day observing his wife, he grew more and more worried about Beret, poor thing. Every day there were new trifles to be noticed.

She, who had always been so neat and could make whatever clothes she put on look becoming, was now going about shabby and unkempt; she didn't even bother to wash herself. He realized that he had noticed it subconsciously for a long time. . . . But now he seldom saw her even wash her face. And her hair, her beautiful hair which he admired so greatly and loved to fondle when she was in good spirits, now hung down in frowsy coils. . . . Wasn't it two days since she had touched her hair? Well—*that* he didn't dare to mention! . . . How could he ever speak of cleanliness at all to his Beret—his Beret who was always so prim and often nagged him for being slovenly and careless about his own appearance? . . . Not that she wasn't pretty enough, just as she was, his Beret-girl; this Per Hansa told himself many times. But one day as he sat looking at her, he suddenly got up, went over to the window, and stood there gazing out; and then he said:

"I really think you ought to go and fix up your hair, Beret-girl. . . . I kind of feel that we're going to have company to-day."

She gave him a quick glance, blushed deeply, rose, and left the room. He heard her go into the stable, where she stayed a long time; he couldn't imagine what she was doing in there at that hour of the day. Her actions made him feel worried and uncertain. When she came in again he did not dare to look at her. . . . Then she began to tidy herself; she took some water and washed, loosened up her braids and combed her hair, and afterward coiled it very prettily. She gave herself plenty of time, and took careful pains. . . . At last he *had* to look at her; his whole self was in the gaze that he fixed upon her; he would have liked to say something kind and loving to her now. But she did not glance at him, and so he dared not speak. . . . In a little while he found an excuse to go out; passing close to her, he said in a tender, admiring voice:

"Now we've got a fine-looking lady!"

All the rest of that day he felt happier than he had been for a long while. . . . Of course his Beret-girl would be all right. . . . Indeed, she *was* all right, as far as that went! . . .

But . . . other days followed. Per Hansa remained idle and had nothing to do but look at his wife. He looked and looked, until he had to face the hard fact that something was wrong.

. . . Had she ever been so brooding and taciturn when she was with child before? He could talk to the boys about the future until they would be completely carried away by his visions; but whenever he tried to draw her into the conversation he failed completely—failed, no matter which tack he took nor how hard he tried. He understood it clearly: it wasn't because she did not want to respond—she *couldn't!* . . . The pain of it surged through him like a wave. God in Heaven, had she grown so weak and helpless! . . . She wasn't even able to take nourishment. . . . There Beret sat in the room with them, within four paces—yet she was far, far away. He spoke to her now, to her alone, but could not make her come out of the enchanted ring that lay about her. . . . When he discovered this, it hurt him so that he could have shrieked. . . .

. . . Another queer thing, she was always losing the commonest objects—completely losing them, though they were right at hand. He had seen it happen several times without taking much notice; but by and by it began to occur so frequently that he was forced to pay attention. She would put a thing down, merely turn around, and then go about searching for it in vain; and the thing would lie exactly where she had placed it, all the time. . . . This happened again and again; sometimes it struck them all as very funny. . . . "It looks as if your eyes were in your way, Mother!" Store-Hans once exclaimed, laughing so heartily that the others had to join in; but Per Hansa soon noticed that she was hurt when they made fun of her.

One day she was looking for the scissors. She had been sitting by the stove, mending a garment; had risen to put on more fuel; and when she sat down again had been unable to find her scissors, which she held all the while in her hand. She searched diligently, and asked the others to help her. Suddenly Ole discovered the scissors in his mother's hand; he ran up to her and jerked them away; the boy was roaring with laughter. . . . Then she burst into violent tears, laid her work aside, threw herself down on the bed, and buried her face in the pillow. All three menfolk felt painfully embarrassed.

And sometimes she had moments of unusual tenderness toward them all—particularly toward Per Hansa. Her concern would grow touchingly childlike; it was as if she could not do enough for him and the children. But it was a tenderness so delicate that he dared not respond to it. Nevertheless, he felt very happy when these moods came; they gave him renewed courage.

. . . Of course she would be all right again as soon as it was over! . . . And now the event could not be far away! . . .

V

Winter was ever tightening its grip. The drifting snow flew wildly under a low sky, and stirred up the whole universe into a whirling mass; it swept the plain like the giant broom of a witch, churning up a flurry so thick that people could scarcely open their eyes.

As soon as the weather cleared icy gusts drove through every chink and cranny, leaving white frost behind; people's breaths hung frozen in the air the moment it was out of the mouth; if one touched iron, a piece of skin would be torn away.

At intervals a day of bright sunshine came. Then the

whole vast plain glittered with the flashing brilliance of diamonds; the glare was so strong that it burnt the sight; the eyes saw blackness where there was nothing but shining white. . . .

. . . Evenings . . . magic, still evenings, surpassing in beauty the most fantastic dreams of childhood! . . . Out to the westward—so surprisingly near—a blazing countenance sank to rest on a white couch . . . set it afire . . . kindled a radiance . . . a golden flame that flowed in many streams from horizon to horizon; the light played on the hundreds and thousands and millions of diamonds, and turned them into glittering points of yellow and red, green and blue fire.

. . . Such evenings were dangerous for all life. To the strong they brought reckless laughter—for who had ever seen such moon-nights? . . . To the weak they brought tears, hopeless tears. This was not life, but eternity itself. . . .

Per Hansa sat in his hut, ate, drank, puffed at his pipe, and followed his wife with his eyes in vague alarm; for the life of him he didn't know what to do. Where could he betake himself? It wouldn't do for him to go from house to house, when things were in such a bad way at home. . . . No, here he was condemned to sit! . . . His temper was growing steadily worse; he found it more and more difficult to keep his hands off things.

He would be seized by a sudden, almost irresistible desire to take Beret, his own blessed Beret, hold her on his knee like a naughty child—just *make* her sit there—and reason with her . . . talk some sense into her!

For this wasn't altogether fair play on her part! Of course it was hard for her these days; but after all, the time would soon come to an end; and *that* was something real to struggle with—something to glory in! Besides, she had her wonted round of duties to perform. . . . But he! . . . Here he was forced to sit in idleness, and just let his eyes wander! . . .

. . . And it wasn't right for him to feel this way, either; but the endless waiting had at last got on his nerves. . . . Strange, how long it took! Hadn't the time ought to be drawing near pretty soon? . . . During these days he often thought about the matter of a name. He immediately decided that if it turned out to be a girl, she should be named *Beret;* that part of it was settled. But suppose she bore him a boy? In that case he wasn't so certain. Two boy's names were running in his mind, but—well, time would tell. . . . If she would only hurry up and bring forth the child, he would guarantee to find a suitable name for it!

He began to feel weak and miserable as he dragged himself about the house. . . . Then, one day, came a fascinating thought: if he could only make a short trip east to the Sioux River, to visit the Trönders! This spell of cold weather was nothing to mind; it was a long way, to be sure, but he felt that he could easily manage it. Hadn't he sailed a cockleshell of an eight-oared boat all the way from Helgeland to West Lofoten in the dark of winter? This would be mere child's play compared to that journey. . . . What great sport it would be to fish with a net through the ice! From the Trönders, who were old settlers in this region, he could get a lot more valuable information; it was really remarkable, what they had told him last time, about the fur trade with the Indians north at Flandreau. . . . Whenever the thought of this journey came to him he could hardly push it aside.

. . . Useless even to dream of such a thing! Here was poor Beret, pottering helplessly about—he must think only of her.

And Per Hansa tried his best to think of her to some effect. He had noticed that she minded the cold; she never complained, but he was well aware of it; from now on he tended the fire himself and kept the stove red hot most of the day. In spite of that he couldn't get the house properly warm when the cold was at its worst; the earthen floor was always cold and Beret's feet seemed particularly sensitive.

One day Per Hansa got an idea which gave him much diversion. While they had been busy chopping the wood he had selected a few of the largest and straightest-grained sticks, trimmed them out square, and stood them behind the stove to dry; he had promised himself that he would make something out of them during the winter. Now he chose the best piece he could pick out; he had decided to make a pair of clogs for Beret; he knew by experience that such shoes were very warm while they were new. For a long while he couldn't think of any material to use for the vamps; then he resolutely cut off a corner of the old sheepskin robe which they used on their bed; he sheared the wool snug, and made the vamps of that. . . . He did a neat, attractive job and felt rather proud when the job was finished.

He brought the clogs to Beret and put them on her feet.

It was plain to be seen that she was touched by the gift; but then she said something that he wished she had left unspoken:

"You might have thought of this before, it seems to me. Here I have gone with cold feet all winter." . . . The words were uttered quietly; she meant no reproach by them, but merely said what came into her mind.

He turned away and went out of the house; outside the door he paused, and stood for a long time gazing off into the evening. . . . Somewhere out there life was still happy. . . . There was no solitude. . . . Didn't it seem to call to him?

Per Hansa felt that now he needed to cry. . . .

VI

A day came when Per Hansa flared up in a rage that frightened even himself; he struck out blindly and smashed whatever happened to lie within his reach. It was one of the Solum boys that brought it about. One forenoon Henry came over and sat chatting for a long while, as if he had nothing in particular on his mind; Per Hansa was glad of the visit, and urged Henry to stay. When the lad finally rose to go he asked if Per Hansa would be willing to keep their cow until the time of the spring planting; he could *have* the calf she would drop in January, so he would be nothing out; and there was plenty of hay left in their barn, which could be hauled over . . . Henry spoke slowly, without looking up; he seemed almost ashamed to explain his errand.

Per Hansa's eyes blinked fast. . . . This was indeed handsome of Henry; imagine his thinking more of Beret and the children than of himself! In fact, it was so generous, and handsomely done, that Per Hansa felt quite overcome; his eyes blinked till they watered. . . . But he mustn't take an offer like this! True enough, Rosie was drying up and milk wasn't very plentiful in their house; but they had learned to get along without it; they made plenty of soup, and that filled the same need. No, it would never do to take the milk away from the Solum boys. . . . "I don't very well see how I can take your cow," Per Hansa answered.

Henry seemed perplexed, looked down at the floor, and apparently did not know how to go on.

—Well, that wasn't exactly the idea, he said. . . . He and his brother had made a sleigh, and now they wanted to try it out. The cow couldn't be left alone after they were gone.

Per Hansa's eyes fairly danced; he leaned across the table, speaking fast and eagerly: The devil you say—going east to the Sioux River, perhaps? . . . What? . . . He wished to the Lord he could go along with them! Couldn't they hold up for just a little while—until he got ready? . . . He threw a swift glance at his wife.

—No, that wasn't exactly the idea, either, Henry confessed, still more embarrassed. Their parents were sitting alone, back there in Minnesota; he and Sam had agreed that they had better go east and celebrate Christmas with the old folks. They had been getting pretty lonesome here, anyway; there seemed to be nothing to do in the dead of winter; but they fully intended to come back in the spring, as soon as the prairie was open. . . . Couldn't he do them the favour of keeping the cow?

For an instant all the light seemed to die out of Per Hansa's face: then it suddenly flared up again in a flame of rage that positively snapped and crackled.

"Take your damned old cow along with you, Henry! We want none of your milk!" . . . His lips trembled like those of one on the point of bursting into tears.

—Well—said Henry, calmly—if that was the way Per Hansa felt about it, he would have to ask some of the others; he certainly didn't want to force the cow on anyone! If they could find no other way out of it, they would have to slaughter the beast; they couldn't possibly take her with them. . . . Without further words he left the house.

It was then that the storm broke loose in earnest. . . . The boys were sitting at the table, each with a piece of charcoal, drawing ponies and Indians on top; those of Store-Hans's were waging war against Ole's; the boys were so taken up with their play that they hardly noticed what was going on in the room. Beret sat by the stove, mending a garment; the child had also been given needle and thread, and was industriously sewing away at a piece of rag. . . . Per Hansa stood at the window, glaring out.

All at once Beret remarked in her quiet manner, without looking up, that it didn't seem a bit strange to her that the Solum boys wanted to leave the place. Why should they lie exiled out here in the wilderness?

It was as if something had suddenly stung Per Hansa; he wheeled quickly and looked at his wife, his eyes hard and glazed.

"Hell!" he snapped . . . "If they were *men*, instead of such god-damned lousy *worms*, they would find something to do!" . . . Quiet fell on the room after this outburst; Per Hansa sank down heavily on the edge of the bench. . . . All of a sudden he burst out again:

—Ha—do! . . . Two strong men! Here lay the finest sleighing that one could wish for! If they had been grownup men, and not a couple of babies, they would now be hauling home logs for their new house! . . . If *he* didn't have to sit there like a sick woman, *he* would have had enough lumber on hand for the finest farmstead, long ago—perhaps would have started to build by now! Did she actually believe there was nothing to do around here? . . .

His words cut through the little room like the harsh grating of a file on a saw blade.

Again there was silence. He got up savagely and stuck his pipe in his mouth, but did not light it; he did not know what he was doing now. . . .

It was Beret who broke the silence; although her question was uttered very calmly, it seemed to cut deeper than his violent outburst:

—Well, why didn't he go to work and do it, then?

Go to work?—he snarled.—Did *she* need to ask why he wasn't doing anything? Was she in such a condition that he could ever leave the house? . . .

—Oh, she was in the condition he had brought her to—no worse and no better—she said. Now her words, too, vibrated with passion.—No, indeed, he didn't need to sit at home on her account! she added sharply.

Per Hansa drove his fist into the table with a terrible crash. The boys jumped up in fright and shrank away—never had they seen their father like this; he looked as if he would strike their mother the next instant. Little And-Ongen threw the rag in her mother's lap, put her hand into her mouth, and screamed in terror.

"You talk like a fool! . . . That only shows how much sense you've got!"

He saw a cap over on a wall somewhere, seized it, found the door, and was gone. . . .

Per Hansa stayed outside nearly all of the day. Before evening had come, however, he had made a pair of skis for each of the boys: they were rather heavy and clumsy affairs, but would serve the purpose; the boys stood looking at them wide-eyed and happy—but still they hardly dared to come near their father. . . . When he finally entered the house that evening the supper stood ready on the table. . . . Beret had gone to bed.

As soon as he had eaten he told the boys that he would have to go on an errand over to Hans Olsa's; he wasn't sure when he would be back; if he stayed late, they must go to bed. . . . No, they couldn't go with him! . . . He gave a glance toward the bed as he went out. . . .

When he reached Hans Olsa's house he asked at once if he might speak to Sörine alone; he seemed bashful and embarrassed—tried to assume a bantering air, but didn't quite succeed. When Sörine had stepped outside with him he asked beseechingly if she would be kind enough to go over and look after Beret—the sooner the better!

—Was there anything going on? Sörine asked.

—No, not exactly *that*—though it must be nearly time now. But Sörine ought to remember that it was pretty lonesome for her, sitting there alone, unable even to go outside the door. Day after day Beret neither saw nor heard another person, outside of the family!

—Yes, certainly—she would be glad to run over!

—Could she go right away?

—Was there such an awful hurry?—Sörine still suspected Per Hansa's denial. If that was the case, he had better go and get Kjersti at once; she didn't care to tackle this job alone!

—No, no—it wasn't that!

Sörine went in for a moment to put on her coat; soon she came out again, ready to start. He went with her for some distance. . . .

—Wasn't he coming along?—she asked, stopping to look inquiringly at him.

—No, he guessed he wouldn't; he needed to have a little talk with Hans Olsa to-night. He only wanted to say this: that she who understood all such things so capably, must look well to Beret now; she mustn't come away and leave her too soon!

Sörine's kind, intelligent face looked straight into his. "I can see that you're worried about your wife to-night, Per Hansa. . . . That's fine of you, I say!"

"God richly bless you for those words, Sörrina!"

Per Hansa suddenly felt like a new person; and yet he lacked the courage to look up.

"But let me tell you one thing, Sörrina: I'm not half so worried about my wife as I am about myself! To-day I nearly laid hands on her—that's how fine I am, and now you know it! . . . Hurry along!"

"You ought to have a whaling for that, Per Hansa!" she said with a laugh, but immediately grew serious. . . . "Alas! life lays a hard hand on all of us! . . . Well, now I'm off. You don't need to hurry to-night—if we need you, I'll send Ola."

Per Hansa stood there in the darkness of the winter night, looking after the disappearing figure. . . . No, her equal was not to be found! She could be both minister and father confessor, that woman!

VII

He had barely entered Hans Olsa's house, found a seat, and lighted his pipe, when another visitor arrived. Tönseten came in, apparently in a bad humour; no, he didn't want to sit down; he was going farther on in a minute or two. Did they know that the Solum boys were about to leave?

"I guess we know as much as you do," said Per Hansa, dryly. . . . "There's such a lot going on around here these days!"

"But this won't do, folks, I tell you—it simply won't do! As Kjersti says, soon we'll have nothing but the snow left!"

"And I hope that'll go in time, too," laughed Per Hansa.

"It probably will!" Tönseten snapped, irritably. "But what I don't understand is, why have you folks let things come to such a pass?"

"*We* . . . ?" Per Hansa asked.

"Yes, *you!* . . . The two of you!"

"We can't very well *tie up* the boys, when they are bent on going," said Hans Olsa.

"I didn't say we could!" . . . Tönseten stood in front of him, waving his arms excitedly. "But we can use common sense, can't we?"

"Very well, Syvert, let's hear your common sense," spoke up Per Hansa.

"You talk like a fool, Per Hansa! Here you both sit around and twiddle your thumbs, doing nothing; but you've got cubs; and will soon have more! Why don't you join forces and hire Henry Solum to teach school for your brats this winter? There's a good enough head on Henry's shoulders, let me tell you; he hasn't had much schooling, to be sure; but the boy was born and raised in this country, and can sling the English like a native—that much *I* know. . . . I haven't any brats of my own to send; but I'll gladly chip in a few dollars when my wheat is threshed next fall!" . . . Tönseten seemed to have the details fully laid out, as usual.

The other two listened in silence. The eyes of Per Hansa began to shoot rapid, sparkling glances, which always betrayed the fact that he was in good humour; but it was some time before he opened his mouth. Hans Olsa sat pondering over the new idea that had just been proposed; it was perfectly true that the children needed schooling; but how did this bear on the case, when the Solum boys were ready and determined to go?

"I see you're still hesitating!" Tönseten exclaimed, snappishly. "Listen here, now: we're all going straight over to the Solum boys and talk them into it right away!"

"It strikes me this way," said Hans Olsa, slowly. "If they have made up their minds, it isn't right for us to interfere."

"Made up their minds!" snorted Tönseten, contemptuously. "What nonsense you're talking, Hans Olsa! How many times have you made up your mind, I'd like to know, and then unmade it again? . . . I can assure you of one thing, fellows: if we let Sam and Henry slip away from us *now*, it's certainly doubtful if we ever see them again—single and unhitched as they are! That's just Kjersti's opinion, too. Then won't we be left in a fine mess, I ask you—for what chance would we stand of ever getting such good neighbours again?"

"We might try it," Hans Olsa conceded. "What do you think, Per Hansa?"

Per Hansa jumped up from his chair. "I'll do whatever you say, friends. We can get no worse than a refusal." . . . But then he remembered something, and hesitated for a moment. . . . "I really oughtn't to be going over there; but—oh, well! who cares!" He grabbed up his cap impulsively. . . . "I might as well give Henry a chance to tell me what he thinks of me! . . . The sooner, the better!"

They held a lengthy conference with the Solum boys that night. Outside of their hut the sleigh waited in readiness; inside the door the chest stood packed; the boys were on the point of going to bed when the three men entered, and were evidently annoyed to see them. . . . The newcomers seemed unaccountably bashful.

Hans Olsa announced their errand.

At this Henry burst out laughing. . . . No, a schoolteacher he could never be, he said; he had other things to think of; back east in Minnesota somewhere, a girl was straying about looking for him; if he could only find her, he too would be needing a teacher by and by! . . .

Then Tönseten began to talk; there was a note in his

voice that put all joking aside, even though they had to laugh at him now and then:

"If you leave this place, you'll have to take Kjersti and me along with you, though I don't know what we would do with ourselves back in Minnesota! She and I crossed the Red Sea, as it were, when we left last spring. . . . For her and me there is no road leading back! . . . What do you think we're going to do, I'd like to know, when you are gone? At Hans Olsa's they don't play cards; and Per Hansa, poor devil—well, he has a sick woman on his hands. . . . God alone knows how that business is going to come off. That's just what Kjersti says, too!"

Per Hansa had been silent ever since he came in; now he knocked the ashes out of his pipe, rose from the chest, and turned to Henry:

"I'll tell you exactly how we stand—and this is gospel truth. If you and Sam leave us now, it'll be so dull and dreary for the rest of us that we might as well hang ourselves. You saw how I went to pieces to-day? You came and made me the finest kind of an offer, and in return I flew right in your face; you know blamed well, Henry, that such is not my way." . . . Here he paused for a moment, and then went on: "What sort of a school-teacher you'll make I haven't the faintest idea; I only know this, that you and your brother are both fine fellows and that none of us can afford to lose you. . . . Now, go ahead and do as your heart bids!"

Per Hansa had spoken with forced calmness; the seriousness of the situation bore in upon them all. Everyone in the room had the same thought: this strong man was likely at any minute to burst into tears.

. . . A long silence fell. Tönseten blew his nose violently between his fingers, after which he wiped them off on his trousers.

At last Henry spoke—his voice was husky and subdued:

"It's harder on us than it is on you. We have only each other; but you have wives and children to squabble with!"

"Children!" cried Tönseten, wiping his eyes. . . . "Good God! what are you saying, Henry?" . . .

"Well, all the same," Henry continued, earnestly, "if

you will undertake to give us supper, one week with each of you, and have our clothes mended, we'll try to hang on a little while. . . . What do you say, Sam?"

VIII

The days wore on . . . sunny days . . . bleak, gloomy days, with cold that congealed all life.

There was one who heeded not the light of the day, whether it might be grey or golden. Beret stared at the earthen floor of the hut and saw only night round about her.

Yes . . . she faced only darkness. She tried hard, but she could not let in the sun.

Ever since she had come out here a grim conviction had been taking stronger and stronger hold on her.

This was her retribution!

Now had fallen the punishment which the Lord God had meted out to her; at last His visitation had found her out and she must drink the cup of his wrath. Far away she had fled, from the rising of the sun to the going down thereof . . . so it had seemed to her . . . but the arm of His might had reached farther still. No, she could not escape—this was her retribution!

The stillness out here had given her full opportunity for reflection; all the fall she had done nothing but brood and remember. . . . Alas! she had much to remember!

She had accepted the hand of Per Hansa because she must—although no law had compelled her; she and he were the only people who had willed it thus. She had been gotten with child by him out of wedlock; nevertheless, no one had compelled her to marry him—neither father, nor mother, nor anyone in authority. It had been wholly her own doing. Her parents, in fact, had set themselves against the marriage with all their might, even after the child, Ole, had come.

. . . It had mattered nothing at all what they had said, nor what anyone else had said; for her there had been no other person in the world but Per Hansa! Whenever she had been with him she had forgotten the admonitions and prayers of her father and mother. . . . He had been life itself to her; without him there had been nothing. . . . Therefore she had given herself to him, although she had known it was a sin—had continued to give herself freely, in a spirit of abandoned joy.

Now she found plenty of time to remember how her parents had begged and threatened her to break with him; she recalled all that they had said, turning it over in her mind and examining it minutely. . . . Per Hansa was a shiftless fellow, they had told her; he drank; he fought; he was wild and reckless; he got himself tangled up in all sorts of brawls; no honourable woman could be happy with such a man. He probably had affairs with other women, too, whenever he had a chance. . . . All the other accusations she knew to be true; but not the last—no, not the last! She alone among women held his heart. The certainty of this fact had been the very sweetness of life to her. . . . What did she care for the rest of it! All was as nothing compared with this great certainty. . . . Ah, no—she knew it well enough: for him she was the only princess!

But now she understood clearly all that her parents had done to end it between them, and all the sacrifices they had been willing to make; she had not realized it at the time. . . . Oh, those kind-hearted parents on whom she had turned her back in order that she might cleave to him: how they must have suffered! The life which she and he had begotten in common guilt they had offered to take as their own, give it their name and their inheritance, and bring it up as their very child. They had freely offered to use their hard-earned savings to send her away from the scene of her shame . . . *so* precious had she been to them! But she had only said no, and no, and *no*, to all their offers of sacrifice and love! . . . Had there ever been a transgression so grievous as hers!

. . . Yet how could she ever have broken with him? Where Per Hansa was, there dwelt high summer and there it bloomed for her. How can a human forsake his very life? . . . Whenever she heard of one of his desperately reckless cruises through rough and stormy seas, on which he had played with the lives of his comrades as well as his own, her cheeks would glow and her heart would flame. This was the man her heart had chosen—

this was he, and he alone! a voice would sing within her. Or when she sat among the heather on the mountain side in the fair summer night, and he came to her and laid his head in her lap—the tousled head that only she could lull to sleep—then she felt that now she was crossing the very threshold of paradise! . . . Though she had had a thousand lives, she would have thrown them all away for one such moment—and would have been glad of the bargain! . . .

. . . Yes, she remembered all that had happened in those days; it was so still out here . . . so easy to remember!

No one had ever told her, but she knew full well who it was that had persuaded Hans Olsa to leave the land and the ancient farm that had been in his family for generations, and go to America. There had been only one other person in the world whom Per Hansa loved, and that was Hans Olsa. She had been jealous of Hans Olsa because of this; it had seemed to her that he took something that rightfully belonged to her. She had even felt the same way toward Sörine, who was kindness itself; on this account she had not been able to hold her friendship as fully as she needed to, either in Norway or here. . . .

. . . But when Per Hansa had come home from Lofoten that spring and announced in his reckless, masterful way, that he was off for America: would Beret come now, or wait until later? . . . Well, there hadn't been a "no" in her mouth then! There she had sat, with three children in a nice little home which, after the manner of simple folk, they had managed to build. . . . But she had risen up, taken the children with her, and left it all as if nothing mattered but him!

. . . How her mother had wept at that time! . . . How her father had grieved when they had left! Time after time he had come begging to Per Hansa, offering him all that he had—boat and fishing outfit, house and farm—if only he would settle down in Norway and not take their daughter from them forever. . . . But Per Hansa had laughed it all aside! There had been a power in his unflinching determination which had sent hot waves through her. She must have led a double life at that time; she had been sad with her parents but had rejoiced with Per Hansa. He had raged like a storm through those days, wild and reckless—and sometimes ruthless, too. . . . No!—he had cried—they would just make that little trip across the ocean! America—that's the country where a poor devil can get ahead! Besides, it was only a little way; if they didn't like it, they could drift back on the first fair western breeze! . . . So they had sold off everything that they had won with so much toil, had left it all like a pair of worn-out shoes—parents, home, fatherland, and people. . . . And she had done it gladly, even rejoicingly! . . . Was there ever a sin like hers?

IX

. . . Then she had arrived in America. The country did not at all come up to her expectations; here, too, she saw enough of poverty and grinding toil. What did it avail, that the rich soil lay in endless stretches? More than ever did she realize that "man liveth not by bread alone!" . . . Even the bread was none too plentiful at times. . . .

Beyond a doubt, it was Destiny that had brought her thither. . . . Destiny, the inexorable law of life, which the Lord God from eternity had laid down for every human being, according to the path He knew would be taken. . . . Now punishment stood here awaiting her—the punishment for having broken God's Commandment of filial obedience. . . . Throughout the fall she had been reckoning up her score, and it came out exactly thus: Destiny had so arranged everything that the punishment should strike her all the more inevitably. Destiny had cast her into the arms of Per Hansa—and she did not regret it! Destiny had held up America as an enticing will-o'-the-wisp—and they had followed! . . .

But no sooner had they reached America than the west-fever had smitten the old settlements like a plague. Such a thing had never happened before in the history of mankind; people were intoxicated by bewildering visions; they spoke dazedly, as though under the force of a spell. . . . "Go west! . . . Go west, folks! . . . The farther west, the better the land!" . . . Men beheld in feverish dreams the endless plains, teeming with fruitfulness, glowing, out there where day sank into night—a Beulah Land of corn and wine! . . . She had never dreamed that the good Lord would let such folly loose among men. Were it only the young people who had been caught by the plague, she would not have wondered; but the old had been taken even worse. . . . "Now we're bound west!" said the young. . . . "Wait a minute—we're going along with you!" cried the old, and followed after. . . . Human beings gathered together, in small companies and large—took whatever was movable along, and left the old homestead without as much as a sigh! Ever westward led the course, to where the sun glowed in matchless glory as it sank at night; people drifted about in a sort of delirium, like sea birds in mating time; then they flew toward the sunset, in small flocks and large—always toward Sunset Land. . . . Now she saw it clearly: here on the trackless plains, the thousand-year-old hunger of the poor after human happiness had been unloosed!

Into this feverish atmosphere they had come. Could Destiny have spun his web more cunningly? She remembered well how the eyes of Per Hansa had immediately begun to gleam and glow! . . . And the strange thing about this spell had been that he had become so very kind under it. How playfully affectionate he had grown toward her during the last winter and spring! It had been even more deliciously sweet to give herself to him then, than back in those days when she had first won him. Was it not worth all the care and sorrow in the world to taste such bliss, she had often asked herself—but had been unable to answer. But—then it had happened: this spring she had been gotten with child again. . . . Let no one tell her that this was not Destiny!

She had urged against this last journey; she had argued that they must tarry where they were until she had borne the child. One year more or less would make no difference, considering all the land there was in the west. . . . Hans Olsa, however, had been ready to start; and so there had been no use in trying to hold back Per Hansa. All her misgiving he had turned to sport and laughter, or playful love; he had embraced her, danced around with her, and become so roguish that she had been forced to laugh with him. . . . "Come here, *Litagod*—now we're gone!" . . . She well recalled how lovely this endearing term had sounded in her ears, the first night he had used it. . . .

But this was clear to her beyond a doubt: Per Hansa was without blame in what had happened—all the blame was hers. . . . He had never been so tender toward her as in the days since they had come out here; she could not have thought it possible for one human being to have such strong desire for another as he held. . . . Who could match him—who dared follow where he led? She remembered all that he had wrought since they had set out on their journey last spring, and felt that no one else could do it after him. He was like the north wind that sweeps the cloud banks from the heavens! . . . At these thoughts, something unspeakably soft and loving came into Beret's eyes. . . . No, not like the north wind: like the gentle breeze of a summer's night—that's how he was! . . . And this, too, was only retribution! She had bound herself inseparably to this man; now she was but a hindrance to him, like chains around his feet; him, whom she loved unto madness, she burdened and impeded . . . she was only in his way!

. . . But that he could not understand it—that he could not fathom the source of her trouble; that seemed wholly incomprehensible to her. Didn't he realize that she could never be like him? . . . No one in all the world was like him! How could she be? . . .

X

Beret struggled with many thoughts these days.

. . . Wasn't it remarkable how ingeniously Destiny had arranged it all? For ten long years he had cast her about like a chip on the current, and then had finally washed her ashore here. *Here*, far off in the great stillness, where there was nothing to hide behind—here the punishment would fall! . . . Could a better place have been found in which to lay her low?

. . . Life was drawing to a close. One fact stood before her constantly: she would never rise again from the bed in which she was soon to lie down. . . . This was the end.

. . . Often, now, she found herself thinking of the churchyard at home. . . . It would have been so pleasant to lie down there. . . . The churchyard was enclosed by a massive stone wall, broad and heavy; one couldn't imagine anything more reliable than that wall. She had sat on it often in the years when she was still her father's little girl. . . . In the midst of the churchyard lay the church, securely protecting everything round about. No fear had ever dwelt in that place; she could well remember how the boys used to jump over the graves; it had been great fun, too—at times she had joined the game. . . . Within that wall many of her dear ones slumbered: two brothers whom she had never seen, and a little sister that she remembered quite clearly, though she had died long, long ago; her grandparents, on both her father's and her mother's side, also rested here, and one of her great-grandfathers. She knew where all these graves lay. Her whole family, generation after generation, rested there—many more than she had any knowledge of. . . . Around the churchyard stood a row of venerable trees, looking silently down on the peace and the stillness within. . . . They gave such good shelter, those old trees!

. . . She could not imagine where he would bury her out here. . . . *Now,* in the dead of winter—the ground frozen hard! . . . How would he go about it? . . . If he would only dig deep down . . . the wolves gave such unearthly howls at night! No matter what he thought of it, she would have to speak to him about the grave. . . . Well, no need to mention it just now.

One day when Beret had to go out she stayed longer than usual. Before she finally came back to the house she went to the spot where the woodpile had stood, visited the curious little fort which they had built of chopped wood, and then entered the stable. . . . It worried her to know where he would find material for a coffin. She had looked everywhere outside, but had discovered only a few bits of plank and the box in which he had mixed the lime. . . . Hadn't she better remind him of this at once? Then perhaps he could go to the Trönders, east on the Sioux River, and get some lumber from them. . . . Never mind, she wouldn't do anything about it for a few days yet.

. . . If he could only spare her the big chest! . . . Beret fell to looking at it, and grew easier in her mind. . . . That chest had belonged to her great-grandfather, but it must have been in the family long before his day; on it she could make out only the words "*Anno* 16—" . . . the rest was completely worn away. Along the edges and running twice around the middle were heavy iron bands. . . . Beret would go about looking at the chest—would lift the lid and gaze down inside. . . . Plenty of room in there, if they would only put something under her head and back! She felt as if she could sleep safely in that bed. She would have to talk to Sörine about all these matters. . . . One day Beret began to empty the chest; she got Per Hansa to make a small cupboard out of the mortar box, and put all the things in there; but she took great care not to do this while he was around.

She realized now the great forethought he had shown last summer in building the house and stable under one roof. They undoubtedly had the warmest house in the neighbourhood; and then she enjoyed the company of the animals as she lay awake at night; it felt so cosy and secure to lie there and listen to them. . . . She could easily distinguish each animal by its particular manner of breathing and lying down. The oxen were always the last to finish munching; Rosie was the first to go to sleep; Injun's habits were entirely different from those of the others; he moved softly, almost without noise, as if engaged in some secret business. She never could hear him, except when the howl of a wolf sounded near by; then he would snort and stamp his feet. It was probably the wild blood in him that made him so different! . . . Beret had learned to love the pony.

When she was not listening to the animals she had

other things to occupy her mind. . . . As a little girl, she had often been taken into bed by her grandmother. This grandmother had been a kindly woman, sunny and always happy, in spite of her great age; each night before going to sleep she would repeat to herself pious little verses from memory. Beret could not remember them all now; but she managed to patch them together little by little, inserting new lines of her own, and repeating them over and over to herself. This she would do for hours at a time, occasionally sitting up in bed to say the verses aloud:

"Thy heavy wrath avert
From me, a wretched sinner;
Thy blissful mercy grant,
Father of love eternal!

"My sins are as many
As dust in the rays of the sun,
And as sands on the shore of the sea—
If by Thee requited,
I must sink benighted.

"Look with pity,
Tender Saviour,
At my wretched state!
Wounds of sin are burning;
May Thy hands, in love returning,
Heal my stinging stripes!

"Weighed by guilt I weary wander
In the desert here below;
When I measure
My transgressions,
Breaches of Thy holy law,
I must ponder
Oft, and wonder;
Canst Thou grace on me bestow?

"Gentle Saviour,
Cast my burden
Deep into the mercy-seal
Blessed Jesus,
Mild Redeemer,
Thou Who gav'st Thy life for me!"

XI

The day before Christmas Eve snow fell. It fell all that night and the following forenoon. . . . Still weather, and dry, powdery snow. . . . Murk without, and leaden dusk in the huts. People sat oppressed in the sombre gloom.

. . . Things were in a bad way over at Per Hansa's now; everyone knew it and feared what might befall both Beret and him. . . . No one could help; all that could be done was to bide the time; for soon a change must come!

"Listen, folks," said Tönseten, trying to comfort them as best he could. "Beret can't keep this up forever! I think you had better go over to her again, Kjersti!"

Both neighbour women were now taking turns at staying with her, each one a day at a time. They saw clearly that Per Hansa was more in need of help than Beret; there was no helping her now, while something, at least, could be done for him and the children. Christmas would soon be here, too, and the house ought to be made comfortable and cosy!

They all felt very sorry for Per Hansa. He walked about like a ragged stray dog; his eyes burned with a hunted look. Each day, the children were sent over to Hans Olsa's to stay for a while; if they remained longer than they had been told, he made no protest; at last they formed the habit of staying the whole day. He did not realize that it was bad for Beret to be without them so much; he tried to keep the talk going himself, but she had little to say; she answered in monosyllables and had grown peculiarly quiet and distant. In the shadow of a faint smile which she occasionally gave him there lay a melancholy deeper than the dusk of the Arctic Sea on a rainy, grey fall evening.

About noon of Christmas Eve the air suddenly cleared. An invisible fan was pushed in under the thick, heavy curtain that hung trembling between earth and heaven—made a giant sweep, and revealed the open, blue sky overhead. The sun shone down with powerful beams, and started a slight trickling from the eaves. Toward evening, it built a golden fairy castle for itself out yonder, just beyond Indian Hill.

The children were at Hans Olsa's; And-Ongen wanted to stay outside and watch the sunset. Sofie had told her that to-day was Christmas Eve, and that on every Christmas Jesus came down from heaven. The child asked many questions. . . . Would he come driving? Couldn't they lend him the pony? . . . Sofie hardly thought so—he probably would be driving an angel-pony!

Store-Hans, who was listening to them, thought this very silly and just like girls. He knew better! . . . Toward evening he suddenly wanted to go home, and was almost beside himself when his godfather said that he couldn't: all the children were to stay with Sofie to-night. They had to hold him back by force. . . . This was *Christmas Eve*. . . . He understood very well that something was about to go wrong at home. Why had his mother looked so wan and worn of late, and his father acted so queer that one couldn't talk to him?

That afternoon Beret was in childbed. . . . The grim struggle marked Per Hansa for life; he had fought his way through many a hard fight, but they had all been as nothing compared with this. He had ridden the frail keel of a capsized boat on the Lofoten seas, had seen the huge, combing waves snatch away his comrades one by one, and had rejoiced in the thought that the end would soon come for him also; but things of that sort had been mere child's play. . . . *This* was the uttermost darkness. Here was neither beginning nor end—only an awful void in which he groped alone. . . .

Sörine and Kjersti had both arrived a long time since. When they had come he had put on his coat and gone outside; but he hadn't been able to tear himself many steps away from the house.

Now it was evening; he had wandered into the stable to milk Rosie, forgetting that she had gone dry long ago; he had tended to Injun and the oxen, without knowing what he was about. . . . He listened to Beret wailing in the other room, and his heart shrivelled;

thus a weak human being could not continue to suffer, and yet live. . . . And this was his own Beret!

He stood in the door of the stable, completely undone. Just then Kjersti ran out to find him; he must come in at once; Beret was asking for him! . . . Kjersti was gone in a flash. . . . He entered the house, took off his outdoor clothes, and washed his hands. . . .

. . . Beret sat half dressed on the edge of the bed. He looked at her, and thought that he had never seen such terror on any face. . . . God in heaven—this was beyond human endurance!

She was fully rational, and asked the neighbour women to leave the room for a moment, as she had something to say to her husband. She spoke with great composure; they obeyed immediately. When the door closed behind them Beret rose and came over to him, her face distorted. She laid a hand on each of his shoulders, and looked deep into his eyes, then clasped her hands behind his neck and pulled him violently toward her. Putting his arms firmly around her, he lifted her up gently and carried her to the bed; there he laid her down. He started to pull the covers over her. . . . But she held on to him; his solicitous care she heeded not at all.

When he had freed himself, she spoke brokenly, between gasps:

. . . "To-night I am leaving you. . . . Yes, I must leave you. . . . I know this is the end! The Lord has found me out because of my sins. . . . It is written, 'To fall into the hands of the living God!' . . . Oh!—it is terrible! . . . I can't see how you will get along when you are left alone . . . though I have only been a burden to you lately. . . . You had better give And-Ongen to Kjersti . . . she wants a child so badly—she is a kind woman. . . . You must take the boys with you—and go *away from here!* . . . How lonesome it will be for me . . . to lie here all alone!"

Tears came to her eyes, but she did not weep; between moans she went on strongly and collectedly:

"But promise me one thing: put me away in the big chest! . . . I have emptied it and made it ready. . . . Promise to lay me away in the big chest, Per

Hansa! . . . And you must be sure to dig the grave deep! . . . You haven't heard how terribly the wolves howl at night! . . . Promise to take plenty of time and dig deep down—do you hear!"

His wife's request cut Per Hansa's heart like sharp ice; he threw himself on his knees beside the bed and wiped the cold perspiration from her face with a shaking hand.

. . . "There now, blessed Beret-girl of mine!" . . . His words sounded far off—a note of frenzy in them. . . . "Can't you understand that this will soon be over? . . . To-morrow you'll be as chipper as a lark again!"

Her terror tore her only the worse. Without heeding his words, she spoke with great force out of the clearness of her vision:

"I shall die to-night. . . . Take the big chest! . . . At first I thought of asking you not to go away when spring came . . . and leave me here alone. . . . But that would be a sin! . . . I tell you, you *must go!* . . . Leave as soon as spring comes! Human beings cannot exist here! . . . They grow into beasts. . . ."

The throes were tearing her so violently now that she could say no more. But when she saw him rise she made a great effort and sat up in bed.

. . . "Oh!—don't leave me!—don't go away! . . . Can't you see how sorely I need you? . . . And now I shall die! . . . Love me—oh, do love me once more, Per Hansa!" . . . She leaned her body toward him. . . . "You must go back to Norway. . . . Take the children with you . . . let them grow up there. Ask father and mother to forgive me! . . . Tell father that I am lying in the big chest! . . . Can't you stay with me to-night . . . stay with me and love me? . . . Oh!—*there they come for me!*"

Beret gave a long shriek that rent the night. Then she sobbed violently, praying that they should not take her away from Per Hansa. . . .

Per Hansa leaped to his feet, and found his voice.

"Satan—now you shall leave her alone!" he shouted, flinging the door open and calling loudly to the women outside. Then he vanished into the darkness.

No one thought of seeking rest that night. All the evening, lights shone from the four huts; later they were extinguished in two of them; but in the house of Hans Olsa four men sat on, grieving over the way things were going at Per Hansa's. When they could bear the suspense no longer some one proposed going over to get news.

Tönseten offered to go first. . . . When he came back little sense could be gathered from what he said. He had not been allowed inside; the women were in a frenzy; the house was completely upset; Beret was wailing so loud that it was dreadful to hear. And Per Hansa himself was nowhere to be found. . . . "We must go and look for him, boys! . . . Haven't you got a Bible or something to read from, Hans Olsa? This is an awful thing!"

. . . There they sat, each occupied with his own thoughts—but all their thoughts were of the same trend. If Beret died to-night, it would go hard with Per Hansa—indeed it would. In that case he probably wouldn't stay out here very long. . . . But if he went away, the rest of them might as well pack up and go, too!

Sam ran over to inquire; then Henry; at last it was Hans Olsa's turn. He managed to get a couple of words with his wife, who said that Beret would hardly stand it. No one had seen Per Hansa.

"Can you imagine where the man can be keeping himself?" asked Tönseten, giving voice to the fear that oppressed them all. . . . "May the Lord preserve his wits, even if He chooses to take his wife away!" . . .

Per Hansa walked to and fro outside the hut all night long; when he heard some one coming he would run away into the darkness. He could not speak to a living soul to-night. As soon as the visitor had gone he would approach the hut again, circle around it, stop, and listen. Tears were streaming down his face, though he was not aware of it. . . . Every shriek that pierced the walls of the hut drove him off as if a whip had struck him; but as soon as it had died out, something would draw him back again. At intervals he went to the door and held it ajar. . . . What did Per Hansa care for custom and decency, now that his Beret lay struggling with death! . . . Each time Sörine came to the door; each time she shook her head sadly, and told him there was no change yet; it was doubtful if Beret would be able to pull through; no person could endure this much longer; God have mercy on all of them!

That was all the comfort Sörine could give him. . . . Then he would rush off into the darkness again, to continue his endless pacing; when daylight came they found a hard path tramped into the snow around the hut.

The night was well-nigh spent when the wails in there began to weaken—then died out completely, and did not come again. Per Hansa crept up to the door, laid his ear close to it, and listened. . . . So now the end had come! His breath seemed to leave him in a great sob. The whole prairie began to whirl around with him; he staggered forward a few steps and threw himself face downward on the snow.

. . . But then suddenly things didn't seem so bad to him . . . really not so bad. . . . He saw a rope . . . a rope. . . . It was a good, strong rope that would hold anything. . . . It hung just inside the barn door—and the crossbeam ran just *there!* . . . No trick at all to find these things. Per Hansa felt almost happy at the thought; that piece of rope was good and strong—and the crossbeam ran just *there!*

. . . A door opened somewhere; a gleam of light flashed across the snow, and vanished. Some one came out of the hut quietly—then stopped, as if searching.

"Per Hansa!" a low voice called. . . . "Per Hansa, where are you?" . . . He rose and staggered toward Kjersti like a drunken man.

"You must come in at once!" she whispered, and hurried in before him.

The light was dim in there; nevertheless it blinded him so strongly that he could not see a thing. He stood a moment leaning against the door until his eyes had grown accustomed to it. . . . A snug, cosy warmth enveloped him; it carried with it an odd, pleasant odour. The light, the warmth, and the pleasant smell overcame him like sweet sleep that holds a person who has been roused, but who does not care to awaken just yet.

"How is it?" he heard a man's voice ask. Then he came back to his senses. . . . Was that he himself speaking? . . .

"You'll have to ask Sörrina," Kjersti answered.

Sörine was tending something on the bed; not until now did he discover her—and wake up completely. . . . What was this? . . . the expression on her face? Wasn't it beaming with motherly goodness and kindliness?

"Yes, here's your little fellow! I have done all I know how. Come and look at him. . . . It's the greatest miracle I ever saw, Per Hansa, that you didn't lose your wife to-night, and the child too! . . . I pray the Lord *I* never have to suffer so!"

"Is there any hope?" was all Per Hansa could gasp—and then he clenched his teeth.

"It looks so, now—but you had better christen him at once. . . . We had to handle him roughly, let me tell you."

"*Christen him?*" Per Hansa repeated, unable to comprehend the words.

"Why, yes, of course. I wouldn't wait, if he were mine."

Per Hansa heard no more—for now Beret turned her head and a wave of such warm joy welled up in him that all the ice melted. He found himself crying softly, sobbing like a child. . . . He approached the bed on tiptoe, bent over it, and gazed down into the weary, pale face. It lay there so white and still; her hair, braided in two thick plaits, flowed over the pillow. All the dread, all the tormenting fear that had so long disfigured her features, had vanished completely. . . . She turned her head a little, barely opened her eyes, and said, wearily:

"Oh, leave me in peace, Per Hansa. . . . Now I was sleeping so well."

. . . The eyelids immediately closed.

Per Hansa stood for a long time looking at his wife, hardly daring to believe what he saw. She slept peacefully; a small bundle lay beside her, from which peeped out a tiny, red, wrinkled face. . . . As he continued to gaze at her he sensed clearly that this moment was making him a better man!

At last he gathered his wits sufficiently to turn to Sörine and ask:

"Tell me, what sort of a fellow is this you have brought me—a boy or a girl?"

"Heavens! Per Hansa, how silly you talk!" . . . Kjersti and Sörine both had to laugh as they looked at Per Hansa; such a foolish, simple expression they had never seen on the face of a living man! . . . But Sörine immediately grew serious once more, and said that this was no time for joking; the way they had tugged and pulled at him during the night, you couldn't tell what might happen; Per Hansa must get the child christened right away; if he put if off, she refused to be responsible.

A puzzled expression came over the grinning face.

"You'd better do that christening yourself, Sörrina!"

—No!—she shook her head emphatically. That wasn't a woman's job—he must understand! . . . "And you ought to have it done with proper decorum, and thank the Lord for doing so well by you!"

Without another word Per Hansa found his cap and went to the door; but there he paused a moment to say:

"I know only one person around here who is worthy to perform such an act; since you are unwilling, I must go and get him. . . . In the meanwhile, you make ready what we will need; the hymn book you'll find on the shelf over by the window. . . . I won't be long!"

The kindly eyes of Sörine beamed with joy and pride; she knew very well the one he intended to get; this was really handsome of Per Hansa! . . . But then another thought crossed her mind; she followed him out, and closed the door after her.

"Wait a minute," she said. "I must tell you that

your boy had the helmet * on when he came! . . . I think you ought to find a very beautiful name for him!"

"What are you saying, Sörrina!"

"Yes, sir—that he had! . . . And you know what *that* means!"

Per Hansa drew his sleeve across his face—then turned and walked away. A moisture dimmed his eyes—he could not see. . . .

Outside it was now broad daylight; the sun stood some distance up in the sky, looking down on a desolate earth. It was going to be cold to-day, Per Hansa noticed; clouds of frosty mist like huge writhing serpents curled over the surface of the purplish-yellow plain. The sunbeams plunging into them kindled a weird light. He tingled with the cold; his eyelashes froze together so that he had to rub them with his mittens to keep them free.

. . . How remarkable—the child had been born with the helmet on! . . . He quickened his pace; in a moment he was running. . . .

"Peace be upon this house, and a merry Christmas, folks!" he greeted them as he entered Hans Olsa's door. . . . The room was cold; the Solum boys lay in one bed, fully dressed; both were so sound asleep that they did not wake up at his coming. His own children and Sofie lay in the other bed, Ole by himself down at the foot, the other three on the pillow; Store-Hans held And-Ongen close, as if trying to protect her. Hans Olsa and Tönseten had moved their chairs up to the stove, and sat hunched over on either side; Tönseten was nodding, the other was wide awake; both men jumped up when Per Hansa came in, and stood staring at him.

Per Hansa had to laugh outright at them; they were looking at him as if they had seen a ghost. But to the two men his laugh sounded pleasanter than anything they had heard in many a year.

* The English equivalent is, "to be born with the caul." Considerable superstition has always been attached to this phenomenon and in Norway especially so; a person born with the helmet on had been singled out by Destiny for something extraordinary.

"How are things coming?" asked Tönseten, excitedly, working his shoulders.

"Oh, it might have been worse!"

Hans Olsa grasped his hand: "Will she pull through?"

"It looks that way."

Then Tönseten suddenly seemed to realize that it was cold in the room; he began to walk around, beating goose with his arms. . . . "I'm ready to bet both my horses that it's a boy! I can see it in your face!" he exclaimed, still beating.

"All signs point that way, Syvert! But he's in pretty poor condition, Sörrina tells me. . . . Now look here, Hans Olsa: it's up to you to come over and christen the boy for me!"

Hans Olsa looked terror-stricken at his neighbour. . . . "You must be crazy, Per Hansa!"

"Nothing of the kind, Hans Olsa. . . . You just get yourself ready. . . . It's all written down in the hymn book—what to say, and how to go about it."

"No, no—I couldn't think of such a thing!" protested Hans Olsa, all of a tremble with the feeling of awe that had suddenly taken possession of him. . . . "A sinner like me!" . . .

Then Per Hansa made a remark that Tönseten thought was extremely well put:

"How you stand with the Lord I don't know. But this I do know: that a better man either on land or sea, He will have to look a long way to find. . . . And it seems to me that He has got to take that, too, into His reckoning!"

But Hans Olsa only stood there in terror. . . . "You'd better ask Syvert to do it!"

Then Tönseten grew alarmed:

"Don't stand there talking like a fool! . . . We all know that if one of us two is to tackle this job, it must be you, Hans Olsa. . . . There is nothing for you to do but go at once; this business won't stand any dilly-dallying, let me tell you!"

Hans Olsa gazed straight ahead; his helplessness grew so great that he was funny to look at; but no one thought of laughing, just the same. . . . "If it only won't be blasphemy!" . . . He finally struggled into his big coat and put on his mittens. Then he turned to Tönseten. . . . "The book says: 'In an extreme emergency a layman may perform this act'—isn't that so?"

"Yes, yes—just so! . . . Whatever else you'll need, is written there too!"

Through the frosty morning the two men walked silently across the prairie, Per Hansa in the lead. When they had covered half the distance he stopped short and said to his neighbour:

"If it had been a girl, you see, she should have been named Beret—I decided that a long while ago. . . . But seeing that it's a boy, we'll have to name him Per; you must say Peder, of course! . . . I've thought a good deal about Joseph—he was a pretty fine lad, no doubt. . . . But grandfather's name was Per, and there wasn't a braver, worthier man on that part of the coast; so it'll just have to be Per again this time. . . . But say, now—" Per Hansa paused a moment, pondering; then he looked up at his neighbour, and his eyes began to gleam. . . . "The boy must have a second name—so you'd better christen him Peder Seier!* . . . The last is after your Sörrina. . . . She has done me a greater service this night than I can ever repay! And now the boy is to be named after her!"

Hans Olsa could think of nothing to say in answer to all this. They walked on in silence. . . .

When they came into the room, they stepped across the threshold reverently. An air of Sabbath had descended on the room. The sun shone brightly through the window, spreading a golden lustre over the white walls; only along the north wall, where the bed stood, a half shadow lingered. . . . The fire crackled in the stove; the coffeepot was boiling. The table had been spread with a white cover; upon it lay the open hymn book, with the page turned down. Beside the hymn

* The name *Seier*, which means *Victorious*, was altogether unusual to Norwegian ears. The English equivalent will be used from now on. As this name plays such an important part in the psychology of Book II the reader would do well to remember the Norwegian form.

book stood a bowl of water; beside that lay a piece of white cloth. . . . Kjersti was tending the stove, piling the wood in diligently. . . . Sörine sat in the corner, crooning over a tiny bundle; out of the bundle at intervals came faint, wheezy chirrups, like the sounds that rise from a nest of young birds.

An irresistible force drew Per Hansa to the bed. . . . She lay sound asleep. . . . Thank God, that awful look of dread had not come back! He straightened himself up and glanced around the room; never before had he seen anything that looked so beautiful. . . .

Sörine got up, went to the table, and bared a little rosy human head.

"If you are going to be the minister here," she said, turning to her husband, who had remained standing motionless at the door, "then you must hurry up and get ready. . . . First of all you must wash your hands."

The next moment they had all gathered around the table.

"Here's the book. . . . Just read it out as well as you can, and we'll do whatever the book says," Sörine encouraged her husband. She seemed to have taken charge of the ceremony, and spoke in low, reassuring tones, as if she had done nothing else all her life but attend to such duties; and it was her confidence that gave Hans Olsa the courage he needed. . . . He went up to the table, took the book, and read the ritual in a trembling voice, slowly, with many pauses. And so he christened the child Peder Victorious, pronouncing the name clearly. Whereupon he said the Lord's Prayer so beautifully, that Kjersti exclaimed she had never heard the like.

"There, now!" said Kjersti with great emphasis. "I don't believe there is a thing lacking to make this christening perfectly correct! . . . Now the coffee is ready and we're all going to have a cup."

But Per Hansa was searching over in the corner; at last he produced a bottle. First he treated Sörine; then Kjersti. . . . "If ever two people have earned something good, you two are it! . . . Come on, now, have another little drop! . . . And hurry up about it, please! Hans Olsa and I feel pretty weak in the knees ourselves!"

. . . After a while both food and drink were served. . . . "It looks as if we were going to have a *real* Christmas, after all!" said Per Hansa with a laugh, as they sat around the table enjoying their coffee.

Book II

FOUNDING THE KINGDOM

I On the Border of Utter Darkness

I

An endless plain. From Kansas—Illinois, it stretched, far into the Canadian north, God alone knows how far; from the Mississippi River to the western Rockies, miles without number. . . . Endless . . . beginningless.

A grey waste . . . an empty silence . . . a boundless cold. Snow fell; snow flew; a universe of nothing but dead whiteness. Blizzards from out of the northwest raged, swooped down and stirred up a greyish-white fury, impenetrable to human eyes. As soon as these monsters tired, storms from the northeast were sure to come, bringing more snow. . . . "The Lord have mercy! This is awful!" said the folk, for lack of anything else to say.

Monsterlike the Plain lay there—sucked in her breath one week, and the next week blew it out again. Man she scorned; his works she would not brook. . . . She would know, when the time came, how to guard herself and her own against him!

But there was something she did not know. Had it not been for the tiny newcomer, who by mysterious paths had found his way into the settlement on Christmas morning, the monster might have had her way; but the newcomer made a breach in her plans—a vital breach!

Most marvellous it was, a sort of witchery. A thing so pitifully small and birdlike. . . . There was no substance to him, really nothing. Only a bit of tender flesh wrapped in pink silk. . . . But life dwelt in every fibre of it. Yet hardly life—rather the promise of it. Only a twitching and pulling; something that stretched itself out and curled up again—so fine and delicate that one was afraid to touch it with rude hands.

Beret lay in bed with the newcomer beside her. . . . She should have been stiff and cold long ago; she should be lying in another place, a place where those fellows who howled at night could find fresh joints to lick and gnaw. . . . But here she was, still in bed. The button-sized, red-tipped nose dug itself into her breast, pushed in to find a good hold, and then lay still with satisfied little gruntings. The movement hurt her, but it gladdened her heart, too; for all the world she would not have had it otherwise. Life was returning; instead of that stiff, cold horror, Beret's body grew warmer and stronger with every day that passed. And the grunts at her side became more and more insistent. . . . Ah, well, she would have to shift him over, then, so that there might be peace for a moment!

. . . "Thank God, you have food enough for him!" said Per Hansa. . . . "I never saw a youngster with such an appetite!" . . .

When Beret had finally awakened on that Christmas day, she had acted exactly like the old woman in the fairy tale. She lay still, peeping out at her surroundings and asking herself: "Am I still here? Is this me?" . . . She could not believe it, and she would not believe it, either. . . . Hadn't she finished with this place some time ago?

But here she was, after all. Daylight shone broadly through the window and lit up the room; wood crackled in the stove; the very walls Per Hansa had whitewashed —so different they were from other walls—rose before her. She saw spots that she recognized; she had had endless trouble with the spots on these white walls, and the boys always so careless. . . . Clothes hung beside the stove, and above it stretched diapers on a line. The smell of wet clothes drying was familiar, but she could not understand where the diapers had come from. . . . Neither Per Hansa nor the children were in sight. . . .

Where could they be? A quick thought crossed her mind: surely Per Hansa would not have let And-Ongen go out without bundling her up? . . . There was a woman working about the stove, but Beret could not see her face. Perhaps it was Kjersti. Wasn't she wearing Kjersti's plaid Sunday skirt? . . . No, no, Beret could not understand it at all. Had Kjersti gone with her, then, when she had departed—Kjersti, who was such a good woman? . . .

. . . Beret quickly grew tired from puzzling over this unsolvable riddle. Through the haze of half-consciousness a word and a number caught her eye . . . "Anno 16—" . . . He had not used the big chest for her, then! Ah no! he probably had felt that he could not do without it. But it hurt her deeply to know it; she had so much wanted to lie in the old chest that she loved.

At last she sank into a doze, hovering gently on the borderline between sleep and waking. . . . For an instant she dropped off into unconsciousness; then she awoke with a start and felt that things were growing clearer. Everything in the house seemed to be in order. But she felt a vague, troubled curiosity to know where Per Hansa was, with And-Ongen and the boys. . . . Probably they had all gone over to Hans Olsa's? . . . Slowly the fragments of thought were finding one another in her mind, meeting and coming together, and taking on natural shape and form. A sense of well-being swept over her, so strong and healthy that it gradually calmed her senses and carried her off into a sound sleep.

She was awakened awhile later by dreaming that she had been borne upward in the midst of something soft and warm . . . in an infinitely large room. . . . "This cannot go on any longer," she thought. "If I rise any farther I cannot possibly reach home by evening time. I must get back immediately. Olamand's pants are almost worn out at the knees; I must mend them to-night or the boy will freeze to death." . . . Making a sudden exertion, Beret was instantly wide awake. . . .

And there stood And-Ongen leaning over the bed, stroking her mother's cheek with a cool hand and stretching up on tiptoe to get a better view of the little wrinkled red face in Beret's arms. Store-Hans was hanging over the foot of the bed, looking at them, while his father was coming in with an armful of wood.

"What have you done with Olamand?" she asked in a natural voice, turning her head and looking about the room.

"He's off with Henry and Sam, hunting wolf tracks," Store-Hans hastened to answer, happy because his mother was awake again. . . . "Won't you let us see Permand?" *

"Please let us see Permand," begged And-Ongen; she left off stroking her mother's face and beamed down at her.

As soon as Per Hansa had brushed the bark and splinters from his clothes he came over to Beret, took her hand, and held it silently a long time. . . . It was difficult for him to speak, but he managed to wish her a happy Christmas and to thank her for her gift. . . . He would not let her hand go, although her arm was growing tired.

No, he would not let it go.

. . . "Ah, Beret, Beret! . . . you know how to choose your time. Here you are with a great big boy at the very peep of day on Christmas morning! . . . Who ever heard of such a woman?" . . . He spoke with a tense quietness; his eyes were nothing but tiny slits in his face, from the great strain he was under. . . . She knew that his heart was crying.

The knowledge brought tears to her own eyes. She lay on her back, and the tears rolled down over both temples. But she did not notice them. A sweet, heavenly peace like summer enveloped her. . . . Warmth and stillness. . . . Sunlight. . . . An Arctic night. . . . Carol of birds. . . . A great sea was throbbing and singing close at hand. . . . Ah, it was good, after all, to be alive! . . .

Per Hansa suddenly found himself; his voice boomed out in strong tones:

"Away from the bed, there, you brats. Can't you see how tired mother is?"

Of that day Beret remembered little else except that

* *Per*, contracted from Peder;—*mand*, diminutive ending like the German *kin;* hence, *Permand* is equivalent to *Pederkin*. *Olamand* is formed in the same manner.

she was weak and tired, that a mildness like summer seemed to remain hovering about her, that songs rose over a quiet sea, that a tender sun shone down, that everything was as it should be, that all the world was good. . . . During the next few days she slept and slept, and never could sleep enough. She slept so much that there was no time left for thinking. Life in the bundle at her side grew stronger, demanded its dues, and would not be denied. . . . It was such a joy to tend him. . . . Per Hansa was always kind now; his eyes were mere short lines in his face as he went about his work; the children were full of happiness; all the people in the world were so kind to her that she could only lie there and be ashamed of herself! . . .

II

Ah, that newcomer! . . . Had the Prairie been possessed of the commonest hobgoblin sense, she would have guarded herself first of all against him. But this wisdom she had not. Glorying in her great might, depending on the witchcraft that had never failed her, she lay there unconcerned. And powerful though she was, the newcomer minded her no more than she did him. Weak and insignificant, he yet bore within him the talisman to set her direst magic at naught. For he beguiled the heavy-hearted folk into laughing, and what can avail against folk who laugh—who dare to laugh in the face of a winter like this one? . . . That winter it was *he* who saved people from insanity and the grave.

Beret began to worry and fuss, thinking they ought to have all the neighbours over on the thirteenth day after Christmas. Hadn't the good neighbours cared for them throughout the holidays, and long before Christmas, too, as if they had been their own kin? But, weak as she felt, she did not know how she could manage the preparations. She mentioned this matter the first time she was up.

Per Hansa thought it a splendid idea. . . . Couldn't he and the neighbour women manage the work? He went over to talk to them about it. Kjersti burst out laughing and offered to come for two weeks if they wanted her.

Sörine was delighted, too. Yes, indeed, they would come, if Beret would only promise to sit still and let them do all the work.

"Oh, there is a way of insuring that," said Per Hansa, with a roguish laugh. He had held Beret on his lap before now, and he was man enough to do it again. . . . "Be sure you come early, all of you!"

And so they came for dinner on the thirteenth day of Christmas, every one, and gathered in Per Hansa's cabin. Tönseten had brought one of the bottles which Per Hansa had carried home for him a generation or two ago. . . . The bottle appeared suddenly on the table, and none of the others knew where it had come from. But they soon guessed the secret; for Tönseten blinked secretively, hinting that his rheumatism was not so bad this winter. Marvellous climate here in the West! Had they noticed it? He felt so much better that perhaps *he* would dare to take a little drink, too. . . . Then there was food; there was coffee; there were the pipes; and much friendly chatting went on in Per Hansa's cabin that day. Time flew; the folks sat on into the night. At dusk the men went out to do the chores, each to his own place; they worked quickly that night. About the huts lay a thick, woolly darkness, black and heavy, with snow drifting softly out of the heart of it. In their hurry to get back to Per Hansa's, the men hardly noticed the weather.

All felt closely drawn together that night. Their chatting became singularly intimate and hearty. When the men returned, there was another bottle on the table, not more than half full. None of them had brought it, and none could guess where it had come from.

"Isn't it remarkable," marvelled Tönseten, "that such things can spring up out of the very ground? This is truly the Promised Land! . . . Ah, that is Beret's work, now. . . . I know the bottle!"

As they sat there chatting through the long evening, they talked of the newcomer—and again of the newcomer—the first newcomer who had found his way to the Spring Creek settlement. Everyone was aware of the many extraordinary things connected with his arrival. . . . Cunningly he had chosen his time—the high and holy Christmas morn! . . . Besides, he had the caul on when he came. . . . And his father had ventured to give him that bold second name . . . *Victorious*—that was not at all a human name! . . .

Tönseten thought that Per Hansa had been reckless and had gone too far in giving the boy that second name. Per Hansa must remember that he himself was only a human being. . . . Where had he been on Christmas night, for instance? That was a thing Tönseten would like to know! He wasn't outside, and he wasn't inside. . . . Tönseten had said a good many things like this to Kjersti when he had first heard about the name.

But that was one time when Tönseten should have kept still! . . . Kjersti had been very angry with him and let him know that it was both right and proper for an unusual child to have an unusual name. So much Tönseten could stand; but what came next was harder to swallow. Kjersti had talked herself into a fit of crying—all about how lonely it was to sit there month after month without ever having anything to give a name to! He was wise enough about other people's children, but she hadn't seen him do much toward getting one himself. What did he think he was made for, anyway? . . . Well, perhaps not, Syvert had said; and he had added, viciously: Did she suppose that *he* could bear children? . . . Oh, he could talk like a fool . . . he could . . . she had cried, stamping her foot on the floor. He could do anything but what he ought to! He was good for nothing in the world, the weak-kneed loafer!

But that episode was forgotten. Now they sat there rejoicing over the newcomer. They all felt themselves to be shareholders in him, but they couldn't agree over the division. . . . The boy undoubtedly belonged to Beret and Per Hansa—that was true enough and as it should be. But it didn't follow from this that they possessed the sole and only rights in him. Had not Sörine and Kjersti stood by while the ship sank? Now, hadn't they? Hadn't they been the sponsors? Did not godmothers have a strong claim on their godchildren? . . . And hadn't Hans Olsa been called out into the cold, grey Christmas morning to take upon himself the holy duties of priesthood? It was he, indeed, who had poured the baptismal water and read the words that should sound over every Christian mortal! . . . All this was beyond dispute, and no one grumbled over Hans Olsa's prior right to the child. . . . But, just the same, protested Tönseten, it was hardly fair play, either to him or to the Solum boys. Not one of them had had a moment's peace on Christmas night; they had just been kept wading back and forth in the snow, for the sake of that confounded baby. For his own part, he hadn't tasted a mouthful of food all day, and hadn't taken his trousers off all night! . . . Tönseten refused to be set aside; in the midst of the company, with all his friends around him, he was less afraid of Kjersti. A sudden fancy struck him—he began teasing Sörine about the name. It was in *his* honour, of course, that the boy had been given that second name, and not in her honour at all! But Tönseten should have been more careful in raising this issue. Sam immediately struck in, insisting that Per Hansa must have taken the name from *him*—he had *two* names beginning with "S"!

. . . No, they could not agree over their claims. Nor did they fare any better when it came to determining the newcomer's destiny.

Henry, with an idea of eventually getting rid of his job, wanted the boy to be a schoolmaster. . . . But no, the godmothers wouldn't listen to the proposal. Schoolmaster! As if that were good enough for such a boy! Besides, they already had a schoolmaster. At this point Kjersti lifted up her voice and announced that he should be a minister. Then Sörine laughed and winked at her husband. Minister? . . . Oh, they already had a minister, too—one of a sort; the boy had been baptized quite in the proper Christian manner! . . . As far as she could see, the newcomer would have to be a doctor. But this proposal started Per Hansa up with a new objection. Hadn't they doctors enough already, too? . . . There was Kjersti, and there was Sörine, and here he sat *himself*. Why, they had nothing but doctors! . . . Sam made them all laugh with his two suggestions: either a hymn writer or a general. . . . It must have been the latter alternative that gave Tönseten his big idea. He had been sitting there craftily pondering how he might outdo the whole of them. Now he arose, knocked the ashes from his pipe, cleared his throat mightily, and said, as if the thing were foreordained and altogether beyond dispute:

"The boy will, of course, be President! He is born in the country—everything points in that direction."

This ridiculous fancy threw them into gales of laughter. But Hans Olsa did not join in the merriment; he remained grave and sat gazing thoughtfully at the wall. Now he stretched, and said, as soon as he could be heard:

"I think we'll be more in need of a good governor out here, Syvert; these prairies will be a state some day."

And there the discussion ended. All felt that at last Hans Olsa had proposed something that bore the stamp of good sense.

Neither Beret nor Per Hansa had taken part in this discussion. They sat listening to it, full of secret elation. . . . Beret's cheeks burned; Per Hansa was on the point, once or twice, of putting in his oar, but managed to stop himself in time. . . . This was the proper occasion for him to hold his tongue. . . . What fun it was to hear them run on! . . .

III

No one knows what might have happened to them that winter if they had not had their school to fall back on. . . . But there it was—a great school, too, a refuge for them all.

At first it was held in the house of the Solum boys, and the plan worked out very well. But then it occurred to Sörine that they ought to find a more practical arrangement. Henry might just as well conduct his school in her house; in which case both she and Hans Olsa could benefit by the instruction. And Sam could come over, too. Both the Solum boys were pleased with the new plan.

A little later, when Beret was quite well again, Per Hansa came one day to inquire if it mightn't be possible to move the school to *his* house every other week—for Beret's sake. It would be interesting for her to listen to the instruction; and, besides, both of them needed to learn English. Why couldn't Henry teach his school just as well over there? . . . They all agreed that this was the thing to do.

But Tönseten, as usual, wasn't quite satisfied with the arrangement; he felt that they weren't being entirely fair to him. So he proposed that they should move the school to *his* house every third week. There was plenty of food for both Henry and Sam. True enough, he had no children; but they should remember that he had fathered the school itself. Think how lonely it was for him and Kjersti to be moping in the hut all by themselves while the others every other week were enjoying company and the glory of learning! . . . Why not be brotherly and share the best with the worst? . . .

Again the new plan was agreed upon, and that became the final arrangement for holding the school.

There was little to do, either outdoors or indoors, during these days. Often the menfolk would sit in the school both morning and afternoon, and the women made a practice of attending every afternoon. They came with their handiwork, and the men with their pipes. At last the school became indispensable to all of them. The men could not bear to lose a minute of it; and as for the women, as soon as they had cleared away the dinner things they would bundle old skirts over their heads and set out in the snowstorm for the house where the school was being conducted.

Never, perhaps, was a school organized along stranger lines, or based on looser pedagogical principles; but—ah, well! It was in reality a flexible institution, with all sorts of functions. It served as primary school and grammar school, as language school—in both Norwegian and English—and religious school; in one sense it was a club; in another it was a debating society, where everything between heaven and earth became fit matter for argument; on other occasions it turned into a singing school, a coffee party, or a social centre; and sometimes, in serious moods, it took on the aspect of a devotional meeting, a solemn confessional. In these ways the school bound subtly and inseparably together the few souls who lived out there in the wilderness. . . . It often happened that both recitation and instruction were broken up for the children because the grown folk interrupted, became absorbed in the discussion, and usurped the whole time.

In the beginning Henry was at his wits' end to know how to fill in the day. There were no books, and no school materials of any kind. In this pass, he resorted to the means that lay nearest at hand—story-telling. Hunting through his memory, he sought out all the tales that he had heard or read; and these he related in either Norwegian or English, making the children repeat them until they had been memorized. In this way they learned both the story and the language—such as it was. Then he proposed to set them the task of writing words and sentences. A fine plan, if they only had something to write on and something to write with. . . . Hans Olsa made a large wooden slate for his girl, and gave her the last remaining stub of a carpenter's pencil which he had brought from Norway. . . . And now that Sofie had a slate, Per Hansa's boys must have something to write on, too. Their father took the two thickest pieces of log that he had standing behind the stove, and whittled each into an object intended to be a writing board; but Ole called his an ox yoke, because it was so heavy to carry around. For pencils they used nails and bits of charcoal. . . . But one day when Store-Hans went on an errand to Kjersti's house, she had a present for him—a great bunch of folded paper bags and wrapping paper. . . . And in the chest she had found a small piece of pencil that Syvert had hidden there. . . . She supposed she would have no use for it herself, she said with a sigh, and she knew of no one she would rather give it to than Store-Hans, for he was a fine boy. She wept a little as she gave him these simple things. Store-Hans was delighted with the gift, and on this account he was for a while the aristocrat of the school.

Before the school became itinerant it had been discovered that Sam could sing. The discovery had come about in the following manner: One day Henry had completely exhausted his knowledge and ingenuity and didn't know what to do next; suddenly he turned to his brother, who sat on the chest listening to the instruction, and ripped out:

"Let's go east, man, and get out of here! . . . This is the devil's own foolishness!"

"Why don't you try singing with them?" Sam answered, bouncing up from the chest with the excitement of his idea.

"I'll leave that job for you," snapped Henry, snatching his cap and running out of the room.

And there stood Sam, looking blankly at the children, whose eyes were fixed on him with an equally blank stare. He couldn't bear to be the object of their ridicule; there was no one else in the room; no other idea came to his rescue; and so he began to sing. He had a good voice, and found himself falling naturally into the methods by which he had been taught. It all came back to him, and because his singing was really good, the scholars caught fire at it and the new idea worked well.

Perhaps this incident saved the school at a critical time. But it did vastly more. That winter they learned to sing many songs. The children learned them, and the grown people learned them, too. There were hymns and national anthems; there were folk songs and war songs; and there were many, many love songs from their own Nordland, with not a few Swedish love ballads as well. . . . By the time the school had become itinerant, Sam had acquired two good assistants; for now it appeared that both Sörine and Kjersti possessed in memory a goodly store of ditties. . . . Everything of that nature was routed out from its hiding place and put into active use.

Tönseten became at times a troublesome listener at these functions. If, as he sat there following Henry's instruction, he thought that he detected heresy, or if he disliked the method of teaching, he said so without mincing words. As to pedagogical methods, Tönseten was very particular. In his opinion, Henry lacked the proper and necessary cunning in formulating his questions; he put the matter too simply. What was the use of asking questions that anybody could understand?

Problems in arithmetic always had to be worked out mentally, on account of the lack of writing materials. One day as they were doing sums, Tönseten arose and informed them that now *he* proposed to try their skill for a minute or two! . . . "Just take a rest for a little while, Henry!" he said. The whole neighbourhood was gathered that day in Tönseten's sod house.

He struck a dignified pose in front of the table.

"Listen carefully now, you numskulls; here is something to try your heads on. Now then: five crows were sitting in a tree . . . five, you understand! . . . A man came by with a gun. He shot one of them. How many were left in the tree?"

Tönseten gave them a severe look as he finished his question.

"Huh!" grunted Ole, who was the brightest student at sums, "you are only fooling!"

"*That* is no problem," said Sofie. "There were four crows left, of course."

"Yes, if they were such dumb crows as you and Ola! . . . Now, Hans, how many were left?"

"None," answered Hans, thoughtfully.

"Right-o! There were none left. . . . But say, Hans, what do you think became of the others?"

"Aw . . ." drawled the boy in his deep voice, "I suppose they flew away."

"Sure they did! . . . Why should they keep on sitting there?" . . .

Tönseten was in a sparkling humour.

"Now we will just try another one. Listen hard now, Sofie; this one is for you. The minister had three daughters, and the deacon also had three; but when the deacon's daughters were with the minister's daughters, there were no more than three. How can that be explained?"

The problem was simply senseless, laughed Sofie; when there were six, there simply must be six, and no way out of it! . . .

"Don't listen to him," said Ole. "He's only fooling!"

"Fooling!" thundered Tönseten. "It seems to me that you are doing the fooling. . . . Well, Hansy, you will have to go at it again!"

None of the grown people had heard this riddle before. They laughed heartily and thought it great fun. Kjersti's knitting sank into her lap. . . . No doubt about it. Syvert was clever at asking questions!

"Hans," said Tönseten, sternly, "put your brains to work!"

"I—I suppose there was only one man with daughters?" submitted Store-Hans, carefully.

"Did you ever see the like of the cleverness in that boy! . . . Yes; you see, the fact of it was that the minister was a deacon in his own church. Very likely there wasn't anyone else who could serve as deacon!"

Tönseten gave Store-Hans a fatherly pat on the head. . . . "There's much good stuff inside that skull of yours. I think you'll be a minister, after all."

And then Tönseten straightened up and turned to face Henry. . . . "*That's* the way to ask questions, Henry!" . . . His face was red from his efforts; he looked ridiculously fierce as he sat down.

IV

Drifting snow and cold . . . a yellow sky . . . grey weather . . . blizzards that lasted for days. . . . If it cleared off for an afternoon, the sun dogs were on constant guard. Everyone knew what that meant! . . .

The winter's supply of wood which the settlers had brought home was disappearing very fast—it had vanished like snow in a warm spring thaw. Now it was almost gone.

Hans Olsa had discovered a new kind of fuel that grew more and more valuable to them as their wood supply ran low. One day as he was clearing the manger of coarse hay which the cow refused to eat it had struck him that this cast-off hay might possibly be put to a practical use. Hans Olsa was a frugal man, who tried to utilize everything that came to his hand. Why wouldn't this hay make good kindling? . . . In order to avoid littering up the floor of the house, he twisted the hay into fagots before he carried it in. It made fairly good fuel, burning fast, of course, but flaring up like birch bark and giving off a fine heat. . . . At once he told his neighbours of the discovery, and they began to burn their hay, too. . . . But it had to be done sparingly; they mustn't run the chance of a cattle famine, in case the spring should turn out to be a long, hard one.

Yet these coarse hay fagots solved their fuel situation for a while.

Along in February, however, there was no way out of it—the fact confronted them that the men would have to go east to the Sioux River for a further supply of wood. The journey demanded great preparations and left little time for going to school. But it was decided that in spite of everything, Henry must keep on with his teaching. Since they couldn't leave the women alone under any circumstances, the school served as a good excuse for keeping him at home. He would have to be the guardian of the whole settlement while they were gone.

Both Tönseten and Hans Olsa thought it impossible for Per Hansa to make such a journey with oxen at this time of the year; they advised him to join forces with them. Then they could all work together, and divide equally whatever they brought home. This sounded like good counsel, and Per Hansa made no objection to it at the time. But for a day or two he went about his work pondering deeply. Before Christmas he had made a sleigh, such as it was. One night he asked the boys to help him after school, and, taking the oxen out, he began to train them for halter-driving. Heretofore he had used only the yoke, shouting "gee" and "haw," like everyone else in those days, who drove oxen.

He had bought his ox team in eastern Minnesota the previous winter, from a Swede who was glad to get rid of them because he wanted to buy horses instead. The Swede had bought the oxen from an Irishman in southern Iowa, and no one knew how many other owners the team had had. The Swede had called them "Tom" and "Buck," but Per Hansa had disliked the names. Bound on a great voyage of adventure as he was, his boats had to be properly christened. So he had gone about thinking for a while, and at length had named the oxen "Sören" and "Perkel." To Sören he had added the prefix "Old," so that the full name of the animal was Old Sören.* And sometimes, when he was in his very brightest mood, he'd prefix the same adjective before the other name,

* Both names are colloquial expressions, peculiar to the dialect of Nordland; they mean the same thing, *viz.*, Old Nick.

too, because that sounded more affectionate. This renaming was an easy process for the oxen, perhaps because the new owner had a temperament so entirely unfamiliar to the beasts; the hide on their loins showed with startling clearness that petting had been an unknown factor in their earlier history.

The boys and the oxen had immediately become firm friends, Store-Hans adopting one of them as his special charge, Ole the other. They scratched the oxen's heads, they rode them like horses, and soon the animals would come trotting after whenever they caught sight of the boys; and as they stood patiently with the children hanging around their necks, giving them a good scratching, and saying "Old Sören" to one and "Perkel" to the other, they must somehow have learned to associate this treatment with their new names, and the words must have sunk in. At any rate, the oxen always responded now when their names were called.

When Per Hansa that cold winter day took them out of the stable to teach them the new kind of driving, they were a pair of ragged and ugly-looking beasts. They stood in the snow before the sleigh and gazed dully over the white prairie, where the snow lay drifting. They didn't know what to make of their new harnesses. All went well for a while, but presently they lurched right into a snowdrift, and stood there motionless, sticking out their tongues and licking the snow. . . . This would never do! . . . Ole shot forward and began scratching furiously; Store-Hans did the same on the other side; and when the oxen had thought it over long enough, and the commands from Per Hansa had taken on a brittle tone, they threw themselves forward into the harness and yanked the sleigh out like a feather, regardless of how deeply it had been lodged in the drift. They kept on training the oxen every day, and got a good deal of fun out of it into the bargain. . . . At last it had progressed so far that one evening, as they unhitched the team, Per Hansa said to the boys:

"There, they are working out splendidly. . . . Now, if you two were worth your salt, you would take this outfit and drive to the Pacific coast for a load of fish for your mother and me!" The boys grinned and said nothing.

But Per Hansa had determined to make the trip to the Sioux River with the oxen. That evening he was very high-spirited and happy. . . . As they were going to bed and Beret was sitting by the stove tending the baby for the night, she said, "I suppose you must make this trip, then?"

"Well, yes, I should say I must, if you and the newcomer aren't to freeze stiff!"

Nothing more passed between them on the subject. Again Beret lay awake far into the night, turning her thoughts over in her mind.

This thing was terrible! . . .

V

The men delayed their trip for several days, waiting for the right sort of weather. The wind veered around uncertainly; the sleighing looked treacherous; the cold was simply fearful—it bit into whatever it could lay its hands on and would not let go.

At last came a morning which gave promise of a clear day. As the sun rose higher and higher a soft breeze began to blow, like the first breath of spring. It seemed to be the very weather they had been waiting for. . . . The men gathered together in a little knot to talk it over, wondering if it would be safe to chance it to-day. . . . Well, yes, it looked all right now, speculated Tönseten, peering into the sky and turning his quid in his cheek; but this sort of weather wasn't exactly dependable. Somehow, it didn't seem natural for this time of year. . . . "It has too sweet a face, I think!"

They had better make a start, counselled Hans Olsa. Already it was late in February; the spring thaw would soon be setting in.

"Well," said Per Hansa, "if we have any idea of bringing a few sticks of wood home before the haying season begins, we'd better get a move on. . . . All the same, I agree with you, Syvert. . . . It looks to me like a weather-breeder. But we ought to be able to reach the Tronders' before anything happens."

Then they began to get ready. There were numberless things to attend to, so that it was past ten o'clock before they set out. They had not burdened themselves with provisions, knowing that they would soon come to hospitable folk; but to be on the safe side they all carried a small supply of food in their pockets.

The four teams formed quite a caravan, each with its own sleigh, trailing in single file across the white plain. Hans Olsa, who had the fastest horses, drove in the van; then came Tönseten; then Sam; while Per Hansa's oxen, shambling along with him and his sleigh, drew up the rear.

The whole settlement was out-of-doors to see the caravan set forth. The children were dismissed from school for a little while; the grown folks left their work. . . . Store-Hans clenched his fists in impotent fury. . . . What foolishness! . . . What an idiotic arrangement! Here they had to sit indoors, he and his brother, in such fine weather, chewing over and over again the stories they knew by heart, while off went the men, bound for all sorts of wonderful adventures! . . . Father would be taking Old Maria along. . . . He might shoot a dozen wolves to-day! . . . Perhaps there would be smooth ice on the river, and a hole in the ice, and fish, and everything! And strangers to be met, and grown-up talk going. . . . Oh, what nonsense, to have to stay here! . . . His brother was in the same state of bitter revolt; that day the boys learned very little in school.

Beret had laid the baby down and gone out with the others; but just as the men were about to start she ran back into the house, her knees trembling under her. . . . The window faced the east and they were going eastward, but she could not bring herself to look out. . . . But what she felt was not exactly fear—was not the same fear that had gripped her the time before when he had left her alone. . . . This was a sense of powerlessness. . . .

The caravan crept away. Sleighs and animals grew smaller and smaller; at last they were nothing but tiny black dots on the endless white expanse of the plain. . . .

All went well with Per Hansa and the oxen. Once the heavy animals had started, they kept the track without any difficulty, and didn't lag very far behind, either. The snow was soft, and it soon proved heavy, slow work to break the track. The three teams of horses had to take turns at it. Though the weather still looked steady, the men pushed on as fast as they could.

Some time after midday the breeze settled down into a mild south wind; the snow was growing more and more soggy under the runners; the air seemed as soft as a May day; in the whole arch of the sky not a cloud nor the trace of a cloud could be seen; the sunshine almost blinded them with its radiant brilliancy.

This lasted without change until after three o'clock. So far everything had gone without a hitch and Per Hansa figured that in two or three hours they would sight the hills over by the Sioux River. But just then, chancing to glance back toward the western horizon, he caught sight of a black, billowy outline above the prairie, looming ominously against the sky. . . . Were his eyes deceiving him? He rubbed them and looked again; rubbed them harder and gazed intently at the sight. . . . Sure enough it was a veritable outline, the form of a low-lying dark cloud. . . . His heart pounded against his breast; he spoke quickly and roughly to the oxen. . . .

The apparition was moving out there—came rushing forward and upward with uncanny speed. The outline had now become a dark, opaque mass . . . it writhed and swelled with life . . . it seemed to be belching up over all the sky, like sooty smoke out of a furnace. Above his head the heavens were still clear; but under the rim of the onrushing cloud a bluish-black shadow had settled on the prairie.

The south wind suddenly died in fitful gasps, leaving a chill in the air. . . . A weird silence had fallen. . . . The thing in the west was possessed of baleful life. It shot outward and upward. . . . Sighs as if out of a cold cavern ran before it. . . . In a twinkling, the day had been swallowed in gloom. . . .

Those in the lead had stopped at the first warning. Hans Olsa had waited until Tönseten and Sam came up; when Per Hansa reached them, the three sleighs were all huddled together.

"It's going to strike us in a minute," said Hans Olsa, soberly. He was standing beside his sleigh, clearing the lashing-rope.

"Looks like it," answered Per Hansa, dryly. "If we ever get out of this—!" . . . He jumped out and followed Hans Olsa's lead, clearing his own rope.

The Solum boy said nothing, but worked frantically to get his rope untangled.

"This is what we must do," said Hans Olsa: "We'll pass a rope from sleigh to sleigh, so that we won't lose each other in the storm. Isn't that right, Per Hansa?"

"Yes, yes!" His sailor instincts were all alive. "It looks as if the storm would travel the way we're going. We'll have to watch the wind. . . . Whatever you do, keep a sharp lookout for the country we know on this side of the river. If we should sail past the Trönders', there'll be hell to pay. . . . Hurry up, now. Damn the luck, that we haven't got a compass!" The words tumbled out of Per Hansa's mouth in a raging flood.

Each man tied his lashing-rope to the sleigh, and gave the other end to the next one behind. Per Hansa ran forward to the Solum boy:

"All ready, Sam? Are you sure your rope is fast? I don't believe I'll be able to keep up with you. . . . But listen: don't give a thought to what lies *behind* you! Do you hear? Hold on like hell to Syvert's rope! It's a matter of life and death. Do you understand? . . . Now we must get a move on!"

Both Per Hansa and Hans Olsa—old Lofot-men that they were—had seen plenty of storms that made up fast; but nothing like this had ever before come within the range of their experience. Like lightning a giant troll had risen up in the west, ripped open his great sack of woolly fleece, and emptied the whole contents of it above their heads.

A squall of snow so thick that they could not see an arm's length ahead of them, a sucking noise, a few angry blasts, howling in fury, then dropping away to uncertain draughts of air that wandered idly here and there, swirling the light snowfall around the sleighs. High overhead, a sharp hissing sound mingled with growls like thunder—and then the blizzard broke in all its terror. . . .

VI

The storm howled and whined, driving the snow before it like giant breakers. A grey-black spume enveloped them, a raging cloud. . . . Instinctively, Per Hansa found himself peering through the murk, knitting his brows and squinting up his right eye—an old habit of his, born of the many times he had looked to see if the mast would hold!

A violent jerk came on his rope, so strong that he almost plunged forward. To save himself from being dragged off his sleigh he was forced to let go his hold. . . . "There goes Sam!" he muttered, grinding his teeth together.

The boat that he steered was behaving very badly; it wouldn't answer the helm; it didn't ride the swell like a seaworthy craft; it had no speed or power to lift itself over the rough waves. The oxen shambled and floundered along, veering before the wind; with every clumsy step they went more slowly; at last, with a great heave, they stood stockstill. Drawing their heads as far as they could into their short necks, they twitched their bodies a little, hunched their backs, and lowered their heavy rumps into the snow, to meet the force of the gale. . . .

There they stood!

"God Almighty!" . . . muttered Per Hansa into the storm. Quick as lightning the thought flashed through his mind: Run your knife into one of them, rip off his hide, wrap yourself in it, and let yourself snow under—it's your only salvation!

No, no, Per Hansa couldn't do that. Old Sören and Perkel had brought him and his family all the way across the plains; they had broken every inch of his fields; if he were ever to have a lordly estate, it would come about through the labor of these beasts. . . . And Old Sören had such kind eyes, and Perkel always came so quickly when they called him.

Per Hansa threw himself out of the sleigh and fumbled his way along the traces till he came to the oxen; he caught hold of their necks and began rubbing their foreheads. While he rubbed, he talked into their ears:

"Now, Old Sören . . . now, damn you, Perkel. By God, you'll have to be good boys!" . . .

With rough caresses he swept the snow off their backs, scratched their rumps a moment, then crept back into the sleigh. Summoning all his force, he shouted in a mighty voice, "Get along now, you devils!" The whip lashed and cracked—the first time since he had bought them that he had ever struck them in real earnest. . . . The oxen gave a tremendous plunge . . . another . . . and off they careered into the heart of the storm. Per Hansa felt as if he were sliding down one huge wave after another; the boat was scudding now with terrific speed! . . . Still on they went, tossing and plunging, down and down! . . .

"Will we ever climb the next wave?" thought Per Hansa.

. . . Why, what in Heaven's name was this? Something had happened very suddenly. He thought that he heard a loud crash, as if two logs had smashed violently together; through the murk he glimpsed a black object flying across the bows and disappearing astern. . . . Wasn't that another? And another? . . . Why! . . . He must be passing the other teams!

"Whoa! Whoa, there!" he bellowed down the wind. "Stop! . . . t-r-r-r-o!" . . . He was so angry that he nearly broke the lines. . . . "Who ever saw such devils! Stop! Whoa!" . . .

But the oxen paid not the slightest attention to him. The spirit of the storm had possessed them; they tore along like mad things; whenever they struck a snowdrift, they plunged through it so furiously that the snow thrown up by their feet and the sleigh was thicker than that which fell from above. Per Hansa could do nothing but cling desperately to the sleigh. . . . This mad race through the inferno of the storm lasted a long time; how long he did not know, but it seemed to him as if it had gone on forever. . . .

But finally the oxen slackened their speed; the wild gallop sank to a trot; the trot fell to a tired jog . . . and then they stopped altogether. He could distinctly hear their exhausted puffing through the roar of the storm.

Per Hansa scrambled down from the sleigh again and

managed to open one of the hay sacks. He tore out a handful of hay, plowed his way forward, and began to rub down the oxen with the dry wisp. . . . The storm was now so terrific that it was impossible to turn one's face against it. The stinging snow drove like icy needles and broke the skin. He rubbed and rubbed, first Old Sören, then Perkel; and when his strength was gone and he could rub no longer, he struggled back to fetch the hay sack, held it under their noses, and let them eat. . . . He stood there holding it so long that he grew stiff with the cold and with the piercing snow that stuck in his clothes like nails. . . . "Hurry now, hurry now, troll-boys! God be praised, you can still wag your jaws!" he spoke in their ears.

At last he got back to the sleigh, loosened the blanket, and wrapped it close around him. He emptied the hay sack and bundled it over his head. . . . Then he shouted a few vigorous words of encouragement to the oxen: now they must get along—now, by God, they must show what stuff they were made of! . . .

But the beasts had a different notion, an idea all their own: instead of rushing off as before, they began to saunter slowly with the wind, moving forward at exactly the same speed as when they were drawing the plow on a hot summer day. Per Hansa tried every means he could think of to start them up; he fumed and swore; he coaxed them and used all kinds of pet names; he grabbed the whip and lashed them mercilessly, but everything had the same effect, or no effect at all. The oxen sauntered along, dragging him and his sleigh as unconcernedly through the storm as if they were on their way down to the creek to drink.

It had now grown pitch dark; the night pressed close about him. Snow was not falling as thickly as in the afternoon, but the cold had become intense . . . it cut into his back like a heavy, dull knife; the wind had risen into a solid blast, so that he had hard work to keep his seat in the sleigh. . . . He sat there, huddled and freezing, and stared out into the blackness. So, this was his last journey! . . .

The thought only made him impatient. . . . God Almighty might have waited awhile longer, until they had seen how their luck would go out here and what sort of a boy Permand would turn out to be. . . . It was a queer thing that He should want to be so cruel to Beret—a sick woman left alone in this terrible place, so far out in the wilderness—and without the oxen, too! . . . A strange fate, this, I'll be damned if it isn't! thought Per Hansa.

. . . By and by he began to feel that he was really freezing. He tied the lines about his thighs and took to beating his arms. It helped his hands, but his back only grew colder; the wind cut through and through. . . .

. . . It seemed to him that by this time he must have gone by the Trönders'—a long way by. The oxen wouldn't stop until they had reached the Atlantic Ocean! . . . He was so cold now that his teeth chattered all the time and couldn't stop.

. . . Then, after a while, the cold seemed to be letting up; the terrible sucking emptiness inside him had gone away; he felt tired and drowsy . . . a good feeling. . . .

He pulled himself furiously together and deliberately chewed his tongue to keep awake. He knew too well what this drowsy feeling meant! . . .

. . . It must not happen—it *should* not happen! To think of Beret alone there with four youngsters! . . . Making a desperate effort, he flung himself out of the sleigh and staggered along beside the oxen, the lines wound securely around his arm.

. . . Struggling through the storm, he felt more and more disgusted with God Almighty. To take him away from Beret now would be a wicked thing, whichever way you looked at it. . . . What could He expect to accomplish by such a wrong? . . . There wasn't a better, truer soul alive than Beret. . . . Was this the way God cared for His own?

"Beret, Beret," he kept sobbing to himself. "I'm going . . ."

The storm raged around him; the cold bit deeper and stronger. He staggered on in the midst of a vast darkness, beset by furious monsters, fighting a battle that seemed to be without respite and without end. . . . On and on he stumbled, on and on. . . .

Strangely enough, he didn't seem tired at all—the fight didn't exhaust him. . . . What sort of a place would he get to if he kept on travelling like this a week or two? . . . A name occurred to him as if it had risen out of the storm—he seemed to see it shining before his eyes: *Rocky Mountains* . . . The Rocky Mountains? What a strange fancy! . . . Floundering through the snowdrifts, this name seemed to be broken in pieces as it ran through his mind: Rocky-ocky-Moun-tains! . . . Rocky-ocky, rocky-ocky . . . Moun-tains, moun-tains! . . . Then he fell down; pulling himself wearily out of the snowdrift, another thought crossed his mind. . . . It was all a mistake—the Rocky Mountains didn't lie in this direction. . . . God! was he going stark mad? . . . He probably wouldn't be able to last much longer. . . . How sweet it would be—what a blessed, infinite relief—to sit down here in this snowdrift and rest a little while! Only a moment . . . it wouldn't take long . . . sleep would so soon overcome him.

Suddenly he was aroused by a new thought that shook him wide awake and stirred his numbed senses: *Sam!* What had happened to Sam? They couldn't leave him in the lurch. . . . Sam was a promising boy. He'd probably make a splendid citizen some day, with his fine voice and all his other good qualities. . . . God above, was he, Per Hansa, going to be blamed for this, too, that Sam would lose his life to-night? . . . If he had kept his mouth shut that evening and let them go on their way, both Sam and Henry might now have been safe and sound in eastern Minnesota with their own folks! . . . But perhaps those who had horses would be able to pull through, since the storm wasn't growing any worse. If only they didn't desert the boy!

Per Hansa was stumbling and falling a good deal now; each time he fell it was harder to get up. The lines were jammed tightly around his arm; the oxen plowed onward without a pause; he had to get up or be dragged through the snow. Neither could he loosen the lines, for his mittens were frozen stiff. . . . Rocky-ocky Moun-tains, Rocky-ocky Moun-tains! . . . Directly behind those mountains lay the Pacific Ocean. . . . They had no winter on that coast . . . no winter, and they fished both halibut and salmon! God! no winter! . . . If he could only gain his way across . . . across the . . . Rocky-ocky Moun-tains! . . .

. . . The devil take it! . . . but this was all wrong!

Steadily onward the oxen plowed, dragging Per Hansa by the arm. Stumble and fall as he would, he had to get up again and struggle along. . . .

. . . What had happened now? The oxen had stopped —were standing still. Per Hansa wasn't being dragged forward any longer.

His first impulse was to sink down where he stood, to snatch a moment's peace, to give up to the weariness that was overmastering him. But deep down within him a voice commanded him to keep on standing. . . . He followed the lines, fumbled his way forward to Perkel, flung his arm across the animal's back, and leaned against his thigh. . . .

What nonsense was this? . . . Day breaking again? . . . Between the heads of the two oxen a yellow eye seemed to be gleaming through the curtain of the driving snow . . . a great yellow eye. . . .

"It must be my death signal!" thought Per Hansa. "Then I'm already across the boundary line!" . . .

Suddenly Old Sören gave a long-drawn bellow. The sound had scarcely died away when Perkel lifted his voice as if to second his comrade's motion. He put such a powerful effort into that bellow that his muscles strained and his whole body contracted. The noise shook Per Hansa out of his grim revery. He felt his way along Perkel's back until he had reached the animal's head . . . it was rammed full-tilt against a log wall! . . .

Here was the corner . . . the corner of a house. . . .

Per Hansa trembled so violently that he could hardly keep his feet. He saw now that the eye shining through the drifting snow was in reality the light from a small window in this log wall. . . . Good heavens! Had he plowed and plunged clear through to Fillmore County? . . . He found his way around the house corner, came to a door, flung it open without ceremony, and stumbled in.

VII

Per Hansa saw nothing as he stumbled into the cabin. The heat of the room seemed to flow over him in a great wave, deadening all his senses. The light blinded him; he could not open his eyes beyond a narrow slit; his face was crusted with snow and ice; his eyelashes were frozen together. . . . But he was conscious, with a deep sense of joy and relief, that this was a safe place and that there were folk around him again—Norwegian folk, his own people. . . . When he had first felt the build of the cornice, out there in the snowstorm, he had sensed instinctively that here lived Norwegians. . . . Out of the jaws of death he had walked in a single step into warmth and life and safety. . . . But it was easier to warm his body than to thaw out his soul. The reaction was too swift and too tremendous; he felt himself growing faint and dizzy and was barely able to stand.

"Give me something to sit down on, good folk," he heard a faint voice saying far away. For a moment, he thought that his senses were going to leave him. . . . He must hurry and say what he had to say! . . . "You'll find . . . two oxen . . . two good oxen outside. . . . Get them under cover at once! . . . I'm all right—but the oxen—!"

Some one shoved forward a chair. He felt vaguely that it must be meant for him, took hold of the back, and let himself sink down. . . . His frozen clothes crackled like sheets of ice, shedding a little flurry of snow.

. . . "There, I'm tracking up your floor! . . . but look after the oxen—the oxen——"

A hubbub of confused, excited voices rose around him. He felt that there must be a crowd of people in the room, but their faces were all a blank to him. A thick haze seemed to surround them, swimming before his eyes.

Then a person got up right by his side—a palpable figure confronted him. Per Hansa gave a start—the voice sounded strangely familiar.

"For the Lord's sake! Is this you, Per Hansa?" it said.

All at once Per Hansa burst into a laugh.

"Where the devil did you drop from, Syvert? . . . Is Sam with you?"

"Can't you see the boy? . . . He's sitting in the chair right in front of you. . . . Thank God, Per Hansa, you're still alive!"

No wonder that they had failed to recognize him, no wonder that he couldn't see, or that his voice sounded weak and strange, for his whole face was covered with a mask of hard-caked snow which had not melted yet in the heat of the room. It was firmly fastened to his eyebrows and beard; it joined his cap to his coat collar and hung down behind over his back in a white sheet. If ever there was a snow king in human form, it was Per Hansa that night as he sat thawing out in Simon Baarstad's cabin.

Little by little his five senses came back to him; and sure enough, there they all were, his good neighbours. He knew the room well, too, and the folk who owned it. . . . He could see Sam plainly enough now—Sam, who could sing so well, sitting close to the stove, beside a fair young girl. . . . He couldn't make out whether he was closer to the girl or to the stove. Per Hansa smiled to himself. . . . Ah, Sam, Sam! . . . No doubt about your being a good man some day! . . .

He listened in deep contentment while Hans Olsa related how they had driven like demons, to save their lives. They had had no idea where they were going nor what lay ahead of them; but at the last moment, when they had almost given up hope, they had gotten their bearings of the country on this side of the river and had arrived at this very spot. That had been two hours ago; it was now past nine o'clock. . . .

Per Hansa heard them as if in a dream. The terrible trip didn't concern him any longer. It was all over now. . . . Something else that was going on in the room interested him a great deal more: beside the stove stood Gurina Baarstad, handling a stewpan. She had filled it over half full of milk; when the milk began to simmer she added a goodly portion of strong, home-brewed beer.

"My dear, blessed Gurina, don't be stingy, now!" Per Hansa teased her. The hot mixture was strong, brown, and frothy. They gave him a large bowlful; he drank and drank. . . .

"God, if a fellow had thirteen barrels of this stuff of yours, Gurina! . . . You don't happen to have another little drop in the pan?" . . . She gave him a second bowlful, which he emptied as greedily as the first. . . . All at once, something occurred to him. He turned to ask a question. . . . Had any of them seen him drive past them in the storm?

Drive past them! . . . "You're talking wild, Per Hansa," said Tönseten, with an anxious look. Per Hansa was off his base to-night!

—Certainly not—nothing wild about that! They had better take a look at Sam's sleigh to-morrow, if they didn't believe him. He had almost run Sam down as he shot by . . . "Say, didn't you see me, Sam?"

Well, Sam remembered that he did see something go by—something black, that flew past like a wraith of the storm. It had been just after the squall broke. He had felt a terrific jolt go over the sleigh and thought he had struck a stone. . . . "Was that you, Per Hansa?"

"Ha-ha! You're damned right! That was my flying oxen passing your good-for-nothing old plugs."

—But where, in Heaven's name, had he been in the meanwhile?—asked everyone at once.

—Yes, they had better wonder about that! . . . Per Hansa was gay once more; he tipped up the bowl rakishly and tried to squeeze another drop out of it.

"If you want to know, I took a little run up to Flandreau to see if I couldn't find a good-looking bride for Henry. I thought that was the least I could do for him, poor fellow. His brother can handle such matters for himself, it seems. . . . Tell me, Sam, are you still as *cold* as all that?"

Sam blushed crimson and hitched his chair away from the girl.

Later a large bowl of porridge was set out on the table for Per Hansa, a mug of hot milk beside it. He ate and ate; it seemed as if he never could get enough. . . . Afterward there was much cozy talk, everyone in the house joining in; they discussed all that had happened so far, and all that was going to happen. . . . Oh, this country had a great future! People who were willing to work could win almost anything out of it! No doubt about that at all!

At last it came time for them to retire. The members of the family lay down in their beds; the strangers slept on the floor, which had been piled deep with hay and covered with many thicknesses of clothes; all four men lay there side by side, and three of them soon slept the quiet sleep of the righteous. . . .

But Per Hansa could not sleep; his mind was numb with weariness, yet he could not sleep. Every nerve of his body was twitching; little spasms passed over him, like ripples on the surface of a smooth, glassy sea. It was very hot in the cabin; the blanket grew so heavy that he had to throw it off. Something remained still frozen, deep down in the centre of his being.

A certain picture stood stubbornly before his mind: a sod house beset by the western storm, a hut with the wind howling around the corners; he could even hear the peculiar note that the wind always made as it sucked around one of these corners. The hut lay far, far out in the heart of the darkness. A woman was moving about there whose sad face was still full of beauty; she carried a child in her arms. Per Hansa's weary, wide-open eyes could see exactly how she held the child. . . . It lay wrapped in a blanket—a red blanket with black borders. . . . He turned over heavily many times, trying to blot out the vision; but the woman continued to pace up and down. He felt that he must speak to her, let her know that all was well—tell her to go to bed now, so that a fellow might have a little peace. . . .

. . . "God Almighty!" sighed Per Hansa. "How Beret must be worrying about me to-night! . . . She ought not to be so foolish. I've told her many times that there are no finer people in the world than these Trönders." . . . But his body kept on jerking; his mind would not let the picture go. . . . It must be cold in her hut to-night. . . . If the boys had only managed to bring enough wood into the house before the storm broke! . . . Surely they must have some heat, or she would not be walking the floor; it would be terrible for her in the cold. . . . He threshed and turned, but the picture followed him. . . .

Along the Sioux River, both above and below Simon Baarstad's place, there was already a considerable settlement, made up almost entirely of Trönders. For those days it was a well-organized community. Some of the folk who lived there thought of themselves as old settlers already; the first had come in '66. Most of them had a good start now, were living in fair-sized frame houses, possessed a good deal of land under cultivation, and were making a comfortable living.

And what adventures they were able to relate about the first few years! How they had had to cross the region that is now the southern part of South Dakota and go still farther westward into Nebraska, to have their wheat ground at the mill; how the Indians had come by in large bands, both winter and summer; and all about many other remarkable things. . . . *Now* there weren't any hardships or difficulties to be met with, said the Trönders; now there were people everywhere, the country was fairly settled, and town after town had sprung up out of the prairie.

Per Hansa liked to listen to these stories. There was about them a certain flavor of genuineness and reliability, as of human experience, and at the same time something that stirred his heart and made his cheeks burn. . . . Surely the things that a Trönder could do were not impossible for a Helgelænding! In olden times it had never been so, and it would not prove to be so to-day, either. . . . "Just wait awhile!" . . .

The next day was clear and still, but bitterly cold. Per Hansa, who on his first trip the previous summer had bought an acre of woodland from Baarstad on time payment, remained on his own lot, felling trees and loading his sleigh; the others went around to different places, buying what wood they could find. . . . The four men stayed in the settlement two whole days, and did not leave for home until the morning of the third day. By hurrying, they might have set out a day earlier, but to hurry seemed almost impossible.

No, it was hard for them to hurry. In many months they had seen few strange faces; this visit was too much fun to cut short. And the Trönders, who were a hospitable folk and had a long story to tell, would not hear of their leaving sooner. . . . The four were easily tempted. These were festal days; the strain of life had relaxed for a moment; and there were a thousand things to consult the Trönders about. Before they left they had ordered all the wheat and oats they would need for the spring seeding. Tönseten had even bought half a sack of barley, a fact which he carefully concealed from his comrades. . . . It would be soon enough to tell them when the time came, he thought. The Trönders knew how to make good beer from barley, and he had received careful instruction from Tommaas. . . . Just wait till fall came around!

Per Hansa, when he had finished making up his load of wood, wanted to try his luck on the river. He coaxed Baarstad until the latter consented to go with him. The two men went at it with a will, chopping their way through the thick ice, while the sweat rolled from their foreheads.

And then Trönder and Helgelænding fished together through the same hole, in the greatest comradeship and with the keenest enjoyment.* . . . At night there was fresh fish on the table, and the two old fishermen sat eating and rejoicing while they told tales of both East and West Lofoten and forgot everything around them as they went back into the past. Per Hansa thought that Baarstad was the finest fellow he had met for many a long day, and Baarstad felt the same way about Per Hansa. For the twentieth time now he had asked him not to wait too long before he visited them again.

As they sat there chatting, a boy came in to speak with the girl of the family. He seemed to be in hot haste, that boy—almost as if it were a matter of life and death.

—What was going on? asked Baarstad.

—Oh, Tommaas had company at his house, and they were going to have a little fun to-night. The girl bustled about, got herself ready, and went away with him.

* During the winter seasons at Lofoten, the two clans, the Trönders and the Helgelændings, had from time immemorial fought many a bitter fight.

Then it occurred to Baarstad that they might as well go, too. He told his wife to hurry up and get ready. . . . "We'll show these Helgelændings how Trönders can dance!"

Awhile later the three arrived at the Tommaas house. As they opened the door, sounds of a scraping fiddle, mingled with the loud tramping of feet, poured out into the frosty night. The house was packed full of people, both young and old. . . . A small lamp with a home-made shade, sitting on a log well up on the wall, tried to keep an eye on all the couples below; but the task was too heavy for such a weak glim. It had to be content with blinking down on the nearest pair. . . . The three new-comers found themselves quickly shoved into a corner, out of the wake of the dancers.

Per Hansa grew restless as he watched, though his rest-lessness was far different from that which had kept him awake the other night. . . . Remarkable how that fiddle sang! He had to admit that the man who played knew his business, even if he was a Trönder! . . .

"Well, I'll be——!" The exclamation had jumped out of Per Hansa before he could stop it. Here came the Solum boy, swinging past him with the Baarstad girl! . . . "Oh yes, he'll be a man, that Sam, if he keeps this up!" . . . Another couple came rocking past—he ought to know that fellow, if he would only stop whirling around. By God! it was Tönseten, tossing along with an apple-round Trönder woman! . . .

"Careful now, Syvert, old man! There are rocks and breakers ahead of you! What do you think Kjersti would——"

"Shut your mouth, Per Hansa! What are you standing there moping about?" Tönseten's face was fiery red; the dance whirled him away before he had time to say any-thing more.

Per Hansa began to breathe hard and fast; his eyes snapped with excitement, narrowing to little slits. Right in the midst of a flock of dancers a big head bobbed up and down, up and down, above all the others, like a buoy on a high sea. . . . Then Per Hansa completely forgot himself. "By all the frolicking seraphims, there's Hans Olsa dancing the schottische!" . . . Waves of spasmodic twitching passed over him, in time to the jigging tune; his eyes blinked rapidly. . . . He looked around for the Baarstads, saw them close at hand, and grasped Gurina's arm.

"Come, show me how the Tronders dance that tune!"

Forgotten was everything else now. With his arm around Gurina, he manœuvred toward the centre of the floor until he had reached his neighbour's side. . . . "Get out of the way, Hans Olsa! I want plenty of room to swing in!" . . .

At exactly eleven o'clock the party was over; Tommaas himself commanded them to stop. . . . No one knew how it came about, but, strangely enough, it was Sam who brought the Baarstad girl home. . . .

The next morning, long before daylight, the four men had left the settlement and were on their way back to Spring Creek.

IX

Sunday afternoon . . . a dim, lurid day . . . a pale sun flickering through the drifting snow . . . an everlasting wind . . . the whole prairie a foaming, storm-beaten sea. . . . Nothing else, to the very ends of the world. . . . The sun dogs were still on guard, one ahead of the sun, the other following. . . .

The whole settlement was gathered in Tönseten's hut that afternoon; a gloomy restlessness had taken hold of them, so that they could not stay at home. Per Hansa had bundled the newcomer up and taken him over; that completed the roll call. . . . Kjersti was serving potato coffee, with potato cakes; but for the coffee to-day she had fresh cow's milk, which made it not so bad, and her store of loaf sugar wasn't entirely gone. . . . Inside the hut the lurid daylight cast a pale, sickly gleam. From out the stove, with its crackling fire, bright streamers of warmer light played about the room.

A heavy mood lay on the folk—too heavy for potato coffee to dispel. . . . It was such a terrible, hopeless day out-of-doors . . and all the days were alike. . . .

Under the strain of this winter the courage of the men was slowly ebbing away. . . . As they sat cooped up in

Tönseten's house, they were discussing the question of how this place would look in two years, or maybe in four years—or even after six years had passed. See how many had come last year—this roomful, where the year before there wasn't a living soul! wouldn't it be reasonable to expect that an equal number of new settlers would turn up another year? They began to figure it out on this basis: next year *so* many, in four years *such* a number; until at last the country would be filled up and the folk would stretch, neighbour to neighbour, clear out to the Rocky Mountains! They foresaw the whole process and calculated correctly—but no one in that company believed in the calculation! They heard themselves speak, and listened to one another, but all realized that there was no fire in their words. . . .

"I don't believe Per Hansa is ready himself to swallow that story," thought Hans Olsa, but he raised no objection. . . . "God save them from making mistakes in their figuring!" ran through Kjersti's mind, as she listened in awe to Per Hansa and Syvert rolling up the total; but she was careful to throw no cold water on the dream.

. . . On a day like this it was impossible to believe in such fine fancies; they all felt it, deep down in their hearts.

But here came Tönseten with a question that made them forget everything else for a while. The conversation had died of its own inertia; no one could find a thought that seemed worth expressing. Then Tönseten straightened up where he sat on the chest, demanding to know what *names* Hans Olsa and Per Hansa intended to adopt when they took out the title deeds to their land.

"Names?"

"Yes, names! . . . That point would have to be settled clearly beforehand," Tönseten explained. "When the deeds were taken out, their names would then be written into the law of the land, and thereafter would be as unchangeable as the Constitution itself!"

. . . But they all had been baptized! How about Tönseten himself? asked Per Hansa, irritably. He couldn't understand why the name Peder Hansen would not be good enough even for the United States Constitution.

. . . This snobbish fastidiousness of Syvert's didn't fit the case.

Tönseten bridled at once and said that sarcasm was uncalled for. He was only, in the capacity of an old American citizen, giving good advice on matters which he understood perfectly. . . . "That's all!" . . . And when Tönseten threw the phrase, "That's all!" into his conversation, they knew that he was offended. . . . Besides, he went on stiffly, it seemed as if anyone ought to be able to understand this much: Hans Olsen and Peder Hansen—why, either a Greek or a Hebrew might bear *those* names! It would never occur to anyone who heard them that they were carried by Norwegian people!* . . .

Hans Olsa laughed good-naturedly, and said with quiet humour: "Then perhaps I had better call myself Olav Trygvason. . . . Wasn't there some one of that name?"

This made everyone laugh: Hans Olsa's shaft had suddenly torn a rift in their mood of depression.

"Well, well," chuckled Per Hansa, "if you want to be Olav Trygvason, I'll be Peter Tordenskjold! But then we'll have to rechristen Syvert, too . . . St. Olaf or Tore Hund.† How would that do, Hans Olsa? . . . If that wouldn't proclaim to both Jew and Gentile that we are good Norwegians, then I'm certainly up a stump!" . . .

* The practice of changing surnames has gone on extensively with the Norwegian-American. Among the common folk in Norway it is quite customary even yet for the son to take his surname from his father's first name; the son of Hans must be Hansen or Hanson. Likewise the girl; if she is the daughter of Hans, her surname becomes *Hansdatter* (Hans' daughter), which she retains even after marriage. When the Norwegians became independent landowners in America their slumbering sense of the historical fitness of things awoke, and so many of them adopted the name of the place they had come from in the old country. Hence the many American names now ending in —dahl, —fjeld, —gaard, —stad, etc. As the Swedes, and the Danes, too, had so many Hansens and Olsens and Johnsons, the change was really a very practical one.

† Olav Trygvason, King of Norway (995-1000); St. Olaf, Norway's martyr king (1016-1030); Peter Tordenskjold, the great naval hero (1690-1720); Tore Hund, St. Olaf's slayer. These names are household words with every emigrant Norwegian.

They were all laughing so hard now that Tönseten had to join them in spite of himself. . . . Then Kjersti and Sörine took up the question; the Solum boys chimed in and expressed their opinions; while the children were busy discussing it among themselves. But Beret sat quietly rocking the baby on her lap, and said nothing.

An earnest liveliness crept into the conversation. Opinions flew thick and fast. At last Sörine spoke up resolutely, as if she had made up her mind, saying that if she had her choice she would rather be called Mrs. Vaag, from their place name in Norway, than Mrs. Olsen.

This sounded so sensible and practical that all the others had to try the idea at once, with their own place names.

"But, look here, Sörrina," objected Per Hansa, "that wouldn't do for my wife! Your notion would make her Mrs. Skarvholmen*—and that nobody shall call her! I warn you!"

"No, that certainly wouldn't do for a Christian woman!" cried Kjersti with a hearty laugh.

"No, I suppose not," admitted Sörine, unwilling to give up. "But how about Mrs. Holm? That seems to me both pretty and practical. . . . I say, Beret, shall we all turn Baptists for a while?" . . . Sörine was laughing in her jolly way, immensely taken up with the idea.

Beret sat rocking the child. She had listened absently all the while, humming a quiet melody to herself. When Sörine addressed her directly she stopped singing and answered that it made little difference to her, if—she choked, and went on—if it was right for a person to take a name other than the one given in baptism. . . . But it made no difference to her.

Sörine grew serious over this point.

"I agree with you, Beret. . . . But here in this country we can't bear our fathers' names, anyway. It wouldn't do for me to sign my name as Sörine Sakkarias'-Daughter!"

* *Skarv* in this compound means cormorant—a rather nasty-looking sea bird; the word is often used in an adjectival sense about a deadbeat or person of low moral qualities. *Holmen* means the holm. Hence *Skarvholmen*—the holm of the cormorant.

"No," cried Tönseten, excitedly, "not if you want to be Hans Olsa's wife!" . . . Remarkable what a bright head sat on Sörrina's shoulders!

This matter of names brought on a long discussion. Hans Olsa, like the others, decided that his wife had made a practical suggestion; Per Hansa found little to say, but his face had a look of quiet elation. . . . He must speak to Beret about this, alone and right away! . . . He sat there trying the name over in his mind, first on her, then on himself, finally on each of the children. As he ran them over, the radiant light in his face grew stronger. . . . Mrs. Holm, that sounded well; Peder Holm, that had a fine ring! . . . Ole Haldor Holm! . . . Hans Kristian Holm! . . . Peder Holm—no, Peder *Victorious* Holm! . . . *Peder Victorious Holm!* . . . He rolled the name on his tongue, biting it off in three distinct parts, as if to enjoy the sound; then he got up suddenly, grasped the waistband of his trousers, and gave them a hitch.

. . . "Sörrina has got it right—that name is both pretty and practical. What do you say, boys—shall we adopt the plan?"

Per Hansa was plainly in a towering humour now; the note of it rang in his voice. There was no opposing him. . . . After that day, each of the two families in question had a pair of surnames. Among themselves they always used the old names, but among strangers they were Vaag and Holm—though Hans Olsa invariably wrote it with a "W" instead of a "V."

That night Beret sat quietly by herself. The chores were long since done and they had eaten their supper. The children were in bed. They had been very noisy to-night, in their excitement over the new name that Sörine had invented for them. But now they were all asleep. Per Hansa was getting ready to go to bed; he moved about abstractedly and took a long time over everything he did. He, too, was full of excitement, thinking about the name. . . .

Peder Victorious Holm—the words sang through his mind; he seemed to expand as he heard them. The song carried him forward into the great, imaginative future where he loved to dwell. . . . "Beret, please come to bed!" he begged, in a low, kindly voice. He caressed his wife affectionately, then went to the bed and lay down.

She returned the caress half-heartedly, as if reserving the better part of it. "Oh yes, I'll come pretty soon," she said, and remained sitting where she was.

She sat there a long time, holding the child in her lap and rocking it gently. Now and then she would open the stove door and stick in a piece of wood. Each time she left the door open a crack, so that she could stare in at the fire. Why did she have to go to bed? The night was long enough, anyway! . . . Well, now they had discarded the names of their fathers, soon they would be discarding other sacred things. The awful spirit that ruled the plains demanded all! . . . She had said nothing to-day. Why should she interfere, to spoil their pleasure? . . . Everything that she said, everything that she did, seemed to be wrong. . . . But, oh, it was a wicked thing that they were doing now! Not that it was any worse than giving the child that terrible second name to start with; for that had been almost sacrilege! . . . But perhaps she was mistaken, after all. Perhaps it hadn't been wrong. Perhaps she was going crazy. The old fear had come back to her to-day—that was why she had kept still. . . . Ah, well, God Almighty had spared her again; He must have some reason for it. . . . Now she could repent of her sins before He took her . . . He had been merciful enough to give her time for that. . . . But sitting here in this mood, she found it impossible to repent. She was only afraid—afraid . . . a timid child in a dark room.

The fire had burned out, but she hadn't noticed it until a draught of frosty air began to circulate through the room. All at once she shivered. . . . The memory of that stormy night some time ago came back to her vividly. The children had been over at Sörine's; they had not come home and she had been unable to go and fetch them. All that night she had walked the floor—walked and walked, until she could walk no longer. . . . And the following two nights had been no better. . . . Again she was overwhelmed by the terror that had visited her at that time. . . . She got up hastily and ran to the bed. . . .

But there was no sleep waiting for her. . . .

No, Beret could not sleep. She lay tense and quiet, thinking of people she had read about, who had been driven out into the desert that they might better please God. After a while she wept silently. If He would only remove the terror that hung like a dark cloud over all this land, she would try faithfully to serve Him even here. But under the shadow of that terror she could not live much longer. . . .

X

The days were growing longer with every one that passed. March came, and the winter seemed to be letting up a little. Per Hansa worked with a desperate energy. If the day was too short for what he was doing, he simply added a part of the night to it. And in the month of March he achieved something that is still told about in the legends of that settlement.

Every time he had visited the Trönders at Sioux River, he had heard fascinating tales about the Indians at Flandreau, where they had a large colony. Their whole winter occupation was trapping, from fall frost to spring thaw, and when spring came they would have large stocks of furs, especially muskrat, though they also trapped mink, fox, and an occasional wolf. They sold the skins wherever they could find a market, and took whatever they could get; but their best prices were no more than a fourth of what the same skins would bring in eastern Minnesota. The price of a muskrat skin was ten cents in this district—never more than ten cents; while in Austin, Minnesota, it would sell for as high as fifty cents. . . . A few people along the river had taken to buying furs from the Indians, and shipping them into Minnesota.

All these facts Per Hansa had heard more than once, and he brooded over them a good deal. Throughout the winter they had been constantly on his mind, but he had said nothing about it to anyone. Now March had come, there must be a great supply of furs stored up at Flandreau, and prices would be running high in Minnesota. . . . The railroad ran east from Worthington. . . . Every day he went about thinking of it; at night he slept with the idea; and all the while he grew more silent and irritable.

There were many things to consider—it wasn't an easy matter! . . . The plan that was slowly forming in his mind was to go alone and trade with the Indians, making what profit he could. God knows, he needed it! . . . And what was to hinder? Flandreau lay only forty miles away; from there to Worthington was perhaps another ninety miles; and there at Worthington stood the train, waiting for him! . . . The days were growing longer; there was nothing to do at home for a while; and the weather wouldn't be too bad for a journey. . . . Here were the furs; in Minnesota lay the profits. Any courageous devil could pull it off. . . . Peder Victorious—the name sang in his ears. Peder *Victorious!*

. . . But he had only five dollars in his pocket! . . . By taking Hans Olsa into the project there would be plenty of capital; that fellow wasn't down to hardpan yet. . . . Still, he couldn't be certain that Hans Olsa would look with favour on such a wild-goose chase. On the other hand, how could he take Hans Olsa and leave out Tönseten? . . . It would be a mean trick to shove him out in the cold. . . . And if the three of them were to join forces, one of the Solum boys would have to be in it, too—Henry, most likely, for he was much more mature than his brother. . . . But that would close the school. . . . And if everyone went, there would be a terrific protest; the women were all more or less timid and naturally didn't want to be left alone. . . .

No, he couldn't seem to hit on the right solution. . . . But it was a thundering pity for that money to lie right at his door—and he in need of another quarter-section of land, with numberless things besides! . . .

The first week of March went by.

One morning Per Hansa got up a little earlier than usual and looked out at the weather. . . . Turning to Beret, he said that this couldn't go on any longer, and stood waiting for her to ask what it was that couldn't go on any longer. . . . But as she made no reply, he had to take up his own story. Seeding time would soon be here—and he hadn't a penny in the world. . . . They needed many other things, a great many, both food and clothes. . . . It was time for him to think of some way of earning a few extra dollars. . . . He couldn't see any other way out of it.

As Beret listened, her heart tightened with apprehension; but still she made no answer.

Then he told her about the Indian colony at Flandreau and how a fellow could easily earn a few dollars there. . . . In the springtime those Indians did a rousing business, so the Trönders had said! . . . Didn't she think it would be a good plan for him to go up to Flandreau and look around? . . . It wasn't far away. . . . While he was asking these questions he did not look at her. Still receiving no answer, he went on hurriedly: Didn't she suppose she could manage with just the boys at home for a little while? The days were getting fairly long now and things were looking better all around. . . . His voice trailed off into silence.

Beret stared vacantly out of the window. She thought: It was true that they needed much; they needed *everything* that people ought to have. Most of all they needed clothes for him and the boys. She had nothing more left to patch with. . . .

. . . "I suppose we'll have to try to keep alive as long as we can. . . ."

That made him very happy. . . . Wisely said! He thought so, too. And now, never fear, they were going to find a solution! . . .

She caught the note of suppressed excitement in his voice. . . . No wonder he was eager to get away! If he would only think of the fact that others felt the same desire!

. . . "When are you going?"

. . . "Well now, Beret, I hadn't made up my mind. But if you think it's all right, I'd better set out to-day! I'm going to take the pony that the Indian gave me. The weather looks steady enough. . . . You'll have to take good care of that newcomer of ours!" . . .

This last remark might better have been left unsaid, thought Beret bitterly; but still she made no answer.

Half an hour later Per Hansa took his departure.

Late at night he reached Flandreau, found his way into a hut, and so saved his life for that night. . . . As soon as he had fed the pony the next morning he took it along with him and poked around the village to interview the Indians. He searched every face; but the one he was looking for and hoping to find was not among them. The savages watched him curiously, returning his stares. They recognized the pony, and seemed to know who Per Hansa was, too. He noticed this quickly and felt relieved. "This scheme is going to work out all right," he thought. . . . Then he followed the plan that he had formed long ago when he had first begun to think about it. Trusting wholly to his instincts, he selected out of the crowd the face that he liked best, beckoned the Indian forward, and uttered the one word, "Fur." As he did this, he gazed inquiringly into the man's face, but kindly, too, as if to inspire confidence in him.

The Indian understood at once. Of course he had plenty of furs! He took Per Hansa into his wigwam and showed him several bundles of fine muskrat skins. . . .

Per Hansa laughed at his success. With the stick he carried in his hand he wrote the figures "10" in the snow, and after them the word "cents." Then he drew an object which was meant to be a man with a bundle on his back. He pointed first to the drawing, then to the figures, and at last made a vigorous gesture toward the Indian; this amused him very much, and he couldn't help smiling as he went through the motions. But all the honesty of his heart managed to come out in that smile, and the Indian saw it. . . . A long period of bargaining followed, with many gestures, and much drawing and writing to be done in the snow. The upshot of it was that he bought as many furs as he judged he would be able to carry away. He arranged them in four bundles and hung them pack-fashion over the pony's back. . . . Per Hansa was still laughing when he left Flandreau.

"Well now, forward, in God's name!" he said to himself, steering his course toward the southeast, in the general direction of a hut where lived a couple of Hallings who used cows for breaking prairie.

He was gone for a whole week on this expedition. When at last he reached home he refused to tell how far he had travelled into Minnesota, or what experiences he had met with on the way. He was worn out and disturbed; such tales had better be left untold where folks were so easily frightened. . . . But he had brought home many of the things they needed—and even so, there were forty dollars left in his pocket! These he gayly counted out on the table for Beret, thinking to amuse her.

He remained at home two days. On the third day he left again. . . . "Understand, Beret, I've got to go and pay the Indian for his furs! . . . Now, don't expect me until you see me heave in sight!"

All together, Per Hansa made three such journeys; the last two took him only six days each; if there hadn't been other pressing things to attend to, he probably would have made a fourth journey. When it was all over he was able to lay one hundred and forty dollars on the table for Beret; besides this, he had brought things for the house on each trip—things that he knew she went about wishing for.

He had returned from the last journey with two frozen toes. These were giving him a good deal of trouble when he and the other men were forced to make the trip to the Trönders' for the seed. . . . It was necessary to get it home while the sleighing lasted; he was not even properly rested when they had to set off.

On that trip he went in company with Hans Olsa. He had a feeling that since they were going so far anyway, he ought to accomplish something besides their immediate errand. Casting his eyes around at Sioux River, he bought a one-year-old heifer from Gurina Baarstad. . . . The heifer was spotted red and white, and was therefore given the name of "Spotty" as soon as he reached home with her.

In all this going and coming Beret had said very little, either when he set out or when he returned. He couldn't help feeling the strangeness of it; she had recovered from her illness long ago, and seemed quite well, as far as he could understand. . . . She might at least have told him that now he was getting on like a man! . . . She would have acted differently if she had known, for instance, how he had ridden one time until he had nearly fallen from his horse with fatigue! And once or twice he had escaped death by a pretty narrow squeak—he had thought that his time had come. But then—better not tell her such things! . . . If she would only say something brave and tender to him! . . . "Ah, well, she would probably be in better spirits when spring and fine weather set in!" . . .

II — The Power of Evil in High Places

I

Per Hansa and the boys sat around the table, sifting the seed; the wheat lay spread in small heaps on the white cloth. This was important work and must be done with the greatest care; every little weed seed and other foreign substance had to be gleaned out. The seed must be *clean,* so the Tronders had cautioned Per Hansa; and now he was attending to it soberly, with infinite pains. If he found a shrunken or damaged kernel, he straightway threw it out—thank you, not that! The best only for new soil! . . . Full kernels will make the bin bulge. . . . "Be careful, boys! Be careful, there! Don't shirk your job!"

It was wonderful to be sitting here playing with these plump, precious kernels; never before had Per Hansa been so absorbed in a task of this kind, yet it made him thoughtful, too. . . . Here, then, was the start! These few sacks of grain would not only supply him and his family with all the wheat flour they needed for a whole year, but would raise many bright dollars as well, a great store of riches. . . . And more than that, seed for the next year, seed again for the year after, and thus down through all the years to come. . . . And always greater and greater abundance of food for the poor, the world over. . . . Here he sat playing with the good fairies that had the power to create a new life over this Endless Wilderness, and transform it into a habitable land for human beings. Wasn't it wonderful?

He began to think of the possibility of selling seed next year. No doubt there would be many new settlers by then, who would stand in need of such things. If he could only afford it, he would store the whole crop—seed wheat brought high prices. . . . Well, he would see; a good many things might happen as time went on! . . .

And here he held in his hand the very promise of all these wonders which were destined to take place! He recalled how the fairy tale started: "Once upon a time. . . ." Not much of a beginning, yet the most startling events would unfold as the story went on—strange, incredible things. . . . Yes, he would have to take every precaution with the seed. His face grew sober at the thought; he spoke in a low tone to the boys, repeating the admonition for the hundredth time: "Boys, look out, now! Didn't I just tell you to be careful!" . . . His wonder grew as he gazed at the kernels; there they lay, so inanimate, yet so plump and heavy, glowing with smouldering flame. It was as if each kernel had light within it—life now asleep. He thrust his hand into the sack and took out a handful of grain; it weighed like lead. As his grasp tightened, the kernels seemed to soften under the warmth of his hand; they squirmed and twisted, slipping against one another; they seemed to be charged with a delicate life that was seeking release. But when he opened his hand and stirred a finger among the grain, the kernels lay there as lifelessly as before—inert, yellowish pale, yet burning faintly with inner, golden light. . . . Reverently he lifted handful after handful from the table, and emptied it into the sack.

As the mild spring weather set in, a feverish restlessness seized him; the work on the seed was done and he could not stay indoors. . . . The chickens were laying finely now; he was finding as many as five eggs a day. They'd better begin setting the hens pretty soon; when fall came, they would have at least fifty fowl on the place! . . . Next minute he was over on the prairie, talking to and caressing the oxen, and feeling of their necks where the yoke would lie. . . . Now if the ground would only dry up! Per Hansa looked at it the first thing in the morning, and felt of it every night before he went to bed. To-day it had made fine progress. Good God—if the sun would only shine as warm to-morrow! . . . He dashed off to the neighbours, to see how the ground was coming on there. No, it was wetter than at his place, where the land lay higher. . . . I'll bet my land is going to be the first to dry up! he told himself.

Beret hadn't seen him in such good spirits since last spring. He walked so lightly; everything that had life he touched with a gentle hand, but talk to it he must; his voice sounded low, yet it thrilled with a vibrant energy; his eyes were drawn so narrow that they could hardly be seen. She felt a force that made her tremble, emanating from him; she tried to keep out of his way as much as she could.

And now the sun bore down on the prairie the whole live-long day. Bright and quivering in the forenoon, he swam through endless seas of blue; across the hazy afternoon he beamed caressingly; toward evening he opened wide his countenance; then the flood of light grew refulgent, only to die in splendour against a mysterious night which also had life.

As the fine weather continued, Per Hansa became more restless, but it only seemed to fill him with greater joy. Suddenly he would be up by the field. Wasn't it dry enough yet? . . . He ought to have had the seeding all done by now; it was high time to begin breaking new ground.

On the 14th of April, the *Sommermaalsdag* of his old fatherland, Per Hansa began seeding the wheat. Three times that forenoon he had been out to test the ground; the last time he made his great decision: *Now we will start!*

No sooner had he finished the noon meal than he rushed out, grabbed the seed bag that he had made for this occasion, and carried two sacks of seed up to that portion of the field where the ground was driest. He had paced off the whole field into one-acre lots, and marked each plot. One and one-half bushels of seed to the acre was the regular measure; but Simon Baarstad had told him that on really first-class breaking, provided the soil was unusually excellent, one and one-quarter bushels might do; and Per Hansa had decided to try the latter amount.

He filled the seed bag, hung it over his shoulder, and was ready. His whole body shook. He paused for an instant and glanced about the settlement. . . . Yes, sir, he was the first, the very first one! There was Hans Olsa hauling manure to his garden patch. . . . That's smart of you, Hans Olsa! . . . Down to the southward he caught sight of Tönseten pottering around his yard. . . . So much for *you!* . . . Then he turned to look in a northerly direction. . . . By God, if the Solum boys hadn't already started breaking! . . . Muttering, "Well, well, well," he strode over to the edge of the field and stuck his hand into the bag.

But just at that moment both boys appeared on the dead run; they had discovered what their father was up to, and wanted to watch the show.

"Go home!" shouted Per Hansa. "Go home! Do you hear me?"

"Why can't we stand here and watch?" the boys remonstrated, their faces gloomy with disappointment.

"Go home this instant! . . . I don't want you tramping around here, carrying off this precious seed on your shoes!" . . . He suddenly realized that it was very wrong of him to be so harsh with the boys in an hour like this. When he spoke again, his voice had grown kinder: "Sowing wheat is such a particular job—each kernel has to lie exactly the way it falls. Be good now, boys, and go straight home—and the first to wake up to-morrow morning shall start the dragging! I'll see to it that one of you covers as much ground as the other—but the first to wake shall start!" . . . With this promise the boys had to be content; they went off homeward in a rebellious mood.

Again Per Hansa thrust his hand into the bag and his fingers closed on the grain. He felt profoundly that the greatest moment of his life had come. Now he was about to sow wheat on his own ground! His hand tightened in the bag; he was on the point of lifting it out, when something queer happened—the kernels were running out between his fingers! He gave another grab, closing his hand still tighter; again the yellow kernels slipped through his fingers like squirming eels. Then Per Hansa threw back his head and laughed. These fellows aren't very anxious to go into the ground after riches for me! . . . He ran his hand around in the bag, stroking the grain caressingly, taking great handfuls and giving them a gentle squeeze.

. . . And now the wheat rained down in yellow semicircles from Per Hansa's hand; as the seed fell, the warm rays of the sun struck full across it, and seemed to wrap it in golden light. . . . Per Hansa restrained himself, working slowly and carefully—the seeding must be even and not too thick. But almost at once he grew very heated; his body was dripping with sweat. He couldn't explain this for a while; it wasn't hard work at all. Oh, well, he thought at last—that's always the way when you tackle a job you don't understand!

Late in the afternoon Tönseten came running up the hill, so hard that his heels seemed to be flying over his head.

"What in hell are you starting here, Per Hansa?" he demanded, breathlessly.

"Can't you see?" laughed Per Hansa; but he hardly dared to look at his neighbour, for fear he would lose his marks.

Tönseten stared at him in amazement. "You're plumb crazy, man, and I don't mind telling you so! . . . The ground isn't half dry enough yet for that—the soil is too cold! Why, damn it all, there's a foot of frost in the ground! . . . Much good it will do you to throw away all that seed!" . . . Into this last, Tönseten threw all the scorn of the man who really knows; in fact, he felt too seriously disturbed to utter another syllable; so, having done his duty and delivered his ominous message, he turned on his heel and stalked majestically away.

As long as the daylight lasted, Per Hansa kept on seeding. . . . After supper he sat at the table without moving; he didn't want to get up; a pleasant feeling of languorous exhaustion had settled on him, the reaction from his excitement. And-Ongen crawled up into his lap and begged for a story, but got no response; the boys came storming in, demanding that he call them both at the same time to-morrow morning. . . . No, he said in a dreamy, abstracted voice, that wouldn't do; there wasn't any hurry; better let the sun have time to warm up the ground a bit before they covered the grain. But the bargain still held; the one who turned out first, yoked the oxen and hitched them to the drag, *he* was to start the dragging! "And now," he added, rising from the table, "I'll tell you this, boys—if we are any good at all, we'll have the whole field seeded and dragged by the time the porridge is on the table to-morrow night!"

The next day Per Hansa worked like one possessed. Now that he had at last caught the trick with the seeding, he made fine progress. When evening fell that day he had finished his task, while the boys had done almost as well, with only the oats left to drag. . . . Per Hansa walked home that night in great satisfaction. Now he had turned a fine trick—he was through seeding and dragging before his neighbours had even thought of beginning the regular spring work! . . .

II

When Per Hansa left the house next morning to finish the dragging, the air was raw and heavy; a penetrating wind blew over the prairie, as if searching for signs of life to wither and blight; not a trace remained of the mildness and pleasantness of the previous days.

Before he had finished covering the oats, the rain began to fall; along with the rain came huge flakes of snow, floating silently down and turning to slush as they struck the ground. After a while the rain ceased, but the snow only came faster; the flakes were firmer now, and fell in a businesslike manner. Before long a veritable blizzard was raging over the whole prairie—there had hardly been anything worse that winter.

Throughout that day and the following night the storm continued with unabated fury. Early on the next morning the weather cleared; but now the cold was so intense that it nipped the skin as soon as one stuck one's head out-of-doors. Spring seemed a thousand miles off.

That night Per Hansa did not sleep a wink. How could

he sleep, with this tragedy going on? He was nothing but an old sailor; he didn't know the least thing about farming. God Almighty! hadn't he good reason to lie awake? . . . Here he had gone to work and wasted all his precious seed—had simply thrown it away, because he was foolish and hasty! And there wasn't even a chance to extricate himself from the mess he had made! Out in the field, under the snow, lay all that priceless wheat, smothered to death and frozen as hard as flint. . . . He could stand the loss of the oats, perhaps—but, God! the *wheat!* Twenty-five bushels he had sacrificed, all the work gone to no purpose, and no possible way of getting a fresh supply of seed. . . . As he opened the door that morning, saw two feet of snow covering the ground, and felt the bitter cold stinging his face, he had an irresistible impulse to fling himself down in the snowdrift and cry like a baby! . . .

He turned around, came into the hut again, and lay down on the bed. . . . No, he didn't want any breakfast! He shouted out the words. All the forenoon he lay silent and motionless. When noon came and he refused to eat any dinner, Beret went to the bed and asked him what was the matter. Did he feel sick? But he only turned his face to the wall, muttering hoarsely that those who felt like eating had better do so. Leave him alone; he'd be all right again—some time. . . . Beret began to feel concerned about him; after a while she brought him a bowl of soup, but he only sat up in bed and commenced to find fault with her like an unreasonable child. . . . For God's sake, couldn't she leave him alone? He had told her he didn't want anything to eat, and wasn't that enough? . . . Well, then . . . Oh, hell! . . .

In the afternoon the sun shone strong and brilliant, but the cold was too intense for it to make any impression on the snow. . . . Per Hansa was still lying in bed; the bright sunshine outside, reflecting on the white walls of the room, seemed to sear his eyeballs; he felt that the only thing that would give him relief would be to get up, strike out wildly, and curse everything around him—for he was fighting an unseen enemy. . . . He had come to his great decision; he had done the seeding; he had felt clearly that it was the most momentous day of his life;

but no sooner had the last kernel fallen to the ground than the very powers of heaven had stepped down to defeat him! . . . Powers of heaven . . . ? A certain image came before his eyes, and would not go away. One Sunday not very long ago, Store-Hans had sat by the table reading to his mother; Per Hansa remembered it vividly, because the words had sounded so awful to him. At last he had gotten up to look over the boy's shoulder; Store-Hans was reading in a loud voice, throwing great emphasis into the words:

"And the Lord said unto Satan, whence comest thou? Then Satan answered the Lord, and said, From going to and fro in the earth, and from walking up and down in it. . . ."

The words would not go away. Per Hansa fell to repeating them. . . . And that night as he lay wide awake, tossing restlessly on the bed, he thought that he saw a beam just inside the door of the stable . . . and there was a rope. . . . Well, if *that fellow* was after him, he might as well give up! . . . Sweat broke out on his body . . . the beam and the rope beckoned him . . . they seemed to call to him! . . .

The snow went faster than anyone would have believed; it began to settle on the day after the weather had cleared, grew soft toward evening, and the next day's sun took all of it away. It seemed to leave very little water; within a short while the ground was drier than before. . . . And now came days when the warm, bright sunshine filled everything between heaven and earth. As the sun sank, he left part of his heat behind him; the nights grew soft and balmy, and stirred with mysterious life. . . . At length evenings so sweet and beautiful began to visit the prairie, that, as the saying is, dead men might willingly step out of their graves and walk about. But all this could not alter the fact that Per Hansa's precious seed grain lay over there in the field, ruined by frost and snow—those marvellous, pregnant kernels, so delicate and sensitive. . . . Damn the luck! . . .

One day as Per Hansa was pottering about out-of-doors, hardly knowing which way to turn, he caught sight of Tönseten, who had commenced his seeding. Like a condemned man about to be executed Per Hansa walked over. . . . Tönseten is an aboriginal American, he thought, bitterly. I might as well let him polish off the damned fool of a newcomer!

But to-day Tönseten was too busy even to talk. Per Hansa didn't feel inclined to open up the subject of his own troubles; he began on a different tack, to head the other off:

"I must say you certainly sow it even!"

Tönseten spat a prodigious distance. . . . "You think so?" . . . But he didn't stop for a moment; his arms continued to cut wide semicircles in the air; golden grain flew out of his hand and rained down to the ground through the warm sunlight, there to begin the mystic dream of life.

This is beautiful! thought Per Hansa. . . . I couldn't sow it as even as that.

"I was a fool for not waiting to get you to do the seeding for me," he observed.

Tönseten spat another great mouthful before he answered:

"Well, some people are bound to cut off their nose to spite their face. . . . But then—this is a free country, you know!" . . . He walked on with measured steps, his arm sweeping in long, graceful curves; the kernels flew far and wide, catching the sunlight a moment as they fell.

Per Hansa turned abruptly, and began to walk toward home. When Tönseten noticed this, he stopped his work and called out:

"Did you want anything, Per Hansa?"

"Hell—no!"

"All right. To-day, you see, I'm a busy man!"

Per Hansa started to answer, choked, and continued to walk away. His head was in a whirl as he went on toward his own field, which seemed to be making faces at him as he drew nearer; it was indeed a forbidding countenance that he saw there, lifeless and black and bare. Reaching the field, he fell on his knees, dug into the soil, and picked up the first kernel he came across; he laid it in the palm of his left hand and turned it over and over with the forefinger of his right; the seed was black with clammy dirt, which clung tightly to it. Slowly and carefully he picked off the particles of soil—and there it lay, a pale little thing, greyish-white and dirty, the golden sheen through which he had read the fairy tale, entirely gone, the magic departed, the seed cold and dead. Per Hansa dropped it without a word, and dug in the ground until he had found another kernel. The one he now picked up had the same lifeless color, but it was swollen and seemed about to burst open. . . . "This is the frost!"—he mumbled, hoarsely. —"It's all begun to rot!" . . . He rose to his feet and stood there as if chained to the spot, the very personification of gloom, gazing out over the face of his dead dream. . . . *"Then Satan answered the Lord, and said, From going to and fro in the earth, and from walking up and down in it."* . . . There can't be much doubt that he's found *this* place, all right—the devil salt and pickle his guts! . . .

III

Over on the piece of field which Per Hansa had broken during the last few days the boys were now busy at work with the dragging. He had set them to the task early that morning, but had not yet made up his mind what to put into the field. Now he walked over to them.

One of the boys was driving; the other sat on the harrow, making grooves with his heels in the loose dirt; on each round of the field they exchanged places. They had quarrelled considerably over who could drive the straightest; now they were trying to decide this momentous question by judging the straightness of the grooves made on each round.

The boys stopped as they saw their father approaching.

"Isn't this piece four acres?" Ole demanded, boisterously.

"It should be," their father answered in a tired voice.

"All right," beamed Ole. "If we plant potatoes in the whole piece and get a hundred and fifty bushels to the acre, we'll have six hundred bushels in all!"

"Then we'll sell 'em!" Store-Hans broke in, his eye snapping.

"Shut up, you! This is my idea!" Ole turned again to his father and kept on with his arithmetic: "We can't get less than thirty cents a bushel, can we? I'll be able to help you haul them to town. And that'll be exactly *one hundred and eighty dollars.* Gee! What a lot!" The boy looked proudly at his father, and added with a grown-up air, "We ought to get the potatoes planted at once—that's my opinion!"

But then Store-Hans had a great inspiration, and flashed out:

"When we get as much money as that, just for potatoes, we'll buy a shotgun. Hurrah!"

"Stop your nonsense and get to work!" said Per Hansa, harshly. "You need a pair of pants to cover your bottom, more than you do a gun. . . . Move on, now, I tell you!"

On the way home that morning, Per Hansa realized one thing more clearly than ever before—unless he could find something to occupy his body and mind, and find it right away, he would go all to pieces one of these fine days. . . . Well, why not do as Ole suggested? Here was this piece of new field, and it had to be put to some use. . . . If *that fellow* was loose around these parts, Per Hansa might as well give him a run for his money! . . .

The minute Per Hansa reached home he opened the root cellar and began carrying out potatoes. He took out all that he judged they could possibly spare and began to cut them up into small pieces; he was determined to have enough seed to cover the whole field. . . . Oh yes, no doubt this was insanely foolish, too, but, damn it all, he might as well come to ruination at once and be done with it! . . .

The planting kept the three of them busy for the rest of that week. When Sunday morning came, Per Hansa rose at the usual time, ate his breakfast in silence, and then went back to bed. And-Ongen crawled into bed with him and stirred up a terrible commotion; he must wake now and tell her a story. Getting no answer, she pulled his hair and pinched his cheek and tugged at his nose.

The carrying-on of the child made a pleasant diversion for him in his dark mood. Beret sat by the table, reading the Bible. To his great relief, she said little these days. . . . As he lay there brooding he was turning over and over in his mind a new idea—mightn't he make another trip to the Sioux River? Perhaps he could yet scare up a couple of sacks of wheat there. The seeding would be far behind-hand, that's true; but barring any more bad luck, he would at least be able to harvest enough seed grain for another year. . . . But it was so late now—too late, really, to think of such a thing. Perhaps he had better go to Sioux Falls or Worthington and try to get work for the summer. Beret and the boys could easily get along without him. . . . No, he couldn't quite make up his mind as to what would be best. . . . All the while And-Ongen was pommelling him because he wouldn't tell her a story.

Suddenly a violent stamping of feet sounded outside; some one came running up, with another close at his heels.

Ole jerked the door open, took one leap, and landed in the middle of the floor. The boy was wild-eyed with excitement.

"Per Hansa!" he cried, calling his father by name. "The wheat is up!" Then he took another leap and stood leaning over the bed. "The wheat is up, I say! . . . Can't you hear me?" . . .

But now Store-Hans came storming in, all out of breath:

"Father Per Hansa—the wheat is *so high!*"

"You shut up!" raged his brother. "I came first!"

"I guess I can tell it, too!" Store-Hans paid no further attention to his brother; he was standing now by the bed, measuring on his finger. "The wheat is *so high*, the oats about up *to here!* . . . Don't you suppose we can buy a shotgun?"

Per Hansa said never a word; he got up, trembling in every limb, and put the child aside. In a moment he had left the house and rushed up to the field. There he stood spellbound, gazing at the sight spread before him. His whole body shook; tears came to his eyes, so that he found it difficult to see clearly. And well he might be surprised. Over the whole field tiny shoots were quivering in the warm sunshine.

Store-Hans was standing now by his father's side; he looked at him in consternation.

"Are you sick, father?"

No answer.

"Why, you're crying!"

"You're . . . so—foolish, Store-Hans!" Per Hansa was blowing his nose violently. . . . "*So terribly foolish!*" he added, softly, and straightened himself up with a new energy.

Store-Hans now began to feel reassured about his father. The boy turned to the field and spoke in a voice thrilled with delight:

"Isn't it dandy?"

The silence continued for a while longer. But at last his father cleared his throat. "Come here, Store-Hans!" Per Hansa placed his hand on the boy's shoulder. "What are you going to be when you grow up?"

"When I grow up?" repeated the boy, wonderingly. "Well, a general . . . one like Grant."

Per Hansa looked at him, a strange chuckling sound issuing from his throat:

"What about being a *minister?* . . . We need a minister more."

"Oh, well," said Store-Hans, indifferently. "I suppose I can be that, too. . . . Don't you think we can get a shotgun pretty soon?"

Per Hansa was a different man when he walked home; the spring had come back to his step. Entering the house, he sat down by his wife, who was still reading the Bible, and said, abruptly:

"You'd better read us a chapter!" Then he cleared his throat and looked around the room. "No more nonsense, boys! Come here and sit down quietly while mother reads to us."

IV

That summer many happenings took place in the settlement by Spring Creek. For those who had been here from the beginning, associations were slowly growing up outside of the day's work. At the very last of May the Irish arrived, with many new land-seekers in their company; they all settled west by the sloughs, so as to have access to water for the cattle. The first part of June the Vossings and Sognings put into port; they, too, brought many new homesteaders with them. The latter folk all settled east of the creek, spreading eastward and southward, to bring them nearer to town. Here the soil was first class, too; and Tönseten assured them that water was no problem, if they would dig deep enough. . . . Water! Why, good Lord! wasn't the whole earth surrounded by water? . . . Talk sense, folks, and get your houses built! . . . Soon one new sod house after another began to stick its head above the waving grass of the prairie.

Among the Sognings was a tall, heavily built man, with a light complexion and rather good looking, but loud spoken and given to bragging. All his words and actions had an irritating arrogance; he was always right; at times he got on everyone's nerves, because he talked so much and with such cocksureness. Luck had been with him, it seemed; he had received a considerable inheritance from the old country; while living in Minnesota he had cleared much land, which he had been able to dispose of at a fine price; rumour had it that he was worth as least three thousand dollars in cash, besides other property; and this report he did not deny. The man had a large family; his name was Torkel Tallaksen.

Not long after the arrival of this man, Store-Hans had a fight with one of the Tallaksen boys. It came about in this way: the boys chanced to meet down by the creek one day, as they were both out chasing the cattle, Store-Hans riding his pony, the other boy a common old work horse.

"Where did you swipe that pony?" the stranger shouted, challengingly.

"I didn't swipe it!"

"Where did you get it, then?"

"Oh, I just got it."

"Can't you tell?"

"Come here, if you want to know."

The two boys dismounted, looked each other over, then sat down and fell to talking. Store-Hans was eager to inform this tenderfoot of the mighty things they had done out here; he related how the pony had come to be his, giving the story a picturesque turn whenever he saw the chance. He and his father, he told the stranger, had rescued an Indian chief—well, it was the highest chief over all the Indians out West. This chief was dying; he was *almost* dead when they found him. . . . What was the matter? Well, there had been a terrible battle; the Indian had been desperately wounded—shot and left for dead. . . . But he and his father had cured him, and they had received this pony as a reward.

The other boy listened scornfully to the story, said "humph—humph" a good many times, and finally declared the whole thing to be a lie; people out here were such awful liars, so his father had told him! . . .

Store-Hans could hardly stand this accusation, for hadn't he himself helped in restoring the Indian to life? So without further ado he pitched into the other boy and the fight was on. It proved a tough battle; clothes were torn and both combatants sneezed gore. The bloody noses didn't matter much, for they could be washed; but it would be more serious to have to explain the tattered shirts. The boys fought it out, however; finally the newcomer had to admit that truth is truth and take back all he had said. This mollified Store-Hans; he let the other boy try the pony, and they became friends. But the same evening he had to tell the incident to his father; after the nose had been washed and properly cooled, it had taken on alarming proportions, which called for an explanation; this Per Hansa got as he sat on the woodpile, smoking his evening pipe, with Store-Hans standing near by.

All the new settlers that spring, with the exception of Torkel Tallaksen, built sod houses; but he had vaster plans in mind. He set up a tent, hitched his four horses to the breaking plow, worked like a beaver, and soon had broken a big field, considering the fact that he had just arrived. He had brought seed enough with him to plant the whole area. Rumours began to spread in the settlement about his plans; when he was done seeding he proposed to go to Worthington after lumber; both his living house and barn were to be built this summer. . . . Per Hansa listened to these rumours and cocked his head on one side, but made no comment.

One day just as they were sitting down to the noon meal at Per Hansa's, Torkel Tallaksen swaggered in and asked in a loud voice if he could hire Per Hansa and the oxen to go to Worthington with him for building materials? All the other neighbours were going, too. . . . "You folks have been here so long now, and have got such a good start that you can afford to lend a hand to a poor devil who is just starting in! I need all the critters that can crawl, with me. I'll pay you in either work or cash—but I prefer cash, for then it's over with! . . . No, thank you, I'm not going to sit down; I just stepped in on my way to your neighbours'. . . . Fine fields you've got on this side of the creek. You ought to get a fairly decent harvest, considering. . . . How big is that field of yours, anyway? . . . Good Lord! Not more than that in a whole year? . . . Well, I'll give you a tip—oxen aren't any good; they're too slow for the way things go nowadays. . . . Fine-looking house you've got, inside, but sod houses aren't much better than dugouts—in some ways, really not so good. . . . For my part, I am through with such poor makeshifts. . . . Well, can I count on you, then?" . . . Tallaksen referred to this trip as airily as if he were asking for a match.

"Are you going to build?" Per Hansa asked, quietly.

"You bet I am. Isn't that what I've been telling you? If I'm to stay here, I intend to live like a human being!" . . . And now he began outlining his building plans and explaining them at length. . . . "Oh yes, there's a lot to do before I get everything ready; but I intend to hire plenty of help and get it done in a jiffy. See? I've come out here to *break prairie*, I want you to know. . . . If crops turn out decently this year, I'll snap up one more quarter by fall, or perhaps two. Really"—here the man grew confidential—"I don't see any nameable reason why a smart man couldn't farm a whole section of land like this—or even more. Why, you've only got to put the plow into the level prairie! . . . But first of all, I want to build a decent house; the painting I'll let go until fall." . . . His voice flowed on in such a steady stream that no one else could get in a word edgewise.

"You're going to *paint?*" Per Hansa asked, and got up from the table abruptly. He was breathing fast.

"Paint? Why, certainly! It would never do to let a house stand unpainted in this climate. It wouldn't look well, either."

A look of innocent curiosity rested on Beret's face as she listened to the great plans being unfolded before her. She seemed lost in thought, and asked in a quiet tone if it were really true that he intended to build a home like that—now, at once, this summer? It would be a fine thing, she added—and there was a note of wistful gladness in her voice—to see a real house once more. It would make the desert look brighter. . . .

At that Torkel Tallaksen had to laugh outright; he had never seen such a houseful of moles! Here he had been explaining till he was hoarse, but apparently they hadn't understood one word of it! What was the use of wasting more breath on them? . . . He turned to go.

"Well," he said to Per Hansa in an important voice, "can I count on you for the trip?"

Per Hansa paused over his answer. They were all looking at him inquiringly when he spoke:

"It seems to me," he began, quietly, "that you are starting from the wrong end." Again he paused, for he found it hard to choose his words. "If you would take the money that you intend to spend in building and put it into cattle and horses and machinery, and hire help enough to run them, then the devil himself couldn't keep up with you. In a few years you'd be the king of all of us—though God knows we'd much rather have another. But this I tell you, now"—prophetic power rang in Per Hansa's voice—"if you start from the other end and do as you've been proposing, then you and I will fight—yes, you and I!—for both the scepter and the crown . . . though all I've got now, God knows, is a pair of pants and a yoke of oxen!" . . .

Torkel Tallaksen laughed overbearingly. "One doesn't need to live in a gopher hole, in order to get ahead! . . . Here, too, will have to come decency and civilized living."

The words stung Per Hansa like a whip lash; in his effort to control himself he felt in his pocket for a match, found one, and hurled it to the floor. . . . "We'll get our decency and civilized living all right—even if you should go back where you came from! . . . And now let me tell you one thing more—it's better to begin in a gopher hole than to end in one." . . .

Before Torkel Tallaksen was able to collect himself for a reply, Beret said, slowly, as if thinking aloud, but in a manner that compelled attention:

"Your wife certainly will have many reasons to be glad. Walls that will shut out all the unspeakable things out here . . . floors that can be washed on the Sabbath eve. . . . I know too well that human beings should not live like beasts! After they have turned into beasts, houses don't matter." . . .

Torkel Tallaksen looked at the woman as if he had discovered her for the first time. . . . Uh-huh, he nodded; here's the common sense of this outfit! . . . "Right you are, and no doubt about it! I wouldn't live like this for all the prairie land in the whole of Dakota Territory. . . . But now things are going to be different, if I have anything to say about it. We're going to build houses that can stand up and be seen; people won't need to wonder whether this is a settlement or a gopher camp!" Suddenly a fresh idea seemed to strike him: "Perhaps you'd like to help my wife weave a few carpets? She's all the time talking about carpets, and I suppose she must have 'em. . . . They save the floors, too."

"I would be glad to try," said Beret, humbly. "One ought to help another get what she cannot have for herself. . . . I think it would be interesting work."

As he listened to his wife, Per Hansa was fumbling in his pocket for another match; at last he brought it out, struck it on the table, and held it until it burned down to the end. The room was swimming before his eyes; words floated across his vision—words that he longed to use, he reached out for them, but they melted into the air; what Beret had said had driven them away. . . . Per Hansa sat down heavily on the chest, his face pale and drawn.

"All right—that's settled, then!" said Torkel Tallaksen. Then he turned to Per Hansa: "We start the day after tomorrow. I'm counting on you, remember—you and the oxen. . . . You'll be needing some one to haul for you pretty soon, when you once get on your feet."

Silence fell on the room. The man stood there, waiting for an answer.

"You'd better count over again!" Per Hansa growled. Without another word he sprang up from the chest and left the house. In a gruff voice he called to the oxen. That day he kept on breaking as long as he could see. When he unhitched at last he walked in slowly from the field, stooping over in thought; he could hardly bring himself to going home. What business had he there—what earthly business? . . . The sod house and all it contained lay in a great darkness, yet he was drawn toward it irresistibly. . . .

. . . Perhaps it was true? What she had said might be more than half right—everything here was a failure, and he himself was no good. . . . A thought cut him to the very quick: "That's the reward you get for fighting and striving—she says you are no good!" . . . To think that she hadn't felt ashamed, that she had been willing to lay bare her troubles to that infernal blabberer and braggart! . . . Had she lost all sense of propriety? . . . "Oh, hell! Get up, there!" he ripped out to the oxen.

But as it transpired, Torkel Tallaksen's great plans ran up against a snag. Tönseten didn't care to go along unless Per Hansa went, for he was fully occupied with his own affairs. And the Solum boys were not overly enthusiastic; they were busy breaking prairie when Tallaksen came, and answered him that they would see how the others felt about it, and let him know. It finally developed that Torkel Tallaksen could engage only two men and two teams, which weren't enough to haul home all the materials for a whole farmstead. And so, in the face of the inevitable, Torkel Tallaksen had to give up building for that summer. . . . Thus it happened that before the fall set in, another sod hut stuck its head above the waving grass of the prairie.

V

That summer many land seekers passed through the settlement on their way west. The arrival of a caravan was always an event of the greatest importance. How exciting they were, those little ships of the Great Plain! The prairie schooners, rigged with canvas tops which gleamed whitely in the shimmering light, first became visible as tiny specks against the eastern sky; one might almost imagine them to be sea gulls perched far, far away on an endless green meadow; but as one continued to watch, the white dots grew; they came drifting across the prairie like the day; after long waiting, they gradually floated out of the haze, distinct and clear; then, as they drew near, they proved to be veritable wagons, with horses hitched ahead, with folk and all their possessions inside, and a whole herd of cattle following behind.

The caravan would crawl slowly into the settlement and come to anchor in front of one of the sod houses; the moment it halted, people would swarm down and stretch themselves and begin to look after the teams; cattle would bellow; sheep would bleat as they ran about. Many queer races and costumes were to be seen in these caravans, and a babble of strange tongues shattered the air. Nut-brown youngsters, dressed only in a shirt and a pair of pants, would fly around between the huts, looking for other youngsters; an infant, its mother crooning softly to it, would sit securely perched in the fold of her arm; white-haired old men and women, who should have been living quietly at home, preparing for a different journey, were also to be seen in the group, running about like youngsters; the daily jogging from sky line to sky line had brightened their eyes and quickened their tongues. All were busy; each had a thousand questions to ask; every last one of them was in high spirits, though they knew no other home than the wagon and the blue skies above. . . . The Lord only could tell whence all these people had come and whither they were going! . . .

The caravan usually intended to stop only long enough for the women folk to boil coffee and get a fresh supply of water; but the starting was always delayed, for the men had so many questions to ask. Once in a while during these halts a fiddler would bring out his fiddle and play a tune or two, and then there would be dancing. Such instances were rare, but good cheer and excitement accompanied these visits.

—Why not settle right here? the Spring Creek folk would ask the west-movers. . . . There's plenty of good land left—nothing better to be found between here and the Pacific Ocean!

—No, not yet. They weren't quite ready to settle; these parts looked fairly crowded. . . . The farther west, the better. . . . They guessed they would have to go on a way, though this really looked pretty good! . . .

And so the caravans would roll onward into the green stillness of the west. How strange—they vanished faster than they had appeared! The white sails grew smaller and smaller in the glow of the afternoon, until they had dwindled to nothing; the eye might seek them out there in the waning day, and search till it grew blurred, but all in vain—they were gone, and had left no trace! . . .

Foggy weather had now been hanging over the prairie for three whole days; a warm mist of rain mizzled continuously out of the low sky. Toward evening of the third day, the fog lifted and clear sky again appeared; the setting sun burst through the cloud banks rolling up above the western horizon, and transformed them into marvellous fairy castles. . . . While this was going on, over to the northeast of the Solum boys' place a lonely wagon had crept into sight; it had almost reached the creek before anyone had noticed it, for the Solum boys were visiting among the Sognings, where there were many young people. But as Beret sat out in the yard, milking, the wagon crossed her view. When she brought in the milk, she remarked in her quiet manner that they were going to have company, at which tidings the rest of the family had to run out and see who might be coming at this time of day.

There was only one wagon, with two cows following behind; on the left side walked a brown-whiskered, stooping man—he was doing the driving; close behind him came a half-grown boy, dragging his feet heavily. The wagon at last crawled up the hill and came to a stop in Per Hansa's yard, where the whole family stood waiting.

"I don't suppose there are any Norwegians in this settlement? No, that would be too much to expect," said the man in a husky, worn-out voice.

"If you're looking for Norwegians, you have found the right place, all right! We sift the people as they pass through here—keep our own, and let the others go!" . . . Per Hansa wanted to run on, for he felt in high spirits; but he checked himself, observing that the man looked as if he stood on the very brink of the grave.

—Was there any chance of putting up here for the night?

"Certainly! certainly!" cried Per Hansa, briskly, "provided you are willing to take things as they are."

The man didn't answer, but walked instead to the wagon and spoke to some one inside:

"Kari, now you must brace up and come down. Here we have found Norwegians at last!" As if fearing a contradiction, he added: "Ya, they are real Norwegians. I've talked with them."

On top of his words there came out of the wagon, first a puny boy with a hungry face, somewhat smaller than the other boy; then a girl of about the same size, but looking much older. She helped to get down another boy, about six years old, who evidently had been sleeping and looked cross and tired. That seemed to be all.

The man stepped closer to the wagon. "Aren't you coming, Kari?"

A groan sounded within the canvas. The girl grabbed hold of her father's arm. "You must untie the rope! Can't you remember *anything?*" she whispered, angrily.

"Ya, that's right! Wait a minute till I come and help you."

An irresistible curiosity took hold of Per Hansa; in two jumps he stood on the tongue of the wagon. The sight that met his eyes sent chills running down his spine. Inside sat a woman on a pile of clothes, with her back against a large immigrant chest; around her wrists and leading to the handles of the chest a strong rope was tied; her face was drawn and unnatural. Per Hansa trembled so violently that he had to catch hold of the wagon box, but inwardly he was swearing a steady stream. To him it looked as if the woman was crucified. . . . "For God's sake, man!" . . .

The stranger paid no attention; he was pottering about and pleading: "Come down now, Kari. . . . Ya, all right, I'll help you! Everything's going to be all right—I know it will! . . . Can you manage to get up?" He had untied the rope, and the woman had risen to her knees.

"O God!" she sighed, putting her hands to her head.

"Please come. That's right; I'll help you!" pleaded the man, as if he were trying to persuade a child.

She came down unsteadily. "Is this the place, Jakob?" she asked in a bewildered way. But now Beret ran up and put her arm around her; the women looked into each other's eyes and instantly a bond of understanding had been established. "You come with me!" urged Beret. . . . "O God! This isn't the place, either!" wailed the woman; but she followed Beret submissively into the house.

"Well, well!" sighed the man as he began to unhitch the horses. "Life isn't easy—no, it certainly isn't." . . .

Per Hansa watched him anxiously, hardly knowing what to do. Both the boys kept close to him. Then an idea flashed through his mind: "You boys run over to Hans Olsa's and tell him not to go to bed until I come. . . . No, I don't want him here. And you two stay over there to-night. Now run along!"

Turning to the man, he asked, "Aren't there any more in your party?"

"No, not now. We were five, you see, to begin with —five in all—but the others had to go on. . . . Haven't they been by here yet? Well, they must be somewhere over to the westward. . . . No, life isn't easy." . . . The man wandered on in his monotonous, blurred tone; he sounded all the time as if he were half sobbing.

"Where do you come from?" Per Hansa demanded, gruffly.

The man didn't give a direct answer, but continued on in the same mournful way, stretching his story out interminably. . . . They had been wandering over the prairie for nearly six weeks. . . . Ya, it was a hard life. When they had started from Houston County, Minnesota, there had been five wagons in all. Strange that the others hadn't turned up here. Where could they be? It seemed to him as if he had travelled far enough to reach the ends of the earth! . . . Good God, what a nightmare life was! If he had only —only known. . . !

"Did the others go away and *leave you?*" Per Hansa hadn't intended to ask that question, but it had slipped out before he realized what he was saying. He wondered if there could be anything seriously wrong. . . .

"They couldn't possibly wait for us—couldn't have been expected to. Everything went wrong, you see, and I didn't know when I would be able to start again. . . . Turn the horses loose, John," he said to the boy. "Take the pail and see if you can squeeze some milk out of the cows. Poor beasts, they don't give much now!" Then he turned to Per Hansa again: "I don't know what would have become of us if we hadn't reached this place to-night! We'd have been in a bad hole, that I assure you! Women folk can't bear up. . . ." The man stopped and blew his nose.

Per Hansa dreaded what might be coming next. "You must have got off your course, since you are coming down from the north?"

The man shook his head helplessly. "To tell the truth, I don't know where we've been these last few days. We couldn't see the sun."

"Haven't you got a compass?"

"Compass? No! I tried to steer with a rope, but the one I had wasn't long enough."

"Like hell you did!" exclaimed Per Hansa, excitedly, full of a sudden new interest.

"Ya, I tried that rope idea—hitched it to the back of the wagon, and let it drag in the wet grass. But it didn't work—I couldn't steer straight with it. The rope was so short, and kept kinking around so much, that it didn't leave any wake."

"Uh-huh!" nodded Per Hansa wisely. "You must be a seafaring man, to have tried that trick!"

"No, I'm no sailor. But fisher-folk out here have told me that it's possible to steer by a rope. . . . I had to try *something*."

"Where did you cross the Sioux?"

"How do I know where I crossed it? We came to a river a long way to the east of here—that must have been the Sioux. We hunted and hunted before we could find a place shallow enough to cross. . . . God! this has certainly been a wandering in the desert for me! . . . But if Kari only gets better, I won't complain—though I never dreamed that life could be so hard." . . .

"Is she—is she *sick*, that woman of yours?"

The man did not answer this question immediately; he wiped his face with the sleeve of his shirt. When he spoke again, his voice had grown even more blurred and indistinct: "Physically she seems to be as well as ever—as far as I can see. She certainly hasn't overworked since we've been travelling. I hope there's nothing wrong with her. . . . But certain things are hard to bear—I suppose it's worse for the mother, too—though the Lord knows it hasn't been easy for me, either! . . . You see, we had to leave our youngest boy out there on the prairie. . . ."

"*Leave* him?" . . . These were the only two words that came to Per Hansa's mind.

"Ya, there he lies, our little boy! . . . I never saw a more promising man—you know what I mean—when he grew up. . . . But now—oh, well. . . ."

Per Hansa felt faint in the pit of his stomach; his throat grew dry; his voice became as husky as that of the other; he came close up to him. "Tell me—how did this happen?"

The man shook his head again, in a sort of dumb

despair. Then he cleared his throat and continued with great effort: "I can't tell how it happened! Fate just willed it so. Such things are not to be explained. . . . The boy had been ailing for some time—we knew that, but didn't pay much attention. We had other things to think of. . . . Then he began to fail fast. We were only one day's journey this side of Jackson; so we went back. That was the time when the others left us. I don't blame them much—it was uncertain when we could go on. . . . The doctor we found wasn't a capable man—I realize it now. He spoke only English and couldn't understand what I was saying. He had no idea what was wrong with the boy—I could see that plainly enough. . . . Ya, well —so we started again. . . . It isn't any use to fight against Fate; that's an old saying, and a true one, too, I guess. . . . Before long we saw that the boy wasn't going to recover. So we hurried on, day and night, trying to catch our neighbours. . . . Well, that's about all of it. One night he was gone—just as if you had blown out a candle. Ya, let me see—that was five nights ago."

"Have you got him there in the wagon?" demanded Per Hansa, grabbing the man by the arm.

"No, no," he muttered, huskily. "We buried him out there by a big stone—no coffin or anything. But Kari took the best skirt she had and wrapped it all around him—we had to do *something*, you know. . . . But," he continued, suddenly straightening up, "Paul cannot lie there! As soon as I find my neighbours, I'll go and get him. Otherwise Kari . . ." The man paused between the sobs that threatened to choke him. "I have had to tie her up the last few days. She insisted on getting out and going back to Paul. I don't think she has had a wink of sleep for over a week. . . . It's just as I was saying—some people can't stand things." . . .

Per Hansa leaned heavily against the wagon. "Has she gone crazy?" he asked, hoarsely.

"She isn't much worse than the rest of us. I don't believe . . . Kari is really a well-balanced woman . . . but you can imagine how it feels, to leave a child *that* way . . ."

The boy, John, had finished milking. He had put the

pail down and was standing a little way off, listening to his father's story; suddenly he threw himself on the ground, sobbing as if in convulsions.

"John! John!" admonished the father. "Aren't you ashamed of yourself—a grown-up man like you! Take the milk and carry it into the house!"

"That's right!" echoed Per Hansa, pulling himself together. "We'd better all go in. There's shelter here, and plenty to eat."

Beret was bustling around the room when they entered; she had put the woman to bed, and now was tending her. "Where are the boys?" she asked.

Per Hansa told her that he had sent them to Hans Olsa's for the night.

"That was hardly necessary; we could have made room here somehow." Beret's voice carried a note of keen reproach.

The man had paused at the door; now he came over to the bed, took the limp hand, and muttered: "Poor soul! . . . Why, I believe she's asleep already!"

Beret came up and pushed him gently aside. "Be careful! Don't wake her. She needs the rest."

"Ya, I don't doubt it—not I! She hasn't slept for a week, you see—the poor soul!" With a loud sniff, he turned and left the room.

When supper time came the woman seemed to be engulfed in a stupefying sleep. Beret did not join the others at the supper table, but busied herself, instead, by trying to make the woman more comfortable; she loosened her clothes, took off her shoes, and washed her face in warm water; during all this the stranger never stirred. That done, Beret began to fix up sleeping quarters for the strangers, in the barn. She carried in fresh hay and brought out all the bedding she had; she herself would take care of the woman, in case she awoke and needed attention. Beret did little talking, but she went about these arrangements with a firmness and confidence that surprised her husband.

Per Hansa came in from the barn, after helping the strangers settle themselves for the night. Beret was sitting on the edge of the bed, dressing the baby for the night;

she had put And-Ongen to bed beside the distracted woman.

"Did she tell you much?" he asked in a low voice.

Beret glanced toward the other bed before she answered:

"Only that she had had to leave one of her children on the way. She wasn't able to talk connectedly."

"It's a terrible thing!" he said, looking away from his wife. "I think I'll go over to Hans Olsa's for a minute. I want to talk this matter over with him."

"Talk it over with him?" she repeated, coldly. "I don't suppose Hans Olsa knows everything!"

"No, of course not. But these people have got to be helped, and we can't do it all alone." He hesitated for a minute, as if waiting for her consent. "Well, I won't be gone long," he said as he went out of the door.

When he returned, an hour later, she was still sitting on the edge of the bed, with the baby asleep on her lap. They sat in silence for a long while; at last he began to undress. She waited until he was in bed, then turned the lamp low and lay down herself, but without undressing. . . . The lamp shed only a faint light. It was so quiet in the room that one could hear the breathing of all the others. Beret lay there listening; though the room was still, it seemed alive to her with strange movements; she forced herself to open her eyes and look around. Noticing that Per Hansa wasn't asleep, either, she asked:

"Did you look after the boys?"

"Nothing the matter with them! They were fast asleep in Sofie's bed."

"You told them everything, at Hans Olsa's?"

"Of course!"

"What did they think of it?"

Per Hansa raised himself on his elbows and glanced at the broken creature lying in the bed back of theirs. The woman, apparently, had not stirred a muscle. "It's a bad business," he said. "We must try to get together a coffin and find the boy. We can't let him lie out there—that way." . . . As Beret made no answer, he briefly narrated the story that the man had told him. "The fellow is a good-for-nothing, stupid fool, I'm sure of that," concluded Per Hansa.

She listened to him in silence. For some time she brooded over her thoughts; then in a bitter tone she suddenly burst out: "Now you can see that this kind of a life is impossible! It's beyond human endurance."

He had not the power to read her thoughts; he did not want to know them; to-night every nerve in his body was taut with apprehension and dismay. But he tried to say, reassuringly: "Hans Olsa and I will both go with the man, as soon as the day breaks. If we only had something to make the coffin of! The few pieces of board that I've got here will hardly be enough. . . . Now let's go to sleep. Be sure and call me if you need anything!"

He turned over resolutely, as if determined to sleep; but she noticed that he was a long time doing it. . . . I wonder what's going through his mind? she thought. She was glad to have him awake, just the same; to-night there were strange things abroad in the room. . . .

VI

The instant the woman had climbed down from the wagon and looked into Beret's face a curtain seemed to be drawn over all the terrible experiences of the last few weeks. She entered a cozy room where things were as they should be; she felt the warm presence of folk who had dwelt here a long time. She took in the whole room at a glance—table and benches and stools; a fire was burning in a real stove; a kettle was boiling; wet clothes were hanging on a line by the stove, giving out a pleasant, familiar odor; and there actually stood two beds, made up with clean bedding! The sense of home, of people who lived in an orderly fashion, swept over her like a warm bath. A kind hand led her to one of the beds, and there she sank down. She mumbled a few words, but soon gave it up; everything about her seemed so wonderfully pleasant; she must keep quiet, so as not to disturb the dream. The hand that helped her had such a sympathetic touch; it took a rag, dipped it in lukewarm water, and wiped her face; then it loosened her clothes and even took off her shoes. But best of all, she could stretch her back again!

. . . Strange that she couldn't remember what had

been going on! Had she told the woman all that she ought to know? About the makeshift coffin, and the big stone beside which they would find him? And that she would have to take a blanket with her, for the nights were chilly and Paul had very little on—only a shirt that was worn and thin? . . . No, she couldn't remember anything except that she had been able to lie down and stretch her back; the warmth of the room, and the knowledge that friendly people were near her, had overcome all her senses with a sweet languor. Her body lay as if fast asleep; but away back in the inner depths of her consciousness a wee eye peeped out, half open, and saw things. . . .

She remained in the same position until three o'clock in the morning. But then the wee bit of an eye opened wider and her senses slowly began to revive; she realized that she was lying in a strange room, where a lamp burned with a dim light. Suddenly she remembered that she had arrived here last night—but Paul was not with her. . . . Too bad I am so forgetful! she thought. I must hurry now before Jakob sees me, because there's no way of stopping him—he always wants to go on! . . . She was fully awake now; she sat up and buttoned her clothes, then slipped quietly out of bed.

For a moment she stood perfectly still, listening; she could hear the breathing of many people; bending suddenly over the bed, she snatched up And-Ongen. She held the child tenderly in her arms and put her cheek against the warm face. . . . We must be careful now! she thought. With quiet movements she wrapped her skirt about the sleeping child; glancing around the room to see if all was well, she glided out like a shadow; she did not dare to close the door behind her, lest it should make a noise. . . . "Here in our wagon!" she murmured. "I mustn't let Jakob see me now; he doesn't understand; he only wants to get on!" . . . Clutching the child to her breast, she started on the run, taking a direction away from the house.

Beret was awakened by a voice calling to her from a great distance; it called loudly several times. What a shame they can't let me alone in peace, to get a little rest! she thought, drowsily. I was up so late last night and I need the sleep badly! . . . But the voice kept calling so persistently that after a while she sat up in bed, her mind coming back to reality; she remembered that strangers had arrived last night, that another besides herself was in deep distress. Well, she had done her best to take care of her. . . . She turned her head to see how the other woman was resting.

. . . "Heaven have mercy!" . . .

Beret leaped frantically out of bed; in a second she had reached the side of the other bed, but no one was there. She did not notice that And-Ongen was gone, too. A cold draught rushing through the room told her that the door stood open; she hurried over to it. She seemed to recall dimly that some one had recently gone out. Hadn't she heard it in her sleep? Beret went through the door and stood in front of the house, but did not dare to make an outcry; she listened intently, then called in a low voice; getting no answer, she ran around the house, peering hither and thither, but the grey morning light disclosed nothing.

Running back into the house, she called her husband distractedly: "She's gone! Get up! You must hurry!"

In an instant Per Hansa was up and had tumbled into his clothes. "Run over to Hans Olsa's and tell him to come at once! Be as quick as you can! In the meanwhile I'll search down by the creek."

When they came out, the first light of day was creeping up the eastern sky; a slight fog floated along the creek; the morning air was crisp and cool. Per Hansa leaped up into the seat of the wagon and scanned the prairie in every direction. . . . What was *that*, over there? Wasn't it a human being standing on the top of the hill? Could she have taken that direction? . . . He jumped down from the wagon, and rushed around to the other side of the house, called to Beret, and pointed up the hill. Instantly they both started out on the run.

The woman did not seem in the least surprised at their coming. When Per Hansa had almost reached her, he stopped stone dead. What, in God's name, was she carrying in her arms? His face blanched with terror. "Come here!" he shouted. In a moment he had the child in his own arms.

And-Ongen was almost awake now and had begun to whimper; things were going on around her that she could not understand; she felt cold, and father had such a queer look on his face. Sleepily she cuddled up in the fold of his left arm, her cheek against his heart, though a hard hand which seemed to be pounding against a wall was trying to wake her up again; she would just let it go on pounding all it pleased. She had to sleep some more! . . . But now mother was here. Hurriedly she was transferred into her mother's arms and squeezed almost to a pancake. She had to gasp for breath; nevertheless she snuggled into her arms as closely as she could, for she felt, oh, so sleepy! . . . But no peace here, either! Here, too, a hand pounded against a wall. Were they tearing down the house? And-Ongen was certainly at a loss to understand all this racket in the middle of the night. . . . But let 'em pound!

As Beret walked homeward, carrying the child, it seemed more precious to her than the very first time when she had held it in her arms; and she experienced a wonderful blessing. Upon this night the Lord had been with them: His mighty arm had shielded them from a fearful calamity.

The other woman was still obsessed by her own troubles; she kept on hunting up there on the hill. . . . Wouldn't these people help her to find Paul? She had to find him at once—He would be cold with so little on. . . . Now they had taken that blessed child away from her; but she didn't wonder—that man had a bad face. She felt afraid of him. . . . But no time to think of such things now; Jakob would soon be coming? She began muttering to herself: "Oh, why can't I find the stone? What has become of it? Wasn't it somewhere here?" . . .

Per Hansa went up and spoke to her, his voice sounding hoarse and unnatural. "Come with me, now! To-day Hans Olsa and I are going to find your boy." Taking her gently by the arm, he led her back to the house. . . . It's very kind of him, to help find Paul, she thought, and followed willingly.

At breakfast she sat very quiet; she ate when they bade her, but never spoke. While they were making the coffin she sat looking on, wondering why they didn't hurry faster with the work. Couldn't they understand that Paul was cold? A little later a handsome woman entered the house—a woman with such a kind face, who lined the coffin inside with a white cloth. . . . Now, that is fine of her; that's just what a woman with such a kind face would do! . . . She would have liked to talk to that woman; she had something very important to confide to her; but perhaps she had better not delay her in her work—the coffin had to be lined! . . .

As soon as the coffin was ready, Per Hansa and Hans Olsa, along with the stranger and his wife, left the settlement to hunt for the body of the dead boy. They took quite a stock of provisions with them. On this search they were gone four days; they criss-crossed the prairie for a long way to the east, and searched high and low; but when they returned the coffin was still empty.

VII

After the return from the search the strangers stayed one more day with them. The morning they were to leave it looked dark and threatening, and Per Hansa wouldn't hear of their setting out; but along toward noon the sky cleared and the weather appeared more settled. The man, very anxious to be on his way, had everything loaded into the wagon, and as soon as the noon meal was over they were ready to go.

But before the man got on his way Per Hansa asked him where he intended to settle.

—Well, he wasn't positive as to the exact place. It was over somewhere toward the James River—his neighbours had told him that.

—Did he know where the James River was? Per Hansa inquired further.

—Certainly he did! How could he ask such a foolish question? The river lay off there; all he needed to do was to steer straight west. After finding the river, of course he'd have to ask. But that part of it would be quite easy. . . .

Per Hansa shuddered, and asked no more questions.

The woman had been quite calm since their return. She kept away from the others, muttering to herself and pottering over insignificant things, much like a child at play; but she was docile and inoffensive, and did what anyone told her. A short while before noon that day she took a notion that she must change her clothes; she got up from what she was doing, washed, and went to the wagon. When she came back she had dressed herself in her best; in a way she looked all right, but made a bizarre appearance because she had put so much on. . . . The man seemed fairly cheerful as they started; he talked a good deal, heaping many blessings upon Per Hansa. . . . If he could only find his neighbours, and Kari could only forget, things would be all right in a little while. Ya, it was a hard life, but—— Well, God's blessings on Per Hansa, and many thanks! And now he must be off! . . . His voice was just as husky and blurred as when he came.

The wagon started creaking; the man, short and stooping, led the way; the family piled into the wagon; the two cows jogged behind. . . . They laid their course due west. . . . Banks of heavy cloud were rolled up on the western horizon—huge, fantastic forms that seemed to await them in Heaven's derision—though they might have been only the last stragglers of the spell of bad weather just past.

After they had gone, Beret could find no peace in the house; her hand trembled; she felt faint and dizzy; every now and then she had to go out and look at the disappearing wagon; and when the hill finally shut off the view she took the youngest two children and went up there to watch. In a way she felt glad that these people were gone; at the same time she reproached herself for not having urged them to stay longer. Sitting now on the hilltop, a strong presentiment came over her that they should not have started to-day. . . . "That's the way I've become," she thought sadly. "Here are folk in the deepest distress, and I am only glad to send them off into direr calamities! What will they do to-night if a storm comes upon them? He is all broken up—he couldn't have been much of a man at any time. And the poor wife insane from grief! Perhaps she will disappear forever this very night. . . .

What misery, what an unspeakable tragedy, life is for some!" . . .

Slowly, very slowly, the forlorn caravan crept off into the great, mysterious silence always hovering above the plain. To Beret, as she watched, it seemed as if the prairie were swallowing up the people, the wagon, the cows and all. At last the little caravan was merged in the very infinite itself; Beret thought she could see the wagon yet, but was not certain; it might be only a dead tuft of grass far away which the wind stirred. . . .

She took the children and went home, walking with slow, dragging steps; she wanted to cry, and felt the need of it, but no tears came. . . . Per Hansa and the boys were breaking prairie; to judge from the language they used in talking to the oxen, they must be hard at it. Her loneliness was so great that she felt a physical need of bringing happiness to some living thing; as soon as she got home she took her little remaining store of rice and cooked porridge for supper; the boys were very fond of that dish.

Toward evening the air grew heavy and sultry; the cloud banks, still rolling up in the western sky, had taken on a most threatening aspect; it looked as if a thunderstorm might be coming on.

After supper Per Hansa was due to meet at Hans Olsa's with the other neighbours, to lay plans for the trip to town which had to be made before harvesting set in. The boys asked leave to go, too—it was so much fun to be with the men.

When she had washed the supper dishes Beret went outdoors and sat down on the woodpile. A nameless apprehension tugged at her heart and would not leave her in peace; taking the two children as before, she again ascended the hill. The spell of the afternoon's sadness was still upon her; her constant self-reproach since then had only deepened it. . . . Those poor folks were straying somewhere out there, under the towering clouds. Poor souls! The Lord pity the mother who had left a part of herself back east on the prairie! How could the good God permit creatures made in His image to fall into such tribulations? To people this desert would be as impossible as to empty the sea. For how could folk establish homes in an endless wilderness? Was it not the Evil One that had struck them with blindness? . . . Take her own case, for example: here she sat, thousands of miles from home and kindred, lost in a limitless void. . . . Out yonder drifted these folk, like chips on a current. . . . Must man perish because of his own foolishness? Where, then, was the guiding hand? . . . Beret was gazing at the western sky as the twilight fast gathered around her; her eyes were riveted on a certain cloud that had taken on the shape of a face, awful of mien and giantlike in proportions; the face seemed to swell out of the prairie and filled half the heavens.

She gazed a long time; now she could see the monster clearer. The face was unmistakable! There were the outlines of the nose and mouth. The eyes—deep, dark caves in the cloud—were closed. The mouth, if it were to open, would be a yawning abyss. The chin rested on the prairie. . . . Black and lean the whole face, but of such gigantic, menacing proportions! Wasn't there something like a leer upon it? . . . And the terrible creature was spreading everywhere; she trembled so desperately that she had to take hold of the grass.

It was a strange emotion that Beret was harbouring at this moment; in reality she felt a certain morbid satisfaction—very much like a child that has been arguing with its parents, has turned out to be right, and, just as the tears are coming, cries, "Now, there, you see!" . . . Here was the simple solution to the whole riddle. She had known in her heart all the time that people were never led into such deep affliction unless an evil power had been turned loose among them. And hadn't she clearly felt that there were unspeakable things out yonder—that the great stillness was nothing but life asleep? . . . She sat still as death, feeling the supernatural emanations all around her. The face came closer in the dusk—didn't she feel its cold breath upon her? When that mouth opened and began to suck, terrible things would happen! . . . Without daring to look again, she snatched up the children and ran blindly home.

After a while the others returned, the boys storming

boisterously into the house, the father close behind; he was evidently chasing them; by the tone of his voice, she knew he was in high spirits.

"Why, Beret," he cried gayly, as soon as he got inside, "what have you been doing to the windows—covering them up?" He was looking at her with narrow, sparkling eyes. "Beret, Beret, you're a dear girl!" he whispered. Then he came over and fondled her—he wanted to help undress her and put her to bed. . . .

"No, no—not *that!*" she cried, vehemently, an intense anger surging up within her. Had he no sense whatever of decency and propriety, no feeling of shame and sin? . . . That's only one more proof, she thought, that the devil has us in his clutches!

After that time, Beret was conscious of the face whenever she was awake, but particularly along toward evening, as the twilight came on; then it drew closer to her and seemed alive. Even during the day she would often be aware of its presence; high noon might stand over the prairie, with the sun shedding a flood of light that fairly blinded the sight, but through and behind the light she would see it—huge and horrible it was, the eyes always closed, with only those empty, cavernlike sockets beneath the brows.

As she went about doing her work, now, she would frequently be seized by a faintness so great that she had to sit down. . . . How was this going to end? she asked herself. Yes, how would it end? . . . Vague premonitions hovered about her like shadows. Many times she was on the point of asking her husband if he saw what she did, towering above the prairie out west; but always she seemed to be tongue-tied. . . . Well, why mention it? Couldn't he and the others see it perfectly well for themselves? How could they help it? . . . She noticed that a silence would often fall upon them when they were out-of-doors, especially in the evening. Certainly they saw it! . . . Every evening, now, whether Per Hansa was away or at home, she hung something over the windows—it helped shut out the fear. . . .

At first her husband made all sorts of fun of this practice of hers; he teased her about it, as if it were a good joke, and continued to force his caresses on her, his voice low and vibrant with pent-up emotion. But as time went on he ceased laughing; the fear that possessed her had begun to affect him, too. . . .

VIII

The month of July wore on. The small patches of fields in the Spring Creek settlement were slowly ripening and made a brave showing. Never had one seen finer fields! The grain had started to head out long ago; the kernels were already formed, tiny bodies wrapped in the most delicate green silk. With every day that passed the wheat filled out more and more; the heads grew heavy and full of milk; as soon as the breeze died down in the afternoon, they would tilt toward the setting sun and slowly drop off to sleep, only to dream of the marvellous life that was now stirring within them.

These days, Per Hansa was behaving like a good boat in a heavy sea—as long as the keel pointed the right way, he would go on. He watched his wife covering the windows at night, and felt both sad and angry; but when he saw how everything was growing on the farm—meadows and fields, cattle and youngsters—then he was filled with an exultant joy that made him momentarily forget his wife's condition. He had a larger field than any of his neighbours, and there wasn't a doubt that his grain was the finest—theirs was just ordinary dumb grain, while his seemed alive! . . . He tried to reason himself out of his serious misgivings over Beret. True enough, she didn't act as a normal person should; yet it was nothing that wouldn't naturally right itself with time. Perhaps he would go to work and build her a house this fall. By thunder, he'd have to see about that! The castle would have to be tackled sooner or later. . . . The lumberman at Worthington was a fine fellow, and Per Hansa wouldn't be ashamed to ask him for credit. Huh! What could the man expect to do with his lumber but sell it? . . . Next spring he would make a big haul in his fur trade with the Indians; he'd buy every damned scalp they had in the place. And when his castle was ready it would be stranger than the devil if such a sensible girl as Beret didn't perk up and throw off her gruesome fancies!

Everything he had planted that spring was blooming like a garden. Why, he could just *hear* the potatoes grow! Already, as early as this, they were having new potatoes every day, while in his neighbours' patches the plants were just beginning to blossom. The oats, too, were standing high; but the wheat—best of all was the *wheat!* The neighbours, and all the east-siders—so the folk who had settled east of the creek had come to be called—and even the Irish from over to the westward, would come to look at his wheat field and say that the sight did them good. He couldn't understand what the Irish were saying, of course, but their joy at the sight of the wheat was written all over their faces. . . . Damned fine people, these Irish. Too bad he couldn't talk with them. But he felt like showing his appreciation of their visits in some tangible way, so he would go over to the potato patch, dig into a row, and give them enough for a meal. . . . Good God! a man as well off as he was must lend a hand to a pack of starving devils! . . .

By this time Tönseten had lost the last vestige of ill-feeling toward Per Hansa for doing his own seeding; he was even willing to praise the other for having had sense enough to get the seed into the ground good and *early*. Now they would be able to cut and harvest the wheat here before the other fields had ripened. . . . "I tell you what, Per Hansa, that's the most sensible thing you ever did in your life—and I ought to know what I'm talking about!" . . . Tönseten's round, fat body bristled with importance, for, of course, it would fall to him to do the reaping for these greenhorns. The Solum boys would have to teach them how to bind. Damn it, he couldn't be expected to do everything! . . . Yes, Syvert Tönseten was a very busy man these days. There was the reaper to overhaul, and the harnesses to be mended; he had to keep a sharp eye on the grain, too, lest they let it stand too long. Such heavy wheat would shell easily! So he waddled back and forth between the houses of his three neighbours, invariably finding some important matter to discuss wherever he went.

Per Hansa was not running true to form these days; he who was always so easily excited and never had patience to wait when something had to be done, seemed in no hurry to start his harvesting. Every evening he would make a trip up to the field, to see how the wheat was coming on, and with each trip his mind was more at ease. "Come up with me and see how fine the wheat stands!" he would coax Beret. And Beret would usually go; she would agree absent-mindedly that the grain looked fine—of course it did; but then she would always remember some task she had left undone at home and would have to hurry back before dark; she seldom seemed to have time to wait for him.

. . . "No, no, there's no hurry yet with the wheat!" Per Hansa thought. When Tönseten insisted that it was time to start cutting he would argue with him: "No, Syvert brother, we'll leave the wheat awhile yet—give her a spell longer to think it over. You'll be able to do the reaping easily enough before the others need you. Don't we all know that your equal in running the reaper isn't to be found in the whole of Dakota Territory?"

Tönseten would give an embarrassed cough: "You mean perhaps in Minnesota?"

"Certainly! Wasn't that what I said?" Whereupon both would laugh like a couple of happy boys.

But one forenoon Tönseten came over in great excitement, declaring flatly that now they would have to start cutting here—and no use talking! He had just come from Hans Olsa's, where he'd been looking at the field; and there, too, the grain was ripening fast. This job had to be gotten out of the way right now, or where the devil would they be?

"Oh, what's your hurry, Syvert? Don't let's get excited; we'll just give her one more night for extra measure!" argued Per Hansa.

Then Tönseten grew goggle-eyed, waving his arms as he talked. "You're a stubborn, ignorant fool, Per Hansa—I don't mind telling you so! No, I'm damned if I do! Here we have eighty acres of grain, and I alone must do all the cutting! In all probability I'll have to help the east-siders, too; they don't seem to have any more brains than they need—some of 'em don't, at least!"

"Take it easy, take it easy, Syvert! Don't you see how nicely the wheat is filling out—just like a young girl budding into womanhood?"

At that Tönseten got mad in earnest. "You make me tired, man! You don't know as much as the nose on your face—no, you don't! What the devil would happen to us if all our grain came in at the same time? Just what would we *do*, I'd like to know? We couldn't save it. . . . Now I've made up my mind: there's to be no more damned shilly-shallying. We start this afternoon, and that's the end of it!"

"As you say, Captain!" answered Per Hansa, meekly, his eyes twinkling.

"All right, then. I'll tell Hans Olsa. You run over and tell the Solum boys."

Per Hansa chuckled aloud. "Are you going to call in all of Dakota Territory to help harvest this little patch of mine?"

"Stop your joking, Per Hansa! You don't know an earthly thing about harvesting in America—no, you don't! You and Hans Olsa couldn't any more take care of the binding, when I once get going, than you could fly! You don't even know what needs to be done; you've never seen a job of binding in your life! . . . Now do as I tell you and get the Solum boys!" . . . Tönseten spoke as if the welfare of the whole country were resting on his shoulders. His neighbour only laughed still harder and did as he was bid.

The moment the noon meal was over, the whole of the little settlement assembled at Per Hansa's wheat field, men, women, and children; Beret had brought And-Ongen with her, and even carried the baby in her arms. Tönseten's shouts and numberless commands put every-one but himself in a festive mood; he felt it to be a solemn occasion, and highly disapproved of the way they took it; but the others only laughed and joked as gayly as if they were in a bridal procession on the way to church, some bright Sunday morning. Some one would think of a funny remark, which straightway would cause some one else to make a still funnier sally; though most of it was aimed at Tönseten, his wife laughed until the tears came. But Tönseten held himself superior to their silly talk; he had matters of weight and purpose on his mind. Fools will snicker and blat! he observed to himself, working steadily on, that's the only way one can keep 'em going.

He was on his back under the machine, sweating streams, hammering away with a heavy monkey wrench, tightening one bur here and another there; now here was a place that needed oiling. . . . "What the devil became of the oil can? Can't you do anything but stand there and grin? Come here and help me!"

But at last he got things so far along that he could hitch the horses to the reaper; taking the lines, he mounted to the throne.

. . . "Now, the Lord help us!" he muttered to himself. He wanted to give more orders, but couldn't get a chance; the mosquitoes were bad and the horses rather uneasy, and new things kept happening all the time. With a great flourish he manœuvred the reaper over to the edge of the field, shouted loudly to the horses—and the first harvest in the settlement by Spring Creek had begun.

The machine roared fearfully as it got its belly full of the heavy grain, but kept calling for more; the horses stepped off at a lively pace and gave it what it called for. Tönseten was now intent on cutting out the first swathe; it had to be straight, and yet it couldn't leave anything along the edge; he was too much taken up with this momentous task even to see the others. But when he had finished the fourth round of the field he felt that he was master of the situation. Stopping the machine, he called in English to Henry Solum—how was *he* getting along? Could he pound any sense into those idiots? Well, Kjersti had been a smart binder in her day. Why didn't he get her to help him with the instruction? . . . And then, turning majestically in his seat, he addressed Per Hansa:

"If this wheat doesn't run forty bushels to the acre, I'll eat my own shirt! By God, I will! . . . Well, anyway, thirty-five . . ."

"You go on with the cutting, brother!" chuckled Per Hansa. "Here's a whole army waiting for something to do! . . . Go on, I say. We'll measure it up later."

All were working; all were having a good time. For the greenhorns the binding proved to be more like work than art; they soon caught on to the trick; there were so many of them at it that the binding this afternoon went like a jolly game. When Beret finally put the baby down on the grass and began tying up bundles of wheat Kjersti felt that she had to come over and speak to her. There wasn't any need of that, she said; the men could easily handle what had to be done. Heavens and earth—five grown men and two boys in a field no bigger than this! Beret and Sörine had better go home and get a lunch ready, Kjersti advised further; the menfolk were never happier than when they had coffee brought to them in the field. She knew them! . . . After a while the two women followed her advice and went home to make their preparations.

Per Hansa was in a rare mood that afternoon. Now he was binding his own wheat, his hands oily with the sap of the new-cut stems; a fine oil it was, too—he rubbed his hands together and felt a sensuous pleasure welling up within him. His body seemed to grow a little with every bundle he tied; he walked as if on springs; a strength the like of which he had never felt before ran through his muscles. How good it was to be alive! He had made a daring throw, and luck had smiled on him! . . . He tied the ripe, heavy bundles, gave them a twist, and there stood the shock! As he looked at them he laughed to himself joyously, stopping a second as he finished each one to draw his hands over his face. . . . He must handle these bundles with care—the heavy kernels might shell out. . . . How absurdly light-hearted and gay he felt to-day! . . .

The men continued working until the dew became so heavy on the wheat that the reaping machine refused to go; it was long after sundown before they quit. Tönseten felt stiff and tired, but he wasn't announcing the fact from the housetops. In Per Hansa's hut stood a table heaped with many good things, though the porridge bowls predominated. Both Kjersti and Sörine had been home to do their own chores for the night, and had returned to help Beret with the supper.

The men were already seated at the table; but they waited for Per Hansa, who had his head in the big chest and was hunting for something or other. "Hold on a minute, boys, before you say grace," came from the cavernous depths of the chest. "Haven't you manners enough to wait for the head of the family?" . . . When he finally emerged and came up to the table, he shook a bottle behind Tönseten's ear, asking, gayly, "Did you ever hear a sweeter sound, Syvert? Can't you just hear her *wink* at you, my boy?" . . . There was enough in the bottle for one round, and then a little drop to swallow on, before the meal started.

Tönseten cleared his throat after the drink; he was anxious to make a little speech:

"What do you plan on doing in the future, Per Hansa, if you're going to get rich on the very first crop? . . . I never in my life saw such wheat! Why, the kernels are like potatoes!"

"How about yourself, then?" inquired Per Hansa in great good humour. "I like to help worthy people who are in trouble; in case you and Kjersti should run short of stockings to keep your money in, you might come to me!"

As the meal went on, the spirits of the men sitting about the table rose higher and higher, and each vied with the other in good cheer.

"Rich?" exclaimed Tönseten. "We'll all get rich; no doubt about it! . . . It's going to be hardest on Sam, poor fellow. He'll have to spend it all in getting married to that fine Trönder girl who's waiting for him over east by the Sioux River! Hard luck, I say!"

"Yes, sir!" drawled Sam, blushing furiously. "But if I were you, Kjersti, I wouldn't let Syvert go to the wedding—no, I wouldn't at all!"

"Why?" laughed Kjersti, innocently.

"Well, you see, he gets sort of strung-up when he's turned loose among the Trönder women—not that I mean anything, you know. . . ."

"Sam, you're a fool!" remarked Tönseten, angrily, laying down his spoon and leaving the table.

IX

By noon the next day they had finished the wheat field. To-day Tönseten was of a different mind—there really was no great hurry; the weather kept cool, and the grain didn't look any riper to-day than yesterday, either at his own place or at Hans Olsa's; if this spell of cool weather should last, the wheat would profit by yet another week; but then they might prepare to harvest a crop unique in the history of wheat growing.

Tönseten felt highly well pleased with himself and the rest of the world; he had now proved his prowess before his neighbours; the field was almost finished here, and it wouldn't do any harm to rest and visit awhile. . . . "Don't fret, boys, I won't need to hurry at all! Those four acres of oats will only be play for the afternoon!"

And Per Hansa felt very much the same way. He and the other men were sitting in the shade on the north side of the house, with their backs up against the wall, enjoying the cool breeze that had sprung up from the west. . . . What was the use of hurrying? . . . Per Hansa had told the Solum boys that he wouldn't need them that afternoon, as he and Hans Olsa could easily bind the oats; but it was so pleasant to rest here and spin yarns that the boys didn't feel like stirring until the others went to the field.

As they got up at last and returned to their work, the northwest breeze struck them full in the face with its cool, fresh fragrance; Tönseten sniffed it approvingly, declaring that if this weather kept on, he and Hans Olsa would be sure to steal a march on Per Hansa in the end; never had the Lord sent finer weather for wheat to ripen in! He chuckled and talked away, his rotund body bobbing up and down with an irresistible merriment. . . . "Well, boys, in my opinion the Land of Canaan didn't have much on this country—no, I'm damned if it had! Do you suppose the children of Israel ever smelt a westerly breeze like this? Why, folks, it's blowing honey!" . . . His festive mood was still possessing him as he began to hitch up the horses; in the midst of it he had to turn around and ask them shyly, "Now, wasn't it remarkable that I should discover just *this* place for you?"

Hans Olsa burst into a laugh. "Yes, it surely was wonderful, Syvert!"

But Tönseten felt that this praise wasn't enough—he wanted to carry the joke a little farther. Turning to his other neighbour, he asked with the same roguish air, "What did you say, Per Hansa?"

Per Hansa remained strangely silent; he was standing a little distance away, shading his eyes with his right hand and looking into the west; an intent, troubled expression had come over his face.

. . . "What in the devil? . . ." he muttered to himself. Off in the western sky he had caught sight of something he couldn't understand—something that sent a nameless chill through his blood. . . . Could that be a storm coming on?

He hurried over to the wheat shock where Hans Olsa was sitting, pointed westward, and asked in a low voice, "Tell me, can you see anything over there?"

Hans Olsa was on his feet in an instant. . . . "Well, look at that! . . . It must be going to storm!"

Tönseten had finished hitching the horses to the reaper, and had just mounted the seat when he saw Per Hansa run over, pointing to the west. Now both his neighbours were shouting at him:

"What's that, Syvert?"

Tönseten turned in his seat, to face a sight such as he had never seen or heard before. From out of the west layers of clouds came rolling—thin layers that rose and sank on the breeze; they had none of the look or manner of ordinary clouds; they came in waves, like the surges of the sea, and cast a glittering sheen before them as they came; they seemed to be made of some solid murky substance that threw out small sparks along its face.

The three men stood spellbound, watching the oncoming terror; their voices died in their throats; their minds were blank. The horses snorted as they, too, caught sight of it, and became very restless.

The ominous waves of cloud seemed to advance with terrific speed, breaking now and then like a huge surf, and with the deep, dull roaring sound as of a heavy undertow rolling into caverns in a mountain side. . . . But they were neither breakers nor foam, these waves. . . . It seemed more as if the unseen hand of a giant were shaking an immense tablecloth of iridescent colours! . . .

"For God's sake, what——!" . . . Tönseten didn't finish; unconsciously he had been hauling so hard on the lines that the horses began backing the machine.

Just then Ole and Store-Hans came running wildly up,

shouting breathlessly, "A snowstorm is coming! . . . *See!*"

. . . The next moment the first wave of the weird cloud engulfed them, spewing over them its hideous, unearthly contents. The horses became uncontrollable. "Come here and give me some help!" cried Tönseten through the eerie hail, but the others, standing like statues, heard nothing and paid no heed; the impact of the solid surge had forced them to turn their backs to the wind. Tönseten could not hold the horses; they bolted across the field, cutting a wide semi-circle through the oats; not until he had the stern of his craft well into the wind could he stop them long enough to scramble down and unhitch them from the reaper.

At that moment two women came running up—Kjersti first, with her skirt thrown over her head, Sörine a little way behind, beating the air with frantic motions. The Solum boys, too, had now joined the terror-stricken little crowd. Down by the creek the grazing cows had hoisted their tails straight in the air and run for the nearest shelter; and no sooner had the horses been turned loose, than they followed suit; man and beast alike were overcome by a nameless fear.

And now from out the sky gushed down with cruel force a living, pulsating stream, striking the backs of the helpless folk like pebbles thrown by an unseen hand; but that which fell out of the heavens was not pebbles, nor raindrops, nor hail, for then it would have lain inanimate where it fell; this substance had no sooner fallen than it popped up again, crackling, and snapping—rose up and disappeared in the twinkling of an eye; it flared and flittered around them like light gone mad; it chirped and buzzed through the air; it snapped and hopped along the ground; the whole place was a weltering turmoil of raging little demons; if one looked for a moment into the wind, one saw nothing but glittering, lightninglike flashes—flashes that came and went, in the heart of a cloud made up of innumerable dark-brown clicking bodies! All the while the roaring sound continued.

"Father!" shrieked Store-Hans through the storm. "They're little birds—they have regular wings! Look here!" . . . The boy had caught one in his hand; spreading the wings and holding it out by their tips, he showed it to his father. The body of the unearthly creature had a dark-brown colour; it was about an inch in length, or perhaps a trifle longer; it was plump around the middle and tapered at both ends; on either side of its head sparkled a tiny black eye that seemed to look out with a supernatural intelligence; underneath it were long, slender legs with rusty bands around them; the wings were transparent and of a pale, light colour.

"For God's sake, child, throw it away!" moaned Kjersti.

The boy dropped it in fright. No sooner had he let it go than there sounded a snap, a twinkling flash was seen, and the creature had merged itself with the countless legions of flickering devils which now filled all space. They whizzed by in the air; they literally covered the ground; they lit on the heads of grain, on the stubble, on everything in sight—popping and glittering, millions on millions of them. . . . The people watched it, stricken with fear and awe. Here was *Another One* speaking! . . .

Kjersti was crying bitterly; Sörine's kind face was deathly pale as she glanced at the men, trying to bolster up her courage; but the big frame of her husband was bent in fright and dismay. He spoke slowly and solemnly: "This must be one of the plagues mentioned in the Bible!"

"Yes! and the devil take it!" muttered Per Hansa, darkly. . . . "But it can't last forever."

To Tönseten the words of Per Hansa, in an hour like this, sounded like the sheerest blasphemy; they would surely call down upon them a still darker wrath! He turned to reprove his neighbour: "Now the Lord is taking back what he has given," he said, impressively. "I might have guessed that I would never be permitted to harvest such wheat. That was asking too much!"

"Stop your silly gabble!" snarled Per Hansa. "Do you really suppose *He* needs to take the bread out of your mouth?"

There was a certain consolation in Per Hansa's outburst of angry rationalism; Kjersti ceased weeping, though it was her own husband that had been put to shame. "I believe Per Hansa is right," she said, the sobs still choking her. "The Lord can't have any use for our wheat He doesn't need bread, anyway. He certainly wouldn't take it from us in this way!"

But her open unbelief only confirmed her husband in his position; clearing his throat, he began to take Kjersti to task: "Don't you remember your catechism, and your Bible history? Isn't it plainly stated that this is one of the seven plagues that fell upon Egypt? Look out for your tongue, woman, lest He send us the other six, too! . . . It states as plain as day that it was because the people *hardened themselves!*" . . .

Tönseten would probably have gone on indefinitely expounding the Scriptures to his wife if Henry Solum hadn't interrupted just then with a practical idea. Turning to his brother, he said, "Go fetch the horses, so we can finish this field; by to-morrow there won't be anything left!"

Per Hansa looked at Henry and nodded approvingly; the simple practicability of the suggestion had touched the chord of action again; he jumped to his feet and walked across to the field, where the work of devastation was already in full progress. As he saw the fine, ripe grain being ruthlessly destroyed before his eyes, he felt but one impulse—to stop the inroads of these demons in any possible way. He began to jump up and down and wave his hat, stamping and yelling like one possessed. But the hosts of horrid creatures frolicking about him never so much as noticed his presence; the brown bodies whizzed by on every hand, alighting wherever they pleased, chirping wherever they went; as many as half a dozen of them would perch on a single head of grain, while the stem would be covered with them all the way to the ground; even his own body seemed to be a desirable halting place; they lit on his arms; his back, his neck—they even dared to light on his bared head and on the very hat he waved.

His utter impotence in the face of this tragedy threw him into an uncontrollable fury; he lost all restraint over himself. "You, Ola!" he shouted, hoarsely. "Run home after Old Maria, and bring the caps!"

The boy was soon back with the old musket. His

father, hardly able to wait, ran to meet him and snatched the weapon out of his hands. Hurriedly putting on a cap, he settled himself in a firm foothold—for he still had sense enough to remember how hard the rifle kicked when it had been lying loaded a long time.

As Hans Olsa caught wind of what he intended to do he tried to stop it. "Don't do that, Per Hansa! If the Lord has sent this affliction on us, then . . ."

Per Hansa glowered at him with a look of angry determination; then, facing squarely the hurricane of flying bodies, he fired straight into the thickest of the welter! . . . The awful detonation of the old, rusty muzzle-loader had a singular effect; at first, as the shattering sound died away, nothing appeared to have happened—the glittering demons flickered by as unconcernedly as before; but presently a new movement seemed to originate within the body of the main cloud; it began to heave and roll with a lifting motion; in a few minutes the cloud had left the ground and was sailing over their heads, with only an intermittent hail of bodies pelting down on them out of its lower fringe; the roaring becoming more muffled.

"Do you suppose you've actually driven them off?" cried Henry, breathlessly, marvelling as he watched.

"Yes, from *here!*" said Hans Olsa in the same solemn tone, as he pointed down the hill. "But see *our* fields . . . !"

Per Hansa was still in the grip of the strange spell that had taken possession of him; he apparently did not hear what the others were saying; without looking again he hurried off to help Sam with the horses. "Let's get the reaper started!" he cried. "No sense in sitting here like a row of dummies!"

His example roused them once more, and without further words they followed his lead; just before sundown that night they finished the oat field at Per Hansa's. All the while fresh clouds of marauders were passing over. As soon as he could get away each man hurried to his own place; they were all terribly anxious to see how much damage had been done at home. . . . Couldn't they start cutting to-morrow, even if the grain wasn't quite ripe? they thought as they hurried on. Wouldn't it be possible to save *something* out of the wreck? What in God's name could they do if the whole crop were destroyed? . . . Anxiety tugged at their heartstrings. Yes, what could they do? . . .

Ole and Store-Hans went home with Hans Olsa to bring back word as to whether it would be possible to start harvesting his field in the morning. Per Hansa walked home alone; the spell had lifted now, and the reaction had left him in a troubled, irresolute frame of mind. The things that had happened that afternoon seemed harsh and inexplicable. . . . To be sure, *he* had saved his whole crop—but how and why? He had saved it—partly because of his own foolish, headstrong acts, and partly because his land chanced to lie so much higher than that of his neighbours, that it had been the first to dry out in the spring. . . . Well, great luck for him! But at this moment gladness and happiness were the last things that he could feel. . . . There were his neighbours—poor devils! Hadn't they worked just as faithfully, hadn't they struggled just as hard—and with a great deal more common sense than he had shown? Why should they have to suffer this terrible calamity while he went scot-free? . . . And there was something else that worried him desperately. Throughout the afternoon, while he had been working, vague misgivings of how it was going at home had visited him, an uneasy sense of oppression and impending disaster; he had found himself constantly watching his own house, and had every moment expected to see Beret come around the corner. But not a soul had he caught sight of in all this time, moving about down there, though the hard labour and the fiends of the air had left him scant chance to think about it till now.

As he approached the house his misgivings grew more pronounced, till suddenly they leaped into an overmastering fear which he tried to assuage by telling himself that she had kept indoors because she had not dared to leave the children, and that in doing so she had acted wisely. . . . The house lay in deep twilight as he drew near; there was no sign of life to be seen or heard, except the malign beings that still snapped and flared through the air; the sod hut, surrounded as it was by flowing shapes, looked like a quay thrust out into a turbulent current; in the deepening twilight, the pale, shimmering sails of the flying creatures had taken on a still more unearthly sheen; they came, flickered by, and were gone in an instant, only to give place to myriads more.

. . . Can she have gone over to one of the neighbours'? he wondered as he came up to the door. No, she hasn't—the door can't be closed from the outside. . . . Per Hansa gasped for breath as he knocked on the door of his own house. . . . He rapped harder . . . called, with his voice tearing from his throat:

"Open the door, Beret!"

He found himself listening intently, his ears strained to catch the least sound; at length he thought he heard a movement inside, and a great wave of relief swept over him.

. . . "Thank God!" . . . He waited for the door to be opened—but nothing happened; nothing more could be heard. . . . What can she be doing? Didn't she hear me? What in Heaven's name has she put in front of the door? . . .

Per Hansa had begun to shove against the panel.

"Open the door, I tell you! . . . Beret—where are you?" . . .

Once more he listened; once more he caught a faint sound; but the blood pounding in his ears deafened him now. Pulling himself together, he shoved against the door with all his strength—shoved until red streaks were flashing before his eyes. The door began to give—the opening widened; at last he had pushed it wide enough to slip through.

. . . "*Beret!*" . . . The anguish of his cry cut through the air. . . . "Beret!" . . .

Now he stood in the middle of the room. It was absolutely dark before his eyes; he looked wildly around, but could see nothing.

. . . "Beret, where are you?"

No answer came—there was no one to be seen. But wasn't that a sound? "Beret!" he called again, sharply. He heard it now distinctly. Was it coming from one of the beds, or over there by the door? . . . It was a faint, whimpering sound. He rushed to the beds and threw off the bedclothes—no one in this one, no one in that one—it must be over by the door! . . . He staggered back—the big chest was standing in front of the door. Who could have dragged it there? . . . Per Hansa flung the cover open with frantic haste. The sight that met his eyes made his blood run cold. Down in the depths of the great chest lay Beret, huddled up and holding the baby in her arms; And-Ongen was crouching at her feet—the whimpering sound had come from her.

It seemed for a moment as if he would go mad; the room swam and receded in dizzy circles. . . . But things had to be done. First he lifted And-Ongen out and carried her to the bed—then the baby. At last he took Beret up in his arms, slammed down the lid of the chest, and set her on it.

. . . "Beret, Beret!" . . . he kept whispering.

All his strength seemed to leave him as he looked into her tear-swollen face; yet it wasn't her tears that drained his heart dry—the face was that of a stranger, behind which her own face seemed to be hidden.

He gazed at her helplessly, imploringly; she returned the gaze in a fixed stare, and whispered hoarsely:

"Hasn't the devil got you yet? He has been all around here to-day. . . . Put the chest back in front of the door right away! He doesn't dare to take the chest, you see. . . . We must hide in it—all of us!"

"Oh, Beret!" begged Per Hansa, his very soul in the cry. Speechless and all undone, he sank down before her, threw his arms around her waist, and buried his head in her lap—as if he were a child needing comfort.

The action touched her; she began to pat his head, running her fingers through his hair and stroking his cheek. . . . "That's right!" she crooned. . . . "Weep now, weep much and long because of your sin! . . . So I have done every night—not that it helps much. . . . Out here nobody pays attention to our tears . . . it's too open and wild . . . but it does no harm to try."

"Oh, Beret, my own girl!"

"Yes, yes, I know," she said, as if to hush him. She grew more loving, caressed him tenderly, bent over to lift him up to her. . . . "Don't be afraid, dear boy of mine! . . . For . . . well . . . it's always worst just before it's over!"

Per Hansa gazed deep into her eyes; a sound of agony came from his throat; he sank down suddenly in a heap and knew nothing more. . . .

Outside, the fiendish shapes flickered and danced in the dying glow of the day. The breeze had died down; the air seemed unaccountably lighter.

. . . That night the Great Prairie stretched herself voluptuously; giantlike and full of cunning, she laughed softly into the reddish moon. "Now we will see what human might may avail against us! . . . Now we'll see!" . . .

X

And now had begun a seemingly endless struggle between man's fortitude in adversity, on the one hand, and the powers of evil in high places, on the other. There were signs of the scourge in the summer of '73, but not before the following year did it assume the proportions of a plague; after that it raged with unabated fury throughout the years '74, '75, '76, '77, and part of '78; then it disappeared as suddenly and mysteriously as it had come. The devastation it wrought was terrible; it made beggars of some, and drove others insane; still others it sent wandering back to the forest lands, though they found conditions little better there, either. . . . But the greater number simply hung on where they were. They stayed because poverty, that most supreme of masters, had deprived them of the liberty to rise up and go away. And where would they have gone? In the name of Heaven, whither would they have fled?

In the course of time it came about that fresh inroads of settlers, just as poverty-stricken as they were, arrived to help them suffer privation and to wait for better times. . . . Beautiful out here on the wide prairie —yes, beautiful indeed! . . . The finest soil you ever dreamed of—a veritable Land of Canaan! . . . One caravan after another came creaking along, a single wagon dropping out to settle here, another to settle there; for it really looked wonderful, this vast expanse of level, smiling plain—the new Promised Land into which the Lord was leading His poor people from all the corners of the earth! . . .

But the plague of locusts proved as certain as the seasons. All that grew above the ground, with the exception of the wild grass, it would pounce upon and destroy; the grass it left untouched because it had grown here ere time was and *without the aid of man's hand.* . . .

Who would dare affirm that this plague was not of supernatural origin? During the spring season, and throughout the early part of the summer, the air would be as pure and clear as if it had been filtered, wrapping and caressing the body like the finest silk; the sky would be as blue as if it had been scoured and newly painted; everything planted in the ground by man would grow as if by magic, filling out with an amazing fruitfulness, as the long warm days passed in endless array, until it bent under its own burden. And then, just as the process of ripening had begun, or perhaps a little before, the plague would descend upon them, suddenly, mysteriously, disastrously! On a certain bright, sunny day, when the breeze sighed its loveliest out of the northwest, strange clouds would appear in the western sky; swiftly they would advance, floating lazily through the clear air, a sight beautiful to behold. But these clouds would be made up of innumerable dark-brown bodies with slender legs, sailing on transparent wings; in an instant the air would be filled with nameless, unclean creatures—legions on legions of them, hosts without number! Now pity the fields that the hand of man had planted with so much care! And the ruthless marauders invariably came out of the clear northwest where the afternoon glow was brightest, most marvellous; more than often toward evening, when the day was sinking to rest and all earth seemed at peace, they would come. To these wandering Norsemen, the old adage that all evil dwells below and springs from the north, was proving true again.*

* An old superstition that goes back to Norse mythology: the Kingdom of Darkness and Evil was located in the far

During the summer of their first visitation, the demons left behind them evil enough to pollute a whole continent. In the plowed fields they laid tiny, frail eggs, having the appearance of fine dry sawdust; although they seemed so delicate, these eggs would lie there unharmed during the wet fall season, and all through the winter, embedded in ice and covered by many feet of snow, thawing and freezing by turns in the early spring; but when the hot sun of summer had warmed them for a while they would suddenly burst open, letting loose a host of voracious, crawling devils. This phenomenon called to mind another saying: No evil is quite so bad as that which man himself fosters. It seemed to be true enough in this case; for these little wriggling demons were not only revoltingly nasty to look at, but they also caused an even greater devastation than those which came flying on the wings of the western breeze.

Not that these others ceased coming now, because man had raised a crop of his own—God, no! It would happen for days at a time, during the height of the pest season, that one could not see clear sky. But not always did the scourge choose to descend; often the locust clouds would come drifting across the sun, very much like streamers of snow, floating lazily by for days on end; then, all of a sudden, as if overcome by their own neglect, they would swoop down, dashing and spreading out like an angry flood, slicing and shearing, cutting with greedy teeth, laying waste every foot of the field they lighted in. At last, perhaps by the time the next afternoon's breeze had risen, they would apparently take the notion that *this* wasn't a fit place to stay in; in a moment they would fly up and be gone in a great cloud, off on the search for new conquests.

Impossible to outguess them! No creatures ever acted so whimsically or showed such a lack of rational, orderly method. One field they might entirely lay waste,

---

north; the way to Hell led downward and in a northerly direction. In the practice of sorcery and witchcraft, whenever water was to be used it must always be taken from streams flowing from south to north, for such water had supernatural power.

while they ate only a few rods into the next; a third, lying close beside the others, they might not choose to touch at all. In one field they would cut the stalks, leaving the ground strewn with a green carpet of heads; in the next they might content themselves with shearing the beard—then the grain looked like shorn sheep with the ears gone. Nor were they at all fastidious: potatoes and vegetables of all kinds, barley and oats, wheat and rye—it made no difference; or a swarm of insects might light on a wagon box, and when it lifted again the box would have been scarred by countless sharp teeth; at one place a fork with a handle of hickory might be standing in the ground, and after a few swarms had passed the surface of the handle would be rasped and chewed, a mass of loose slivers; somewhere else a garment might be laid out on the ground to dry—a swarm would light on it, and in a moment only shreds would be left; if the annihilating devils were in the proper mood, they would take anything and leave nothing.

The folk looked on helplessly, in grim despair and awestricken wonder; the more timid ones among them were oppressed by a growing fear, while the godless swore so that the air smelled of brimstone; the pious would assemble in homes and churches, entreating the Lord to deliver them from famine and pestilence; but the brave did not lose heart, and kept on busily inventing all sorts of devices with which to drive the demons away. Many odd expedients were tried in different places; simple-minded people would take a washtub and a rolling pin, and beat until they were tired, but never a ripple did such a din cause in the current's steady flow.

And all the while the folk tried to comfort one another. . . . It will be better by-and-by, you know! . . . This plague must leave *some time*—it can't go on forever! . . . The Sognings were a people of even temperament, not easily flustered; they bore the affliction with remarkable calmness and fortitude. Of course this thing would have to stop! They had faith to believe it —how could it well be otherwise? . . . And their cousins, the Vossings, would always agree with them.

Yes, indeed! Why, such things always seem hardest to bear at the first—don't we know *that?* . . . Some one would think of a hallowed consolation with which to comfort the others. Wasn't it pretty bad in Egypt?—But what did the Book say? Didn't the plague vanish there? Why, it had lasted practically no time at all! . . . I'll bet my last dollar, some one else would venture, that next year everything will be all right! . . . And when it turned out to be just as bad the following year, the same person would be even more confident. Now, see—we've had this thing with us two years already—this is the end! Who ever heard of a plague lasting forever? Don't you remember the Black Death? That finished up in half a year, didn't it, and was never heard of again? . . . And even when the third summer came, and there was no let-up in the awful visitation, some bright head would remember the indisputable fact that *all good things are three*. So there!—Now let's thank the Lord that we're through with it at last! Just wait awhile—the soil out here is first class; if we hang on, we're sure to make a clean sweep! . . . On the fourth summer the plague raged worse than ever before; but now it had begun to lose its power over the people—they feared it no longer. We're getting used to it, they would say with a bitter laugh. It takes neither man nor beast—let's thank God for *that* anyway! . . .

III The Glory of the Lord

I

A day in June, of quivering, vital sunlight. . . . The irregular shadows of fleecy clouds drifting across an endless plain. . . . Sun and irregular, fleecy clouds—nothing but these all day . . .

Over the prairie, making toward the settlement by Spring Creek, rattled an old, dilapidated cart, antique of build, in a state so wretched that it seemed ready to fall apart at the next tussock it might encounter.

The nag in front was in perfect keeping with the vehicle: long-shanked and rawboned, and so lean and lanky that one could have counted every rib. Originally its colour might have been a light grey, but now it was no longer definable: dirty grey, rusty, yellowish-brown—it might have been any one of these, or just as accurately something else. Only a few miserable hanks were left of what probably had once been a flowing mane. Above the shoulders rose a big hump; when the animal stretched out its neck, one was reminded of a dromedary. Undoubtedly it had once been an authentic horse, but that must have been a long time ago.

The man in the seat was of even more uncertain age than either horse or vehicle. He might be forty-five, or he might just as likely be sixty-five. But for his beard and stoutness, one would be inclined to guess the former figure, for the expression of his face was still youthful, the eyes bright and sparkling with something boyish in their gleam. But the beard clearly suggested a more advanced age; it stretched from ear to ear, forming a thick fringe around the chin; it was perhaps an inch long, heavy and stiff, originally blond in colour, but now streaked with grey. The clothes, too, testified to the man's advanced age; especially the coat, which seemed to be neither coat nor jacket, but something out of the ordinary —a garment of thin black cloth, loosely fitting, too long to be called a jacket, yet not long enough for a topcoat.

The horse trudged slowly on, the cart jolting and rumbling behind; the man on the seat allowed him to dawdle as much as he pleased, and hummed tunes to himself to pass the time. After a long while the sod huts by Spring Creek began almost imperceptibly to lift their heads out of the ground; and not a bit too soon, for evening was fast coming on.

A couple of frame houses, one large and square, the other smaller and with a high gable, had long been visible. They seemed strangely conspicuous in the bare, level landscape; one could not help wondering if they really belonged here in the wilderness. The man on the cart, however, apparently paid no heed to them; as the sod huts came more and more within the range of his vision, his humming gradually grew fainter and more intermittent.

"Hm . . . hm. . . . Well, here they are. Move along now, King!" came coaxingly from out of the fringe of beard. "We must try to scratch gravel, you see, and get there before the folks go to bed. Go 'long, I tell you, go 'long!"

The sun had already set when the horse came to a standstill in front of one of the huts; the traveller did not get down.

"Anybody at home here?" he shouted in a strong voice.

Sounds of sudden movement were heard within. A stout, toil-worn, red-faced man came hastily out, an equally stout but rounder woman rolled after him, both with their mouths full of food; the red-faced man was wiping his beard; both he and his wife were staring at the stranger.

"I asked if there were people here," repeated the man, unconsciously falling into the idiom of his native tongue and using a phrase that carried a special meaning. Behind the fringe of his whiskers beamed a broad smile.

"Oh, the devil! Are you Norwegian, then?" shouted the red-faced man, jovially.

"So, so! Do you call on *that fellow* around here?"

The man on the ground immediately grew serious; he and his wife were staring at the stranger.

"Have you any more food than you need for supper, and a place to put up a tired horse that's been on his feet all day?"

Without waiting for an answer, the speaker threw down the lines, stepped out of the cart, stretched himself, and sighed with relief.

"My, my! How stiff one gets from all this shaking! . . . What's your name, my good man?"

"My name is Syvert Tönseten. What kind of a fellow may you be?" Tönseten came close up and looked inquiringly at the stranger, who had now turned to the woman:

"Have you got any food in the house, mother?" And ignoring the man, the traveller took from his cart a large, old, and well-worn satchel, which he deposited on the ground.

"Why, yes . . . of course . . . if you will take what we have!" said Kjersti, slowly. There she paused; moving behind her husband, she took her hand from under her apron and gave a pull at his jacket; she had now looked the stranger over and didn't feel altogether relieved. . . .

Tönseten was too preoccupied with himself to notice her. "I am asking you," he said with pompous dignity, "what kind of a fellow you are and what you are after. Are you looking for land?"

The stranger put his hands against his sides, looked straight at them, and said, impressively:

"I am a minister. As for you, my good man, you ought not to stand there swearing into the face of strangers! . . . Now let me ask you again: May I stop here to-night?"

"Good heavens!" exclaimed Tönseten, letting his

breath go as if some one had hit him in the stomach.

"Oh, my! Oh, my!" wailed Kjersti, awe-stricken, yet overwhelmed with joy. "Is the man crazy? Can he really be a minister? . . . Of course he must stop here, if he can only eat the stuff we have!"

"Don't worry about that, mother." He turned to her husband. "And now you and I will attend to the horse."

Tönseten's knees were weak from penitent zeal; he trembled with eagerness to help; he wanted to talk, but his voice failed and the words would not come. But the horse was wonderfully well cared for; he even went back a second time, after they were through, to spread another layer of straw for bedding. While they worked the minister had many questions to ask; they took their own time about coming in.

At last Tönseten ushered the minister into the hut, placed a chair at the farthest end of the table, and bade him be seated. The table now was laid with a white tablecloth, on which had been placed a superabundance of food for only one person; there were *römmekolle* and *flatbröd*, fresh milk and boiled eggs; there were coffee and cakes; but even so, Kjersti thought it too little to offer such a distinguished visitor; now she was busy frying a couple of egg pancakes. Thank goodness, there was plenty of what she had! She had hurriedly tidied up the room; it looked cozy and comfortable inside the hut, and the minister could not refrain from expressing his admiration.

Finally he sat up to the table and began to eat, praising everything that he tasted and helping himself bountifully, like a healthy person whose hunger has been sharpened by a long fast.

Tönseten remained standing in the middle of the floor, talking with the minister; his manner was humble almost to the point of unction, his voice had taken on a tone of great solemnity. Kjersti hung in the background by the stove, where the room lay in shadow, listening closely to the conversation; she was more concerned about what her husband said than to follow the minister's discourse—Syvert was so easily excited, poor fellow, and had so little experience in talking to people of quality! She watched the minister as he helped himself liberally to the food, and felt the blessing of it descend upon her. How kind of him to say the nice things he did about the food she had prepared! . . . And he chatted with them so pleasantly and naturally! No traces of sermonizing in his talk! Why, he and Syvert were just discussing ordinary everyday things—about conditions as they were around there, about crops and prospects, about the best way to run a farm. . . . Now and then Tönseten would turn their conversation toward the future; he was more interested in visualizing how things were going to turn out than in making a bare statement of how they actually were; *that* was something he could enlarge upon to the minister! And the minister seemed to have much good advice; thus they ought to do with that, he said, and so with this, but differently with the other. . . . At length he inquired about the religious life of the people in this locality. Tönseten cleared his throat at the question, which he had been expecting, and answered emphatically that that was a subject on which he wasn't very well posted; you couldn't expect a common farmer to know much about such matters. And then he began hurriedly to ask the pastor which way he had come, and whether he had seen many settlers in the parts through which he had travelled. This, in turn, gave him an opportunity to tell how the country looked hereabouts when he had first arrived six years ago; he waxed so eloquent on this point that it seemed difficult for him to stop. . . . Kjersti realized that he was now on extremely dangerous ground!——

At last the minister had finished his meal.

"Now then, my good man, be silent, and we will thank the Lord for this day."

"Yes, yes—of course!" . . . Tönseten blew his nose vigorously; but not knowing what to do with himself next, he stuck his thumbs inside his trousers-band, and stood where he was in the middle of the floor, utterly unnerved.

Kjersti sank down on the wood-box, and wiped her eyes with her apron. . . . She wanted to tell her husband to sit down, but simply couldn't screw up her courage to do it.

Placing his folded hands on the table, the minister

began in a quiet way, as if addressing some one they could not see who stood very near; he seemed to be well acquainted with this unseen being, for he spoke in a low voice and very intimately, as to a dear friend who, unexpectedly, had done him a good turn. He thanked Him for the day that now was past, nevermore to return, entreating Him to cast into the ocean of grace all sins committed on this day; he prayed long and earnestly for the people out here, for the house in which he sat, and especially for the man standing there who was so prone to swear; in one way or another He must come to him and remind him constantly of what His holy law provided with respect to this grievous sin. But He must not be too severe with these poor people, for they had wandered far from home and some had gone astray, and long had they dwelt out here in the Great Wilderness, without a shepherd and without care. Truly, life had not been easy for them! . . . After saying amen, he remained silent for some time, with hands still folded; from the candle on the table a pale glow was thrown over his face, touching the fringe of his beard with pure silver. . . . Peace had fallen on the room.

Then the minister arose.

"Praise be to God, and thanks to you, good people, for this sumptuous feast!"

Tönseten again blew his nose violently; then, overcome with confusion, he wheeled about and walked out of the hut.

Kjersti sat on the wood-box, weeping with mingled emotions. The minister came over and took her by the hand. "A fine meal you prepared for me, mother, and here are my heartfelt thanks!"

"Oh, well—that's nothing!" . . . She shook her head speechlessly, but could not let go his hand.

In a moment Tönseten returned. . . . This would never do, he wanted to explain. He wasn't such a bad case as the minister seemed to think. He ought to hear some of the others when they let themselves go! . . . But as soon as he stood in the presence of the pastor, confusion overcame him again; he merely stuttered and stammered, and found nothing to say.

The minister now opened his satchel; first of all he

took out a large, fat pouch, and then an ancient pipe, which he carefully cleaned and promptly filled. "A little incense, I think, will now be blessedly enjoyable. . . . No, just remain seated, mother."

II

The sleeping quarters assigned to the minister were the spare sod house, a structure which was now to be found on every farm. Clothes were hung in it, and food was stored there, as well as tools and farm implements; it might even contain a blacksmith's shop and a carpenter's bench, if the size of the room was sufficient; but nearly always there was a bed, made and ready for use.

But the minister seemed more anxious to visit with them than to go to bed; he smoked pipe after pipe, striking it against his toe to knock out the ashes, each time filling and lighting it anew. He asked them all about their life, and the struggle they had had since they came to this place. This was rich for Tönseten; he never tired of telling. . . . Finally the minister knocked out the ashes of his pipe for the last time, got up, and laid it carefully aside.

"Well, now the day is done, and a fine, blessed day it has been; the night is approaching, so let us enjoy sweet repose. . . . Where do you intend to put me up for the night, mother?"

Both Kjersti and Tönseten felt that they must accompany him to the other hut. There stood the bed, with a small table at its side, covered with a rose-coloured cloth; the room was small and crowded, but seemed cozy and cheerful withal.

"Oh, here it will be sweet to stretch one's weary limbs!" exclaimed the minister, joyfully.

"What a wonderful man he is!" thought Kjersti. She began to make many excuses because they had nothing better to offer.

With a mixture of jest and earnestness the minister rebuked her for such talk; soon they were all three laughing together, and it was so pleasant that the hosts could hardly tear themselves away.

Tönseten had aged considerably in the last two years; one who had known him before that time would scarcely recognize him now. He had struggled with a bad cough for two consecutive springs; this spring it had been so violent at times that he feared the end had come; but Kjersti had finally managed to boil and dose it out of him. It had left its mark, however; he became easily tired now, and needed a lot of sleep in order to keep going.

But to-night he didn't get much sleep; and what little there was brought no rest. Serious things to think about had suddenly come forward. . . . Oh, my God! . . .

He would have liked to stay with the minister for a private and confidential talk; but he knew that Kjersti would never go away and leave them alone. While she was clearing the table, after they had gone back to their own house, he slipped out and walked over to the other hut; but when he got there he realized that it was too late; he couldn't talk to the minister to-night—it would never do to disturb him now.

At last they went to bed together, Tönseten and his wife. Kjersti lost consciousness almost at once; but Syvert lay awake a long while, pondering over how he might be able to gain the ear of the minister. . . . "To-morrow morning," he thought, "before the minister shows up, I'll take some wash water over to him. I'll sit down in the doorway while he washes, where I can see if anyone is coming; then, maybe, I'll get a chance to talk with him. . . . I'll tell him everything. There's going to be the devil to pay! Useless to try any tricks here—I can't get out of it. His eyes are too keen—they see right through you! . . . But suppose Kjersti comes along while we are talking? Well, there you are! He would be likely to refer to it again when we go over to the house, and that would give the whole thing away; he's a terror when he begins asking questions! No, this thing has always been my own worry, and it shall continue to be. . . . O Lord! I dread it like hell! If he could make such a fuss over that little innocent word I dropped, just speaking *naturally*, what will he say about *this?*" . . .

Cold sweat was standing on Tönseten's forehead. . . . "No, it will probably be better to wait till he leaves; then I can go along with him a little way—get out of range of those eyes of hers."

This decision brought him something like peace, but no sleep; for now he had to consider how to present the case in the best light possible. No sooner had he begun to think that over than the whole wretched business stood clearly before his eyes; there he lay, wide awake, staring at his great sin. . . .

Tönseten was indeed in a terrible plight; none but himself knew how utterly heinous and desperate it was. Until last spring he hadn't known it, either; but at that time, when he was lying prostrate and the cough was threatening to make an end of him, he had come to a full realization of the enormity of his deed; since then it had hung over him like a dark shadow, growing deeper and deeper the longer he turned it in his mind. . . . Just imagine a perfectly innocent man getting himself into such a fix! But had anyone, innocent or guilty, ever committed a sin like the one that lay at his door?

This minister seemed to have a lot of sense, though; perhaps he might understand that it wasn't altogether Syvert's fault, in a manner of speaking. . . . They had come to him, you see—he couldn't get out of it. He had been legally elected, too; and one of the specified duties of his office was to do just *this thing*. Surely those who had laid down the law and forced ignorant people to perform such acts ought to be made to bear part of the blame! . . . Of course, he might have objected. Oh yes, that was just it—he might have refused. That was probably just what the minister would say; he felt it in his bones. Great God, what a mess! . . . The picture of it passed before his mind in rank and file, clearly and distinctly; he could both see and hear the actors of that hateful drama; and so he lived it over once more to the last detail, muttering to himself, and turning alternately hot and cold.

It would be just four years the coming fall since this transgression had taken place. . . . It had even happened on a Sunday afternoon. . . . Well, perhaps that wasn't so bad. The whole crowd had come walking up toward the hut; nearly all the east-siders were in the procession, with Johannes Mörstad and his girl, Josie, in the center. . . . Halvor Hegg had explained their errand—Halvor, he was a pretty decent fellow. Tönseten couldn't remember the exact words now, but their import was something like this: "You are a justice of the peace, Syvert Tönseten, and that is a very important office." He remembered one thing distinctly, that Halvor had emphasized the word *important*. "Now, Johannes and Josie, they want to get married and live together, because Johannes, he needs help the way he is hustling; and there isn't anyone else but you to perform the ceremony. According to law and justice, you'll have to do it, too, as near as you can in the Christian manner; you realize that yourself." That was the trend of Halvor's remarks. . . . Tönseten groaned aloud, for he well remembered how frightened he had been when he had finally waked up to the grim fact that Halvor meant what he said. Since last spring, when he had lain there fighting with death, he had scarcely thought of anything else. . . .

And that Sunday afternoon he had married the couple! If he could only be sure, even, that he had done it properly according to law! But he had been unable to find the papers and instructions furnished him for such an occasion; not that they would have helped him much, for they were all in English. . . . The neighbours had elected him justice of the peace when they organized the town; the regulations called for such an official, and they had poked a lot of fun at him about his important office. At that time he hadn't dreamed that it would ever call for legal or technical action, least of all for anything like *that*. . . . How could he, an ignorant layman, have dared to go to work deliberately and do such a sacrilegious thing! Tönseten spat on the floor and rolled over in bed; he was absolutely convinced that the heaviest sin one could commit was that of meddling in sacred matters. . . . He *had* excused himself—he *had* tried to get out of it! He had insisted that he didn't know how—the neighbours could testify to that! . . .

The worst of it was that the young people had made merry with him about it, both then and afterward; they had hurrahed for the "parson" as well as for the bridal couple, and had applauded the whole ceremony as if it were a joke. . . . And Johannes and Josie had moved at once into a house of their own and had lived together as man and wife ever since. . . . What infamy! The minister would simply *have* to do something about it! . . . Oh yes, he recalled the whole damnable business. . . .

Why, hadn't the two principals themselves, Johannes and Josie, stood before him without a sign of seriousness in their attitude; hadn't they even laughed right into his face? . . . And he couldn't be certain that he, too, hadn't smiled, although he had tried hard to keep his face straight. . . . Then he had taken her hand and placed it in Johannes's. . . . No, now let's see, it must have been the other way around; it had been Josie, however, who had taken the notion that he wasn't doing it right, and had insisted on changing the hands—the others had laughed and shouted fit to kill. . . . With that settled, in a deep silence he had pronounced these words: "Now, Johannes, you take this woman standing by your side—yes, I say, take her now, and use her decently and honorably, as is befitting good Norwegian folk!" After that he had uttered the word "amen" in a loud voice—for the life of him he couldn't think of anything else to say. And Josie had looked up brightly into his face, her eyes snapping with mischief—she was such a pretty girl and had laughed so happily! . . . Since then these two had lived together as man and wife—in infamy! But after all, no serious calamity had befallen them, save that the children had come so terribly close together; at any rate, they were all pretty and well shaped! . . . Huf! Huf! . . .

Tönseten turned over for the twentieth time. Oh, well, he would confess to the minister in the morning, let the chastising be ever so severe. He *must* be absolved of this sin! If that cough should return next winter, there was no telling what might happen! . . .

Since children baptized at home could be rebaptized by a minister, as if the religious ceremony had only been postponed, there was no logical reason why a matter like this couldn't be mended!

At breakfast next morning the minister kept asking a

host of questions; he inquired at length about everything that his brief survey had shown him: Who lived in this hut and who lived in that? Who had built the big houses? How had those men happened to prosper ahead of the others?

Tönseten sat at the opposite end of the table, where he was served separately. This morning he didn't seem to have any appetite—he couldn't relish his food. . . . It was astonishing how many things the minister found to ask questions about. . . . Throughout the breakfast Tönseten sat in the grip of a silent fear, afraid of what might come next; as soon as the meal was safely over, he found a pretext for leaving the room.

A few moments later the minister came out into the yard, with his satchel in his hand, and glanced around at the neighbourhood where he had arrived. In his wake came Kjersti, bashfully tripping out of the house; Tönseten walked restlessly about the yard, handling one thing after another, but did not approach the minister; then the latter called out to him:

. . . Who lived directly west of them?

. . . Why, that was Hans Olsa—that is to say, Hans Vaag.

. . . And to the north?

. . . That was Per Holm—or rather Per Hansa, as he was called.

The minister scrutinized closely that part of the settlement visible from where they stood; then he went on with his inquiries about the people.

. . . Where was the largest house?

. . . Did he mean the biggest room? Well, that was at Per Holm's; he had gone ahead and built on a big scale the very spring he came out; people had thought him crazy for putting up such a sod house, but it had turned out that he wasn't so crazy, after all. . . . Torkel Tallaksen was now building a grand house of lumber, that would surely be a mansion when it was finished; but it wasn't done yet. . . .

"Well, now, let's get to work," said the minister, resolutely. "First of all, my good man, I must get you to help me. Will you hurry around to all your neighbours and tell them that to-day, at two o'clock, I shall conduct divine services at the house of this man Per Holm. Everyone must be present—tell them that they have to come! And you, mother"—he turned to address Kjersti—"I think it would be a kindness of you if you were to go over and help Mrs. Holm get the house ready for the service; it need not be anything extraordinary, but the place in which the Lord's blessings are dealt out ought at least to be clean and tidy!"

They gazed at the minister in alarm, but for a while said nothing.

"Well—poor Beret!" sighed Kjersti, compassionately.

"Beret? . . . So that is her name? What is the matter with the woman? Are they so very poor?"

Suddenly Tönseten forgot his reserve and spoke up emphatically: "I'll tell you about it. This Per Hansa—that is to say, Per Holm—he has got rich out here; he has done better than anyone else, though he came here without a cent to his name. And why shouldn't he have done well? He has plenty of help in his own family, so he never needs to hire; and besides that, good luck has followed him right along. The first year we settled, for instance, the grasshoppers came and made a clean sweep of the rest of us; but Per Hansa saved his whole crop! The same year he made a big haul with his potatoes . . . why, he must have sold for a thousand that year, and nobody knows how much he has made these years on the fur trade that he's carried on with the Indians. . . . He is now settled on three quarters of land!"

"Well, well! that's fine! But what ails his wife?"

Now it was Kjersti's turn; she shook her head sadly as she related all the distressing circumstances. Now and then Tönseten, fearing that she hadn't made things clear enough, would put in a word. The minister prompted them with questions. After a while he had learned the whole sad story about Beret Holm. . . . His face clouded as he listened; it was as if the sun had suddenly darkened over a beautiful landscape, until it became drab and desolate to look upon. For a long time he stood there absorbed in thought, the two gazing at him apprehensively; they dared not speak to him in this mood. At last he said, quietly, "I think we had better arrange it this way, mother: I will go over there first, and you follow about noontime. As for you, my friend," turning to Tönseten, "try to do your errand well! Remember that they must bring all the children requiring baptism. Don't forget that! And tell them to be sure and bring their hymn books, too."

The minister was now making his preparations to go to Per Hansa's; as the distance was so short, he had decided to leave his horse.

Tönseten fussed about uneasily, delaying his errand; he assured the minister that he needn't worry—he would get the message around to everybody in good season—it would only take a minute or two! . . . His red beard caught the sunlight every time he moved his head, which now kept bobbing around in a ridiculous way.

At last the minister took his departure and Tönseten was on hand to go along with him.

"Let me carry that satchel for you. . . . I'll begin here on the north side and work east—that's the shortest way."

They walked on side by side, the minister deeply absorbed in thought; after a while Tönseten fell a little way behind.

"I want to talk to you about something," he tried to say casually. His voice was so faint and low that the other could hardly catch it.

The minister stopped short and looked at him. Tönseten glanced this way and that; his eyes fell to the ground and he made nervous dashes here and there, as if seeking escape. . . .

"Well?" . . .

Too late now! . . . Tönseten took a deep breath, summoned all his courage, glanced once at the minister—then turned his head away. . . .

"I just wanted to ask you if . . . well . . . if it's possible to marry a couple who are already married? Because in that case, I'd ask them to come, too."

"You mean, they are divorced?"

"No, indeed, not divorced! Heavens! I should say not! But maybe it wasn't done just right, you see, when the ceremony was performed. . . ."

"I am afraid I do not understand you."

Tönseten spat out a huge mouthful of tobacco juice, and looked up into the sky.

"You see, it happened here," he confessed in a desperate voice, "that we had to organize the township; so we had to have officials, you see. Well, they went ahead and elected me justice of the peace. . . . How could I help it, I'd like to know? . . . And then, you see, there wasn't a minister to be found in all Dakota Territory—there simply wasn't one in sight!" Tönseten waved his hand with a wild gesture, still looking off into the sky.

The minister's face expanded into a broad smile.

"And so you had to serve as minister?"

"You've hit it—that's *exactly* what happened! . . . You see, this fellow, Johannes Mörstad, and his wife, they couldn't wait any longer—they should have been married long before, for that matter. And so they pounced upon me! . . . I refused point blank, of course . . . I have witnesses to *that*. But then, you see, I really was justice of the peace; and at last I had to give in. . . . That's the worst sin of all!" . . . Tönseten could only whisper now.

"And so you married them?" said the minister, slowly.

"Well, yes—I pitched in and did the best I could. . . . But now you've got to fix it up properly!" begged Tönseten.

The minister's smile suddenly became a loud chuckle; Tönseten listened incredulously; that chuckle descended on the anxious old fellow like a warm shower; it gave him courage to glance again at his companion. So great was his thankfulness that the feeling surged through him: for that man he could gladly die!

He spat and sputtered, blowing his nose in stentorian tones; but he could not take his eyes off the other man's face.

"Was it long ago?"

"It will be four years this coming fall. . . . It was the third Sunday after Trinity, to be exact. I put a mark in my hymn book."

"You did what the law prescribed?"

"Of course I did! . . . Well, that is to say . . . I'm only an ignorant man . . ."

"Are there any children?"

"Children! Don't talk about it! There are three of them already, with a fourth well on the way. As far as that part of it is concerned," Tönseten observed in all seriousness, "everything seems to have been done properly enough! But . . . well, you'll just have to do it over again!"

"No," said the minister, still smiling, "that is your job, and I'll have nothing to do with it. But tell them to bring the children with them. . . . And now see that you get started!"

"But wasn't it a sacrilegious thing to do?"

"Yes, under normal conditions—undoubtedly. But at the time, as you say, conditions were far from normal out here, and you had been duly elected to perform certain official duties. . . . The Children of Israel wandered about in the desert; at first they used the barren desert for their house of worship, then came the tabernacle, finally the temple. And so with our people in this country. Such marrying practices as some people have here are sacrilegious and must be discontinued . . . you're right in that."

"Do you think the Lord will ever forgive me?"

"That I truly believe He will! This probably is not the worst sin you have committed!"

Tönseten's joy and relief were almost suffocating; he wiped his eyes as he gazed at the minister. . . . What a marvellously sensible man! . . .

"I'll hurry right off and tell them! . . . But, please, I beg of you, don't mention this at home. You see—well, Kjersti is not very strong." . . .

And now Tönseten was speeding along in great excitement from farm to farm, announcing to all the people that a pastor had come to them at last and that they must gather to hear him, he was such a wonderfully able man. And the farther and faster he went, the easier became the road and the more wonderful did the minister grow in his mind, a fact which he emphasized at every place he came to and enlarged upon whenever he could stop long enough to draw breath. And he forgot neither the children nor the hymn books; he even found other items to bring to their attention. . . . All the while he was thinking: Just imagine, even *he* could splice a couple together so that it was all right with the Lord! Well, well, that certainly was a most remarkable thing! . . .

III

The minister stood in the corner next to the window, arrayed in full canonicals. The gown was threadbare and badly wrinkled, as a result of its many journeys inside the old valise; the ruff might have been whiter, perhaps; but such trifles were not noticed now, for here stood a real Norwegian minister in ruff and robe! . . . It was undoubtedly true, what Tönseten had said about him—he was an altogether remarkable man. The vestments which he wore seemed only to emphasize the strength of his features, whose youthful vigour, in spite of the grey-streaked beard, appeared at this solemn moment to have taken on a new glow of life.

The table, spread with a white cloth, had been placed so close to the window that the minister barely had space to stand behind it; on the table stood two homemade candles, one at either end; the candlesticks, too, were homemade, cut from two four-inch pieces of sapling, with the bark left on and painted white; at a little distance they looked like curious works of art. The candles were not yet lighted; a Bible and a hymn book lay between them.

The time for the meeting had come. The people filed slowly in and took their places, settling down wherever space was available; on the beds sat women crowded close together, strung along the edge like beads; these were mostly the mothers, and behind them sat and lay the children all over the beds; on the big chest eight in all had taken their seats, running from big to little; the chest had been pulled out from the wall, so that people could sit on all four sides; the six rough benches which Per Hansa and Hans Olsa had hastily nailed together were now filled to capacity, mostly by women, young children, and older people who were not able to stay on their feet so long.

The beds stood in one corner of the room, the stove in another; in the third were the minister and the table; in the fourth, and on every available part of the floor, people were packed like sardines. As many as the room would actually hold had crowded in, eager to see the minister. But not all who had come could gain an entrance; quite a crowd had to remain outdoors: some stood along the walls; others had settled down on the grass. From those outside the house came the subdued sound of talk and laughter.

The women had dressed up in their best for the occasion, and most of the men, as well; but here and there one saw a man who had come straight from his work in the fields, his face covered with sweat and grime. . . .

In the dense cluster of people by the door some one cleared his throat loudly; another was heard to mutter that it was a good thing they didn't have to be particular about the floor! This latter remark caused a slight disturbance in the group; a voice laughed outright, and a couple of men tried to push the people ahead of them forward a little, so that they could clear a space to spit in. . . . The minister glanced up sharply, searching the crowd for the one who had spoken; the youthful look on his face changed to sternness as he rapped on the table:

"Let us have silence, good people! We will begin at once." He raised his voice: "Those who are outside must keep perfectly quiet!"

And now a deep silence descended on the closely packed room; through this silence the sound of quiet breathing rose and fell, gently yet perceptibly, like the rise and fall of a heavy ocean swell.

The pastor read the opening prayer. Then he announced the hymn which they were to sing, and himself led the singing; a few joined in at first, one voice after another straggling along, like waves on a calm sea; but before the first stanza was ended every voice had picked up the tune and the room was vibrating to a surge of mighty song. After the hymn the minister chanted, conducting the full service just as if it had been in a real church. . . . How wonderful it seemed! . . . Before long the men had to slip their coats off, it had grown so warm in the room.

The minister preached on the coming of the Israelites into the Land of Canaan. He began by reminding his hearers of the dangers which the Children of Israel had been obliged to pass through, and of the struggles and tribulations which they had been forced to endure. He set forth what had been promised them if they would remain faithful to the heritage of their fathers and obedient to the law which the Lord had given them as their guide.

Then, in powerful strokes, he sketched the history of Israel. First of all, how had the ten tribes fared? They had been taken as prisoners to a strange country; they had remained there and had forsaken their gods; and then they had disappeared, leaving no trace, like the morning dew on the face of the Great Prairie. Where were the ten tribes now? Not a word nor a sign remained of them—not even a chance name, here or there, to indicate where they must have been! Was it not significant that a whole people could disappear so completely? . . . How different the story of the two-tribe peoples! They, too, had been put in chains and treated as slaves; but they had been held in bonds of loyalty to their race and to Him who had nurtured them; and they had endured and prospered. And so, at last, they had come back to rebuild the ruined walls of Zion—and from their loins had sprung the Saviour of mankind.

Then the minister shifted the scene, applying the parable to those who stood before him; they, too, had wandered in search of a Land of Canaan; from the ancient home of their race they had fared forth, far away over the ocean into a foreign country; here they had settled now, here they proposed to strike root again; and here their seed would multiply from generation to generation, ages without end. True enough, they had no hostile nations to fight against—and for that they should thank the Lord! Yet there were other battles, for the powers of darkness never rested; here were the long journeys to town, with their strong temptations; here was the force of heathendom, which constantly threatened them; and here, in all probability, would soon come wealth! Here was the endless prairie, so rich in its blessings of fertility, but also full of a great loneliness—a form of freedom which curiously affected the minds of strangers, especially those to whom the Lord had given a sad heart. Even the bravest would find it hard to face and conquer the strangeness of it all, the hopeless chill, the overwhelming might of this great solitude.

The minister was now spinning out his thoughts and holding them forth in the light for the people to see; he grew in greatness and power before their watching eyes, as he showed them their own feelings during the lonely hours. But when he even came to the grasshoppers at last, then Tönseten could no longer restrain himself; he had to make manifest his approval in some way or other. With a firm hand he pushed against the back of the person in front of him, gaining the room to spit which he greatly needed; then he looked around at the others triumphantly, as if to say: "Well, didn't I tell you—isn't he a wonderful minister?" . . . But there was no time to waste on such thoughts now!

For now the minister was busy with their future. . . . Did they fully understand what the Lord had given them here—and were they sufficiently grateful to Him for it? The minister towered high and mighty before them. . . . In what manner had they thought to make use of the unbounded liberty which the Lord in His mercy had granted them? Here they were about to build a new kingdom—themselves to lay the foundations, themselves to raise the whole structure from the ground up. Had they begun to realize the greatness of that glorious responsibility which He had placed on their shoulders, and did they have sense enough in their heads to thank Him for it on bended knee? . . . He had spread before them here an opportunity the equal of which was unknown in human history; and here it would be tested out whether they could measure up to it—whether they were sprung from good stock or not—whether they were the children of free men or slaves. . . . Were they not glad of the chance? . . . Oh, they ought to sing like the birds of the plain in the morning sunrise—and then thank God, thank Him in all humility! In truth, they had not come here out of captivity and bondage—that, too, they should bear in mind in giving thanks. But they had found here the fairest promise that the Lord God had ever given to any people. . . .

The words came with thrilling meaning; they took on a richer glow, a brighter texture, as the minister fired to his subject. . . . There was one point, he cried, where they and the ancient Children of Israel paralleled each other in a striking manner. For the kingdom which they were founding here would be a work of praise, a blessing to coming generations, only in so far as they remained steadfast to the truths implanted in them as children by their fathers. There was no other foundation to build upon; indeed, what other refuge did men have? . . . And now he stood here in their presence on this great day, a frail messenger of the Lord, to bring them this solemn question: Would they do as the ten lost tribes of Israel did, and disappear out of the world, or would they do as the two tribes had done, and never perish among men? . . .

The minister's voice had sunk low, but his words bore in upon them with irresistible power; his eyes glowed with a secret light; his cheeks burned with the flush of his inspiration; all his boyish youthfulness had gone, and in its place was speaking the authority of ripe, mature experience.

The people sat and stood about while he was preaching, hanging on every word he said. Only a few were competent to climb the ladder of reasoning that he had raised for them. The others realized that he was preaching well, and let it go at that; it gave them a simple satisfaction just to listen; they rejoiced in their hearts that such a man had come here to-day; they felt that he wished them well. And it was so fine and jolly, too, this gathering together; now there would be some excitement in the settlement. . . . One was thinking about the congregation that they would have to organize; another about the location of the new church; still another about the cemetery, as to where it would probably be located; and to everyone the thought came that men would be needed to manage these activities; well, they would show him that they could govern themselves, that they were a well-conducted people! . . . One woman had it in mind that they would of course start a ladies' aid, now that they had a minister; and that would be great fun, with meetings and cakes and coffee and sewing and all the rest; she proposed to begin some embroidering at once! But those who had not yet been confirmed dreaded the ordeal a little, though at the same time they were glad; at any rate, there would be a change in the daily monotony, and they would of course have some fine new clothes for the confirmation! . . . Tönseten had fallen into deep and serious thought concerning a matter of great importance—of very great importance. He was wondering how he could manage to help the minister out in the most valuable way. . . . Now, when the congregation was organized, they would as a matter of course have to elect a *klokker!* * Well, if he had been able to splice a couple so that the knot held even before the Lord, he certainly ought to be able to serve as *klokker*. . . . He would have to see about it later on. . . .

In the farthest corner by the stove sat a pale, delicate-featured woman, almost hidden by those in front of her. As soon as the minister began to talk she bent her head forward and a little to one side, until she had found an opening through which she could get a glimpse of his face. She listened intently to the sermon—at first with a wondering, happy look, which slowly grew skeptical and sad; all the while her eyes did not release their hold on the speaker. As the sermon progressed, the expression on her face became covert and cunning; her lips moved as if she were making objections, but no sound came. . . . "That! No, that shall not happen—it shall not happen!" was what the face seemed to say. . . . "He is playing us false . . . this man . . . he will lead us to something that is not good."

By her side sat a man with a handsome, fair-skinned

* A church official having partly the duty of cantor and partly of sexton. During the seventeenth and eighteenth centuries a *candidatus theologiæ*, when deemed too great a blockhead to receive ordination to the holy ministry, was often appointed *klokker*.

little boy in his lap; the boy had sparkling blue eyes, which flitted about from face to face, looking at everyone, laughing mischievously when the look was caught and returned. . . . Now and then the man laid his hand on the woman's shoulder, as if to reassure her; then she smiled strangely; she had no time to look at him, but the smile seemed to say: "Don't worry, he shall not deceive me. . . . I understand it all. . . . He is *sly*, though, isn't he?" . . .

When the hymn following the sermon had been sung, the minister said to them:

"Now, it is my advice that those who have been sitting all this time, and have the strength to stand, change places with those who have been standing; in this way we may help to bear one another's burdens. Let the change be made with order and decency. . . . We shall now perform the holy act of baptism. I should appreciate it if all you grown people would remain, and thus call to mind your own sacred covenant with the Lord. . . . First let all unbaptized children come forward; and afterward those who have been christened at home."

At this a considerable disturbance arose in the crowd; some people got up and pushed their way out of the door, talking in low tones as they squeezed through the throng; at the same time several who had remained outside during the sermon pushed their way in; hitherto they had heard only the voice, but now they wanted to get a glimpse of the man. . . .

Sörine came in with a basin of water which she placed on the table, and laid a clean towel beside it.

Those who were to hold the children now took them in their arms and came forward; the sponsors stood up and looked around; there was scant room to move in the stifling crush, and several people had to go out at this moment; but little by little the disorder subsided, so that the ceremony could begin.

Most of the grown people knew the baptismal hymn by heart, and although the air was heavy and close in the crowded hut, the singing rose with great fervour. There were fourteen children who had not been baptized, one of them only three weeks old—a tiny being whose arrival had been looked for in the fond hope that it might turn out to be a baby girl, as indeed it had, and who now lay sweetly sleeping in its mother's arms.

The first child to be baptized was four years old—a big, fat, dark-haired, hungry lump of a boy, who talked out loud and wanted to get down and run over to his mother. He didn't seem to appreciate in the least what was about to be done for him, and aroused a good deal of merriment among the onlookers. However, the ceremony soon went on with all proper calm and decorum. . . . Josie, the one for whom Tönseten had performed the marriage rite, came last of all; she had three children, and had striven hard to get them ready for this service; she carried the youngest in her own arms. Tönseten regarded her and her offspring with a certain fatherly pride, and folded his hands devoutly as she came forward.

Then came three children who had been privately baptized by laymen. Sörine advanced first, holding up for his second christening the child at whose birth she had been present and for whom she had once before stood sponsor; the boy awakened in the arms of his godmother, turning two bright blue eyes toward the minister; he laughed aloud and asked Sörine who that man was with the whiskers and the long black skirt? Sörine tried by petting him to hush him up. . . . "He doesn't have any pants!" said the boy, still laughing and putting his arms around her neck; those who stood near enough to overhear were doubled up with mirth.

But as the pastor asked the child's name and she gave it, and he repeated it clearly and distinctly, so as to be heard throughout the room—"Peder Victorious, dost thou renounce—" . . . something extraordinary happened. From out that pale face over in the corner came a sound of anguish. Beret rose up and pushed her way violently through the crowd, which moved aside in sudden alarm to let her pass, then closed immediately in behind her; Per Hansa tried to follow, but found it hard to make a passage through the throng, which now was crowding forward in order to get a better view; and all at once her voice, shrill and vibrant, pierced the room: "This evil deed shall not be done!" . . . She was already halfway there. Some blocked her passage; others tried to silence her. . . . "Oh, let me go!" she cried. "This sin shall not happen! How can a man be *victorious* out here, where the evil one gets us all! . . . Are you all stark mad?" Her cries were shrill and piercing; they rose with a wild tremor of anguish, striking terror into the hearts of the men who stood about, not knowing what to do; the women hid their faces and did not dare to look; some of the weaker-nerved began to weep hysterically; on one of the beds a little girl had thrown herself face downward, crying and screaming; two half-grown boys, overcome by the horror of it, silently pressed their cheeks against the sod wall; the doorway was now crowded with curious faces, one tier above another. All wanted to see what was going on.

The minister paused in the service.

"Take your wife outside, Peder Holm! The air in here is close and bad for a sick person. I will talk to her afterward. . . . And the rest of you—please keep quiet!"

It took some time to calm the morbid excitement. Per Hansa had finally reached Beret; he lifted her in his arms, but the people crowded around so densely that it was difficult to get through, and all the while Beret was striking out wildly, pulling and pushing in a frantic effort to escape. She foamed at the mouth. . . . "This is the work of the devil!" she muttered through clenched teeth. . . . "Now he will surely take my little boy! . . . God save us—we perish!"

The meeting lasted inordinately long. When the pastor was finally through he announced divine services again two weeks from the following Sunday; at that time he would return to them and conduct Communion. "There must be many of you who need to unburden your hearts before your God and Father in Heaven!" he went on impressively. "We shall begin the service here in this room, promptly at eleven o'clock." Hesitating for a moment, he looked around at the people and a tired smile crossed his face; in a lower voice he continued: "It would not be amiss, I think, if you men were to dress up a little; to the Lord it makes no difference, but it would seem more like the Lord's day for you, and you would be edified thereby."

IV

After the service the people remained standing around in groups out in the yard, talking about the minister and the sermon, and discussing in low tones the sad thing that had happened that day. The latter event claimed most of their attention. Everyone felt great sympathy for this family on whom adversity had laid such a heavy hand; some thought it was very wrong for Per Hansa to keep a person like Beret at home; a tragedy might happen at any time—and then it would be too late; various incidents of this kind were recalled; some remembered also that Per Hansa himself was a hard-hearted sinner who needed serious admonition; but they were all sorry for him, just the same.

None of the people of the house were to be seen. The crowd outside stood looking around, as if waiting for something to happen; no one wanted to leave until he knew. . . .

A few women were still inside the house; they had planned to stay and help put things in order. Among them was Sörine, still carrying the child in her arms. The women were plainly anxious and disturbed; they talked in subdued voices, and couldn't seem to take hold of the work with any heart.

The minister had seated himself at the table, folded his hands, and laid his head upon them; thus he sat for a long while in silence; then, as if noticing the people in the room for the first time, he got up and walked over to the group of women.

"I would suggest," he said, gently, "that you all go home. Only let some one of you who is well acquainted here remain to help; if more are needed, we will send for you. . . . Let me have that fine little boy awhile," he said to Sörine. . . . "Of course, I think it would be better if you all came often to see her, but never more than one at a time. And never ask her how she is feeling; just take it for granted that everything is as it should be. To me, things do not look entirely hopeless here; I believe it will all come right in the end. Yes, I truly believe it." . . . He took the boy on his knee, and began to play with him.

"God grant that it might happen as he says!" sighed Kjersti.

The minister heard her.

"In His name, nothing is impossible! . . . Now I should leave at once, if I were you. Let the one who is best acquainted here, stay behind."

Then the minister took the boy in his arms and went out into the yard; he approached each group standing there, talked to them quietly, and advised them to go home and keep to themselves as much as they could. . . . "For the word of God," he said, "is like seed put into the ground; it must be undisturbed, if it is to germinate and bear fruit; but if it is too deeply covered, it will fail." . . .

"We were just talking about organizing a congregation, you see." The speaker looked in astonishment at the minister. Could it be wrong to discuss that idea?

"The time for that will come later on, without a doubt." . . . The minister raised his voice. . . . "Now I will ask each one of you kindly to go to his own home, remain quiet the rest of the day, and think about what you have heard."

"Well, yes—that's probably all right, of course . . . but anyhow . . ."

The minister turned away and went to another group; the man had to quit talking and make the best of it. But he thought to himself: this must be a funny sort of minister who hasn't time to discuss such an important matter as organizing a congregation!

Group after group broke up and melted away; people moved slowly homeward, and soon there was no one left in the yard; the day had closed and night was fast coming on.

The minister remained outside for some time, walking about the yard, still clad in his canonical robe; the boy toddled along beside him, hanging on to the black gown as if it were a great joke, and thoroughly enjoying himself with this queer man.

At length the minister bent his steps toward the new sod stable, from which seemed to come the sound of voices and the whimpering cry of a child; he took up the boy in his arms, went over to the door, pushed it open, and stepped inside. The room had no windows; it was so dark in there that as he peered about, coming straight from the twilight, he could not make out the objects clearly. He was at once aware, however, of the presence of people; he walked farther in, looking around for what he knew was there.

They were sitting on a bundle of hay—Per Hansa and Beret, she with her face pressed close against his, he with one arm about her neck and the other about her waist; And-Ongen clung to her father's shoulder, her arms clasped tightly around his neck.

"The sweet peace of God be upon you!" said the pastor, gently, as soon as he had discovered them. "The people have all gone. And now, Mother Holm, I should like very much to have you cook us a good cup of coffee, if there is any in your house; I want to take supper with you."

The sound of his voice startled Beret. She sat up, brushed her hair back, and looked around with a puzzled expression. She felt abashed, just like a modest person with too few clothes on who unexpectedly finds himself in the presence of others.

"Oh, is this where we are?" she muttered, bending over and covering her eyes.

"I want something to eat!" cried the boy, tearing himself from the minister as soon as he heard his mother's voice.

She seized the child frantically and hugged him close to her; pushing her face down in the hollow of his neck, she drank and drank. . . .

"No, no, Beret—don't be so violent!" begged her husband. "Please be careful!"

Then she threw back her head, the pale face flushed and distorted. "Am I not to love my own child!"

The minister came up to her and laid his hand on her head.

"That's quite right, Mother Holm! Love him all you can; but do not forget to thank Him who has given you this precious gift. There is the promise of a splendid man in that fine boy; you will surely have much joy in him!"

Beret ceased caressing the boy and sat bent over

him, listening to the words of the minister. Then she rose hurriedly and smoothed down her dress; again the minister got the impression that in some curious way she felt ashamed. Without saying a word, she took a child by either hand and walked out of the stable.

Per Hansa remained sitting on the pile of hay, resting his head on one hand; his hair and beard were unkempt, and quite grizzled now; his face was deeply furrowed, as if by the marks of a ruthless hand; his whole figure seemed fearfully ravaged and broken, like a forest maple shattered by a storm.

The minister sat down beside him; he began to confess Per Hansa with all the gentleness of a sympathetic and understanding pastor.

"Now tell me everything. Two can carry what one alone cannot lift. Tell me everything from the beginning."

Without changing his position, Per Hansa looked down at the hay, sighed, and began to talk in broken accents: "I don't understand it myself, you see. . . . I only know that damnation has come down upon us. . . . It can't continue much longer—I'll probably have to *send her away*." Again he sighed, and then became silent.

It seemed to the minister as if the sum total of human tragedy sat talking to him. . . . A chill had entered the dimly lighted room.

"Perhaps you are right . . . otherwise, the cross might become too heavy for you to bear!"

A long pause fell.

"But she is not entirely deranged, is she?"

"Partly or entirely—what difference does it make? If the fiddle is cracked, it's cracked. . . ."

"Maybe so . . . yes, yes. . . ."

Still looking down at the hay, Per Hansa continued: "I don't know that I am guilty of any other wrong toward her than that our oldest boy came before we were married; but in that matter we were equally to blame. . . . And then I brought her out here. I suppose that there is where the real trouble lies. . . . I don't believe she grieves much about that other affair. . . .

No, it's this business out here—and for the life of me I can't see any sin in it."

"I think I understand," said the minister, gently.

"But is a man to refuse to go where his whole future calls, only because his wife doesn't like it?" . . . The question sprang out of Per Hansa's soul, as if he were for the first time opening the door to many years of pent-up suffering. He turned his strong, resolute face toward the minister, begging for an answer.

"Indeed he may, my good man," said the minister, earnestly. "But it would be better if they were both agreed upon it."

"Agreed, yes—easy enough to say! . . . When the only disagreement, for instance, was that she advised waiting another year! . . . And it isn't so much what she has *said* since we came out here. . . . Now, I wish you would tell me—" Per Hansa spoke softly, almost diffidently. "Suppose a husband and wife cannot agree—what, then, is *he* to do?"

The minister felt through the question the aching need of the man for relief and comfort.

"*Therefore shall a man leave his father and mother, and shall be joined unto his wife, and they two shall be one flesh,*" he quoted. "There you have the Lord's decree. But if the law applies to man, it must apply to woman as well. Between you two there has, as I understand it, been no real disagreement?"

Per Hansa shook his head; the words came with great difficulty:

"I sometimes wonder if there ever were two people who cared quite as much for each other as we do. . . . But that hasn't made things any easier; you can't lift the ocean, whether it rages in a storm or lies quiet in a flat calm. . . . And now, please tell me, you who are a minister and understand the Scriptures, *What is the man to do?*" Per Hansa grasped the minister by the arm, clutching hard in his terrible agitation.

"He shall humble himself before the Lord his God, and shall take up his cross to bear it with patience!" said the minister, impressively.

"Ha-ha!" Per Hansa suddenly burst out in a bitter

laugh. "That's too scanty a fare for me to live on. You'd better put that kind of talk aside. . . . I ask as an ignorant man, and I must have an answer that I can understand: Did I do right or did I do wrong when I brought her out here? And what should I have done instead, when I saw nothing else ahead of me in the world?"

"That time you undoubtedly did right, my good man, if what you have told me is true; a man must go whither his heart and mind lead him, unless the Lord comes and says no. . . . You did right that time; but since then you have let yourself sink into the mire of a great sin, as I am told. And now you grumble—like those Israelites of yore—because the Lord is leading you on paths that you do not wish to follow. . . . You are not willing to bear your cross with humility!"

"No, I am not; and let me tell you something more." Per Hansa's voice hardened. "We find other things to do out here than to carry crosses!" Then he fell silent. The minister tried to find words with which to reprove him; but in a moment Per Hansa began again—and now it was he who rebuked the minister: "My experience has been that it is mighty easy for one to talk about things he has not tried! . . . I have sweat blood over this thing—and now I'm no longer equal to it. . . . Have you ever thought what it means for a man to be in constant fear that the mother may do away with her own children—and that, besides, it may be *his* fault that she has fallen into that state of mind?"

When the minister finally answered, he had become all gentleness again. "No, thanks and praise to God, such affliction He has spared me!" He put one arm over Per Hansa's shoulder. "Tell me how all this came about."

Per Hansa sat for a while without answering; he seemed like a man trying to climb a steep hill, whose strength has given out; all at once he got up and went over to the door, standing there and looking out a long time into the darkness of the night. The minister followed him. . . .

"There isn't much to say about such things," Per

Hansa began. "She has never felt at home here in America. . . . There are some people, I know now, who never should emigrate, because, you see, they can't take pleasure in that which is to come—they simply can't see it! . . . And yet, she has never reproached me. And in spite of everything, we got along fairly well up to the time when our last child was born. . . . Yes, the one you baptized to-day. . . . Then she took a notion that she was going to die—but I didn't understand it at the time. . . . She has never had the habit of fault-finding. . . . She struggled hard when the child was born, and we all thought she wouldn't survive—or *him*, either. That's why we had to baptize him at once. In my heedless joy, after the worst was over and things had turned out all right, I went and gave him that second name. . . . And then everything seemed to go to pieces!"

"That name . . . ?"

"Yes, the second name. It was very wrong of me, I know. I see that now."

"What are you saying, man? Such a beautiful name!"

Per Hansa looked at him. . . . "Do you really mean it?"

"Of course I mean it! It is the handsomest name I can ever remember giving to any child. *Peder Victorious* —why, it sings like a beautiful melody!"

"Please tell me—is it really a human name? And wasn't it a sacrilege on my part?" asked Per Hansa, incredulously, hardly daring yet to acknowledge his joy.

"My dear man, have you worried about that, too?"

"Have I? . . . Don't mention it! . . . You mean that the name is all right?"

"Yes, indeed," said the minister without hesitation. "There is nothing unusual about it, except that you have happened to find a more beautiful form than I have yet heard; the name itself is common in all languages."

Per Hansa gazed at the minister, bringing his face close up in order to see him better in the growing dusk of the evening. Slowly his eyes began to light with a new courage; he took a deep breath, and straightened his body up for the first time in many a long day.

"I must ask you again, for I am an ignorant man: Is this really true? . . . And won't you please tell her the same thing, too—as soon as you can?"

"I certainly will. . . . So she does not like the name?"

"No; that's the trouble. . . . She believes it is an idea that the devil himself has given me in order to get us more completely in his power—but this we didn't realize before her mind began to cloud. Now she can't bear to hear the name; that's why the attack came on her this afternoon, when you fastened it on the boy for good. . . . I was afraid, too, that something like that might happen."

"Well, well! Is this possible? How long has she had these attacks?"

"It began with the grasshoppers. . . . However, she's always had the heavy heart to fight against. . . . And then, those fears of hers—just utter fancies! Can you understand how a person gets possessed by fear, right on the level, solid ground?"

"You say it began with the grasshoppers?"

"Well, sir, I came home from work one evening to find a crazy woman! . . . She thought it was the devil himself who had cast the plague upon us—and maybe she wasn't far wrong in that, either! . . . Pretty soon she began to see visions of her mother, who had been dead for some time then, though we hadn't got the news. . . ."

"What's that you are saying?"

"Yes, sir, she saw her mother; and, will you believe it, she knew that her mother was dead half a year before the letter came! . . . Oh, you can't imagine how bad it was!" The terrors that he had lived through seemed fairly to choke him as he remembered the awful scenes.

"She could not have actually seen a dead person! She must have been seriously deranged."

"Yes—may God help us!—she both saw her and talked with her! . . . One night I lay asleep, the first summer after the grasshoppers had come. I had saved my whole crop and got it in. Suddenly I was awakened by some one talking aloud in the room. And there she was, pacing back and forth in the middle of the floor and talking to her mother, exactly as though she were sitting by her side. . . . I know that she saw her, I tell you; and the child—she was carrying the child in her arms!" . . . Per Hansa's breath failed him for a moment. . . . "'It's no use, mother,' she said. 'The boy can't come to you with a name that Satan has tricked Per into giving him!' Those were the very words she used. I got up, lighted a candle, and as I watched her pacing there, with the little fellow in her arms, then, at last, I saw how it was with her . . . I saw it then. Until that time I had refused to believe it. . . . Pastor," whispered Per Hansa, "do you know what it means to feel the skin creep up your back?" . . .

"Did she try to harm the child?"

"Not then." He shook his head. "I can't say whether she had such thoughts or not; but she took the notion that her mother wanted the child with her. . . . The rest came later." Per Hansa pulled himself together with a strong effort. . . . "It will be two years this summer; it happened toward evening, one day when the grasshoppers came in such numbers that it was hard to see the sky. If Sörrina, our neighbour woman, hadn't been making us a visit, it's hard telling . . . but there she sat, holding the child."

"The Lord show mercy unto you!"

"Well may you say it! . . . That afternoon, when the grasshoppers began to beat like hail against the walls, she remembered that some of the little fellow's clothes were lying outside to dry. She ran out to get them, but when she picked them up there was nothing left but a few tatters of cloth. . . . Then the spell came over her in an instant, you understand. She ran into the house like a mad woman, wailing: 'Now the devil has come for your clothes. . . . He'd better have you, too. . . . Until he gets you we will have no peace!' . . . Then she grabbed for the child!" Per Hansa groaned aloud. . . . "But what might have been in her mind I cannot say. I forgot to tell you," he went on, controlling himself once more, "that the very night before, her mother was in the room with her; Beret talked with her just as plainly as I now stand here talking to you. She had got up and dressed herself, and was telling her mother all about everything, the way women do . . .

and, would you believe it, she wanted to cook coffee for her! . . . 'We aren't so poor as all that!' she told her mother."

"And how was it afterward?" the minister asked, deeply moved.

"Well, you see," said Per Hansa, wiping his eyes, "I had to do something about it. So I persuaded her to let Sörrina take the child during the summer."

"You got her to agree to that?"

"Yes, after a while; at first she wouldn't hear of it, but finally she gave in. And now I don't know whether I did right or wrong; I believe it hurt her terribly to have the little fellow gone. I saw how she wandered about the room, as if longing to care and do for him, but he was not there. . . . And one night after the plague came—I couldn't lie awake every night, you know—she got up quietly and stole over to the house where he was. . . . She wanted to get the child. Whether she intended to do him harm or not, none of us can be sure. She told Sörrina and Hans Olsa that visitors had come from afar, asking to see the boy, and so she must have him; there wasn't any way out of it. Yes, that's what she said!"

"The Lord has certainly laid a heavy cross upon you! But remember, He will remove it in His own good time! . . . Now, tell me, how is she between these attacks?"

"Well, you see, she may be all right for months; one who had never known her well would hardly suspect that anything was wrong with her during this time; she does her work like all the rest of us. In the dead of winter, of course, when the blizzards are raging and we don't see any other folks for weeks at a time, she has days when she seems to go all to pieces; but I hardly reckon that as the disease—that sort of thing happens to a good many of us, let me tell you!"

"What do you intend to do about it this summer?"

"This summer?" . . . Per Hansa's face was drawn with fear as he turned to the minister. . . . "If Satan lets his hosts loose upon us again this summer, then I don't know what will happen!"

The minister patted him on the shoulder:

"Take no thought for the morrow! The plague cannot last forever. And remember that the Lord is always near. As the number of thy days, so shall thy strength be. And now take this advice from me: From now on keep close to her; be toward her as you were during those happy days when you first got her; let your affection warm her into the understanding that it is good to be human; and lighten her burdens in every way. . . . Above everything, do not take her child away from her again. You will simply have to be as watchful as you can. . . . And now I will perhaps stay here to-night; arrange it so that I can be alone with her awhile to-morrow." . . .

The minister gazed before him in deep thought, his heart wrung with pity and compassion. "Perhaps the Lord will allow me to reach her mind with a clarifying idea. His word is living life and can move mountains. . . . When I return you must take her to Communion."

His hand was patting the shoulder on which it rested. Per Hansa wept, his sobs coming in short gasps that shook his frame; he experienced a blessing descending upon him, and his burden grew lighter. There was much more he wanted to say, but just now he could not speak. . . .

A long pause followed; then the minister spoke again: "Let us not stand here longer in fear and darkness, talking about sad things; our bodies need nourishment."

They walked across the yard in the quiet prairie evening, Per Hansa so happy that he could gladly have offered the minister his whole crop as it stood in all its beauty . . . and he had a hundred acres seeded in, counting it near and far.

Just as they reached the door of the hut somebody rounded the corner on the run and called in a quick, scared voice, "*Father!*"

Both men jumped, so suddenly had the figure come out of the darkness.

"Is that you, Ola? What are you up to, anyway?"

"Father, come here!" The boy grasped Per Hansa by the arm and tried to pull him along. "Hans is sitting up on the Indian mound, crying and taking on! I can't get him to come home!"

"Is he sick?"

"No!"

"What's the matter with him, then?" The father shook the boy.

"He is afraid of mother . . . you must come right away!"

The boy sped away into the darkness.

Per Hansa gave the minister a look which seemed to say: "Now you see how things are here!" . . . And all the radiance that for a moment had lighted up his soul was suddenly gone out. He asked the minister to enter. . . . "Tell them that I and the boys will be right along." . . . Then he too disappeared.

The minister stood there for a while in deep uncertainty; at last he turned toward the door, made the sign of the cross in front of it, said a prayer, then opened it and went in.

. . . But across the fields ran Ole, and the father went after him.

"Where is he?"

"Over there!"

"You run home. I guess I can find him. Is it over there by the grave?"

"Yes . . . here . . . "

Ole vanished on the other side of the mound.

"Store-Hans, where are you keeping yourself?"

A smothered cry came through the darkness.

Per Hansa followed the sound and almost stumbled over a writhing form which lay on the ground; he bent over and lifted it up in his arms.

"Hansy-boy, what's the matter?"

The father sat down with the limp, slender body of the boy in his arms, rocking and lulling it.

"Is . . . is . . . mother queer again?"

"No, indeed! Mother is all right, and now supper is ready."

"Did . . . did she . . . kill Permand?"

Per Hansa took a firmer hold of the boy, got up, and started to run.

"Did she do it?"

The father spoke harshly:

"I don't want to hear any more of such wicked talk!

Mother is all right . . . all of us are . . . and now she has supper ready, and everything." He stopped and set the boy down. "Now wipe your face—we can't come into the house this way." . . . The father began to dry the boy's tear-stained face. "You must wash yourself as soon as you get in the house," he said, gently, taking the boy by the hand.

V

Nothing out of the ordinary happened that evening. When the minister came into the hut he greeted them in an even voice, "God's peace upon this house!" Then he took off his vestments, folded them up and put them in his valise, looked around for a chair, and sat down. And now that he had removed his official garb he looked like a different man; the special odour of sanctity that had rested on him seemed to have departed; he sat there quietly, having little to say, looking like a man who has just passed through a great hardship and is very tired. . . . The table was set for supper; upon it had been placed one candle, and another stood on a little shelf by the stove. Sörine was still in the house, bustling about and helping with the meal; And-Ongen sat on one of the beds, playing with her baby brother, who had been washed and dressed for the night and was now ready to be put to sleep. Sörine kept talking and laughing with the children as she worked, and an air of cheerfulness had come over the room.

Beret stood by the stove, bent over, washing some pots and pans; she glanced once over her shoulder at the minister as he sat down; but very soon she had to look again. And then she did something that she often wondered at afterward: she wiped her hands, took a clean bowl from the cupboard, filled it with fresh milk, and offered it to him, saying: "Have some milk, please, to stay your hunger while you wait."

The minister took the bowl without looking at her; he emptied it at one draught, put it down, and thanked her in a few brief words.

Almost immediately Beret grew bashful and uneasy over what she had done; in her nervousness she picked up a shirt that she was making for one of the boys, sat down by the candlelight near the stove, and began to sew as hard as she could; but she kept her face turned away from the minister.

Per Hansa and the boys came in; Sörine announced that supper was ready; the four men sat down and began the meal. The minister looked at the younger boy; his face was swollen, his eyes were red with weeping; a heavy veil seemed to hide his handsome features. At the sight of the boy the minister felt more like crying than eating; a sudden revulsion overcame him. Laying down his knife and fork, he asked for another bowl of milk, which he emptied slowly, and then waited for the others to get through. When he thought they had finished, he folded his hands on the table and began to pray to the unseen one whose presence was always near.

So quickly did he begin, that at first Per Hansa didn't realize what was going on and was on the point of asking the minister what he said. The same thing happened to the others: Ole had just discovered that he wasn't quite satisfied, and was reaching for another piece of bread; Sörine was about to offer them all more coffee. But Beret sat bowed over her sewing, trying to catch every word; she took a few stitches, and then the work dropped to her lap; something compelled her to turn and look at him. The light of the candle cast a reddish gleam over his face; his beard seemed more silvery than ever; the countenance was that of a good child who is tired and wants to be put to bed. . . . His voice was gentle and low. . . . He is really a fine man, thought Beret, and kept on listening. . . .

During the summer there are at times dark days on the prairie; the rain is cold, the fog dreary and dank, sticking to one's clothes like wool. But it may happen that toward evening, just as the day is nearly done, a curtain is suddenly drawn aside; in the western sky appears a window—not built by the hand of man—all luminous with splendour; out of it shines a radiance clearer and more glorious than anything the eye has ever beheld; all around the window night and darkness hang suspended like draperies—they too radiating a glory not of this world. . . . Thus was the splendour which now pervaded Per Hansa's sod house. All had folded their hands without knowing it. Over on the bed the play continued; happy laughter arose, though it did not seem to disturb the prayer. But after a while that also quieted down. . . . Then Permand heard the voice of the one he had been playing with earlier in the evening; it tempted him so hard that he could not resist; clad in his little nightdress, he crawled out of the bed, toddled across the earthen floor to the minister, put both hands on the knees that rose before him, and looked up merrily into the man's face. All who saw it felt shocked at the impropriety; they wanted to stop the child, but only feared a greater impropriety in anything they might do. Per Hansa was on the point of speaking sharply, but his voice failed; Sörine thought of snatching the child away, but only remained motionless and aghast. . . . "I suppose I shall have to do it myself," thought Beret —yet she, too, could not get up from her chair. . . . The child had entered a glory where no one dared to follow. . . . Without interrupting his flow of words, the minister lifted the boy onto his knees, folded the baby hands within his own, and went on with the prayer. . . . "Oh, this is too bad!" cried Beret to herself, struggling to rise. "The child's nightshirt is dirty —he mustn't sit there!" But still she could not get up from her chair: the one with whom the minister was talking stood too near. . . . The words flowed on without a pause, softly and sweetly, like the warm rain of a summer evening. It was as if the minister had much to confide to that other one; the other one seemed to be objecting, as if He hesitated to do what was asked; then the minister prayed more fervently; not that he raised his voice—the words came with the same gentleness—but he threw his whole soul into them, as if he refused on any account to give in.

At last he came to the little boy who sat there on his lap—the child he had christened that day. And it seemed almost uncanny to listen to what he said; one could hardly make out whether he was talking to the unseen being or to the boy himself; at times it sounded as if they might be one and the same. . . . He laid his hand tenderly on the child's head; his eyes seemed closed, but the words had caught a new inspiration; to those who listened, it seemed a wonderful thing . . .

"Set him aside, O God," the pastor prayed, "as Thou didst formerly with Thy chosen ones in times of yore! . . . Set him aside, and consecrate him as a true Nazarene! . . . Let him indeed fulfill the promise of his splendid name and become a true *victor* here, both over himself and for the salvation of his people. . . . And now may Thy blessed peace rest on this house, for ever and ever . . . Amen!" . . .

He sat with closed eyes for some time, his hand still resting on the boy's head; the others were very still. Beret trembled throughout her body; a choking feeling came over her, and at last she had to cough. She glanced down in confusion at her sewing.

"I haven't done this right!" she thought, distractedly, trying to calm herself. She looked at the sewing again, got up to fetch the shears, and ripped out what she had been doing.

Then the minister began to play with the boy, in a natural, happy way; and in a little while they both seemed to be having great fun. But he didn't have anything to say to the others; and they, in turn, couldn't find anything to say to him.

But the next morning, as they sat at the breakfast table, the minister was both merry and talkative, and helped himself so liberally to the food that it was a pleasure just to see him do it. He asked many questions regarding the life and conditions in that vicinity, and showed himself so well informed about farming that Per Hansa asked, without thinking, whether he had ever been a farmer. . . . Then he suddenly remembered what the minister had told him to do the evening before; he got up hastily, called to the boys, and they left the house together.

The moment they were gone Beret grew very uneasy; she found her sewing again, and sat down with it in a furtive, embarrassed way. The minister could see nothing unusual about her, except that her face was so singularly childlike; this impression came mostly from the way she used her eyes; it was hard to find them, because she kept looking down in extreme bashfulness and timidity;

nor could he seem to easily draw her into conversation.

He came over and stood beside her chair.

"Well, now, Mrs. Holm, I have a request to make of you. Two weeks from next Sunday I shall return; and then I plan to conduct Communion services here in your house."

Beret was so astonished to hear these words, that she forgot herself for a moment and looked straight at him.

"Here in our sod house?"

"Yes, right here in your house, where you live every day. . . . Don't you think it would be a blessing for you to come to the Lord with your sins and taste the sweetness of His mercy?" he said in a quiet voice.

"Here . . . ?" she asked, greatly agitated. "Oh no—that would never do—oh no! . . . It's too filthy and dirty here. . . . There's too much . . . it's *unclean!*" . . . She stopped abruptly, blushed scarlet, and looked down into her lap again.

"No doubt there is much sin here," resumed the minister. "That I am sure of. But the Lord will sanctify the house for us. . . . And now I want you to plan how nicely we can arrange it for His blessed purposes. Let us consider the matter before I leave." He looked around the room. "The table had better be taken out—that will give us more room. That big chest we can perhaps use as the altar—that is, if your husband could fix up something for railing. We could probably find some fitting material to cover both that and the chest; perhaps you had better talk to the neighbour women about it." . . . The minister talked on as if everything were decided, with only the responsibility for its execution left in her hands.

She gave him a quick look; her cheeks were flushed.

"That is my father's chest . . . it is a nice chest, too."

The voice had grown querulous again and bore the same childlike expression; the minister made no reply. He took her hand, thanked her briefly for her hospitality, and hurried out of the room. When he got outside his forehead was damp with perspiration. He saw Per Hansa coming in his direction, but turned away to avoid him. . . .

When Beret sat down awhile later to dress the little

boy she felt that she could sing aloud to-day—felt that she had to sing, that she could not help it. Both words and melody seemed to rise in her throat; it was the baptismal hymn that they had used the previous day, and she sang all the verses. . . . While she sang she handled the boy so gently . . . as if she were almost afraid to touch him. . . .

VI

There was much stir and activity all through that summer and fall of '77; many schooners sailed across the wide prairie, and with them came always excitement. The greater number of them, however, went drifting past, pushing still farther westward into the sun glimmer; but there were others that anchored in the settlement and tied up for good. Many were there already, and sod houses grew up like ant hills. . . . Prospects seemed favourable here, they said, especially if one would take the time to look around. The soil was probably just as good here as farther west. . . . Well, why not try it here? . . .

The Sognings in particular were clever at hanging on to prospective settlers: "No use talking, you couldn't find better land than this, if you searched clear to the Pacific coast! As far as *land* is concerned, you might just as well settle here. . . . And this is an old settlement now, the community well organized, with schools and everything. . . . You can easily get help for both plowing and building." . . . The Sognings were practical folk, and good talkers, besides; and so they had elected a committee to advise all land seekers that passed through the settlement; this committee had informed itself—at least, it talked that way—about every quarter section that was not yet taken.

The grasshopper plague had raged frightfully that season, but they would probably soon be rid of it—and, thank God, it took neither man nor beast! This year, too, the hay was spared, and some of their crops had been saved from year to year; several of the farmers even had a little ready money left, after buying the absolutely necessary articles of food and clothing. The herds of live stock were growing constantly, and now the flocks of poultry, larger and larger each season, helped to pay for many of the things that one had to buy.

One fine day a strange monster came writhing westward over the prairie, from Worthington to Luverne; it was the greatest and the most memorable event that had yet happened in these parts. The monster crawled along with a terrible speed; but when it came near, it did not crawl at all; it rushed forward in tortuous windings, with an awful roar, while black, curling smoke streaked out behind it in the air. People felt that day a joy that almost frightened them; for it seemed now that all their troubles were over, that there could be no more hardships to contend with—at least, that was what the Sognings solemnly affirmed. . . . For now that the railway had come as far as this, it wouldn't take long before they would see it winding its way into Sioux Falls. Indeed, if this wasn't a place fit to live in now, where would one find it?—that the Sognings would like to know. . . . Good neighbours, schools, the finest kind of land, a railroad and everything—what more could anyone wish? . . .

That summer a number of houses went up to the westward of Spring Creek. Before the minister had come the first time, Hans Olsa had already hauled the materials for both dwelling and barn; now he was building. After the first year he had gone into stock raising; he had the largest herd in the settlement, and was doing very well—for those days. . . . And Tönseten, after receiving absolution for his great sin, had become all aglow with high ambitions; his prospects were bright of being elected *klokker*—perhaps *deacon*, too; life for him was positively glorious, just one grand song. All day his head was full of the idea that he, too, ought to build himself a respectable house. But the plan never seemed to materialize; he still lived in the old sod house. At last Kjersti would lose her temper whenever the project was mentioned. The hut was good enough, she said; besides, they had no one to build for! This latter fact, however, she didn't refer to oftener than seemed absolutely necessary; it only made her husband sulky, and then he would call her names, like "whimpering Jane" or "weeping willow." . . . He probably wasn't to blame, poor fellow, after all. . . .

In the fall Henry Solum built an immense barn; he saw that Hans Olsa had done well by raising cattle, and intended to follow his example; the dwelling house could wait until he got some one to take care of it—and that might be next summer, if everything went as it should. . . . East of the creek, too, framed houses were rising above the sod huts. The Irish, west by the sloughs, were a little slower about building; there things made scant progress until the following year. The pest had raged worse in that locality than anywhere else, because the land lay lower. And the Irish acted with native caution. They have a wise proverb which says that a good barn may perhaps pay for a decent house, but no one has ever heard of a fine dwelling that paid for a decent barn . . . These words of wisdom they believed—and put them into practice.

The new houses seemed so out of place, standing up on the open, bare prairie. Did they really belong there? They looked so defiant! . . . And that was exactly what the savage storm thought when he came along, winter or summer, found these unheard-of objects in his way, puffed and wheezed, took firm hold, and roared in anger. Well, perhaps he did more than that; it happened now and then that a house would be toppled over, or shattered and torn to pieces; but no matter how hard the storm raged and fumed and growled and took on about it, most of the houses remained standing, and their numbers steadily increased as the years went by. And the groves of trees which the settlers had striven so hard to plant and rear—they stretched and spread, they grew in height and breadth and richness every summer. As they grew they hid the houses, except where the driveway was to come in, when plans and visions became reality. There were settlers, even, who wooded themselves in so completely—perhaps to keep out all evil—that their houses could not be seen at all until one came inside the grove. . . .

VII

The weather was beautiful on the Sunday of the Communion service; the pest had already begun, but only that form of it which bred in the soil there at home; nothing had come yet out of the sky. To-day a light breeze was blowing from the southwest; there was just heat enough to be comfortable; the air swept one's face like a soft, silken veil. The young people felt like taking off their clothes; the sun quivered down through a greenish-blue haze far off in the deep sky; and over on the prairie the first meadow lark had sung that morning. Both the lark and the robin had found their way out there the second summer after the settlers came.

Several folks had arrived ahead of the appointed time, and were standing in little groups around Per Hansa's house; most of them had walked over, but those who lived farther away had come jolting along in a lumber wagon, the load and the jolting apparently increasing together. The people were all laughing and talking together, full of life and fun; from their actions no one would have gathered that they were on their way to church.

Old Aslak Tjöme, who lived just northwest of Sam Solum, brought his wife in a wheelbarrow. She had fractured her hip on the ice that spring and was still unable to walk. . . . "God only knows when she's going to get well again!" said Aslak. "It's too bad, because even when she is well I have no more help than I need." . . . And Aslak was bringing his wife to church for this reason: he had a notion—just a notion—that if the minister would lay his hands on her she might gain faster. . . . Anyhow, there was no harm in trying. . . . Aslak, with his wife in the wheelbarrow, made a funny sight; he had rigged up a high back-rest for her and had fixed a seat in the barrow, covered with a sheepskin rug; on this she sat like a queen on her throne. On either side of the wheelbarrow he had fastened short poles, connecting them with a rope. The woman clung to the rope with one hand; in the other she held a hymn book wrapped in a white handkerchief.

Folks passing them stopped and laughed, and offered to push awhile. "Oh no, thank you!" said Aslak, merrily. "Now I can manage her alone, but it hasn't always been thus—no, indeed!" Then he laughed again as he pushed on, and looked lovingly at her. She nodded and smiled, laughing back at him. . . . "You take my place and let me push awhile!" . . . That gave them a good laugh together.

The minister had reached the settlement the evening before and had stayed overnight at Per Hansa's. That morning they had been up early, had hurried through the breakfast, and immediately after had started to put the house in order for the service. It had been thoroughly cleaned and tidied up before he came. All kinds of wild flowers that were to be found on the prairie had been gathered and hung in bouquets of various sizes under the ceiling, or put into glasses and bowls that stood around in every conceivable place. There was something strange and haphazard about it, as if it had been done by children in play. . . . As the minister looked around, a chill hand seemed to clutch his heart. . . .

The table had been carried outside and the big chest placed diagonally in one corner, just as he had directed on his first visit. Per Hansa had constructed a long, low bench, made up of several small benches; this ran along in front of the chest and was covered with two rugs that Sörine had brought over; the chest itself was draped with a white cloth. The minister took the paten and the chalice and placed them on the improvised altar; he also asked for the two candlesticks he had noticed the other time, and when they had been brought and fitted with candles, he set them on either end of the chest. Over the cold stove they spread another rug; yesterday the boys had stripped off a whole tubful of willow leaves; these were now brought in and scattered around on the floor.

The result was satisfactory. The minister looked around; he had scarcely spoken since he came. . . . "Now I am going over to the other hut to dress for the service; I shall be there until it is time to begin, and would rather not be disturbed." . . . He glanced at the wife, then at the husband, and said as he went out, "God grant to both of you a blessed Communion!"

Entering the other hut, where he had slept the previous night, the minister slowly began to put on his canonicals. His lips moved in prayer; his brow was wet with perspiration. When he had dressed he sat down on the edge of the bed and leaned his head on one hand. As he sat there, his bowed figure seemed strangely powerless and insignificant; the strength that he had so fervently prayed for at this hour, he had not received. When he finally took the books from the valise his hand trembled. His face looked pale and tired; now he felt the need of a strong faith—and when he sought it he sought in vain! . . .

. . . *In him* the faith was lacking; of that he was painfully aware.

With a supreme effort he got up from the bed and went out into the yard.

When he reached the other house it was packed full of people; the elders had found places in the front of the room; there also sat Aslak Tjöme with his wife, the invalid woman comfortably propped up at his side; Per Hansa and his wife sat on the very first bench, right in front of the improvised altar. The minister scanned the crowd, paused for a moment, then came forward and spoke calmly to Per Hansa: "Now, when the service begins, you two will please come forward first. As soon as you have received Communion, you had better go outside, for it will be hot and stuffy in here." Then he went from person to person, writing down the names of the communicants; at once a deep silence fell on the room.

As the text for the Communion sermon the minister had chosen *The Glory of the Lord;* rather, he had not chosen it—it had suggested itself powerfully to him on the day he had gone away after talking with Beret. He had at once recognized the fitness of the theme. And now, to-day, it had returned to him with overwhelming force; here sat people who, perhaps for many years, had had no chance, no single opportunity, to confess their sins before the Lord and receive His blessed remission. Among them was one soul, sore perplexed, that he must try to reach. . . . He had seen clearly on his last visit—at least, he thought he had seen—that what the woman needed above everything else was the gladness of salvation, the abiding joy that issues out of the faith and the firm conviction that life is good because the Lord Himself has ordained it all. . . . Until he faced her he had felt so happy over the theme. . . . Ah, well, perhaps the Lord would vouchsafe unto him the necessary strength . . . yes, if he only could find the faith within his own soul! . . .

He asked the assembly to keep quiet and remain seated during the Communion service, and began the service at once.

But as he started to preach the words he wanted would not come; in those that came there seemed to be no power; to-day something had happened to him which he could not control. He heard himself speak, and it seemed like the voice of another. He could not fathom it; here he stood before a remarkable congregation, under the most inspiring circumstances; he had been given a text more wonderful than any servant of the Lord could rightly hope to find; in all ways he was better prepared to conduct Communion services to-day than he had ever been before. . . . And yet he could not preach . . . the words would not come! . . .

They were failing him utterly now. Here he was preaching about the Glory of the Lord—and stuttering like a child! . . . "I must go a little slower and try to collect my thoughts; that may help me; perhaps it will bring the words I need. . . . It makes no difference if I don't speak so loud; the people can hear me well enough, if I can only express myself simply and clearly!". . . He struggled to find the right words, the aptest illustrations; his face grew flushed with the unusual exertion; great beads of sweat stood out on it and began to roll down. . . . But all to no purpose. . . .

. . . "If I am not careful," he thought, "I will break down completely; I'm not saying a thing that is worth while!" . . . And he spoke even more slowly, making long pauses between his sentences, so that it sounded like a sort of conversation—a one-sided argument against a silent adversary. . . . The man who had looked forward with such fervour to preaching this sermon on *The Glory of the Lord* was making a sorry mess of it as he rambled on in disconnected phrases.

But he must keep going; he had asked the people to remain seated, and they were expecting a long discourse; to disappoint them would be a scandal.

. . . "The Glory of the Lord—what is it? One might

suppose it to be too wonderful for us to talk about. . . . Nothing to that remark!" he thought, as soon as he had said it. . . . "Nothing but empty words about holy things!" . . .

He began to enumerate all the examples from the Scriptures that he had been striving for two weeks to cull and arrange; everything calculated to show the real wonders of the Glory of the Lord:

. . . "Did not Adam and Eve behold the Glory of the Lord as they walked in innocence in Paradise? The Lord spake to them in the paths of the Garden; that was in the morning of time, when the world was still young and everything in it was pure and beautiful. . . . And Enoch who was translated that he should not see death. . . . Abraham and Sarah, as they saw the promise made to them fulfilled before their eyes in such a wonderful fashion. . . . Jacob, who fought with the Lord and wrestled with Him as man to man—what was he allowed to see? . . . And that man of God, up on Mount Sinai, as he stood face to face with the Lord of Hosts. . . . and Jonah, and all the rest?" . . . The speaker toiled through the entire Old Testament and pushed his way into the New. . . . "What was it that the little band of disciples experienced when they sat at table with Him and He Himself brake the bread for them and handed them the cup?"

The minister paused, wiping the perspiration from his face. Every time he drew one of these word pictures for them, the idea came to him more and more forcibly: "These people, sitting here in front of me, are Sognings and Vossings; the man of the house and his wife are fisher-folk from Nordland. . . . How can they understand the things that happened to an alien people, living ages ago, in a distant land? The Israelites were an Oriental race; they didn't know anything about Dakota Territory, either; they had no experience of the hardships out here!" . . . He could have wept aloud in his sore distress; here he stood, an old and tried servant of God —and now he had preached himself through the whole Bible without finding the Glory of the Lord! . . .

. . . "This will never, never do!" he thought, and continued doggedly to speak in slow accents, like one who goes about looking for something while he talks aloud to himself. His eyes roamed helplessly over the rows of faces; they fixed on a fly buzzing around the room, and followed it while he talked. A little way off sat a young woman with three small children; she was a fine, bright-looking woman, tanned and burned by the sun; that must be the girl that Tönseten had married, he thought. The oldest child leaned up against her, the second lay with his head on her thigh; he seemed to be sleeping, for the minister saw only the curly head. She had the youngest child in her lap. He had been restless for a long time, and the mother had unbuttoned her clothes to nurse him. The fly buzzed and buzzed, made a turn in the air, and settled on the nose of the nursing child; the mother raised her hand and swept it away, and as she did so she drew the hand caressingly over the face of the child.

The minister kept on looking at the group. . . . He had talked himself into complete bankruptcy respecting all things great and beautiful, without finding a message that seemed to apply here. Now, taking a sudden shift, he began to address the little group directly before him; not that he actually pointed to the sunburnt, healthy woman who sat there watching the fly, too busy to listen to him; but he commenced to speak of the love of mother and child. And all at once he did something that he had never done before in a Communion sermon—he told a story; it was a sentimental story, too—and he had always despised sentimentality in preaching:

Once upon a time, he said, a Norwegian immigrant woman landed in New York City; her name was Kari—she was widowed and had nine children. . . . New York is a terribly large city. Imagine the difficulties a poor immigrant woman meets with there—one who can neither speak nor understand the language! And this woman hadn't a single friend in all America. When she landed, and saw the great throngs of people, and looked at the whirlpool of traffic, she got terribly frightened, poor soul! She had been told that in this foreign metropolis almost anything might happen to a mother coming alone with nine children; and so she had prepared herself in her own way. Around her waist was wound a long rope; this she now unrolled, tying all nine children to it in single file, but keeping the end still securely fastened around her waist. In this fashion Kari plodded through the streets of the great city, a laughingstock to all passers-by. But just the same, she reached her destination at last, with all her nine children safe and sound! . . . Wasn't that rope a fine illustration of a mother's love?

It occurred to the minister that he had come down to very commonplace things—yet he spoke straight out, from the fulness of his heart. . . . The people were listening intently; the woman with three little children stopped chasing the fly; he longed to tell her to go on with her duties and not mind him. . . . But all at once she seemed to become his own mother, as plainly as if he had seen her in the flesh; and he remembered how she had struggled and suffered as a pioneer woman, first in Illinois, afterward in Minnesota. He was profoundly moved as he caught this reflection of her destiny; his words came faster, pouring forth without a trace of effort. . . . "But when such love exists between a poor pioneer woman and her plain, ordinary children, what must it not be when it rises to Divinity—the love of Him Who is the source of love itself—of Him Who cares for all life, yea, even for the worm crawling in the dust? The love of mother and child can be only an infinitesimal part of that other love; yet, small and imperfect as it is, it still carries a breath of the Divine omnipotence. . . . If you, pioneer mothers, have not seen the Glory of the Lord, then no preacher of the Gospel will ever be able to show it to you! . . . And now come forward to the altar of God and taste that He is good. . . . Come, with all your sorrows. . . . Bring Him your trials and your grief! Love itself, eternal and boundless, is present here. He is ready and willing to lighten your burdens, just as a mother cares for her nursing child. . . . Come and receive freely of the abundance of grace. Come and *behold the Glory of the Lord!*" . . .

The minister ended his sermon, looked at his watch, and his brows knit in a puzzled frown. How had this happened? According to the watch, he had been speaking for an hour and fifteen minutes. Could it be possible?

The people came forward, knelt down before Per Hansa's big chest, and received an assurance so gracious and benign that they could hardly credit its reality. . . . Many eyes filled with tears during that hour. . . .

The absolution took a long time. The minister looked again at his watch; he still couldn't understand where the time had gone. In his heart he blamed himself bitterly; not only had he spoiled the Communion sermon, but he had also made it so long that no time was left for the regular sermon of the day!

And so he omitted the sermon altogether, brought the Communion service to a close, and ended with a fervent admonition to the communicants to go directly home and remain quiet for the rest of the day. . . . They mustn't stop anywhere to gossip and talk! . . . He would return at the end of four weeks, at which time he intended to take up the question of organizing a congregation.

He refused to stop for dinner; having hastily drunk a bowl of milk, he got into his cart at once and drove off. . . . The cart shook and rattled; the old nag ambled along; the minister sat immersed in a deep gloom. . . . "Never before," he thought, "have I failed so miserably in any service!"

VIII

It rained both Monday and Tuesday, but not so hard that Hans Olsa had to stop building. With two carpenters to help him, he made such good progress that the day was gone even before it had begun—or so it seemed to him. Which was hardly to be wondered at, because from morning till night could be heard rumbling out of the caverns of his bulky chest a continuous monotone that was seriously meant to be a song; as steady and deliberate as everything he did—as he himself was, for that matter—the vocal performance droned and rumbled on and never came to an end; and so each day proved too short, both for himself and his song.

Yes, now Hans Olsa was building himself a real house, and he sang all day at his work. And why shouldn't he sing? This was going to be a beautiful house, larger—

very much larger, in fact—than he had originally planned; it was to have a roomy kitchen, both a dining room and a parlor, with three bedrooms upstairs and two downstairs.

Concerning the matter of bedrooms on the ground floor, there had been a long-drawn argument between him and Sörine; not a serious disagreement, exactly, but —well, they had talked about it a great deal! Hans Olsa was never in the habit of saying unkind things to his wife; and Sörine always smiled, even when she was provoked; so a real quarrel between the two was hard to raise. But in this instance she held tenaciously to her idea that there must be a bedroom downstairs, no matter how many others he might build elsewhere; and that plan called for an addition to the house, which seemed a needless extravagance. And it was so unlike her—she was never known to be extravagant! So he had tried to reason the idea out of her head; but he finally had had to give it up as a bad job. And since there was no way out of building an addition, while he was about it, he thought, he might as well extend it clear across the house. Thus it had come about that there were to be two extra bedrooms downstairs. . . . Very unwise, a needless expense, and so utterly unlike her; but there stood the framework, all complete. Nothing to do about it now.

That Sörine was a real gift from on high no one knew better than Hans Olsa himself and now, this particular summer, there was nothing that he would not gladly have done for her. Ever since last spring, when she had confided to him that she was with child, he had been in a state of blissful anticipation—this time he felt sure that it would be a boy. Hence the new house—hence the song. As soon as she had told him the great news he had come to the decision that *that* event should never take place in the old sod house; and if it meant such a lot to her to get that room downstairs, she certainly should have it, no matter how unreasonable it might be.

Hans Olsa was fully aware, these days, how everything was arranging itself for his benefit, and he walked about in a state of blissful contentment and thankfulness; his herd had steadily increased from year to year; every season he got more and more land under cultivation; there must be an end to the plague some time, so all wise men said; here, where there was not a human being to be seen the year they came, large settlements were now springing up; the soil was good, the rain and the sunshine were plentiful. And now he was building a mansion for him who was coming. . . . How marvellous it all was! . . . Hans Olsa was both a sensible and a serious-minded man; but he would gladly have built two more rooms if she had asked for them, just to show his gratitude. . . .

He had been present at the service last Sunday, had taken part in the Communion; and the longer the service had lasted the stronger and deeper had grown his felicity. He was only a common, uneducated man, and probably lacked a proper conception of the wonders the minister preached about; yet this he knew for certain, that nothing so glorious as that Communion service in Per Hansa's sod house had he ever before experienced, and the happiness of that hour was still glowing with steady warmth in Hans Olsa's heart. . . . As Per Hansa and Beret had knelt before the chest, he had looked at them, thinking of many things. Beret's sad condition could easily be seen in her face. Ah no, when reason once leaves a person, it seldom returns! . . . And Per Hansa himself had become an old man long before his time: his hair and beard were grey; his face was thin and worn; not till then had Hans Olsa fully realized the terrible struggle his lifelong friend was going through. He had gazed at the kneeling couple until his large, heavy features drooped with sympathy. Could he at that moment have shared his own happiness with his friend, he would have handed it over to him without a question.

Coming home from the service that day, he had wandered about the place, pondering over an idea which he wasn't ready to mention to his wife until he had given it more thought. But on Monday night he broached the subject to Sörine: Shouldn't they offer to take Per Hansa's youngest child? . . . Did she suppose that would be too much for her? . . . You see, he wasn't any too sure about it, himself. . . . And now he told her all his thoughts of the previous Sunday. . . . What did she say—should they offer to take the child? . . .

Sörine laughed and asked him teasingly if he didn't think he'd soon have enough with his own? The next instant, however, she too became serious; and now she confided in him that for a long time she had been thinking about this very same thing, herself. But she hadn't mentioned it to Per Hansa because he knew that she was only too willing; had he wanted to bring it about, he would only have had to ask her. . . .

They couldn't be sure of that, her husband objected; Per Hansa knew that she was soon going to have one of her own, and he was not the kind of a man to impose on others. . . . He doubted very much, as a matter of fact, if Per Hansa fully realized the seriousness of Beret's condition. Should the plague return this summer and that awful spell come over her again, there was no telling what might happen. . . . "Isn't it really up to us, who can see the true state of affairs?"

Sörine gave an unexpected answer to this question: "I believe that Beret is jealous of me because I'm so fond of her little boy. . . . I think I've noticed it."

Hans Olsa pondered this information awhile. . . . Perhaps his wife was right; and there were other difficulties, too. . . . Suppose they did take the boy. Could they be certain that he would thrive better here? And if he didn't, where would be the gain? . . . And would it be fair to the parents even to suggest such a thing? . . . At any rate, if things came to such a pass that Per Hansa had to send Beret away—which wasn't at all improbable—then some one would have to take the child permanently. . . . And just now, wouldn't it be too great a burden for Sörine? . . . No, Hans Olsa couldn't quite see his way clear. . . .

Sörine only laughed at him. . . . Certainly she would undertake to be a mother to that blessed dear little boy —it would be only one more—that is, if it ever seemed necessary. But she doubted very much if Per Hansa would consent to the plan; he thought more of that boy than of any of the other children, unless she was much mistaken. . . . They discussed the matter at great length that evening.

IX

Wednesday afternoon of the same week a faint mist floated before the sun. A light, warm rain fell at intervals from drifting shreds of clouds. Between showers the sun peeped through the clouds to see what was going on down on the prairie; and he set the rainbow here and there as a sign that he was well pleased. There was a big blue heaven behind it all, the air very still . . . beautiful weather.

Beret sat in the old sod barn which Per Hansa long since had made over into a workshop and storehouse, sewing a shirt for little Permand. The door was open and she sat where she could look out. She had sent And-Ongen to the field with some water for the boys, who were hoeing the potatoes. Per Hansa was repairing the roof of the new barn. It had been leaking there since the frost went out of the ground last spring, because the willow poles used for supports had not been heavy enough. She could not see him from where she sat, but she could hear him working.

"Yes," she sighed, looking up from her sewing, "he can manage his work all right. I only wish I could do mine as well." . . . Her face carried the same childlike expression that the minister had noticed, her eyes had the same dreamy, far-away stare; they seemed to be seeing something she did not want to behold, looking for something that would never happen; hence the strange sadness that always shone through them.

She felt perfectly happy, however, but felt so tired and drowsy; it had been this way every day now since that remarkable man had placed his hand on her and in his prophetic voice had assured her that from this time forth she was released from the bonds of Satan. . . . That any man could have such power! . . . Yet she knew positively now that he hadn't been deceiving her, because burden after burden had been lifted from her soul—she felt so light that she could almost float in the air. . . . But after a while this drowsiness had come on. She could not imagine what ailed her; she slept well at night, and yet was so sleepy during the day that it was a constant struggle to keep awake; to-day she had lain down right after eating and had fallen asleep immediately. . . . A blessed man he was, indeed. . . . And the way he had got them to sing! She had to smile as she remembered it. . . . Just imagine! he had made them sing exactly the same hymns here in this sod house as the people sang in the churches in Norway—yet no harm had befallen the house on that account. . . . Melodies were yet hanging throughout the room; yesterday while at work she had heard them everywhere. She had even caught one up and followed it—had sung until Per Hansa came rushing in, to ask her what was the matter; he had looked at her so queerly . . . He ought not to get frightened just because she sang!

As she recalled the incident now, snatches of the song came back to her again, and she began humming. . . . No, no—this would never do! She might scare some one again—people seemed so easily frightened here. . . . This had turned out to be a rather hard piece of sewing, but the child was going to look fine in his new shirt. . . . Would she be able to hear him in the other hut when he woke up? . . . Well, he had a pretty good voice! . . .

. . . Surely, now, mother will stop asking for him when she hears he is going to be a minister! . . . The smile on her child-like face broadened and lighted up. . . . A minister in the family—I, the mother of a servant of God—why, that is exactly as it is in the Bible! . . . Her hands trembled as stitch followed stitch. But thoughts were crowding rapidly on her now; she laid down her sewing.

. . . When mother comes—and she can be expected at any time now—I shall tell her all that has happened here lately. And then I shall say: "You would never have become the grandmother of a minister if I had remained in Norway. Such miracles do not happen there." . . . But very likely she'll not believe what I tell her. . . . Beret's expression became thoughtful and troubled; she rested her hands idly in her lap. . . . Then I must tell her that now we have a church, right here in our house. At that she'll only laugh and shake her head, and she'll probably say: "Now, Beret, you don't know what you are talking about!" That's just what she'll say. . . . But

I will have to answer: "Now, mother, I certainly do. Listen to me: We have a real church. There is an altar with candles on it, and the altar is father's *big chest!*" . . . That will astonish her still more. . . . "Beret, my child," she'll say, "you are too foolish—you must guard your speech. One doesn't say everything that comes into one's head, you know!" . . . But then I'll show her how Syvert and Kjersti, Hans Olsa and Sörine and all the rest, knelt down before the chest and there partook of the Glory of the Lord. I shall describe it all. . . . She knows Hans Olsa and Sörine—she will believe them. . . . I must show her just where the chest stood. . . . Let me see if I can remember the exact words he used:—"the gracious forgiveness of all thy sins." . . . Yes, he said *all* . . . *all* . . . I am sure of that . . . I remember it distinctly. . . .

For some time Beret sat deeply absorbed in her thoughts, her sewing in her lap, her hands resting on it without motion. . . . Mother will sit by the stove, just as she always has done when she has been here. "Well," she'll ask, "are you sure now, Beret, that he is going to be a minister? Don't draw hasty conclusions—you've always been so impulsive!" That's exactly what she'll say. . . . Then I must answer: "Yes, mother, you needn't doubt it any longer; for I myself sat here and heard how this wonderful man argued about it with the Lord—and how he got his way, too. And both Per Hansa and Sörine heard it also. You can ask them if you don't believe me." . . . Then mother will look at me in her kind way, for a long, long time. At last she'll say: "Well, if God can use him, it certainly isn't proper for me to want him; though I would like to have some one of yours with me. But now you must take good care of him, my child!" . . . "Yes, mother, how can I help it? How can I ever forget that he is to go out into the world to give of the Glory of the Lord to the children of men?" . . . Then mother will get up to go. . . . I must say to her: "Don't forget to greet father! You might just as well tell him all this, about his big chest." . . .

Beret's face had gradually grown very serious. But the sound of heavy steps in the yard brought her out of her reveries. Some one stopped at the barn, and then went in; in a moment she heard the voice of Per Hansa. . . . What can they want of him now? . . . Hm, hm—it's Per Hansa this, and Per Hansa that! First one comes and takes him away, and then another; they never leave him a minute in peace! Can't they understand that I need him at home? . . . And he is so easily talked around—he can't say no to anyone. . . . I suppose it's some more hauling—and then he'll be gone for a long time. . . .

She picked up her work again, but the sewing failed to claim her attention. . . . It took a long while over that errand. Who could it be?

Putting the work away, Beret stepped quickly out of the door, stealthily crossed the yard to the side of the new barn, and pressed herself close to the wall. . . . Oh, this was Hans Olsa! It was all right, then—he certainly didn't need any more hauling.

She was straightening up to return, when something arrested her—kind words spoken slowly in a deep voice. . . . Hush! hush! They ought not to talk that way about her when she was listening!

. . . "Should Beret get another spell, you know what might happen—a calamity none of us could get over. We've all seen enough of such things. . . . Now, we will take the boy and care for him as though he were our own flesh and blood. . . . Sörrina and I have talked it over."

Beret's childlike features suddenly took on a peculiarly covert expression. . . . Ah-ha! So that's his errand? . . . Hush! Hush! There is Per Hansa speaking! . . . His voice sounds so queer—can he have been frightened again? . . .

. . . "That's more than good of you and Sörrina—I realize it all; but matters will have to take their own course. . . . She is the mother, and I can see how she clings to him. . . . This spring I worried a lot about what I ought to do when summer came; but now I've decided that she shall keep the child with her. If she doesn't get well by having him at home, it certainly won't make things any easier for her to have him away—that I know. . . . She risked her life for him once, and she shall not be bereft of the happiness of having him with her now, no matter what happens. . . . There's a Destiny that rules us all—it's bound to overtake us, whether we are here or there."

. . . "Now I'm afraid you are taking too great a responsibility upon yourself," said the other voice, slowly. "Remember what might have happened last summer when she had the spell."

A short silence fell in the barn. Beret's features grew tense. Bending over with a quick, fierce movement, she snatched up a piece of stake and grasped it tightly.

. . . "No," came Per Hansa's voice in meditative tones, "that's just what none of us can say for certain. She might have escaped the attack altogether if the child had been at home. . . . I remember how pitiably she seemed to miss him. I'm not at all sure that isn't what brought on the spell. Perhaps that burden, added to everything else, became too much for her. . . . And even if the spell had come on with him here at home, she might not have harmed him—I doubt it very much. . . ."

As Beret drank in these words the tenseness all left her; the weapon she had seized dropped from her hand; her body straightened up; she looked about in wide-eyed wonder. . . . Were those church bells she heard? . . . But the voices were beginning again on the other side of the wall. . . . Hush! Hush!

. . . "Do you really think so?" asked Hans Olsa, seriously.

. . . "Well, I tell you, Hans Olsa, there's hardly an angle to this affair that I have not considered. I'm thinking of nothing else, when I'm asleep as well as when I'm awake. And this I do know," he added with great certainty, "that a kinder person than Beret the Lord never made; there's nothing but kindness in her. . . . I've come to the conclusion that even in her beclouded moments she has meant no harm to the child—no matter how things may have looked to us. . . . When all is said and done, it's my own fault from beginning to end."

"O God! How beautiful these bells ring!" thought Beret.

. . . "Because," Per Hansa went on, sadly, "I should not have coaxed and persuaded her to come with me out here. . . . Perhaps it was her misfortune that we two ever met. . . . You remember how it was in Nordland: We had boats that we sailed to Lofoten in, big crafts that could stand all kinds of rough weather, if properly handled; and then there were the small boats that we used for the home fishing; the last were just as fine and just as good for their own purposes as the other kind for theirs, but you couldn't exchange them; you couldn't sail to Lofoten with the small boats, nor fish at home in the larger ones. . . . For you and me, life out here is nothing; but there may be others so constructed that they don't fit into this life at all; and yet they are finer and better souls than either one of us. . . . There are so many things we don't comprehend."

. . . "I certainly ought to know Beret," remarked the other voice, thoughtfully. "We were playmates, she and I." . . .

. . . "I doubt that very much," interrupted Per Hansa, "though you are an observing man. I have lived with her all these years, yet I must confess that I don't know her. . . . She is a better soul than any I've ever met. It's only lately that I have begun to realize all she has suffered since we came out here. The minister was probably right; no one can ever fathom the depths of a mother's heart. . . . The urge within me drove me on and on, and never would I stop; for I reasoned like this, that where I found happiness others must find it as well. . . . . But you see how things have turned out! . . . The finest castle on earth I was going to build her—and here we're still living in a mole's hole—all my dreams have been crushed in misery. . . . But this I've decided, that she shall keep the baby—though I thank you for the offer." . . . The sadness in Per Hansa's voice had grown deeper and more profound than the grey autumn evening that falls on the bleak prairie.

. . . "You mustn't feel hurt about the offer," put in the slow voice of Hans Olsa. "We only thought it might do a little good."

Beret listened no more; she walked away like one in a dream of happiness; she did not know where she was going nor what she did. In the southern sky floated transparent little clouds; rainbow ribbons hung down from them. She saw the rainbow's glow; her face was transfigured; she walked on in ecstasy. . . . "Are there signs for us in the sky? . . . That is the Glory of the Lord now . . . *See!* . . . The whole heavens are full of it! . . . There . . . and there again . . . everywhere!"

She reached the other house, came to the door, and would have gone by, but in the house a child was crying loudly. Beret stopped short and passed her hand across her face, as if trying to wake herself from a dream that possessed her; then she went quickly into the house. Over on the bed sat Permand, crying as though his heart would break. Beret hurried to the bed, threw herself down on it, took the boy in her arms, and hugged him close; she felt as if she had got back a child that had been irretrievably lost; she wept as she fondled him, while wave upon wave of gratitude welled up within her.

The boy was so astonished at his mother's strange behavior that he stopped crying immediately and lay quiet; then he wriggled out of her arms and threw himself on the pillow, one of his forefingers in his mouth, the other pointing out into the air, as children often will do when they don't know whether to laugh or cry. There was something so irresistibly comical about him as he lay there pointing at nothing, that a sudden surge of playfulness swept over her and she threw herself down beside him on the pillow. Then he gave her his very biggest smile, letting the finger that had been hovering in the air fall on her face. At that they both burst out laughing—she so boisterously that he withdrew the finger and gave her a frown. She stopped laughing at once, petting and fondling him until she had won him completely.

X

As Beret lay there playing with the child she was suddenly overcome with drowsiness; it seemed to her that she simply could not resist snatching a little sleep—it would feel so delicious! In a moment she had dozed off and was carried away into an infinite, glittering blue space with rainbows hung all around it. The air felt soft and warm about her. A voice, loud and clear, yet very beautiful, was speaking through the sky. . . . She could not have slept long, for when she awoke there sat the boy close by her side, poking a wet finger into her eyelid. She hastily raised up on one elbow and rubbed her eyes, unable to bring herself fully awake. . . . "My, how I must have slept!" she thought. . . . She gazed wide-eyed at the child beside her, and rubbed her eyes again, but could not seem to be able to connect things in her mind. . . . "Why, what am I thinking about?" she said, half amused. "This is my own little Permand!"

She sat up on the edge of the bed, lifted the boy tenderly, and put him down in her lap. To her own surprise, she was trembling in every limb; she felt a sudden overwhelming bashfulness, like a lover who for the first time comes close to his beloved.

"I want something to eat now!" murmured the boy in a voice that was full of well-being.

—Of course, this little fellow needs food! she thought.

The boy wriggled out of her arms and slid down to the floor. . . . She could hardly take her eyes away from him; she began to feel almost frightened because of all the vigorous life in that sound little body.

She hastily left the bed and started to find something for the child to eat. It was in her mind to get some milk from a shelf in the corner; but instead of going there she remained standing in the middle of the floor, looking about the room, her eyes still large with wonder. . . . Everything looked so strange in here to-day! What could have happened? It seemed to her that she hadn't been here for a long time. . . . The child was growing impatient; he took hold of her skirt, shook it, and wanted her to hurry. . . . It confused her dreadfully to stand here like a stranger in her own house! . . . Well, anyway, there was the bowl of milk she had been looking for. . . . Where was the spoon, now, that she always used for skimming? . . . And used she not to have a special cup for the child? . . . And the bread

—he had to have a slice of bread with his milk! . . . Where was the bread always kept in this house? . . .

Beret went searching about in her own home like a housewife who had been away on a long visit and returns a partial stranger. But the feeling of home-coming filled her with such joy, that she could only laugh at her bewilderment. . . . She found one thing here, another there; at last the boy had eaten his fill and was satisfied.

All at once another thought struck her; she glanced around with puzzled anxiety. . . . Where were the rest of the family to-day? . . . Surely Per Hansa was somewhere around. Hadn't she just been talking to him? . . . And where could the children be keeping themselves? . . . It exasperated her, yet she couldn't help laughing; here they had all been with her only a moment ago, and now she couldn't recall the least little thing! Was she walking in her sleep, in broad daylight? . . . Thinking vaguely that she must try to get things cleared up, she went out of the door and looked around.

The mildness of the afternoon greeted her like a friend. She breathed in the pure air deeply, straightening her body, throwing back her arms. . . . What fine weather, these days! . . . The trees around the yard caught her eye; again she had the feeling of having just returned from a long journey. The idea! Look how big that grove is getting to be! . . . Over on the prairie, some distance away, rose a half-finished house. Well, that's Hans Olsa's. It will be fine for Sörrina to move into that new house! No matter how good care you take of a sod house, it's never very satisfactory—dust and dirt keep falling from the ceiling all the time, especially when it gets old. . . . But who was that tall, stooping man coming out of the barn? Now he had greeted her quietly in a deep voice and walked on. . . . Beret began to be worried. Wasn't that Hans Olsa? Didn't she know her own neighbour? . . . Hearing some one still in the barn, she hurried across the yard and peered in.

"Are you in there?" she called.

A stocky, broad-shouldered man appeared in the

barn door; his face was deeply furrowed; his hair and beard, heavily sprinkled with grey, were now full of dust and straw. As she looked at him she felt strangely uneasy and disturbed; but she couldn't help giving him a bright smile:

"What in the world has happened to you, Per Hansa?"

He stood staring fixedly at her, unable to stir a muscle. No power on earth could have taken his eyes away from her face at that moment; he caught hold of the jamb of the door to steady himself. . . . God in heaven!—what had happened? . . .

Beret saw his great agitation. Now her disturbance increased—her concern over him grew genuine. "Are you sick, Per Hansa?" she asked in tones of deepest sympathy, coming closer to him. "You mustn't keep on with this work when you aren't feeling well; there can't be such a hurry about it, you know."

Per Hansa cleared his throat to speak, but no words came . . . he could only look at her.

She noticed his pale, haggard face, and her anxiety grew insistent. "You've got to quit right now! . . . I'll run in and boil some milk for you!" . . . She hurried off to the house, too full of her new-found solicitude to wait for an answer.

In the open door Per Hansa stood gazing at her as she went; he longed to follow her, to touch her, to talk to her, but he dared not do it. . . . There was a spade standing beside the door; he picked it up and set it down inside. . . .

"No, it better not stand in here." He picked it up again and put it back. . . . His eyes rested on a hammer lying on the floor—the one he had been using a moment ago. "I must remember to put that hammer away before it gets tramped into the ground." . . . Next moment he forgot all about it. . . . He was shaking violently from head to foot; he had to lean up against the wall. . . . "God be merciful! I haven't seen her like this for many years!" . . . Then he sighed wearily. . . . "But I don't suppose it means anything."

Beret came into the house, moving with purpose and confidence now, and hurried to light the fire. The boy was still sitting at the table; no sooner did he see her than he wanted more to eat. But she had no time to bother with him; she put a pan on the stove and filled it with milk. . . . "Poor fellow, he must have caught a cold, in all this rainy weather," she thought. "And summer colds are hard to get rid of, unless they're taken in time. I'd better mix some pepper with the milk. . . . If I could only persuade him to lie down so that I'd have a chance to cover him up and get him good and warm, I'd soon have him all right again. . . . Colds don't usually last very long with him."

As she was tidying up the bed she chanced to get a glimpse of herself in the mirror that hung on the wall behind it; she had to take a second look. . . . "Good gracious! What a sight I am to-day! No wonder he looked worried—he who always wants me so nice!" . . . While she was waiting for the milk to simmer, she washed her face and combed her hair; that done, she opened the big chest, found her best Sunday garments, and hurriedly put them on. . . . Now then, she wasn't quite so much of a scarecrow. . . .

The milk boiled; she lifted it off the stove, went to the door, and called Per Hansa. . . . As a timid child enters a stranger's house and does not dare to put aside his cap, so now Per Hansa stepped across his own threshold. Permand was still sitting by the table; his father caught sight of him there, and walking over to him, picked the boy up and sat down in his stead; then he put him on his lap and gently stroked his hair. . . . His voice was gone—it would not come. . . . All the while he was casting furtive glances at his wife; big beads of sweat stood on his forehead.

She brought him a cup of the steaming milk. "I put pepper in it; now you must get it down while it's still hot. . . . Then you shall go right to bed and get good and warm!"

Without protest he did as she bade him, sipping cup after cup of the strong hot mixture; he couldn't keep his eyes off her face. . . . But still he found no words to say to her; whenever he tried to speak his throat closed. . . .

While he was drinking she came and sat down by his side, telling him innocently how topsy-turvy things had seemed to her to-day. Why, she had just lain down for a moment with the child, and when she woke up it had seemed as though she had been gone for years and a day! She laughed merrily as she told him about it.

Per Hansa listened in silence, looked at her, and drank of the hot mixture until the tears rolled down his cheeks. . . . She chatted on unconsciously, her voice low but full and very sweet; as he gazed at her, he saw in her face only intelligent concern—only loving solicitude—exactly like the dear Beret-girl that he used to know! . . . When he found it impossible to swallow another drop of the hot pepper-and-milk, she insisted that he lie down at once; if he would only take a good sweat, this cold would soon pass off. Per Hansa obeyed like a docile child, while she herself came and tucked the quilt around him. . . . "Now try to drop off to sleep. . . . Don't worry—you'll soon be all right."

He turned his face to the wall, crying silently; he had clasped his hands together with a grip of iron, but soon he had to break the grip, to wipe the tears away. . . .

He lay thus until the paroxysm had passed and he felt that he could master himself. Then he flung the covers aside, sat up suddenly on the edge of the bed, and looked intently at Beret, long and slow. . . . He began to believe . . . and as he looked, he felt his old self returning. . . .

"Are you getting up already?" she asked, greatly surprised. "I really think you ought to stay in bed the rest of the day."

"Oh, well . . . !" He laughed boisterously, rose to his feet, and stretched himself. "I guess I'd better hurry up and get that rickety roof fixed. . . . We must begin building here as soon as Hans Olsa can find time to help with the hauling! . . . By God, we're not going to live like moles all our days! . . . That drink of yours was pretty good. Have you got a drop left?" He came forward and began pacing up and down the room. . . . "*God!*" . . . But then he checked himself in time, caught Permand in his arms, and flung him up to the ceiling again and again, until the boy shrieked with delight.

"My, my, how funny we all are to-day!" smiled Beret as she stood there with the bowl in her hands, waiting for them to come to their senses.

IV *The Great Plain Drinks the Blood of Christian Men and Is Satisfied*

I

Many and incredible are the tales the grandfathers tell from those days when the wilderness was yet untamed, and when they, unwittingly, founded the Kingdom. There was the Red Son of the Great Prairie, who hated the Palefaces with a hot hatred; stealthily he swooped down upon them, tore up and laid waste the little settlements. Great was the terror he spread; bloody the saga concerning him.

But more to be dreaded than this tribulation was the strange spell of sadness which the unbroken solitude cast upon the minds of some. Many took their own lives; asylum after asylum was filled with disordered beings who had once been human. It is hard for the eye to wander from sky line to sky line, year in and year out, without finding a resting place! . . .

Then, too, there were the years of pestilence—toil and travail, famine and disease. God knows how human beings could endure it all. And many did not—they lay down and died. "There is nothing to do about that," said they who survived. "We are all destined to die—

that's certain. Some must go now; others will have to go later. It's all the same, is it not?" The poor could find much wherewith to console themselves. And whisky was cheap in those days, and easy to get. . . .

And on the hot summer days terrible storms might come. In the twinkling of an eye they would smash to splinters the habitations which man had built for himself, so that they resembled nothing so much as a few stray hairs on a worn-out pelt. Man have power? Breathe it not, for that is to tempt the Almighty! . . .

Some feared most the prairie fire. Terrible, too, it was, before people had learned how to guard against it.

Others remembered best the trips to town. They were the jolliest days, said some; no, they were the worst of all, said the others. It may be that both were right. . . . The oxen moved slowly—whether the distance was thirty miles or ninety made little difference. In the sod house back there, somewhere along the horizon, life got on your nerves at times. There sat a wife with a flock of starving children; she had grown very pale of late, and the mouths of the children were always open—always crying for food. . . . But in the town it was cheerful and pleasant. There one could get a drink; there one could talk with people who spoke with enthusiasm and certainty about the future. This was the land of promise, they said. Sometimes one met these people in the saloons; and then it was more fascinating to listen to them than to any talk about the millennium. Their words lay like embers in the mind during the whole of the interminable, jolting journey homeward, and made it less long. . . . It helps so much to have something pleasant to think about, say the Old.

And it was as if nothing affected people in those days. They threw themselves blindly into the Impossible, and accomplished the Unbelievable. If anyone succumbed in the struggle—and that happened often—another would come and take his place. Youth was in the race; the unknown, the untried, the unheard-of, was in the air; people caught it, were intoxicated by it, threw themselves away, and laughed at the cost. Of course it was possible—everything was possible out here. There was no such thing as the Impossible any more. The human race has not known such faith and such self-confidence since history began. . . . And so had been the Spirit since the day the first settlers landed on the eastern shores; it would rise and fall at intervals, would swell and surge on again with every new wave of settlers that rolled westward into the unbroken solitude.

II

They say it rained forty days and forty nights once in the old days, and that was terrible; but during the winter of 1880-81 it snowed twice forty days; that was more terrible. . . . Day and night the snow fell. From the 15th of October, when it began, until after the middle of April, it seldom ceased. From the four corners of the earth it flew; but of all the winds that brought it, the south wind was the worst; for that whisked and matted the flakes into huge grey discs, which fell to the ground in clinging, woolly folds. . . . And all winter the sun stayed in his house; he crept out only now and then to pack down the snow; that was to make room for more. . . . Morning after morning folk would wake up in the dead, heavy cold, and would lie in bed listening to the *ooo-h-ooo-h-ooo-h-ing* of the wind about the corners of the house. But what was this low, muffled roar in the chimney? One would leap out of bed, dress himself hurriedly in his heaviest garments, and start to go out—only to find that some one was holding the door. It wouldn't budge an inch. An immovable monster lay close outside. Against this monster one pushed and pushed, until one could scoop a little of the snow through the crack into the room; finally one was able to force an opening large enough for a man to work himself out and flounder up to the air. Once outside, he found himself standing in an immense flour bin, out of which whirled the whiteness, a solid cloud. Then he had to dig his way down to the house again. And tunnels had to be burrowed from house to barn, and from neighbour to neighbour, wherever the distances were not too long and where there were children who liked to play at such things.

In the late spring, when all this snow had to thaw, the floods would come, covering all the land. Once again it would be just as it had been in the days of Noah; on the roofs of houses, on the gables of barns, in wagon boxes, even, people would go sailing away. Many would perish—for there was no Ark in those days! . . .

The suffering was great that winter. Famine came; supplies of all kinds gave out; for no one had thought, when the first snowfall began, that winter had come. Who had ever heard of its setting in in the middle of the autumn? . . . And for a while not much snow did come; the fall was light in November, though the days were grey and chill; in December there was more; January began to pile and drift it up; and in February the very demon himself arrived. Some had to leave their potatoes in the ground; others could not thresh the grain; fuel, if not provided beforehand, was scarcely to be had at all; and it was impossible for anyone to get through to town to fetch what might be needed.

In the houses round about folks were grinding away at their own wheat; for little by little the flour had given out, and then they had to resort to the coffee mill. Everyone came to it—rich and poor alike. Those who had no mill of their own were forced to borrow; in some neighbourhoods there were as many as four families using one mill.

That winter Torkel Tallaksen had two newcomer boys working for their board; he also kept a hired girl; in addition to these he had a big family of his own, so that his supply of flour was soon exhausted. Now, he owned one mill, but he wasn't satisfied with that, so he went and borrowed four more; one might as well grind enough to last for a time while one was at it, he maintained. And so they ground away at his house for two days; but at the end of that time they were all so tired of it that they refused to grind any more.

When the mills had to be returned one of the little Tallaksen boys put on his skis and started off for Tönseten's with the one they had borrowed there. The slight thaw of the day before and the frost of the previous night had left a hard crust on the snow; in some places this would bear him up, but more often it was so thin that he broke through. Down by the creek the snowdrifts lay like mountains. Here the boy let himself go, gathered more speed than he had expected to, and went head over heels into a huge snowdrift. His skis flew one way, the mill another. When he tried to recover the mill he broke through the drift, and then both he and the mill were buried in snow. He dug himself out, began to hunt wildly for the mill, broke through again, floundered around, and at last managed to lose the mill completely. After hunting until he was tired, he had to give it up; there was nothing to do but to go to Tönseten and tell him what had happened.

"You haven't lost the mill?" gasped Tönseten, seriously alarmed.

"No," said the boy, laughing. He knew exactly where it was, but he just couldn't find it.

"And you laugh at that, you young idiot!" Tönseten was so angry that he boxed the boy's ears; then he pulled on his coat and rushed off to ask his neighbours to help him hunt for the lost treasure. It was on this occasion that he coined a saying that later became a by-word in the settlement—"Never mind your lives, boys, if you can only find the mill!"

But the greatest hardship of all for the settlers was the scarcity of fuel—no wood, no coal. In every home people sat twisting fagots of hay with which to feed the fire.

Whole herds of cattle were smothered in the snow. They disappeared during the great early storm in October, and were never seen again; when the snow was gone in the spring, they would reappear low on some hillside. After lying there for six months, they would be a horrible sight.

And the same thing happened to people: some disappeared like the cattle; others fell ill with the cough; people died needlessly, for want of a doctor's care; they did not even have the old household remedies—nothing of any kind. And when some one died, he was laid out in what the family could spare, and put away in a snowbank—until some later day. . . . There would be many burials in the settlement next spring.

III

The third quarter-section which Hans Olsa owned lay near the creek, north of Solums'. This he had fenced in and was using as a pasture for a large herd. During the summer he did not need to look after the cattle at all, except to give them salt; the grass was plentiful up north and they could drink at the creek. The preceding year the herd had pastured there until late in the fall. This year he had hauled over all the straw he could spare, and had bought more where he could find it. Then he had built a shed of poles and banked it in with the straw, with the intention of wintering the cattle on that quarter. He had finished the shed before winter set in; and now that he had managed to keep the cattle there until February, he felt fairly safe; surely the winter would be over pretty soon. . . . But the winter had only begun!

The 7th of February dawned bleak and cold. Large, tousled snowflakes came flying out of the west, filling the whole sky with a grey, woolly blanket. As the wind stiffened steadily throughout the morning, the flakes grew smaller and finer; but for all that, they fell in a thicker cloud. By noon, heaven and earth were a swirl of drifting snow. The west wind cut in more and more savagely; it waxed to a fury at times, driving the snowflakes before it with such violence that they were pinned to the walls. . . . As the afternoon wore on, the weather became so bad that Hans Olsa thought it best to go over north and look after the cattle. Had he not been so familiar with the lay of the land, or had he not known how to take his bearings by the direction of the wind, he would never have been able to find the place.

Things were in pretty bad shape there. Most of the straw had been blown away from the west side of the shed. The cattle had left the open inclosure, and had sought what shelter they could find to leeward of the straw stacks on the north side. At a glance he saw that unless he could repair the shed at once and get the animals under some sort of protection, he would find himself a considerably poorer man on the morrow. So he set to work as hard as he could to carry straw and fill it in between the poles, in order to shut out the wind; that done, he spread more straw all over the floor.

It was dark by the time he had got the shed into fit condition to drive the cattle in again. In the meanwhile they had been standing behind the stacks. But now his trouble began in earnest; the moment he drove the beasts far enough away from their shelter to feel the full force of the wind, they wheeled sharply, put their noses close to the ground, and headed back for the stacks. This would never do! He waited awhile until they were quiet again, and then he led them over one by one, taking the biggest first; the smaller animals he literally picked up and carried in. These had burrowed themselves so far into the stack that it was difficult even to get them out. With the snow beating on him, and the wind constantly taking his breath away, he found this a tough job; but he kept on at it without pause, though the sweat was pouring from him in streams.

The evening was gone when he had finished. Round about him lay the night, full of a whirling menace thicker, more desperate, than he had ever seen before—a surge which the wind drove before it in roaring breakers; in the eddies around the corners it was impossible to keep one's eyes open. . . . Hans Olsa stood at the door of the shed, his work done, looking out at the storm; he was so weary that every limb trembled. At last he started out mechanically, walked a few steps, but had to stop to catch his breath. Then he began to realize that in this darkness, with such a blizzard raging, he would never be able to steer a straight course home. He felt his way back to the shed, went in again, and remained standing in the door. . . . His mind was too exhausted to think clearly; something kept telling him that he had done well to save the cattle. If they had been left outside, there wouldn't have been many of them alive when the storm was over. If they only had a little more straw under them, they would really be quite comfortable now.

After he had been standing there a short while a succession of light shivers began to run through his body. He wasn't exactly cold—it was only that his muscles wouldn't keep quiet. Now they tautened and cramped convulsively; now they arched and slacked up like released steel springs. . . . "If I lie down close to the animals, I'll easily be able to keep warm," he thought. "Day will soon come, and then I can go home to Sörrina and the children. I suppose she'll have sense enough to go to bed and not sit up to wait for me all night."

He felt his way over to where the herd had snuggled together, and lay down with his back close up against a large bull. He recognized the animal by a broken horn which his hand happened to fall on. His underclothes were so wet that they stuck to his body; but the warmth of the bull soon penetrated to him, and then he felt better. He lay there thinking how fine it was that he had saved the herd. About hurrying home he needn't worry, for all was well there. . . .

He did not intend to go to sleep—wasn't aware that he was dropping off, either. He merely felt a heavy drowsiness stealing over him, and surrendered himself to it for a moment. It seemed so restful after that strenuous labor. Behind him rose the sound of quiet, regular breathing—*up . . . down; up . . . down*—like a light undertow on a summer's day. If only he could have such pleasant warmth in front of him, too! Involuntarily he stretched out his arms, caught hold of the first creature he came to, and raised himself up sufficiently to drag it close to him. Fearing that he might have hurt the poor thing, he began to pet it and talk to it. . . . Really, now, he was as comfortable as a man could expect to be on such a night—anywhere but at home. Hans Olsa settled back and curled himself up snugly between the animals.

The gusts of wind shook and tore at the frail shelter. The storm raged terribly; all evil powers were loose that night. The worst of it was that it had turned so bitterly cold. Through every crack in the shed the snow came whirling; it settled everywhere, piling itself up in little mounds, which the wind alternately levelled and raised again, as it sucked and swirled through the place.

. . . Hans Olsa began to twitch violently; he thought that he felt some one pricking his arms and legs. Next instant he *knew* there must be somebody there—somebody who was using both hands on him; one hand was working upward from the legs; the other from the elbow toward the shoulder. When these two hands met, he jumped—a shock seemed to go over him. . . . With great difficulty he heaved himself up and stood on his knees; the heavy mantle of snow slipped off him, shedding an icy shower which struck him full in the face. . . . Now, what was this—had he lost his feet? . . . And where were his hands? . . . With infinite pains he raised himself and stood unsteadily on his legs. Then he tried to go to the door, to look at the weather; but in a moment he was down again; at the first step he had stumbled against a living mound under the snow, which reared up wildly and then was gone in the impenetrable darkness. With each movement now, a blast of wind and snow struck his face. This happened many times.

He could not understand it—what had happened to him? He knew that he wasn't drunk, but his legs would not carry him. And one of his arms was gone. . . . Well, here was the wall. He leaned against it, and stood there, panting. . . . What! Was his hand frozen? . . . He pulled the mitten off his good hand, took hold of the fingers of the other and bent them—yet he could not feel them move. He saw them bend, too—but he could not feel them. . . . This would have to be attended to at once! He let himself sink down, and began to rub the hand with snow—he breathed on it hard, and rubbed. Now he began to feel himself frozen through and through; his teeth were chattering; his whole body was shaking violently; well, there was no time to waste in idle thinking. . . .

Even now he was trying to make the best of it. "As soon as this hand is all right, I'll have to get my feet thawed out. If I don't get that done, I'll be a cripple for life." . . . In his usual level-headed way, he tried to pull his boots off, but couldn't accomplish it. Then he took out his pocket knife, and ripped them both open—first one, then the other, and placed them methodically against the wall. The socks came off easily enough; these he stuck in the bosom of his shirt.

He got up and started to run in his bare feet, holding to the wall; he stumbled a good deal, but kept on with his shambling run. After a spell of this, he sat down and chafed his feet. He rubbed a long while, got up again and ran—ran as hard as he could, and then sat down again to rub anew. His mind was calm, but it worked very slowly—his thoughts seemed to be far away; he saw them in bright letters against the darkness: "I had better be careful—I've often seen people rub the skin from a frozen limb. . . . If I only had some cold water, this would be easy." . . . He pulled his socks on again, and found his boots. In one corner of the shed, he remembered, stood two crotches, which he had bound together with steel wire. He felt his way there, unfastened the wire, and wound it around his bootlegs.

Then he began to stamp up and down along the wall . . . to beat his arms . . . to run. The pricking seemed to be going away, he thought . . . everything seemed better . . . yet he wasn't certain of anything at all. His thoughts were working somewhere outside himself; they stood and stared at him through the whirling drift. . . . "It is certain," said something away there in the dark, "that if you stay here to-night, you're done for. . . . If the wind continues steady, you ought to be able to find Henry's fence—you know where that takes off in the direction of Per Hansa's—you follow it from there on, and then you come to your own—that runs right to the cattle barn at home. You might as well freeze to death out there, as here." . . . "Well, well," he assented, as if tired of arguing. "That may be right—it may be." . . . Pulling himself together, he went out of the shed and started off before the wind. . . .

IV

That night Hans Olsa received his death blow. He stumbled into his own house in the small hours of the morning; he was then so exhausted that he could not get his clothes off unaided. . . . Sörine had been up all night, well-nigh crazed with fear; twice she had started to go to Per Hansa's for help, but the storm had driven her back each time; then she had lighted a candle and placed it in the window, in hopes of its doing some good. She had fed the fire with desperate resolution, trying to face the fact that now the worst had happened and there was nothing to do about it, for Fate is inexorable.

As soon as she had got him into the house she began tending him with frantic haste. She made him drink several bowls of hot milk with black pepper in it; then she put him to bed, warmed the clothes and tucked them around him. But he lay there shivering, in spite of all she did, so that the whole bed shook. Later in the day he began to cough—a dry, rasping cough, it was, that seemed to grate on something hard as iron down in the bottom of the chest. During the night that followed he was delirious; he wanted to get up all the time and go north to look after the cattle. Sörine had all she could do to quiet him and keep him in bed. When the cough came from deep down in his lungs it seemed to scrape off flecks of rust that stuck in his throat and threatened to choke him.

Day came at last, after a long, dismal night; and then he seemed better. Between the coughing spells he talked calmly to his wife, telling her what she and Sofie had to do about the chores. He felt condemned that they should be left to do all the outside work alone. As soon as they had gone out, he tried to get out of bed and put on his clothes; but the chills grew so violent that he could not stand on his feet. He fell back on the bed. . . .

For two full days the blizzard raged. During the forenoon of the third day the snow ceased falling and the storm abated; but the air was still grey and bitterly cold. As soon as Hans Olsa saw that the storm was really letting up, he told Sofie to put on her skis and go over to get Per Hansa. "This will never do," he said to his wife. "For three day and nights you haven't been out of your clothes. I may be a long time in getting over the cough." . . . He wanted to say more, but the words were lost in a paroxysm of coughing.

Per Hansa and the oldest two boys were making hay twists out in the barn when Sofie brought the first news that her father had been out in the storm the other night and was now very sick. Per Hansa immediately dropped his work and went back with her. Sörine looked worn out and very much worried. She turned her head aside when she spoke to him, saying that things didn't look very well. Then she went to the stove, put her apron up to her eyes, and murmured again—things didn't look very well! But Per Hansa's coming cheered her up a little and even seemed to take away some of her anxiety. In a moment her old buoyancy had come back; she dried her eyes and asked him to follow her into the bedroom.

In a hut on the border of the Irish settlement lived an old woman who was so queer at times that she was called "Crazy Bridget." In fact, she had brought this name with her to the settlement; Tönseten long ago had picked it up from her countrymen, and had translated it into Norwegian—he made it *Kræsi-Brita*. All the Norwegians called her that now. This Bridget had come west with her son, had taken the quarter of land next to his, and had herself put up the hut in which she now lived. Very little was known about her except that she was extremely religious, and that as a rule she spoke a language which none of the Norwegians had ever heard before, and which, apparently, few of her own people understood. She seldom visited the other settlers of her own accord; but many—especially those of her own race—came often to her for help in time of sickness. She had a great store of old-fashioned remedies, both for humans and for beasts, and she gave of them freely, without pay. Most of the Norwegians had consulted her at one time or another, in spite of the fact that they went on saying she was only a fraud. And though they said it, they all had to admit, when it came down to known cases, that she had a remarkable way with sick folks.

When Per Hansa saw how seriously ill his neighbour was he went out into the kitchen and said to Sörine that some one must go and fetch Bridget. They ought not to scorn her powers at a time like this—she might be able to help; at least, they must try every chance that offered.

Suiting the action to the word, he went for her himself. A little later the old woman came trudging over on snow shoes, carrying an odd-looking bag on her back. She warmed herself at the fire, went into the bedroom, and looked at the suffering man. Then she asked for a kettle and opened her bag; first she took out four large onions; these she cut into tiny bits and dumped into the kettle; then she opened a bottle of vile-smelling stuff and poured some of its contents on the onions; at last she set the kettle over the fire and let it boil awhile. From this mixture she made thick poultices, which she put on Hans Olsa's back and chest; but before she put them on she took out of her pocket a small rusty crucifix, mumbled some words over it, and stuck it into the poultice which was to lie on his chest. As she fixed these applications she made the sign of the cross over his chest and back. All the while she was muttering strange words, in a language they did not understand—whether a prayer or something worse they could not say. These poultices were to be kept on for twelve hours, she explained in broken English, and hot cloths must be put over them to keep them warm. When the twelve hours were gone they must make a fresh poultice. She instructed Sörine how to make it—with onions, a cup of linseed oil, one cup of fresh milk, and some flour. They must take good care of the crucifix, she said; she would hold them responsible for it. After giving some more good advice, she wished them God's blessing, put her bag on her back, fastened her snowshoes, and trudged away.

Both Sörine and Hans Olsa had faith in the woman and were glad that she had come. . . . One must try such remedies as one had. . . .

Per Hansa was very busy that forenoon; there was much to do at his own place, and more at his neighbour's. He had hurried home from Hans Olsa's after going for Bridget; had called the two boys, and taken them with him at once to look after the cattle up north. Before he left he told Beret briefly how things were at their neighbour's, and asked her to arrange her own work so that she could go over toward evening and stay there for the night. It might be late before he could get back. . . .

At supper time Tönseten called at Per Hansa's as he was going by. He was on his way home from the east part of the settlement, and just wanted to drop in to see how they were after the storm. When he heard the news about Hans Olsa—how he had come down with such a bad cough, that it was doubtful if he would pull through—he decided to go over at once and tell Sörine what to do. If anyone in these parts knew all there was to know about a cough, he was the man! Tönseten was in an extraordinarily bright humour that evening. He told Per Hansa not to worry, if it was nothing worse than the cough; put on his skis and started off for Hans Olsa's.

Out in the bedroom lay the sick man, propped up by pillows; Little-Hans sat at the foot of the bed with his playthings; Sörine and the daughter had finished the chores and were now working in the kitchen; Beret sat in the bedroom, taking care that the poultices were kept hot and that the patient's shoulders were covered up warm; she had her knitting in her hands and was singing a hymn when Tönseten came in.

On entering the room Tönseten greeted them both cheerily; but instantly he began to feel ill at ease. . . . No need, surely, to begin the funeral before the man was in the coffin! . . . He managed to hold his tongue, however. Since Beret had recovered, he couldn't stand her. She had become so pious that if a fellow made the most innocent remark, she was sure to preach at him. And never a drop of whisky would she tolerate, either for rheumatism or for cough. . . . One ought to have some sense, even if one was going to be religious. Surely he who was both *klokker* and deacon ought to be privileged to talk a little sense into her! . . . But such was the respect which she commanded, that even though he had thought about it for two years, he had never dared to say the first word.

To-night Tönseten could think only of how serious things looked for Hans Olsa; he went straight to the bedside, and said in a tone of voice that was meant to be cheerful: "I'm surprised at you, Hans Olsa! . . . What do you mean by lying here like this, *you slugabed?* And here you have the finest ski-slide the Lord ever made, clear from your housetop all the way down to my place!" . . . The sick man's face brightened as he looked into Tönseten's merry eyes; a breath of fresh air flurried from out the red, icicled beard; the whole face bending above him radiated good humour. . . . "I'm glad you came, Syvert," said Hans Olsa in a faint voice.

Tönseten now began to feel that the right atmosphere had been established; he hummed a tune, took a chair, and sat down beside the bed. Without further prelude, he started to relate what had happened to him that day. . . . Yesterday morning, when Kjersti had tried to make the fire, the stove wouldn't draw and the room had filled with smoke; not being able to manage the thing, she had come and roused him. He had got up, had dressed, and then tried to open the door, only to find that the whole house was snowed under; from the hillside to the creek stretched one huge, solid drift, and the chimney itself was packed full of snow. . . .

Well, he had succeeded after a while in getting a hole through, so that at last they could have their morning coffee. It was simply terrible how much snow there was down his way. Yesterday he had been busy all day, making steps in the snow down to the house; these had packed fairly well during the day, but to-day they were as solid as ice. . . . And this morning when Kjersti had come along carrying a pail of water, she had been so unfortunate as to slip on the top step—"ha-ha!" . . . She had thrown the pail into the air, her feet had shot out from under her, and she hadn't stopped until she'd landed on her backsides in the middle of the floor! . . . "ha-ha-ha!" . . . There she sat. . . . "What in Heaven's name are you up to, Kjersti?" he had said, when he saw that she hadn't hurt herself very much; and then he naturally had gone off into a fit of laughing. This had infuriated Kjersti; and when he saw that he'd tried his damnedest to stop—but for the life of him he couldn't! He'd laughed and laughed, and the more he'd laughed the worse things had got; until finally she had lost her temper completely and just driven him out of the house. . . .

Well, this is what he had done next; he had put on his skis and gone over east in the settlement—had spent the whole afternoon there—just to visit around and see how folks were getting along. At last he had dropped in to see Johannes Mörstad and his wife Josie—Josie was about to have her fifth child, you know, and was expecting it any day now; Tönseten felt compelled to keep himself posted on the intimate progress of that family. So he had sat there gossiping with them a long while, and had just been telling them what had happened at home that day, when there!—he'd burst out laughing again, and laughed so hard that they all had to join in. And this had thrown Johannes into such a good humour that he had hunted up a bottle which he was saving for the coming event, and had given Tönseten a drop or two—perhaps it was three—well, it may have been four—if one must be accurate. . . . All this about the stove, and the steps, and Kjersti, and about how he had had to take to his heels in order to find péace, he related in epic detail to Hans Olsa—there seemed to be need of something jolly here! . . . But the number of drinks he really had had, he didn't fully reveal.

There was something so infectious about Tönseten's good spirits that they almost coaxed Hans Olsa into a brighter mood. But then a spell of coughing came on; he choked it back and asked if Kjersti hadn't hurt herself pretty badly?

"Oh no, boys, never you fear!" hiccoughed Tönseten, wiping his eyes with the backs of his hands. "She's all right, except for a few scratches here and there in the bottom—*here* and *there*—but they'll heal up in a little while. . . . Everything grows so big and fat around here, you know!" . . . Tönseten went off into such another gale of laughter that he almost fell out of his chair.

"Well, well!" . . . he said as soon as he could control himself, getting up to leave. "To-morrow I shall bring Kjersti over here with me. You just wait—we'll get the cough boiled out of that chest of yours! Kjersti knows how to treat a cough, I can tell you!" . . .

V

Beret had stopped her singing abruptly when Tönseten came in. As he rambled on she sat and watched his face —something made her look at him in spite of herself. She listened to his half-maudlin laughter—and it seemed to her she never had realized before how disgusting his laugh was. His breath smelled of whisky. At first she felt furious with him and wanted to order him out of the house. Didn't the fool know that it was unseemly to talk that way at a deathbed? . . . But she only took her chair and moved farther off, as a child draws away from one of whom it is afraid.

When Tönseten had at last gone the air of the room seemed close and foul to Beret; filth and pollution had entered in where all should have been the serenity and holiness of a Sabbath. In a vision of startling clearness she saw how evil besmirches all life. What a degraded thing man's life on earth had become! Here was one neighbour calling on another at the point of death; if ever there was need of godly speech, it was at this moment; and yet there had been nothing but vileness in his mouth! She felt a physical desire to cleanse the place of its corruption; folding her hands, she began to sing, soft and low:

"O Jesus, see
My misery:
God's image out is blotted,
And with snow-white leprosy
Sin my soul has spotted.

"Once heavenly bright
Thy own delight,
It was—a new creation;
Now, because of sin's dread blight,
Under condemnation.

"In death's dark night,
Devoid of light,
It sought to find its pleasure;
All in vain, since it did slight
God, its greatest treasure.

"No tongue can tell
How low it fell
In sin's dire degradation;
By forgetting heaven and hell,
It sought consolation.

"Thus it was found
In darkness bound,
With all its powers shattered,
Led at will by Satan round,
And with filth bespattered.

"O Christ, in Thee,
Who cam'st to be
A ransom for us given,
Is our only sanctity
And our way to heaven.

"Thy mercy be
My only plea;
Thy light my soul enlighten,
That it God again may see,
And life's pathway brighten.

"Let morning rays
Of Thy mild grace
Upon my heart be streaming,
And from death my soul thus raise
By Thy love redeeming.

"O sinner's friend,
Whom thorns did lend
Death's scornful coronation,
Grant me peace with God again,
And with it salvation."

She sang the whole hymn through before she got up again to change the cloths; that duty done, she went out to help Sörine and Sofie in the kitchen.

All that night Beret sat by the bedside. Though the sick man seemed no worse, the specks of rust that he raised from the depths of his chest appeared to her to be larger and more numerous. He slept little, but she didn't wonder at that—he must have solemn things to think about now. She wanted to talk them over with him, but did not like to disturb his thoughts yet awhile. During the early part of the night they exchanged few words. But along toward morning the paroxysms of coughing became more frequent and violent; there were times when they almost choked him. Once she grew frightened and got up to hold his head; his face was turning blue as he struggled for breath; then she said, slowly: "Now I think you must prepare yourself, Hans Olsa."

He turned his head sharply and looked at her. . . . "Prepare myself?" . . .

"You will hardly be able to stand this very much longer."

The big bulk of Hans Olsa lay very quiet; only his hand was moving nervously over the cover; his eyes had a questioning, startled look. . . . "Well . . . many have got over the cough." . . .

She did not answer him. After a while he added, thoughtfully, "It will be worse for those who are left." . . .

"You ought not to say that, Hans Olsa—their time has not yet come. But remember that for you the day of grace is nearly over." She spoke quietly and compassionately, in a tone of voice which, whenever she used it, always carried conviction by its confident faith.

For a long time Hans Olsa made no reply; he turned his face to the wall and closed his eyes. Beret stood looking at him. . . . "He does not like what I said. That's how we are, we sinners. But I am glad I said it. I don't believe he will ever get up again."

. . . "Oh, well," murmured Hans Olsa after a while. "He has had mercy on many a sinner before. I suppose there will be a little left for me, too." . . .

A great eagerness suddenly welled up in Beret's soul. . . . "If only you will bring him a contrite heart! But how can one forgive the erring child who does not repent? . . . Woe unto you that are rich!—For ye have received your consolation. . . . Woe unto you that are full!—For ye shall hunger. . . . Woe unto you that laugh now!—For ye shall weep and mourn. . . . Oh no, we cannot only comfort ourselves with the belief that there is mercy enough—that it is free!" . . . With firm hands, she changed the cloths again.

One severe coughing spell after another began to

attack him now, and nothing more was said; but after a prolonged struggle he got his breath again; completely exhausted, he turned his face to the wall, and it looked as if he might drop off to sleep. . . . He lay perfectly quiet a long time.

Beret knit steadily until her hands grew tired; she wondered if she couldn't find something to do for Sörine, took the lamp and went into the kitchen. Here she found a great pile of coarse hay stacked against the wall; she set to work at once, making twists of it for the fire. All the while she was thinking about her conversation with Hans Olsa. . . . "It will seem strange not to meet Hans Olsa in the hereafter—that it will. In the old country we grew up together. . . . They are good folk, both he and she. . . . And now he is starting out on his long journey—and will not pass through the heavenly gates! . . . His mother, Ellen, was a very Godfearing woman; his father I didn't know, but I never heard a word against him. . . . Now they have waited there for him these many years; it will be hard for me to meet them some day and tell them how it all happened here. . . . Perhaps I will be to blame, too; I certainly haven't done what I should. . . . Oh, how can he hope to get in? Not many from the Dakota prairie will ever stand in glory *there*—that I am sure of! . . . For here Earth takes us. What she cannot get easily she wrests by subtle force, and we do not even know it. . . . I see what happens in my own home. . . . It is awful! . . . Here he lay at the point of death, enjoying Tönseten's ribaldry! . . . With thoughts like this, he is now to meet his God!" . . .

The lamp burned low. The room was growing cold. She got up and threw some fagots into the fire, waited until it burned up briskly, then put on a couple of sticks of wood—there were not many left in the box. . . . "It will not be easy for Sörrina when he is gone. . . . But nothing else matters, if only he could reach the Heavenly Home! We can take care of things here." . . .

She went into the bedroom again, to see if she could do anything for the sick man. He was awake when she came in; his manner showed that he had been waiting for her.

"How is the weather outside?" he asked, slowly. "Would it be possible for a man to travel in it?"

"What do you say?" She came close to the bed.

"Could we try to get the doctor, do you suppose? . . . Others out here have had him." . . .

"We shall see when daylight comes. . . . But how about the minister, Hans Olsa?"

"The minister?"

"Yes—when the Lord's hour is at hand, man's help is of no avail; for from His wrath no man can flee! . . . What you need most of all is Communion, Hans Olsa!"

"Communion . . . ? Well . . . yes . . . I suppose so . . . that is true."

"It is terrible to fall into the hands of the living God," said Beret, quietly, and looked into his face with sorrowful despair. "There is nothing but evil in us—yes, nothing! But when He comes to us in Holy Communion, laying His merciful hands benignantly upon us and assures us from out the Gates of Eternity that all our sins are forgiven—oh, there is no moment so great as this for the sin-burdened soul! Then we may rest in peace." . . .

Once more he turned his face away, gave a light cough, and looked fixedly at the wall. Beret felt intuitively that his cough was forced this time. . . . "How strange we are—we erring mortals! Here I stand, telling him of the truth and the light and the way. Now he is wandering in the dark—he does not know which way to go. But when I tell him, he coughs the word away! . . . Thus it is to be dead in the midst of life!"

He lay still awhile, and then he said, wearily, "All my life I have thought it would be blessed to come Home."

Tears came to Beret's eyes. . . . "But are you ready to journey on? Do you dare now to meet Him as you are? . . . Here you have lived all these years, in error and sin, and have not taken time to give Him any thoughts at all."

"Oh no," he sighed, heavily. . . . "But that isn't so very strange, is it?"

She felt uplifted by what she had been able to say; it gave her greater courage to go on. . . . "That's why you must seek Him here, before you meet Him face to face yonder!" she cried, exultantly. "Now I will pray for you." . . . Without waiting for his consent, she knelt beside the bed and began to pray earnestly, with sweet compassion vibrating through her mellow voice, that he who now lay here might be given the grace to see his sin and to repent before the door had closed.

But she had hardly begun when something stopped the prayer. . . . Hans Olsa had reared himself up on his elbows when she had sunk to her knees beside the bed, and had remained in this position, staring at her wide-eyed. As he heard how she pleaded for him he was seized with a sudden convulsion of coughing; he sat up frantically in bed, gasping for breath. The bedclothes fell off him, the poultices slipped down, and Beret had to leave her praying to attend to him. And when he was quiet again he asked to have his milk warmed; then he had to get up; from that he got an attack of chills, and Beret had to call Sörine to help her warm the clothes once more and tuck him in.

With the first grey light of dawn Johannes Mörstad arrived, begging and begging that Beret go with him—Josie was coming down; he had tried to get Kjersti, but she had lamed herself so badly the other day, that it was impossible for her to walk that far. . . . "This is certainly the work of the devil!" thought Beret. "Just now . . . !" But she went out of the house full of the same great exaltation, like one whose sins had been laid bare before the whole congregation. . . .

VI

A little while later Per Hansa dropped in to see how they were getting along. He said that he would arrange with the Solum boys to help him carry hay and water to the herd up north; that done, he would go to Gjermund Dahl's, to get him to come and help Sörine with the chores. This evening he would come back to make a report about everything. Now he must be gone. . . .

People were hard at work throughout the whole settlement; the weather continued threatening, and there was much to be done after the storm; hogs and cattle, as well as human beings, had to be safeguarded against another onslaught of winter. On most of the farms the outhouses were still of primitive construction, built either of sod or of poles and straw. The last storm had buried some of them entirely; from others it had stripped off the straw so completely, that the tops of the poles poking through the snowdrifts resembled nothing so much as bleached bones sticking out of the ground. Of some of the farmhouses only the roofs could be seen; of the sod huts, only the chimneys; down at Tönseten's, the smoke came right out of a hole in the snowbank. If one wanted to go to his neighbour's, he had to put on skis or snowshoes, and keep on top of the drifts. There were homes where no other food was left than dry corn and the little milk that the cows gave. On the outskirts of the settlement, where the latest newcomers lived, they sometimes didn't even have that much. But the people there would borrow a sack of wheat from anybody who had one; and if they had no coffee mill in the house, they would use a mortar, or improvise one from a kettle. Folks were cheerful about helping one another in those days. What one didn't have, he borrowed; if one got a new idea, he passed it on to his neighbours. The scarcity of fuel caused the most suffering, for hay burned like hay, even if twisted.

Tönseten was sitting in the bedroom at Hans Olsa's when Per Hansa came back after supper. He was downhearted and quiet to-day. Kjersti had been in bed most of the time because of the stiffness and soreness from her fall; and she was so cross, he explained, that if a fellow as much as looked at her she would bite his head off. He had had the devil to pay, with taking care of both her and himself and doing the chores besides. . . . As he noticed how flushed Hans Olsa's face was and heard how he struggled for breath, he wondered if his own cough had ever been as bad as this. If this was *worse* than he had had it three years ago, the man would never be able to throw it off. . . . But he kept the thought to himself.

Things had been in a bad way with Hans Olsa all that day; the coughing spells had come oftener; he had been restless and fretful; had asked first for one thing, and then for another, and was always inquiring about the weather. At that moment he happened to be quiet; when all at once he began to talk about the inevitable. . . . He asked both of his neighbours to help Sörine when he was gone, and to give her their best advice about running the farm, just as he would have done for them, if either one of them had been in his place. . . . "Per Hansa, stay with me to-night! Sörrina must have some sleep; she has had all the work to do outdoors, and needs some rest. It may take a long time with me yet—perhaps we shall need help from all of you!"

Thus it came about that Per Hansa watched with him that night. Sörine lay down in the other room, fully dressed. The door between the rooms stood open. She intended to doze only a minute and not lose herself so completely that she couldn't jump up to help when the worst spells came on; but she had tramped about working in the snow nearly all day, and was so worn out that she soon dropped off into a sound sleep.

After all had been quiet in the house for some time, Hans Olsa looked up and asked, in a needlessly loud voice, if his wife was asleep. When no answer came from the other room, he lay still for quite a while, gazing up with his eyes fixed on space; then he began, in a calm, matter-of-fact way, to tell Per Hansa how he thought everything ought to be arranged after he was gone. He mentioned first a couple of little debts which he had in Sioux Falls; then he spoke of several of the new settlers who owed him for seed and cattle, and stipulated how much each was to pay. It transpired later that in every case he had stated less than what was owing to him. . . Sörine ought to hold the farm and keep on living here; for this was the country of the future—of that he was certain. Per Hansa would hereafter have to be her chief counsellor; if he could hire an honest and capable manager for her, she and the children would get along all right. . . . And then there was Little-Hans—it was hard to go away and not see what this seedling of manhood would grow up into. If he showed any aptitude for his books, they would have to send him to St. Olaf College. . . . Or if the Lord had destined him for the ministry— But that was probably expecting too much. . . .

He talked with great difficulty. Every now and then he had to stop for breath. Per Hansa only nodded his replies; all he could think of to say was: "Don't worry. . . . Is there anything else now? . . . I will take care of everything."

Little by little Per Hansa got the feeling that his friend had something on his mind; he could not tell exactly why he felt that way, but the impression grew stronger and stronger. Every time a pause came over the sick man's talk, he expected to hear what it was. But there seemed to be nothing more. At last Hans Olsa fell silent; he was still looking straight ahead of him; but now he began to be very restless. A violent fit of coughing shook his frame. From out that great chest of his came a dreadful wheezing, grating sound, as from an old pair of leaky bellows when they are blown up hard.

When the cough had eased itself, Hans Olsa began once more his frightened groping among the things of the future; but now he spoke less coherently. After midnight he had a quiet spell when he lay as if exhausted and said nothing; but off and on he would glance at his neighbour out of the corners of his eyes; there was something unusual and urgent in the look—something that made a man afraid. . . . Per Hansa wondered if the end were at hand. . . .

But suddenly the sick man began to talk again. It was hardly what Per Hansa had expected to hear. He merely raised his eyes and asked in a low voice:

"Is the snow very deep?"

"Between our farms," said Per Hansa, "it doesn't lie less than four feet anywhere; and it's as deep as that on the level all over the prairie. Down near the creek, by Tönseten's, it must be as much as twenty feet deep! . . . It snowed just a little, I want you to know!"

"Is it as bad as that?" . . . The sick man sighed heavily, his hands fidgeting with the covers; then he repeated in a low voice: "So—is it as deep as that?"

"Was there something on your mind?"

"Then it isn't possible to get anywhere!" . . . The

powerful jaws closed; drops of sweat stood out on the great, shiny face.

Per Hansa's heart stirred with a nameless dread; he felt himself grow dizzy, but he cleared his throat and said, firmly:

"What is it that you want, Hans Olsa? . . . Do you want the doctor?"

The sick man turned toward him.

"Oh—it's the minister I need!" . . . Then, after a moment, he added: "But don't you think the weather will be better in a day or two?" . . .

He lay perfectly still. When he got no answer he looked up and repeated, imploringly:

"Don't you think so?"

Per Hansa rose to his feet and began pacing back and forth across the floor. It must be very close in here . . . he felt so faint. Thinking of how it was outdoors, he suddenly found himself bathed in perspiration. . . . God pity him who had to travel the prairie these days!

He came back to the bed.

"You feel that you must have him?"

"It is terrible to fall into the hands of the living God!" . . . The large, kindly features were drawn and trembling, with fear of the unknown. Per Hansa could scarcely endure it to look at him; he had to lean against the back of a chair for support. . . . In broken words, his friend repeated: "It is terrible . . . terrible . . . to fall . . . into His hands!" . . .

"Hush, now! Hush, now, man! Don't talk blasphemy!" cried Per Hansa. "Lie down, now. . . . See here . . . the covers are falling off you!"

The bulky form had reared itself violently up in bed. Through a paroxysm of coughing Hans Olsa whimpered:

"Tell Sörrina to come here!"

It looked for a moment as if he were passing away in the midst of the attack. Hans Olsa himself thought so. In wild alarm, Per Hansa resorted to pounding the sick man's back, just as one does with children when they have swallowed the wrong way. But after a while the spell gradually left him, as the others had done. He settled back, and a little later fell into a deep sleep, which lasted till morning.

The first rays of daylight woke Sörine. Her husband was already awake by that time, and seemed better. Per Hansa put on his coat and prepared to go; he had all his own work to do at home, besides Hans Olsa's cattle up north to look after.

Hans Olsa watched him get ready, following all his movements with a pathetic sadness like that which stands in a dog's eyes when he watches his master go away without him. Then he called him over to the bedside and asked him again what the weather was like. There was an odd little quiver in his voice as he said, almost as though he were ashamed:

"I suppose it's still impossible to get anywhere?"

Per Hansa felt like laughing at such childishness in a grown-up man; he scarcely knew what to answer. But answer he must; so he braced himself, buttoned his big coat, put on his mittens, and said, firmly: "You ought to lie still and sleep awhile longer, Hans Olsa. . . . During the night you slept like a rock—and see how much better you are already! . . . I promise you that I'll be back some time later in the day."

"You don't think it can be done?"

Nameless dread again seized Per Hansa. He stepped back and said, hastily: "Calm yourself now, Hans Olsa! . . . We'll have to see about it—you understand."

The sick man reached out toward him, caught his hand and held it tightly, with something of his old strength. . . . "Oh, Per Hansa!" he cried. . . . "There never was a man like you . . . !" and fell back on the pillow, exhausted.

VII

All through the latter part of last summer and early fall Per Hansa had done a full man's work plus a bit more; nor had he spared the boys, either. And he had hired a number of men besides. He needed all the help he could get; for there was the new house to be built, the crops to be harvested, the fall plowing that must be done, and in addition, all the other work about the farm.

But he had gone about his duties in a mood that made any task easy both for himself and for those who worked with him. His wife's improved condition had relieved him of whole loads of worry and anxiety. During the years that her mind had been beclouded he had treated her as a father would a delicate, frail child that, by some inexcusable fault on his part, had been reduced to helplessness. So solicitous had been his watchful care over her through all these years, that this paternal attitude had become fixed with him. Even now that she was well again, it didn't change.

Her growing religious concern didn't alarm him; that, too, he took as a notion on the part of a frail child. He either would meet her admonitions with silence, or else laugh kindly at her eagerness, or he might throw himself into the work all the harder. The fact that she now was quite all right again, that he no longer needed to watch over her in constant dread, but that she, on the contrary, could take care of the house in a capable way and even find time to help with the outside work, was a constant source of thankfulness to him. To him she was still the delicate child that needed a father's watchful eye. To desire her physically would be as far from his mind as the crime of incest.

Shortly before the Christmas holidays they had had a set-to over religion. She had insisted that he as the father of the family should conduct daily devotion. At this demand he had laughed, not unkindly but humorously, as if she had sprung a good joke on him. . . . He conducting devotion—the idea! She had become insistent; her voice was full of deep sorrowful concern over his seemingly total depravity. She had entreated him earnestly and yet so kindly that he, too, was touched. And so he had said, as one yields to an unreasonable whim of a dear child, that that he would not do, but he would be glad to have her do it, for she could read so beautifully, which was true. Feeling that it would be dangerous to his temper to argue the matter any longer, he had gone out of the house to find some work outside. From that time on she had been conducting devotion each day, but both of them had studiously avoided a new discussion, with the result that the relation between them was less frank than before; each seemed to feel the guardedness of the other.

As time passed her devotional exercises became less and less pleasing to him; at times they would get on his nerves. In the prayers she began to offer there would creep in more and more of concern for him; and little by little it got to be almost exclusively for him. As he sat there listening it sounded to him as if he were the most hardened sinner in all Christendom; he would feel ashamed before the children, would find some pretext to steal out of the house. But he couldn't bring it across his heart to speak to her; for how can one reason with a child that is so delicate as she, he thought.

In the grey light of dawn Per Hansa returned from the bedside of Hans Olsa, looking like a man who had reached the end of his rope. He hung up his coat and hat and sat down at the table in the large kitchen to eat his breakfast. Off and on he glanced out of the window. While Beret brought him his food, she asked how things were over at Hans Olsa's. At first she got very little satisfaction; his answers were short and taciturn, and he seemed engrossed in his own thoughts. He ate slowly and took a long time over the meal; all the while he kept looking out of the window.

At length he got up from the table, crossed to the stove, turned his back to it, and put his hands behind him, as though he still felt cold and needed the warmth of the fire. . . . "Well," he said, meditatively, "I suppose he doesn't expect to get over this sickness—and it's more than likely he won't. He just lies there and whimpers about having the minister. . . . There's something uncanny about him. I can't understand it at all." . . . These remarks were not directed at Beret; he stood looking straight ahead of him, as if thinking aloud. Beret had stopped working when she heard him; her face lighted up as she answered, with an unmistakable ring of exultation in her voice: "But *I* can understand it! . . . Now may God be near and hear his prayer! Some one must go for the minister at once."

Per Hansa did not move; he was staring off into space.

Beret crossed the floor, her hands full of dishes, and stopped directly in front of him. . . . "You must persuade some one to go with you. This is terrible weather! . . . Could you try going on horseback?"

"Huh—horseback! How you talk!"

"But it is an awful thing for a soul to be cast into hell when human beings can prevent it!"

Per Hansa seemed amused at this idea. "Well, if Hans Olsa is bound in that direction, there'll be a good many more from here in the same boat! . . . He'll land in the right place, don't worry."

The words sounded so blasphemous to Beret that she could not repress a shudder of horror. Greatly wrought up, she set the dishes down on the table and said, fiercely: "You know what our life has been: land and houses, and then more land, and cattle! That has been his whole concern—that's been his very life. Now he is beginning to think about not having laid up treasures in heaven. . . . Can't you understand that a human being ever becomes concerned over his sins and wants to be freed from them?"

"I suppose I don't understand anything, do I?" said Per Hansa in a tone of disgust. "Perhaps I don't understand, for instance—though God knows it would not be difficult for any grown person to see it—that no man could cross the prairie from here to the James River, as things are now, and come out alive— . . . As for Hans Olsa, the Lord will find him good enough, even without either minister or *klokker*—that I truly believe!"

"The God of this world hath blinded the minds of them which believe not! . . . Here lies one who is about to receive his sight, and we will not reach out a hand to help him!"

"Hold your tongue, Beret!" cried Per Hansa, sharply, anger at the hopelessness of the argument getting the better of him. "Do you want to drive me out into the jaws of death?"

"What horrible things you say, Per Hansa!"

"Horrible—well! Don't you suppose the good Lord would have provided other weather if he had intended me to make this trip?"

She gave him a quick look.

"It's possible to try, isn't it?" she said with cold persistence. "Why can't you get some one to go with you? You could take Indi—he is light-footed, and we could wrap things around all four legs, so that he wouldn't sink through the snow. They say that has been done before—I've read about it. . . . Henry has a sleigh; and you could turn back at any time, if you couldn't make it. . . . The Lord would forgive us then for what we couldn't possibly do—if we had tried!"

"He had better do that right now!" growled Per Hansa, a gust of hot anger nearly choking him. Without another word he went to the stairs, called Ole and Store-Hans, and told them to get into their clothes right away. Pulling on his coat, he slammed out of the house to do the morning chores.

Beret looked at the door through which he had just disappeared. . . . There he leaves in a fit of temper, fuming and cussing! . . . She took up the morning work, her thoughts busy with many things. Before she realized it she was absorbed in what had so often been on her mind lately: What had happened to him, anyway? What had made him so different? . . . His warm playfulness, his affectionate tenderness—what had become of it? . . . Oh no, no! she caught herself, how can I be thinking of such things again! The sweet desires of the flesh are the nets of Satan. . . . How deeply sin has besoiled all life! . . . Beret went about her work with a greater determination; but her sad mood did not lift.

A hundred things were waiting for Per Hansa outside, but he was so angry that he scarcely noticed what he was about. . . . The world seemed upside down to-day. . . . That grown people couldn't see an inch beyond their noses! Here lay Hans Olsa, driving himself out of his mind because he couldn't have a minister—when there was no better man than himself in all Christendom! . . . And here was Beret insisting that he leap right into the arms of death—she who had a heart so tender that she couldn't harm a mouse! . . . People could certainly twist things around in a queer way! All his life he had worked and slaved in order that she and the children might be made comfortable . . . and now it was flung in his face and he was taunted with being only a blind mole who saw nothing but the hole he had burrowed himself into! . . . "By God, it's a strange world we live in!" . . . If this went on much longer, he would go out of his mind himself—if he wasn't a little crazy already! . . . He dashed from one thing to another in a frenzy, leaving everything half done.

When the boys came out they all put on their skis and started across the snowdrifts to Hans Olsa's north quarter. The day was bleak; a cold air was drawing in from the west. To Store-Hans, all these fields of snow were glorious; now he could skim like a bird over the drifts. Little by little Per Hansa forgot his temper as he caught the infection of the boy's exuberant joy.

While they were working over the cattle, Per Hansa talked in a steady stream to the boys. All this snow, he said, promised a bumper crop next summer—you could depend on that! . . . One of his moods of high good humour had come over him now with a rush; and as was customary with him in that frame of mind, he discussed things with the boys as if they had been grown men. He outlined at length how they could manage their place in order to have the very finest of farms. If all went well, they would build a big barn next fall; but they certainly wouldn't be such damned idiots as to build a horse barn and cow barn separate, as that fool Torkel Tallaksen had done! It made a fine show, all right, but it was hardly practical; besides costing a good deal more, the barns were cold. . . . But they were going to have a real show barn, just the same—red with white cornices, because he always thought those colors looked the best. . . . Then he told them how he had read in the *Skandinaven** that the big farmers in the East now built a track under the ridgepole, along which they hauled the hay right into the barn loft. They would have to investigate this idea, for it sounded practical. . . . They found plenty to do up north; they saw to it that the cattle had water and hay enough; they carried in more straw; they stuffed the cracks in the walls; and all the while they talked and worked together like three grown men. Per Hansa felt the need of throwing off the great burden

* Norwegian-American newspaper published in Chicago.

that weighed him down; and for the moment he seemed to be succeeding fairly well. But at last they had finished everything that needed to be done; then the skis went on in a hurry, and off flew the boys like two great sea gulls soaring across the fiord. . . . No more time for talk! They struck off directly for the highest hill in sight; from there they could slide all the way down to the creek. . . . Wasn't it wonderful . . . all this snow!

Just as Per Hansa reached the yard at home Sörine was coming out of the kitchen door; she went over to the wall of the house, took a pair of skis that stood there, and put them on. He noticed that she was very thinly clad. She had a shawl over her head, but wore no other outdoor wrap. He concluded at once that she must have left home in a hurry, and feared that the worst had happened. . . . Was anything wrong? he asked. . . . No, Hans Olsa didn't seem much worse; she thought he looked a little better. But her face was sad and she looked down as she spoke. . . . Bridget had been to see him again and had said there was no hope. . . . "And I guess there isn't, either," she went on. "But I had to come over and ask your advice, Per Hansa. . . . He said that you were going after the minister for him. And I suppose that might be a good thing to do; at any rate, he is very happy about it. . . . But now, of course, I see that it's impossible to go anywhere. . . . Still, I was thinking that if you *did* intend to try, it might be better to get the doctor instead. . . . I don't suppose you can think of it in this weather, but I had to come over, anyway. . . ." Not once did she look up as the obvious pleading went on.

Per Hansa glanced down at his skis. Her voice had a thin, timid sound in this piercing wind. He felt the cold himself and remembered how thinly she was clad.

"You must stay awhile and get warm before you go," he said, quietly.

"No, I must hurry home. I know I shouldn't have come, but—" her voice suddenly left her. In a moment it came back, and then she went on, bravely: "It is so hard to see him go, without being able to help! And then we all have a feeling that nothing is ever impossible for you—and I thought that perhaps you might find a way out of this, too!" . . . All at once her pleading had taken on a frantic urgency.

"Did he ask you to come to me?"

"No—he didn't exactly do that. But he kept wondering if you weren't getting ready—if you wouldn't be starting soon. I could see plainly enough that he wanted some one to come over."

Per Hansa said nothing more, nor did he look at her again. She went away at once. When she had gone, he took off his skis, beat the snow from them, and set them up against the wall. But he did not go in immediately . . . His thoughts followed her who was now walking across the snow, passed her, entered the house before her, saw his friend lying there—saw the great face staring up at him, the frightened eyes imploring him like those of a kindly dog. He stood still in his tracks a long time, gazing off into vacancy, without the will to move. . . .

On the kitchen floor Permand was playing at threshing. When the father came in he hailed him, giving off orders like a man: "Come here and help me, you; we've got to get this work done before evening!" The boy's heart and soul were in his play. Seeing that dinner was not yet ready, the father hung up his coat and hat and sat down on the floor beside his son. In a moment they were both absorbed in the play.

During the meal the two parents scarcely spoke to each other, and never once did their eyes meet. As soon as they had finished the boy came and wanted his father to play with him some more; the father willingly agreed, and soon they were hard at it again. It was a serious question as to how they could get a lot of threshing done today; all the while they were laughing and talking about it, making a great deal of noise.

As the mother cleared the table she kept looking at them in wonder and dismay. . . . Here he sat and played with the child, just as if there were nothing serious in the world for him. The day was wearing on. Didn't he really intend to try to do anything? She could have cried aloud in her anguish! Had he become stone blind? . . . When she had finished washing the dishes she went to the window and stood there awhile, looking out;

then she crossed to the wall where her outdoor clothes hung, and began to put them on. This attracted Per Hansa's attention.

. . . Was she going out? he asked.

. . . Yes. . . . She put on one of his coats over her own wrap, then pulled his big stocking cap over her head.

He looked up a second time.

"Are you going far? You seem to be wrapping up a good deal."

She waited a moment before she answered.

"I have to talk to Henry. . . . *Some one* must go on this errand for Hans Olsa!" Her face was flushed with determination and her eyes shone with a quiet light.

Per Hansa burst into a laugh and scrambled to his feet.

"You'll have to behave yourself now, woman," he said, like a man trying to talk reason into a naughty child. "You ought to know that this is no weather for a woman to be out in."

"It's no weather for men to be out in, either, by the way it looks in here!"

He whirled on her suddenly, his face white with passion; the eyes that stared at her fiercely, burned with a lambent flame.

"God help me!" she thought. "Now he's going to lay hands on me! . . . But I only spoke the truth!"

"I want no more damned nonsense about this!" he burst out, hoarsely. "If you . . . if you have something to say to Henry, you'll have to say it here in this house. . . . You can't go chasing from farm to farm today!" . . .

Before she knew it he had gone out of the kitchen.

VIII

In front of the steps stood the forward part of a sleigh, on which the boys had tried to haul hay to the house; it was a clumsy, homemade affair, so heavy that the boys couldn't budge it after it had stood awhile, and so they had left it where it was. Per Hansa had noticed it earlier in the day, and it had angered him at the time to think that the boys were so careless. . . . When he came out now this object was the first thing he saw. He rushed at it; wrenched it out of the snow with a violent jerk, and flung it so hard into a drift that only one runner remained in sight.

"*There!* . . . God damn the thing!" he muttered.

With that passionate outburst his temper seemed suddenly to have left him, but his face was still very pale. His skis leaned up against the wall where he had placed them; he put them on and stood still for a moment, lost in thought; then, staff in hand, he started off. . . .

In the east part of the settlement lived two Telemarking* boys, who had come over a couple of years before. They were skilled skismiths; last winter each one had made himself a pair with straps and staffs, the finest ever seen in this part of the country. This year they had made two trips to town on them before Christmas. . . . It was to these boys that Per Hansa now went. In about an hour he returned with one pair of skis on his shoulders, and another on his feet. Neither pair was his own.

Beret, greatly agitated by her husband's hasty departure, walked back and forth across the kitchen floor. . . . "Now I have brought things to a sorry pass!" she thought. "I know I said too much—but what could I do? Some one has to go, and I had no one else to ask." . . . When she saw him returning with the skis she felt relieved. . . . "It's sensible of him to go on skis; it's the only way he can possibly get along. . . . I wonder who he intends to take along with him? He ought to have thought of the plan more seriously this morning; the boys and I could have managed with the chores. . . . I must hurry up and make him a cup of coffee; he must have something hot to drink before he leaves. . . . They'll hardly get far to-day." . . . She put the coffeepot on the stove and began to set the table. . . . "I guess I'll put on a tablecloth to make things nice for him. . . . He mustn't think that I hold any hard feelings." . . .

The oldest two boys were busy digging a tunnel from the cow barn to the pigsty—the latter had been com-

* People from the mountain district of Telemarken, Norway.

pletely snowed under. Per Hansa went over there first; he talked to them as if he were in no hurry, and when it seemed to him that they were losing interest, he went down into the tunnel where they were. . . . He said that now he was going away, and that it was uncertain when he would return. Could he depend on them to look after things while he was gone? . . . The boys were absorbed in their task and didn't pay much attention to what he said. Certainly he could go. They would look after everything. They went on with their work, and soon fell into a quarrel about how long it would take them to reach the pigsty. . . . He left the boys, took his skis, and went into the granary; there he rubbed one pair of skis with some tallow which he kept for the purpose, and put a piece of the tallow into his pocket. He also had to adjust the straps a little before he could start. . . .

While he was doing this Peder Victorious came trudging in and announced that mother had made coffee. She said father must come in before it got cold.

"What?" . . . Per Hansa's face brightened. "Did mother really say that?"

"She said coffee was ready."

"Oh! . . ."

Per Hansa had now adjusted the straps as he wanted them, and stood looking around for a rope with which to strap the other pair of skis on his back.

"Did she send you out and tell you to say that?" . . .

"She said—she said—coffee was ready, she said!"

The father looked at his son. "You haven't got enough on, Permand," he said in a low, tender voice, stroking the boy's cheek with his hand and running his finger down into the soft warm neck. The boy screamed when it tickled. Per Hansa laughed to hear him. "Hm—hm—cold as an icicle! Pack yourself in this minute! . . . So mother has the coffee ready, you say?"

He carried the boy out lovingly, set him down with a lingering touch, and went back after his skis. One pair he tied to his back; the other he put on.

The boy waited, watching him.

"Aren't you coming, father?"

"Get into the house with you!" the father said with

mock severity. "I'll probably be along in a little while." . . . Then, as he straightened up and put on his mittens, he suddenly remembered something:

"Permand!"

"Ya?" . . .

"There's a ball of nice twine in the bedroom. Ask mother to find it and give it to you to play with. . . . And now you must be a good boy, and get a lot of threshing done before I come back!"

"Yes, father," said the boy as he trotted away.

Per Hansa stood motionless, watching him until he had passed from sight inside the house. Then, with a staff in either hand, he started off. . . . Was that a face at the window that he saw? . . .

He did not look at the house again. In a moment he had passed the place where the boys were digging the tunnel; he longed to talk with them once more, but crushed the feeling down. . . . He struck out westward. Something tugged and pulled at his heart, trying to make him turn back; it was as if he had a bridle on and the driver were pulling hard on one of the reins. He had to bend his head forward against this unseen force in order to hold his direction. . . . "No—not now—not now. . . ." he murmured, bitterly, wiping his mitten across his eyes.

In the kitchen window Beret stood watching him; her soft, kindly eyes grew large and questioning. . . . Wasn't he coming in? Had Permand forgotten to tell him? . . . Surely, surely, he would come. She had fixed things so nicely for him. . . . Oh, this would never do! She must find out at once who was going with him! . . . She hurried to the door, flung it open, ran out on the steps, and tried to call to him—he simply mustn't leave this way! . . . But he had already gone beyond the range of her voice; the westerly gusts, driving full against her, snatched her words away. Her eyes filled with tears, so that she could scarcely see him now. Furious blasts came swirling out of the grey, boundless dusk, sweeping the snow in stinging clouds, whirling it round and round, dropping it only to pick it up again. Per Hansa soon disappeared in the whirling waste. . . . The wind was so cold that it penetrated to the very marrow of her bones.

A little later Per Hansa turned in at Hans Olsa's; he sat and talked with them awhile in the bedroom. Their words were few and far between. Per Hansa felt that there was nothing more for him to do here. At length he got up and said that now he was going—what sort of a trip he would have he did not know. If luck were with him, he would bring back the minister. In the meantime Hans Olsa must behave himself and rest as much as possible, for he really had nothing to worry about. . . . The sick man groped for Per Hansa's hand, and did not seem to want to let it go. He acted like a child who has teased and teased until it has finally got its way. . . .

"I didn't dare to ask you right out," he said, as if in explanation. "But I knew you would go as soon as it was possible—that's always been the way with you. . . . Now I can sleep in comfort." . . .

Out in the kitchen Sörine sat waiting at the table; when she heard this she hurried to pour the coffee, intending to make him sit down and have a cup before he left.

"Must I have coffee here too? . . . No, no," he said, jerking up his head. "I've had enough for to-day!" . . .

With these words he went out.

He put on his skis, straightened himself up, and remained standing there for some time; as he pulled on his mittens he took one glance homeward. He could just make out the house in the dim distance. Then the whiteness all around it thickened—rose up in a cloud—seemed to be piling in. Whirls of snow flew high over the housetop—sometimes the house itself disappeared. . . . He sighed deeply, brushed his eyes with his mitts, and started on his way.

He took his bearings from familiar outlines of the landscape, and laid the course he thought he ought to follow. . . . Perhaps it wasn't so dangerous, after all. The wind had been steady all day, had held in the same quarter, and would probably keep on. . . . Oh, well—here goes! . . .

He thought no more about his course for a while; but instead he began to wonder if he had done wrong in not going in to drink the coffee, when Beret had taken all the trouble to make it. . . . "Now she'll go around feeling unhappy, just because I am so touchy; and she'll be so melancholy that she'll have little patience with the boys. . . . Such high-spirited colts need to be managed with a careful hand. She doesn't understand that at all!" . . . Thoughts of home continued to come, warm and tender; he laughed softly at them. . . . "You may be sure she'll get Permand to remember me in his prayers to-night, if he doesn't think of it himself. . . . It would be fun to listen to them!" . . .

He moved slowly on with steady strokes, taking note of the wind at odd times. The picture would not leave him. . . . "It would be fun just to look in on them. . . . Oh, Permand, Permand! Something great must come of you—you who are so tenderly watched over!"

The swirling dusk grew deeper. . . . Darkness gathered fast. . . . More snow began to fall. . . . Whirls of it came off the tops of the drifts, circled about, and struck him full in the face. . . . No danger—the wind held steady. . . . At home all was well . . . and now mother was saying her evening prayers with Permand. . . . Move on!—Move on! . . .

IX

About halfway across the stretch from Colton to the James River a cluster of low hills rear themselves out of the prairie. Here and there among them a few stray settlers had already begun to dig in.

On one of the hillsides stood an old haystack which a settler had left there when he found out that the coarse bottom hay wasn't much good for fodder. One day during the spring after Hans Olsa had died, a troop of young boys were ranging the prairies, in search of some yearling cattle that had gone astray. They came upon the haystack, and stood transfixed. On the west side of the stack sat a man, with his back to the mouldering hay. This was in the middle of a warm day in May, yet the man had two pairs of skis along with him; one pair lay beside him on the ground, the other was tied to his back. He had a heavy stocking cap pulled well down over his forehead, and large mittens on his hands; in each hand he clutched a staff. . . . To the boys, it looked as though the man were sitting there resting while he waited for better skiing. . . .

. . . His face was ashen and drawn. His eyes were set toward the west.